A Pirate's Lesson in Love

She stared at him, a sense of captivity descending over her as he continued to hold her imprisoned. Lord, but he was handsome. Too handsome. Handsome as Lucifer himself and just as dangerous.

His hand held her firmly, the forceful pressure evenly distributed, not hurting her, but reminding her of her capture.

"Now for your first lesson, Catherine." He paused a moment, stared down at her then lowered his face to hers with each word spoken. "I never make a request twice. I'm always obeyed the first time."

His lips sat a mere breath away from hers, waiting.

She lifted her head a fraction preparing to hastily deposit a kiss on his lips when her senses were assaulted. He smelled of the sea, fresh and salty and temptingly lickable. Without thought or reason she slowly lifted her head and captured his frowning lips. Gently, almost worshippingly, she brushed across them, testing, feeling their velvet smoothness.

Lucian hadn't expected this slow and torturous assault on his senses. His passion flared like a roaring fire. Heat coursed through his veins, his blood boiled, his body soared to life.

He had intended to teach her a lesson and she had taught him one. She had taught him just how erotic a gentle kiss could be . . .

The Buccaneer

Donna Fletcher

JOVE BOOKS, NEW YORK

THE BUCCANEER

A Jove Book / published by arrangement with
the author

PRINTING HISTORY
Jove edition / July 1995

ISBN: 0-515-11652-1

A JOVE BOOK®
Jove Books are published by The Berkley Publishing Group,
200 Madison Avenue, New York, New York 10016.
JOVE and the "J" design are trademarks
belonging to Jove Publications, Inc.

PRINTED IN THE UNITED STATES OF AMERICA

10 9 8 7 6 5 4 3 2 1

For my son Matthew
for always being there, for always caring,
for always loving . . . you're a true hero

Prologue

"LUCIFER!"

The man standing ankle deep at the ocean's edge wearing only white, wet breeches turned slowly though his name had been called in haste. "What is so important, Santos, that you see fit to disturb my late morning swim?"

Another man would have immediately retreated with a hasty and sincere apology for Lucifer's commanding tone would have set the fear of the devil himself in him. Not Santos. He had been friends too long with the infamous pirate Lucifer. "The letter you've been waiting for." Santos held the sealed paper out to him.

Lucifer wasted not a minute. He approached Santos in sure and steady strides, his hand reaching out and snatching the letter. He broke the wax seal and scanned, more than once, the contents.

"She's agreed."

This time Santos shivered. Whenever Lucifer spoke so calmly and so in control, it presaged trouble, serious trouble. "My friend, think—"

"Think?" Lucian's soft but powerful tone interrupted. "I think all right, Santos. I think of the hell that bastard put me through. And I think of the revenge that will be mine."

Santos tried unsuccessfully to stop his knees from trembling. Lucifer's anger once unleashed was an uncontrollable force, not easy to harness, and Santos could tell he was close to losing the slender grip he still held on it.

"I have waited too many years," Lucifer whispered

harshly. "I finally hold the key to retribution in my hand." He raised the letter, crumpling it.

Santos cringed as the paper crinkled loudly in protest. He stared at his friend's arresting features, his long blood red hair, the taut, heavy muscles in his arms and chest and the sheer overall size of him. It was easy to understand why men quaked in his presence and women trembled with desire for him. "Are you certain this is what you want, Lucifer?"

Lucifer stared at Santos for a full minute before he turned and walked to the water's edge.

Santos read his silent command correctly and followed him.

"Do you know how much I hated the sea at one time?"

Santos simply nodded.

Lucifer continued, not taking his intent glare off the deep blue water. "I sometimes prayed to die, but then . . ."

Santos remained silent having lived through the same hell as Lucifer and understanding his pain.

Lucifer laughed briefly. "The Lord saw fit to send me a reason to live. He sent me the name of the man responsible for condemning me to a living hell. Now it is his turn to suffer."

"But she is—"

Lucifer turned to Santos, the anger so visible in his eyes that it forced Santos to retreat a step. "*She* belongs to me."

Santos once again chose silence.

"Ready the ship. We sail tomorrow," Lucifer ordered, and dropped the crumpled letter into the sea. He walked farther out, the strength of his body easily pushing through the water. He stopped and the sea rushed around his waist like a greedy woman happy at his return.

He turned, the sun's rays directly behind him and lapping at him like the fires of Hades. He looked at Santos and spoke in a tone of a man who would not be denied. "Catherine Abelard is *mine*."

⚜ 1 ⚜

"You sold yourself," Charles Darcmoor, Earl of Brynwood, said, dabbing furiously at his perspiring brow.

"You're standing too near the hearth, Charles," Catherine Abelard cautioned.

Charles stepped away from the flames and continued to dab at his brow. "I must voice my protest over this matter most vehemently."

"So you've told me on several occasions. I clearly understand your position. Now you must understand mine."

Charles's tall, lean body stiffened at her demand and his face plainly registered his disdain. "You should leave such matters to those who know better."

Catherine resented the same old argument, fearful that there might be some validity to his words. But what else was she to do? There had been no avenue of help she had not sought, nor offer of help she had refused. "You mean to the barristers in all their learned wisdom who assured me my father's innocence could easily be proven. That the charges of treason brought against him were preposterous and could never be corroborated."

"Really, Lady Catherine, the gentlemen did their utmost to help the marquis. Your obviously disparaging opinion is uncalled for."

"Uncalled for?" Catherine said, attempting to retain her anger. "These same men who filled my hopes with such promise now cry for my father's neck at Charing Cross."

"The evidence—"

"The evidence was obviously planted by someone filled

with deep hatred for my father, and God only knows for what reason."

"So you turn to a *pirate* for help!"

"Must I remind you that it was he who offered it. And at a most opportune time, when the officials were pounding on the door, demanding Father's immediate imprisonment. And he upstairs in bed barely recovered from his first heart seizure. Where were my father's so-called friends then?" The reminder of that day, a few short weeks ago, brought a chill of fear to her. If it had not been for the papers the captain had sent, her father would now be languishing in the Tower of London. An almost certain death sentence, given his fragile health.

"There are some—"

"There are none who feel the Marquis of Devonshire innocent of treason. They all ran like cowards, deserting him at a time when he needed their friendship and support the most."

"I stayed and offered my help," Charles said patiently.

"Yes, Charles, you did and I'm grateful." A soft smile demonstrated her sincerity for his dauntless, though recent, friendship. He had only been in residence at Brynwood estate, the neighboring manor, for a few years. "If it wasn't for you, I don't know how I would have made it through these trying times."

Charles walked over to her, sitting beside her on the white brocade settee. "I never doubted his lordship's innocence."

"I never thought you did," Catherine said with a reassuring pat to his hand.

He took her hand in his and squeezed it. "Catherine, I fear for your safety."

"I have no choice. There are no options left to me. Captain Lucifer offered evidence. Something no one else has been able to do."

"I still don't like it. Even his name disturbs me."

Catherine tried to soothe his doubts as well as her own, for in fact his name caused her to tremble. "I doubt his given name is Lucifer."

"Granted, I think some of the pirates choose names they feel will most frighten people, but it doesn't matter since their barbaric actions alone cause fear. Please, Catherine, rethink this."

She couldn't give herself the luxury of thought. The doubt she harbored would only grow stronger. "I have given my word. I cannot go back on it."

Charles sprang to his feet, raking his hand furiously through his brown hair. "My God, Catherine, how can you worry about giving your word when the man you gave it to has no morals or convictions?"

Catherine suppressed the flutter of fear that his words had caused. She calmly stood. "Do you have evidence to present to the Crown that will clear father's name?"

Charles's mouth dropped open prepared to speak then snapped shut. He sadly shook his head.

Catherine appreciated his concern and support. He had proved a true friend, and she had admired his courage in standing by her father when so many friends had abandoned him. Her father had often commented on his intelligence, handsome features, and charm. Attributes, he reminded her, to consider when searching for a husband. She had to admit he was attractive in a common way and his temper was even and controlled. She supposed he would prove a kind husband, but *she* wasn't interested.

"I insist you allow me to send someone along, presumably a large man, to protect you, just in case. . . ."

She didn't care for the way he purposely let his words trail off. "You know the terms he insisted upon. I was to come alone. He promised my safety."

"He's a pirate! A scourge of the sea," Charles shouted. "His word means nothing."

Catherine wasn't able to control the shudder of fear that raced through her.

Charles was instantly contrite. "Forgive me, Catherine. It was unkind of me to speak so."

"I have no choice. No choice," she repeated as if convincing herself. "I must do this." Tears filled her eyes and she fought gallantly to control them.

Charles slipped a comforting arm around her shoulder and drew her against him. "When you reach his island you will post a letter to me on the first vessel sailing."

She agreed with a nod.

"If I do not hear from you soon . . . I shall sail after you myself."

And he would, Catherine thought.

"Understood?" he asked, releasing her and standing.

"Understood, but I'll be fine," she assured him as well as attempting to assure herself. "I'll write immediately."

"Good," he said, sounding relieved.

"You will make certain father doesn't learn of any of this until the appropriate time, as we discussed?"

"Don't worry, I'll take care of everything."

"The only thing that matters right now is his health. The physician says that he is making a remarkable recovery and that his heart is growing stronger every day. I want him to continue to improve."

"I agree, Catherine. It would do his health little good if he learned of this."

"As soon as Captain Lucifer and I marry, he promised he'd give me the remaining proof of father's innocence. I will send the papers to you immediately."

"And what then?"

"Then all will be settled. And I'll hear no more. I have but two hours time before my coach leaves. I have much to do." She did not want to think beyond the wedding. The prospect was too frightening.

Charles nodded reluctantly. "As you say."

Catherine walked over to him and kissed him lightly on his cheek. "Thank you for being such a good friend. I feel safe knowing you will be here to protect father."

"Do not worry about your father. He'll be fine. He's a fighter, a survivor."

Catherine smiled and patted his arm. "So am I."

She remained in the small sitting room after Charles left. The fire toasted the room to a simmering warmth and the heavy green velvet drapes, though drawn back, kept the chill of winter at bay. She felt safe and secure as she had upon first arriving here fifteen years ago at the tender age of four.

Her mother having been a widow for two years had found herself in an arranged marriage with the Marquis of Devonshire. Catherine had been nervous about meeting her new father and her mother had warned her repeatedly to be on her best behavior. But she needn't have worried. It was love at first sight for the little girl, who had been scooped up into the marquis's strong arms and hugged and kissed. At that moment Randolph Abelard had become her knight in shining armor and her love and admiration for him had grown over the years.

Especially when she had found her lessons difficult and her tutor had brazenly informed the marquis that his stepdaughter was stupid and unteachable. The tutor was dismissed immediately with no letter of recommendation. It was then that Randolph Abelard had begun to teach Catherine himself.

It had been hard for her to learn. The letters never looked the same to her and the numbers confused her, but Randolph

Abelard would not give up nor would he allow her to give up. He repeatedly, and with great patience, explained to her that she should take her time and think things through. Great minds, he had informed her, never hurried.

To this day she was forever grateful for the world of knowledge Randolph Abelard had opened for her. And to her he would always be her *real* father. She often found herself still listening to his advice to "think things through." Which is precisely what she had done when the letter with the offer of help had come from Captain Lucifer.

She had thought and debated and considered her options. There had been none. She had had no choice. Three weeks after receiving the captain's letter she had sent one of her own, simply stating that she agreed to his terms.

Catherine stood and reprimanded herself for reminiscing. "Enough. You have much to do before you leave."

Dulcie, her personal servant, was busy filling Catherine's traveling case with her toiletries as she entered her room on the second floor. Short and plump, Dulcie was a ball of energy and gossip. Her hands worked as fast as she spoke. And her face, though full, was pretty, with thick dark lashes, rosy cheeks, and a saucy smile. Dulcie had her fair share of male admirers and though the same age as Catherine, she was wise far beyond her nineteen years. Dulcie's present companion Henry routinely followed her around like a love-starved puppy.

Catherine found her actions and stories entertaining and she was going to sorely miss Dulcie. "Everything packed?" she asked.

"Yes, my lady. My lady?" The servant's tone was shaky and reluctant as though nervous to speak.

"Yes, Dulcie." Catherine turned to face her.

"I fear for you, my lady." Dulcie began to cry. "I know

I've only been working here two years, but I like you. You've been the kindest lady to me. And I kept my word and didn't tell anyone about where you're truly going, but I've heard stories. Horrible stories."

Catherine took her hand, noticing both their palms were clammy. "What stories?"

"They ain't fit for a lady's ears," Dulcie insisted in protection of her mistress's virginal sensibilities.

"But you heard them," Catherine argued, tired of being treated like a lady who would learn nothing of intimacy until her wedding night.

"I ain't a lady highborn like you."

"Please, Dulcie. Tell me, or I will leave on this trip ever fearful."

Dulcie looked at her mistress, nodded, and then anxiously glanced about the room. Seeing the door open she rushed over, closed it, and bolted the lock. She hurried back.

Catherine sat on the bed and patted the spot next to her, impatient to hear all. "Sit and tell me."

Dulcie sat and lifted the cross, hanging on a chain around her neck, to her mouth. She kissed it and mumbled a quick prayer for protection before she began. "It ain't right that you have to do this. Pirates are evil beings, especially Lucifer. He ain't named after the devil himself for nothing."

"Many of them are poor unfortunate souls who had no choice in the matter of becoming a pirate," Catherine said, seeking to believe her own assumption.

Dulcie slowly shook her head. "Pirates ain't got souls."

Catherine was stunned. "Nonsense, everyone has a soul."

"No, my lady, evil beings don't have souls and them pirates are evil. I heard tell—" Dulcie stopped, covered her mouth and widened her eyes fearfully as though if she spoke the words an avenging demon would strike her dead.

"Tell me, Dulcie, nothing can harm you here," Catherine said, though oddly enough sensing a tingle of fear.

Dulcie's voice was soft and her tone low as she began. "I heard tell that a man captured by a pirate had his ear nailed to the mast because the captain wanted to make certain he'd stay put. And another had a man buried alive up to his neck near the water's edge so when the tide rolled in the man would drown." She crossed herself and shook her head. "Only the crabs got to him first."

"These are just stories probably made up by bragging men to entertain each other at the local public house," Catherine said with more conviction than she felt.

"No, my lady, these stories have been told by men who've seen it with their own eyes. And they say Lucifer's the worst. He was so angered by one of his prisoners for talking too much that he had the man's lips sewn shut and left him on a deserted island. He died, mum."

"Then who told the story?" Catherine asked, finding the story too preposterous to believe.

"One of the other men that was captured with him. He got away at one of the ports and made his way back to England."

Catherine covered her mouth with her hand, thinking of all the times her tongue got carried away, rattling on about nonsensical things.

"And the women, my lady," Dulcie said, shaking her head and kissing the cross once again.

Catherine's skin crawled with gooseflesh. "The women?"

"Oh, yes, mum, the women. Captain Lucifer is known for his fondness of them though it's been heard it isn't always fondness he treats them with."

If not fondness then what? Indifference? Savagery? Contempt? Catherine did not care for her musings. "And you've heard stories regarding this?"

Dulcie nodded her head vigorously, her brown curls bobbing along her forehead from beneath her mobcap.

"Tell me," Catherine insisted, needing to learn all she could before her marriage.

"My lady, excuse me for saying so, but you have no experience in such matters."

"Granted I've no firsthand knowledge, but I'm not ignorant of the basic act that goes on between a man and woman," she said, wishing most fervently that she was knowledgeable beyond the basic act. She had no idea how a wife should act, react, or feel, and the lack of information greatly disturbed her.

"Lucifer enjoys more than the basic act, mum. According to tales, one captured lady failed to entertain him to his specifications, so he had her thrown overboard and he was heard to yell, 'since you can't please me, you'll please the bloody sharks.'"

Catherine didn't know whether to laugh or cry. Whether what Dulcie was telling her were truths, or tales. "I can only assume that Captain Lucifer's exploits are overly exaggerated and that he would not think of treating his wife in such a barbaric manner."

Dulcie chewed on her lower lip, uncertain if she should speak, but unable to keep still. "Oh, my lady, forgive me for saying so, but how can you be certain he'll marry you? And why does he wish to marry you? Him being a pirate. How would a marriage to you benefit him?"

"We've both signed an agreement of marriage. And I can only assume he wishes to better his station in life. By marrying me perhaps he will attain some respectability. Why else would he send for me?" Catherine asked, not wanting to consider what other motives Lucifer could possible have.

"To ruin you, my lady. You mustn't go. I have a bad feeling."

"Hush now. Why would he wish to ruin me? What would that accomplish?"

"It don't matter, my lady, don't you understand? He has no soul. He doesn't care." Dulcie's tone rose in pitch to emphasize her point.

"I don't believe Captain Lucifer has no soul," Catherine said, attempting to calm her servant though seriously doubting her own remark. "And I don't want you to worry, when I am settled and all matters are taken care of, I'll send for you. If you would prefer not to come, I'll understand." Although she prayed Dulcie would join her, suddenly feeling terribly alone.

"Oh, my lady, I'll come and I'll help protect you, no matter how fearin' I am."

Catherine hugged the young girl, relieved that she would eventually join her. "I shall miss you, Dulcie."

Dulcie wiped the tears from her eyes with the corner of her white apron. "I'll pray for you, my lady, night and day."

"Good, then I won't be afraid since I know your prayers will protect me," she said, offering Dulcie and herself what little comfort she could muster.

"God love you, my lady. You're so innocent of the world."

Dulcie quickly left the room to conceal her flowing tears and to see to the removal of the trunks. Catherine remained sitting on the bed absorbed in her own thoughts and fears.

Had her decision been wise? Or had she foolishly allowed her love for her father to cloud her wisdom?

"My lady, your father calls for you," Dulcie said, peeking her head in the room.

"I'll be right there," she said, and hurried to her dressing table to check her face. Her eyes were shiny with unshed tears and her cheeks pale. She pinched life back into them, then dabbed at the corners of her eyes to clear them.

She sprinkled rose water on her neck and fluffed the white ruffles that ran along the square neck of her dark green wool gown.

She hurried out of her room and down the hall.

She was all ready to see her father . . . and say goodbye.

Courage is a strong and not always easy virtue to maintain. Her father had repeated that often to her these last few months. She called upon his words now as her hand reached out to grasp the metal latch. She took a deep breath, released it slowly, then opened the door and walked into her father's room.

A rush of heat from the blazing hearth flushed her face as she walked to his bed. "You look wonderful, Father." She leaned over and kissed his cheek. He did look wonderful. Health bloomed once again in his face.

"And I feel wonderful, Catherine. After speaking to Charles this morning and realizing that we are finally getting somewhere in proving my innocence . . . well, it has given me a renewed strength."

"Yes, things do look better," she smiled in agreement.

"I told Charles that we must go over the information we have. I want to see the papers he spoke of, the ones that show I wasn't using my merchant ships to send supplies to enemy countries."

Catherine fussed with the heavy quilt covering him, folding its edges neatly back. "You must rest first. You may view the papers all in good time."

The marquis took his daughter's hand in his.

Catherine couldn't help but notice how thin and frail he felt. He had been a tall, strapping man and although he still retained his almost six-foot height, his weight had dwindled and it would be months before he regained his full stamina. His once-dark hair was heavily streaked white and gray and his face, though still handsome, betrayed his fifty-nine years.

He roughly cleared his throat as he had done so often when she was young and he was about to have a serious discussion with her. "Catherine, these last few months have been difficult for you. I am sorry."

"Nonsense, Father," she said, trying not to look directly into his blue eyes, so close was she to the verge of tears.

"It isn't nonsense. You have worked hard helping Charles. He told me how determined you were to prove my innocence."

Catherine fussed further with the quilt, keeping her hands busy, so worried was she that her father would notice their nervous trembling. "Charles shouldn't have disturbed you with that news."

"You can't carry the weight of my burden on your shoulders. It isn't right or proper," he said, covering her hand.

"When you are well I shall gladly give the burden back to you," she said with a forced smile, cherishing his touch as she had as a child. It had always brought with it a feeling of comfort and safety. And she wondered when next she would feel it.

"I am well enough now. The burden is mine. And I feel confident that this matter will be settled in a few months. By then I shall be feeling my old self, and we can head to London for a holiday. And to find you a husband. It is about time I tended to my fatherly duties."

Catherine choked back her emotions. He had always seen to her well-being. Always. Now it was her turn. "You have been the best father in the world to me."

Tears blurred the marquis's vision. He wiped at his eyes and coughed. "Must be the smoke. I tell Dunwith not to use damp logs, but he never listens."

Catherine laughed, the first time in months. "You couldn't do without Dunwith. He's been your manservant as long as I can remember."

Her laugh was infectious and he chuckled along with her. "He's been my manservant as long as *I* can remember."

Catherine was glad to see him smile again, to see him free of worry and concern for the future.

The marquis squeezed Catherine's hand tightly. "All will go well, you'll see. And then I will arrange a most wonderful marriage for you."

She leaned over and kissed his cheek once again. She braced herself against the lie she was about to tell him. She had never lied to him before and it disturbed her to do so now. "I will be away for a few days. Aunt Lilith is insisting I visit with her. It's been so long since I've seen her."

"It will do you good to get away from here for a few days even if it's only with my unconventional sister." The marquis attempted to stifle a yawn, but wasn't successful. "I am tired. You will visit with me later?"

She gently placed a kiss on his forehead, knowing this was her farewell, for how long she could not say. "I will visit with you soon."

His eyes closed contentedly as Catherine walked to the door. She stopped a moment and without turning around she whispered, "I love you." And walked out the door, closing it quietly behind her.

She stood there a moment in silence, her head resting against the door, tears trickling her lashes. She wiped them away and turned.

"Dunwith!" she said, her hand flying to her chest, surprised by his sudden appearance.

"Lady Catherine," he said.

She looked up into his face. She knew he had to be well into his seventies, but his face was ageless. A few lines and wrinkles worn well. And a voice so articulate one would think him an aristocrat. "I was visiting with father."

"He is improving," Dunwith said matter-of-factly.

"Yes, very much so," she said softly, her bottled emotions close to erupting.

"He is strong as is his daughter," Dunwith said, his face not betraying a hint of emotion.

Catherine suddenly felt her throat constrict and her eyes flood with unshed tears. "You will take care of him? Of course you will. It was foolish of me even to ask such a thing." She wiped at her eyes with her hand, then bravely and most unseemingly flung her arms around Dunwith, hugging him. "I shall miss you. Tell father I love him."

She released him and ran down the hall without glancing back, else she would have seen the single teardrop fall from Dunwith's eye and splatter upon his white shirt.

The trip had been more difficult than Catherine had thought. Not so much physically, for she was treated well and her comfort seen to at the various stops along the way. It was her emotions that had caused the most problems. Now standing here on the dock, she looked up at the massive ship that would take her away and deliver her to a complete stranger, and she felt her confidence fade away completely.

"Lady Catherine?"

Catherine turned her attention to George, her father's stable master for the last twenty years.

"I talked with Captain Morley. He says your cabin is all ready and he'd like you to board as quickly as possible, being the tide is perfect for him to set sail."

"My trunks are aboard?" she asked, feeling a bit fearful of being on her own.

George nodded, twisting his worn cap in his hands. "Lady Catherine, are you certain you'll be all right? You know a fine lady as yourself shouldn't be traveling alone. It isn't proper."

"I appreciate your concern, George, but circumstances warrant that I must."

"It isn't safe on the open seas with pirates and such."

"I'm sure Captain Morley will provide safe passage for me, and I shall arrive at my destination without incident."

George nodded his head reluctantly as though he didn't entirely agree with her. "If you say so. You won't be gone long, will you? Your father will be missing you terribly."

The cold winter wind grew blustery at that moment, causing Catherine to wrap her wool-lined cloak more tightly around her. "And I'll be missing him," she answered, deciding it was best she didn't comment on the unlikelihood of her return anytime soon.

One of the sailors from the ship hurried toward them. "Excuse me, but the captain, he wants to be sailing now."

Catherine was glad for the interruption, since she was finding it difficult to say good-bye to George and the last remnants of her life in England.

"Keep well, George," she called as the young sailor took her arm and assisted her up the gangway.

"Be careful and God bless," George yelled.

But the wind carried his blessing away and all Catherine heard was "be careful."

She was shown to her cabin. It was small but adequate. Her baggage had been stored in the ship's storage and she had been left with her traveling case. It held enough clothing and essentials for the journey. Her destination was Jamaica, where she would be met by an emissary representing

Captain Lucifer. Captain Morley knew naught of her true
reason for her journey, only that he was to deliver her safely
to Jamaica.

The ship pitched and rolled considerably and Catherine
quickly seated herself on the narrow bed, holding firmly to
the wooden sides.

They were sailing. The men had released the ropes,
setting the ship free, and it was headed to the open sea away
from England.

Catherine let the tears come then. The ones that had
remained locked away these many months. They burst forth
and raced down her cheeks. She hugged her cloak around
her and gave voice to her greatest fear. "Captain Lucifer
must have a soul. He must."

❧ 2 ❧

It was a tiny black speck floating in the distance. Catherine could barely make it out. Craning her neck and widening her eyes she focused on the natural beauty of the watery landscape surrounding her. An endless sea met a forever, deep blue sky, rich with thick white clouds. It resembled a perfect painting with the exception of the speck.

The crew was obviously disturbed by it. Although she felt they were a safe distance away from the vessel, if that was what the speck was, the crew appeared to think otherwise. Their eyes strayed often to the horizon and their movements seemed strained and fearful. Odd, since these were experienced sailors accustomed to all the variables of the sea, and the two weeks they had been at sea, the crew had been congenial and relaxed. Yet now something was frightening them beyond reason. She herself could feel it. Its presence was tangible and as Catherine sniffed the salty air she could almost smell the sickening odor.

Fear.

She was all too familiar with it. These last few months fear had been her constant companion, feeding off her day and night. But here on the ship it was no companion. It was their adversary. An adversary that was far stronger than any human opponent. But what or who caused it to spread and lurk with such intensity?

Catherine walked toward the quarterdeck, steadying her step with each pitch and sway of the ship. Her eyes stole glances at the crew members, and her apprehension grew as she watched sailors cross themselves in protective prayer. The strange mumbling disturbed her even more for she could only hear snatches of their conversation and what she did hear heightened her own fears.

"Pray it ain't the *Black Skull*."

"Hell holds a better fate."

"Bloodthirsty lot."

"No soul."

Catherine turned in such haste she almost lost her balance. Had she heard Dulcie's warning or had one of the crew voiced the same fear?

Tension filled every muscle and fiber of her body like a band that had been strung too taut. She wrapped her cape snugly around her not to ward off the chill, but to keep her alarm at bay. She would go to her cabin and read. If she kept her mind busy and focused, this uneasiness would dissipate.

She continued walking in unhurried steps. She didn't wish to show that her misgivings equaled the crew's. It was better to keep her emotions in check. After all, her worries might be for naught and she didn't wish to appear a fool.

Catherine smiled congenially at the sailors busy in their duties as she passed them. Their returned smiles were pleasant though forced and the odd look in their eyes didn't help her own highly nervous state.

She was about to go below to her cabin, her hand already on the wooden frame when for some unexplainable reason she turned her head slowly to the right. Her feet took her in quick strides to the balustrade. Her hands gripped the scarred wood. Her heart uncharacteristically fluttered like a woman about to swoon. But swoon she didn't. She just stared in amazement at the speck.

It had grown considerably. She still couldn't make out a form, but it was closer, larger, even darker in its strange presence.

Catherine heard it then. It was more frightening than any clamor she could remember. It was stillness. No sailor spoke. No sails flapped. No wind blew. The ship had suddenly stilled in the sea.

She shivered as though desperately wanting to rid herself of a horrible premonition of doom.

Captain Morley broke the thick silence with a loud command that sent the men scurrying. Sails were raised and small barrels were carted and stacked near the cannons, prayers were no longer whispers.

Catherine watched the chaotic action, stunned by what it represented. The captain obviously expected an attack. She stood stock-still until a sailor softly offered to see her to her cabin.

The young man closed the door behind him. Catherine remained standing in the dark interior uncertain what to do. It was several minutes before she forced herself into action and convinced herself to stay calm. She lit the oil lamp on the table next to her bed and removed her cape.

A book would ease her worries. She sat on the bed and reached for one of the two books on the table. She hadn't thought of what book would best entertain her, and she found comfort in the fact that her hands had chosen her Bible. She would find peace within its pages.

She opened the book and one name jumped out at her. *Lucifer.* She snapped it shut hard, closed her eyes tightly, and tried to calm the thunderous pounding of her heart.

Several hours later supper was delivered to her room. The sailor who brought it smiled apologetically and assured her all was well. The captain just felt it was best she kept to her quarters for extra protection.

Catherine didn't question his explanation. She had thought on the matter and realized that if the drop in wind had slowed them it had also slowed the speck.

She decided it was best to sleep in her clothes, not knowing what early morning might bring. She doubted sleep would visit her this night anyway and sat herself up in her bed to face the long evening ahead.

The deep pitching of the ship woke Catherine from her unexpected sleep and the sound of the slapping water against the wood brought a smile to her face. The wind had picked up and they were finally slicing through the water once again. Captain Morley was an able, experienced seaman. He would outmaneuver the speck and in the morning it would no longer be visible on the horizon. The watery landscape would be perfect again after all.

The blast sent Catherine flying out of bed, landing in a heap on the floor. She quickly scrambled to her feet upon hearing another blast.

Attacked! My God, they were being attacked.

Catherine jumped, her hand flying to her chest in fright as a frenzied pounding shook her locked door.

"Lady Catherine! Lady Catherine!"

Catherine opened it to an anxious young sailor. His pale face wore a mixture of perspiration and gunpowder.

"Captain Morley says to bolt your door and push what furniture you can in front of it. And he says to take this."

He shoved a pistol into her hand.

"This isn't necessary," she protested.

"Yes, it is. The captain says to use it one way or another. These are mean ones we're dealing with, real mean ones." He added in a whisper as though afraid to speak the fearful words, "It's the *Black Skull* that's attacking us."

The ship suddenly felt as if it were rammed, sending Catherine and the sailor tumbling to the side.

The sailor helped Catherine up, then pushed her into her

room. "Bolt the door! Hurry, we're being boarded!" he shouted, and ran to join his fellow crew members.

Catherine slammed the door shut and secured the crude iron bolt. She dropped the pistol on the bed, giving no thought to the danger of it discharging. Her only concern at the moment was to barricade herself in her quarters and pray Captain Morley and his men would succeed in besting the pirates.

From above she heard the clash of steel against steel as she dragged the heavy wooden chest across the cabin floor and shoved it against the door. She sat on top of it, her breathing labored from the exertion.

Screams, which turned one's blood cold, pierced her ears and sent a shiver through her. How ironic this attack, when she herself was on her way to marry a pirate.

No soul.

Dulcie's warning rang loudly in her ears, driving all sounds of the battle away.

Was the young girl right? Did all pirates actually lack souls? They must since they held such a blatant disregard for life. My God, what had she gotten herself into?

A vicious blow to her door sent her falling to the floor. She scrambled on her knees to the bed, reaching for the weapon.

"Break it down!" came the harsh order.

She fumbled with the pistol, trying to recall what she had been taught about firing one. But she was frightened and confused and couldn't remember.

"Calm down, Catherine. Calm down and think," she warned herself, her hands shaking badly. The splintering of wood warned of the pirates' imminent entrance.

She looked at the pistol in her hand. Did she use it on the pirates or escape her certain capture by death?

She concentrated and cocked the pistol. She'd not desert

her father now. She would face her attackers and demand she be ransomed to Captain Lucifer.

The wooden door splintered into pieces from the forceful blows. Catherine stood, pointed the pistol at the door, and sent a hasty prayer above that she would fire it correctly.

A man came crashing through the broken door, his one fist punching away the remaining barriers of splintered wood while a cutlass was grasped firmly in his other hand.

Catherine gasped at the size of him. He was a giant, so large that his shadow completely devoured her. He raised his cutlass, pressing the sharp tip to the back of Catherine's shaking hand that held the pistol.

"Drop it," he ordered. His voice was deep and harsh, and to ensure her immediate compliance he pricked the back of her hand with his cutlass.

Catherine cried out, letting the pistol fall to the bed. A thin trickle of blood ran down her hand to catch at her wrist and seep into the cuff of her mauve dress. With strength and courage her chin shot up and her eyes met his directly.

Cold and unmerciful they were, yet sharp and striking in their gray-blue color. She searched deep within them, hoping and praying she would catch a glimpse of his soul.

He said nothing and his silence frightened her even more than did his size. He was tall, several inches over six foot. Shoulders broad and muscles that had to have been developed by years of hard labor bulged from beneath his half-opened white linen shirt. His legs were the width of mighty oaks that stretched the black material of his breeches to the limit, demonstrating every bit of prowess his body had to offer.

And his hair? Lord, but it was sinister, long and uncommon in color, *blood red,* with a single braid that ran down the side.

But it was his face so rich and ample in features that made

her catch her breath. Aristocratic features, she thought. A strong jaw. Sculpted cheekbones. Narrow nose. Lips that were sleek and wide. And then he smiled. Not a nice smile. A dangerous one. Handsome, much too handsome, and that was when she knew without a doubt his identity.

He removed his cutlass from the back of her hand, placing the tip on the floor and leaning his two hands upon the handle. He spread his legs slightly apart. His easy stance plainly demonstrated his arrogant confidence.

She placed her hand against her midriff, ignoring the small wound that had already stopped bleeding and took a deep breath before she spoke, gaining some courage. "There was no reason for you to attack the ship, Captain Lucifer. I was on my way to you with all intentions of keeping my part of the agreement."

"Aye, my lady, but I have no intentions of keeping mine."

Catherine stared at him a moment. His voice was smooth and his tone distinguished. She did not expect such articulation from a pirate, nor those particular words. "I don't understand."

"But you will," he said so dangerously softly and calmly that it made Catherine shiver.

"Take her topside," his voice boomed, and the group of men peering in through the broken door rushed forward.

Catherine backed up, but hands reached out and grabbed her.

They pulled and yanked and pinched her skin as each tried to direct her to the door. Captain Lucifer just stood by, his cutlass draped at his side, watching with indifference.

She was shoved toward the door and before she stepped over the chest and through the gaping hole, she caught the captain's eyes.

"Why?" she asked in a choked sob.

"Revenge," he said harshly.

Catherine was pulled roughly through the broken door. The strange answer filled her head with confused thoughts. *Revenge*. But for what?

She tripped several times going up the steps, unable to control her balance with the many hands that pulled at her. She felt like a puppet whose movements were being controlled by more than one puppeteer.

She fumbled over ropes and charred wood as they continued to drag her along. Where were they taking her?

Her fear and anxiety soared and she attempted to twist herself free. The firm hands would have none of her feeble actions and jerked her forward. Her feet hit a solid form and she began to tumble. The men quickly released her and down she went with a thud.

Her first thought was that at least she was free of all those groping hands and she scurried to right herself. But when she turned to push herself up, her eyes connected with those of the young sailor who had come to warn her.

He lay beside her. His head was bleeding. His eyes were wide with fright.

"Dear God," she whispered, and turned to survey the carnage. Crew members lay moaning, their faces and limbs bloody. The once-billowing white sails were torn in shreds and the masts were split.

"Help me."

The barely audible plea returned Catherine's attention to the injured sailor. She scrambled to her knees and ripped the hem of her petticoat. She gently wiped the blood from his head. "Easy now, you'll be fine."

The young sailor kept his eyes fixed upon her.

She smiled, trying to offer encouragement as she continued to clean the wound. "It's not as bad as it looks, really."

"It hurts."

"You have a large bump, but the wound itself isn't deep,"

she said, relieved his injury wasn't as fatal as she first believed.

A tear came to his eye.

"You'll be fine, really. I'm not fibbing," she said with a smile, trying to reassure him.

He shook his head slightly, but it hurt so he held it very still. "You didn't use the weapon."

Catherine realized what had brought the tears on. He was frightened for her, not for his well-being. "I didn't—"

Her words caught in her throat as she was yanked viciously away from him and swung around by her arm to face Captain Lucifer. His hand bit into her flesh and she had to tilt her head back to look up into his face. She regretted her actions.

His eyes were cold gray. His long hair hung wildly about his shoulders, and his mouth was open enough for Catherine to see white even teeth. She shut her eyes against the disturbing sight, having sworn they were sharp and about to snap angrily at her.

"I gave you no leave to tend the injured," he said, his fingers biting more deeply into her flesh.

"You're hurting me." She refused to plead or cry for her release.

"No, not yet I'm not."

Catherine was shocked by his response. It was delivered with such calmness and self-assurance that she wondered exactly what he meant.

"Clean up here," he ordered with a shout to his crew, then dragged her along beside him.

She tripped a few times, but his firm hold and strength prevented her from falling. He stopped next to the balustrade on the side of the ship. He raised his leg, placing the sole of his black knee-high boot on the scarred top. The muscles in his thighs bulged and Catherine was certain their strength alone could easily crush a person.

He looked down at the dark water lapping angrily against both ships. Then he looked up and over at his ship. Then he looked at her.

Though she was frightened, she held his intense stare. For a moment she had thought he intended to throw her overboard, but then she recalled his reason for attacking the ship. *Revenge.* He wouldn't obtain his revenge by feeding her to the sharks.

"Santos," he yelled, still holding her eyes with his. "We're coming aboard."

Catherine snapped her head to look over at his ship. A short, barrel-shaped man stood on deck. A thick hemp rope that hung from one of the masts was held firmly in his hand.

"You need help?" the man called over with a laugh, and the pirates on both ships joined him in laughter.

"Throw the rope, Santos," he ordered in a rough tone that brought the merriment to an abrupt end.

His free hand caught the rope, coiling it around his arm like a snake before his fingers locked onto it. He released her arm, but before Catherine could rub her sore skin his arm wrapped around her waist and hoisted her up flat against his chest.

"Hold on," he ordered, "unless you want the darkness of the sea to be your grave."

Instinct to survive such a heinous fate brought her arms up and around his neck quickly. She tried to keep her head away from his chest, but when he stood on top of the balustrade and swayed, she hastily relented.

As they swung off the ship, Catherine tightened her arms around him even more. Her face she pressed as hard as she could against his chest. It was warm and the steady beat of his heart sounded reassuring. It wasn't thudding rapidly in fright, but evenly and strongly and in confidence of his ability to deposit them both safely. A sobering thought to Catherine.

A robust cheer rang out from the pirates as they landed on the deck of the pirate ship. She held on until he had steadied them both and then she swiftly dropped her hands and took a step away from him.

He allowed her the distance. She supposed it really didn't matter since he now had her safely on his ship. Where could she go?

He grabbed her arm once again and propelled her toward the quarterdeck. She hopped over coiled ropes and small kegs, almost falling several times had it not been for his strength that held her firm.

"You must—"

He stopped abruptly, swinging her around. She held her hand up, pushing against his chest to stop herself from slamming into the solid wall of flesh.

"I give the orders. I don't take them."

"I only wish to talk with you." Her voice shook upon hearing the brutality in his tone.

"When I'm ready," he said. "Santos, hurry the men. I want to be under way in ten minutes."

"Aye, Captain," Santos called back, then raised his voice in language that wasn't fit for a lady's ears.

Catherine had no choice but to continue following the captain. Down a flight of steps she was drawn and along a dark passage to the end where he grasped the latch to the door and threw it open, dragging her in behind him.

He released her, walked behind her, and fastened the bolt.

The solid thud made her jump and move away from him. She was amazed that the back walls of the cabin held a row of four large windows. The view was astonishing, the sea spread endlessly out before her. A potent reminder of her captivity.

She swung around. "Revenge for what?"

He smiled. A smile that raised the corners of his lips slowly, heightening his handsome features so provocatively that Catherine found her breath catch in her throat.

"When I'm ready," he said, his smile fading.

Catherine felt chilled although the cabin was filled with the warmth of the morning sun. He would give her no answers, of that she was certain. *When he was ready.* Then and only then would she learn the reason behind his brutal actions.

She stood still and silent in the center of the room. If he wouldn't answer her questions then she would wait. She had no other choice.

He walked to the bed, large enough for two people and secured to the floorboards like the other furnishings in the cabin. He pulled his white shirt off, throwing it to the floor, then unwrapped the black sash that circled his waist until it fell, joining his shirt.

Catherine, alarmed by his actions, took a step back.

He loosened the fastenings of his breeches just enough for the material to slip slightly from his hips.

Her eyes were caught by the width of his chest, his flat midriff and narrow waist, but she refused, absolutely refused, to allow them to stray any lower. It was bad enough his navel peeked at her. She would see no more, positively no more.

"The sword is a powerful revenge," he said softly.

Her eyes widened considerably. He couldn't mean . . .

She had heard Dulcie speak of the prowess of Henry's sword. She had foolishly asked to see a demonstration. Dulcie had turned scarlet as did she when Dulcie reluctantly explained the part of the male anatomy that was referred to as a sword.

Catherine opened her mouth to once again ask why.

"Don't," he ordered harshly.

"When you're ready?"

"When I'm ready," he said as he walked toward her.

Catherine remained perfectly still. Perspiration, brought on by fear and uncertainty, prickled her skin and caused her dress to stick to her damp flesh. Her mouth was dry and speech difficult, but she attempted to defend herself in any way she could. "Honor? Keeping one's word? There is none of this among pirates?"

"None," he answered without hesitation, and walked slowly around her in quiet perusal.

"Then you had no intention of honoring our agreement from the beginning?"

"None."

"And the evidence proving my father's innocence?"

"You will earn it."

She shut her eyes against the thoughts his words suggested.

Calm yourself, Catherine, calm yourself and think.

He had stopped close in front of her. She could hear his breathing, even and strong, and she could smell the stinging odors of battle—gunpowder, sweat, and blood. He was not only in total command of the situation, but of himself as well. This man never doubted his ability to attain what he desired, and the idea of such superior confidence and strength terrified Catherine. She was no match for him.

His bare arm brushed against the sleeve of her dress as he walked past her.

"You have but twenty minutes, madam."

She opened her eyes and turned. He stood by the door, his hand on the latch. "Twenty minutes?" she repeated.

"Precisely. Twenty minutes to strip and get into that bed."

Fury swept through Catherine at his outrageous demand. "I won't."

Captain Lucifer stood there a moment, his eyes set intently upon her and his mouth grim and tight. Then he released the latch and marched toward her.

Catherine took several quick steps back, but his arm reached out, grabbed hers, and yanked her toward him.

"You will do as I say."

"I wo—"

His free hand grabbed her other arm and he shook her like a disobedient child who needed to be taught a lesson. "You will never say 'I won't' to me again. You will never say no to me. You will never deny me what I demand of you. You will obey my every command. Now strip and get into that bed, or when I return I will take immense pleasure in ripping your clothes from your body."

He released her and walked to the door.

"Why?" she asked, attempting one more time to make some sense of this nightmare.

"To pay for your father's sins," he said. "I will use you until I grow tired of you, if you please me I shall provide you with the evidence of your father's innocence. Then you shall return to England as *used goods*. How shall the marquis feel then with a daughter who's been the whore of a pirate?"

With his explanation delivered he walked out the door, locking it behind him.

Catherine lowered herself slowly to the floor and wrapped her arms tightly around her middle. What made no sense before made even less now. Why was he using her as the instrument of punishment? What sins did he think her father had committed against him? She knew her father to be a fair man. What fool's thought drove Captain Lucifer to such heinous actions?

Think, Catherine, think!

Her thoughts were jumbled and confused. Her mind refused to think rationally. Fear. It was the fear that caused the confusion. Fear of what Captain Lucifer had planned for her and fear of how his actions would destroy her father, perhaps cause his death.

Put them aside, Catherine, and think.

Captain Lucifer felt by dishonoring her he would hurt her father. And of course that was true. Society wasn't tolerant or forgiving when a young woman made an error in judgment, even if it had been forced upon her. It was still her fault. Of course the married or widowed women had their little dalliances and they were acceptable although not spoken of openly.

So the price Captain Lucifer sought was her virginity. But what if she had already given it away? The notion intrigued her and gave her pause to ponder on it.

If he thought her used goods already, what then? Would he be so fast to make her share his bed? Or would he find her an obstacle in his path of punishment? And what of the evidence proving her father's innocence? She would take one step at a time. The first was to convince him she was soiled property, so to speak.

Of course she would still need to undress, appear naked before him, and she must convince him that it didn't disturb her in the least. That she had shared many a bed with a man and quite enjoyed it.

"Naked," she whispered. How in heaven's name was she going to be able to appear before him without a stitch of clothing on her? Those cold eyes of his would scrutinize her. Would they see her deception?

What was it her Aunt Lilith had so often told her?

Something about a lady always being dressed if she wore . . . what?

Catherine suddenly grabbed the hem of her dress and tore at it. "Please, oh please, let this be the dress." Her fingers tugged frantically at the material until . . .

"Yes!" she said triumphantly as she pulled a long strand of white pearls from the torn hem. "A lady wasn't completely dressed unless she wore her pearls. Thank you, Aunt Lilith, for never letting me forget that bit of advice."

The pearl necklace would save her from feeling naked in front of Captain Lucifer. They were the last item she always put on after she dressed. Therefore when she undressed and placed the pearls around her neck she wouldn't feel so naked. She would feel fully clothed.

Thank God the pearls were sewn, for safekeeping, in the hem of this particular dress. It was fate. Fate was on her side. Her pearls were there for a definite reason—to protect her.

Catherine's hands shook as she stood and unfastened the ties to her dress that would be replaced by what . . . a string of pearls.

She giggled. She couldn't help it. She was nervous and somewhat doubtful that her plan would work.

Catherine removed her clothes and carefully folded her garments on the top of the chest near the window. The sun beat down upon her naked skin through the window and she hugged herself, realizing just how vulnerable she was without clothing. She hurried and slipped the single strand of pearls around her neck. Cool and virginal white, they fell just below her navel.

"My cloak of protection," she whispered, and fussed with the pearls as if they were a dress needing preening.

She then gave attention to her hair. The silver strands were in tangles and she ran her fingers through them until her hair fell over her shoulders and down her back in natural waves.

"All ready," she announced to herself, and walked to the bed.

She stopped near the side a bit dubious of the prospect of climbing in it. This was it. Her one and only chance. She had to convince him. She had to make him think she looked forward to his lips upon hers, his hands intimately touching her, their bodies uniting. She shivered at the thought of his large body smothering hers.

"Stop, Catherine," she warned in a soft whisper.

She climbed into the bed. The blankets were toasty warm and welcoming. She snuggled her backside into them and braced her back against the pillow. But she didn't feel comfortable.

She felt stiff and unnatural. A woman waiting for her lover wouldn't lie so. She would strive for a seductive pose.

But what was seductive?

Perhaps not showing too much, lying to the side, one leg up and across the other, only allowing a small amount of the blond hair to peek from between her legs in temptation.

Catherine blushed terribly. Dear God, what was she thinking? Temptation? She didn't want to tempt him. But she did. She must. She must make him believe her capable of tempting him, wanting him.

She tried again, positioning herself just so, to the side, her leg up slightly and lying across the other one. Her hand was splayed on her hip, her full breasts peeked through the strands of her silver hair, and the pearls were draped over the side of her waist, brushing across her firm backside like a gentle kiss.

She was ready, or at least she hoped she was.

⦿ 3 ⦿

"MOVE YOUR USELESS asses!" Captain Lucifer bellowed, stomping across the deck.

The men scurried like frightened rats to get out of his way. Having sampled his wrath on more than one occasion, they wanted no part of it.

"Bones!"

A skinny man, long in limbs and short on teeth, tripped over his own feet rushing to the captain's side. "Aye, Captain, what is it you be wanting?"

"Your hide!" he yelled, sending the man stumbling backward from the strength of his voice. "If those men aren't off that ship in five minutes."

"Aye, Captain, aye," Bones said.

"And I want this vessel moving as soon as the last man's foot touches deck."

"Last foot, under way," Bones repeated. "Aye, sir, aye."

"Don't 'aye, sir' me, get it done, now!"

Bones turned and collided with a fellow pirate. "Move, you brainless bastard. There's work to be done."

The captain left Bones screaming at the top of his lungs and men running about, preparing the ship to cast off. He secured the fastenings on his breeches, fitting the material snugly to his hips as he walked toward Santos.

"Don't say a word," the captain warned, then turned to the barrel filled with rainwater next to the main mast and dunked his head in it down to his shoulders.

Santos smiled.

The captain lifted his head, snapping it back and shaking

the water from himself. He ran his large hands through his wet hair and over his face, ridding himself of the stench of battle as best he could.

"She's beautiful," Santos said.

"She's *his*."

"But beautiful."

"She's here for a purpose and shall serve that purpose well."

"At least the task won't prove difficult. Young, beautiful, untouched. You should enjoy bedding her over and over. Of course it would be wise to go slow at first. It will take her time to grow accustomed to your size and—"

"Enough!" the captain bellowed. "You think because she is young and innocent that I should spare her?"

"Lucian," Santos said.

The captain turned angry eyes on him. Santos never referred to him by his given name except in private. "I was young and innocent once . . . before her father so carelessly took it from me."

"So robbing her of what he robbed from you will right the situation?"

"We've been through this before, Santos. You are opposed to my decision, but nonetheless, it will stand. I will have my revenge."

"At what cost?"

Lucian glared at the short, stout man who had been his friend for the last eight years. "You forget what we have been through together?"

Santos shook his head. "Never, my friend, never do I forget that. We both have the scars to remind us. But I need no reminder."

"And revenge? Do you still wish this?"

"Yes, Lucian, I will want revenge against the man who made us suffer far more than the torments of hell."

"But?" Lucian asked, knowing all too well something disturbed him. His dark eyes and thick bushy brows always narrowed when troubled.

"But dishonoring the young lady is no way to settle this matter."

"Why? Because she is a woman of pure virtue and noble breeding? Her delicate senses would not take kindly to such treatment?"

"She will be hurt a—"

"I hurt, Santos. Every time I felt the sting of the lash tear my flesh. Every time I ate the food laced with weevils. Every time I smelled my own stink. Every time I remembered it was the Marquis of Devonshire's signature that had condemned me to rot in hell."

Santos made no move to interrupt his tirade of pain. His friend's suffering had been too great. Revenge was the catalyst that would heal his wounds, or so Lucian thought.

"Taking Catherine Abelard's innocence will not cease your nightmares."

"No, it won't, but it will be the start of nightmares for the marquis."

"If he is the monster you think he is, why would he care what you do to his stepdaughter? Why not just let the damaging evidence you planted against him send him to rot away in the Tower, or better yet meet his fate at Charing Cross?"

Lucian leaned against the mast, folding his arms across his bare chest. "That would be too easy, my friend. I want him to taste humiliation as I did."

"But he has," Santos insisted. "These past months he has lost many friends and colleagues. He has been tried and convicted by his own peers. Isn't that enough?"

The defined features of Lucian's face hardened. "No. Now his suffering will begin. It is well known he holds a special spot in his heart for his stepdaughter. He cares deeply for her and would never see any harm come to her. How do you think he will feel when she returns to him in disgrace? How do you think he will feel when he learns that she was the infamous pirate Lucifer's whore? Do you think he will hurt? Do you think his heart will break?" *As mine once did.*

Santos's displeasure was apparent on his grim face.

Lucian moved away from the mast and placed his hand on Santos's shoulder. He towered over his friend. But there was no fear in the short man's eyes, only concern.

"I know you do not approve of this, but I must repay him for the torment he has made me suffer. I cannot let go of the anger and hate. It feeds within me and grows. Perhaps this will be its final meal and I shall then, finally, be free."

"I hope so, Lucian. I hope so," Santos said, and walked away.

"Mind those ropes, you bloody idiots. We're under way!"

Lucian's feet held firm to the deck as the ship pitched away from the merchant ship lying still in the water. He turned away from it and looked out on the clear horizon.

Lucian Darcmoor existed no more. He had been an arrogant young fool, the son of an earl, pampered by wealth and social status until . . .

His eyes squeezed shut against the hurtful memories as he recalled the feel of the lash upon his back the first time. The thin leather lashes ripped like sharp talons into his skin. And just . . . just when he thought it was over the whispering of the leather lashes would sing in the air once more, striking him again and again and again.

After being tied to the mast for several hours, an example to others who disobeyed, he was cut down and cold seawater thrown on his raw open wounds. His screams were loud—the first time—but after repeated abuses he learned to hold back the cries and disengage himself from the ordeal.

Inner strength and mastery over his emotions were the two major lessons he had learned from the beatings.

Finally, the lashes ceased to threaten, but the captain, whose thirst for another man's blood and pain was unquenchable, devised other ways of torture. Lucian had learned by then to hold his tongue, especially when one sailor lost his over a minor infraction.

He walked to the balustrade, gripping the wood. His eyes watched the sea but instead saw his first battle with pirates. He was actually relieved to see the bloodthirsty crew attack the merchant ship he was on. Desperately wanting freedom, he had fought with the pirates. Before the captain took his last breath Lucian demanded a name. The name of the man responsible for his being sold into the captain's servitude for so-called debts.

The captain, his life slipping away, breathed the name Abelard.

Lucian burned the name into his memory and a day didn't go by that he didn't think of the marquis. He was given the choice of joining the pirates, or death. Death wasn't an alternative to him, although some chose it, having lost the will to survive.

Five long years of filth and more suffering followed until he was skilled enough to seize his own ship, and begin the destruction of the Marques of Devonshire.

"Excuse me, Captain," Bones said hesitantly.

Lucian turned his head slowly to the side to look at Bones.

The skinny man's knees began to quake. "Where you be wanting the lady's trunks?"

"Ship's storage. She won't be needing them," he answered, and turned his attention back to the sea.

Bones snickered as he walked away, his smile showing the gaping hole where his two front teeth should have been.

"What are you smiling about, Bones?" a man as fat as Bones was skinny and with a thatch of bright red hair asked.

"The captain wants the lady's trunks in storage. She won't be needing them," he said, poking Jolly in his protruding belly.

Jolly scratched at the stubble on his chin. "She don't look the captain's type."

"The captain don't have no type. If he wants a woman, he takes her."

Jolly shook a chubby finger in Bones' face. "You know damn well the captain don't force no women."

"He don't have to," Bones said proudly of his captain's prowess with the ladies.

"Yeah, they all fall under his spell sooner or later," Jolly agreed.

Bones looked about him, checking to see if anyone could overhear their conversation. "It's his eyes," he whispered.

Jolly stared at him as if he were daft. "His eyes?"

"He's got that look that's real evil. That's why he's called Lucifer. But the look affects the women differently. They get captured by it and soon they're wanting him like mad."

Jolly leaned closer to Bones. "Do you think we could learn to give that look? To women, I mean."

Bones thought for only a moment. "It's sure worth a try. Especially if it works and women start falling all over us."

"That would be a welcome change," Jolly said with a hearty laugh.

"We'll watch his eyes and practice," Bones suggested, trying to squint his wide eyes into the evil look he so often saw the captain wear.

Jolly followed his lead, squinting his eyes and causing his full cheeks to bulge.

"Problem, men?"

Bones and Jolly jumped, startled by the captain's stern voice beside them. Both turned at the same time, a definite mistake since Jolly's belly bumped Bones and knocked him on his backside.

"Get to work," the captain ordered. "And save the nonsense for later."

Both men stared at him as he walked away and shivered at the sight of the thin pale scars that crisscrossed his back.

Jolly held his hand out to Bones to help him up. "I think we should forget the look."

Bones agreed with a nod. "Evil, ain't it?"

"Worse than evil," Jolly whispered. "He's got demons inside him, he does."

Bones and Jolly watched Lucifer walk toward the quarterdeck. They then looked at each other, nodded, and walked in the opposite direction.

Lucian stood outside his cabin door. All his hard work, his carefully laid plans, had finally brought him to this. He would have his revenge though it would not be through rape he achieved it. Matching her innocence with his experience in pleasure would be all that was necessary to reach his objective. In her naivete she would hand her father to him on a silver platter.

His hand reached out, grabbed the latch, and without hesitation he walked into the cabin.

The sunlight played off her pale skin, pure white and blemish free. Lucian stopped in his tracks at the end of the bed, his breath caught in his throat. She was gorgeous. Her five foot four height complimented her every shape and curve. And her hair . . .

God, he thought, only angels possessed hair of that shimmering moonbeam color. Long and silky, it fell over her shoulders, allowing just so much of her breasts to peek through. And they were perfect in size, the type a man could cup gently in his hand and feast upon.

A narrow waist gave way to round hips and a firm backside that molded into shapely limbs. He couldn't help but smile, wicked though it was, at the pearls that tantalized her delicate skin as they lay across her firm derriere.

His eyes hastily made their way to her face and he was captured by it. Her wintergreen eyes were warm and sensuously stunning, especially framed by brows arched like raven wings, yet so extreme in color. Her soft cheeks were flushed pink and her lips were tinged with moisture. Lucian felt a shiver run down his spine as he thought of her small tongue that had probably only moments before slipped across them, staining them with a glistening wetness.

"I'm ready, Captain. Don't be naughty and keep me waiting."

Lucian wasn't certain he heard her correctly.

"Well, do hurry, sir. It has been a week since I've last had a man fill me and I find myself . . . aching."

His look grew menacing, but Catherine continued the charade. She sat up, the pearls rolling down to lie over her breasts and stomach in protection. "Are you having a problem?"

Catherine didn't understand the implication of her question. She only knew it made him more angry, his eyes darkening to a dangerous gray.

"You've had a lover?" he asked in a tightly controlled tone.

"Oh, several."

"Several?" His response was a rough choke of disbelief.

"Yes, did you wish an exact count? It would take me a few moments for I'm not certain if you just wish my lovers, or the few stable boys I've enjoyed from time to time."

"Stable boys?"

"Yes, well, the need strikes at the oddest times."

"Your father?" he asked, unable to complete his question, so confused was he by her actions.

"My father? Good heavens, no! My tastes don't run to the perverse."

"Damn it, woman! I didn't mean that," he yelled. "Your father, he knows of these liaisons?"

Catherine retained the false smile with difficulty and hoped the answer she chose would suit the situation. "Yes, indeed he does. You see there were one or two times that necessitated my farther compensating a gentlemen in return for his silence."

Lucian was shocked into silence.

Bravely Catherine pushed on. "Have you changed your mind, Captain? I'm sure you'll find me entertaining enough. My lovers have often commented on my extraordinary skill."

Lucian lunged forward, grabbing her by the arms and roughly lifting her up to him.

She was inches from his face. Her heart beat wildly. She had gambled and lost. Now he would take her and discover her lies and then what? *You can't give up Catherine. You can't.*

He brought his face closer to hers. She could feel his warm breath. Smell the dampness of his blood-red hair, see the anger in the depths of his cold gray eyes, and taste, oh, God, she could almost taste his lips full and wet with anticipation.

Her eyes grew soft and languid, her mouth opened faintly and she prayed. Oh, how she prayed she would say the right thing.

"Taste me, Captain. Please taste me."

Lucian felt as though he'd been skewered by a cutlass, so

sharp was the pain. He released her hastily as though in disgust, pushing her back upon the bed.

Catherine couldn't speak. Her emotions were strung taut and about to burst. She wouldn't even direct her gaze his way.

He stood staring at her, seeing his weapon of revenge dissolve before his eyes. The anger that had shimmered beneath his controlled surface erupted and spewed forth. "I should have known that the Marquis of Devonshire's daughter would be a whore."

He walked from the room, slamming the door behind him.

"I'm not a whore," Catherine whispered, and with relief buried her head in the pillow and cried.

∂ 4 ∂

Lucian stormed into Santos's cabin, slammed the door behind him, and walked to the table secured to the far wall. A single chair rested beside it. His powerful body took the seat like a dead weight, the wooden legs creaking in protest. His eyes instantly captured Santos's dark ones.

Santos stood a safe distance from him, but still he took a hasty step back, his legs bumping against his berth. He had been privy to that strange look many times. Lucian had worn it often during sea attacks or when he had questioned captives even remotely associated with Abelard.

His eyes would narrow, the scant specks of blue would flare like icy sapphires and his voice . . .

Santos shivered recalling the calm control with which Lucian spoke before issuing orders. His frigid tone rang with the indifference of a man who possessed no soul. Santos made a hasty sign of the cross.

"She's a whore."

"No! Impossible," Santos said, finding himself protecting the young beauty while a chill raced up his spine.

Lucian's voice was as calm as the sea before an angry gale. "She looks like an angel. Innocent and pure of heart." Lucian leaned his head back against the wall and laughed, a low timbre that rumbled deep in his chest like the roar of a mighty predator out for a hunt. "She's far from pure. She's even sampled her father's stable boys."

Santos shook his head more to satisfy his own disbelief than to convince Lucian. "She plays a game with you."

"No!" Lucian yelled, and slammed his fist down on the table. The aged wood trembled from his mighty blow.

His head remained flat against the wall and his eyes slowly closed shut when he spoke. "Her body was made to give and receive pleasure. Her breasts are plump and ripe." His eyes drifted open and stared at his hand on the table. He cupped his fingers. "She would spill over in my hand so plentiful is she. Her skin is a creamy white like that of rich, thick cream you want to lick until full to bursting with its sweet taste. She was fashioned to drive a man to madness— and she knows precisely how to produce insanity."

Santos dropped down on the edge of his unkempt bunk, pushing the crumpled blanket out from beneath himself. "She's demonstrated her skills?"

"She was most certainly willing. Actually it was more like a craving she needed quenched." Lucian sat forward, shaking his head in disbelief. "She enticed me further by wearing a long strand of pearls that fell below her belly as though pointing the way to her treasure."

Santos's eyes widened and were joined by a huge grin. "Remember that whore in Madagascar and what she did with the pearls she wore?"

"All too well, my friend," Lucian said, and shifted uncomfortably in his seat.

"Damn, I'm hard just thinking about that talented lady. Do you think this one possesses the same skill?"

Lucian's nostrils flared in fury as he jumped up. "I have no intentions of finding out."

"Why not?" Santos asked, still wearing his grin. "How else will you satisfy that bulge in your pants?"

Lucian reached for the pitcher of warm ale on the table as he returned to his seat and poured himself a tankard. "That bulge won't be satisfied between Catherine Abelard's legs."

Santos joined Lucian at the table, filling his own tankard

with ale. "I don't understand. Why deny yourself the pleasure?"

"She'll benefit from my pleasure."

"Benefit?"

Lucian explained. "Once she returns to England and her exploits are discreetly discussed, there isn't an aristocrat who wouldn't jump at the chance to bed her. Imagine the tales they could exchange having sampled the infamous Lucifer's fare."

Santos wiped away the ale from his mouth but his grin remained. "Then what do you intend to do with her?"

Lucian downed the last bit of his ale. "One thing is certain. I don't intend to touch her."

Santos laughed heartily. "I wouldn't wager money on that if I were you."

Lucian broke a brief smile. "You have such confidence in me, Santos."

"That I do, my friend. Tell me that remembering the delights of those pearls won't torment you. Will you be able to view them without thinking of the lady from Madagascar and recalling the exquisite pleasure you shared with her? And tell me—tell me honestly—that you won't be tempted to use those pearls on Catherine Abelard."

"I won't teach her new tricks to entertain her lovers. She stays with me until I can find a solution to this unforeseen problem. And I won't *honestly* touch her. I don't wish to be added to her list of conquests."

Santos found his grin fading. "I still find it difficult to believe that she has a list of lovers."

"A long and varied one," Lucian assured him.

"But hasn't your source in England provided you with a detailed report on her?"

"Ladies, though the term is misused, have a way of being discreet concerning certain affairs."

Santos's grin returned in full. "You mean affairs of the heart?"

Lucian smiled broadly this time. "The heart isn't the part of the anatomy the *ladies* seek to satisfy."

Santos filled both their tankards again. He raised his in a salute. "You should know, you've satisfied enough women."

"But how many have satisfied me?" Lucian said with a regretful shake of his head.

A frown lined Santos's mouth. "You found no satisfaction with these women?"

Lucian found it easy talking with his friend. They had shared so much together, pain, sorrow, degradation, that there wasn't anything he felt he couldn't confide in Santos. "I found release from my lust, but satisfaction?" He shook his head once again.

"Of what satisfaction do you speak about?"

His answer came quick to his lips. "The satisfaction you find when you crawl into Zeena's bed."

Santos's smile was filled with pure delight. "Then, my friend, you must fall in love to find such contentment."

Lucian spoke with a hint of sadness. "I lost the ability to love many years ago."

"You didn't lose it," Santos insisted. "You closed your heart against such strong emotions. One day—"

Lucian interrupted abruptly, not wanting to hear once again of Santos's prediction of how he'd find love one day. "Never."

"When you least expect it," Santos continued as though uninterrupted. "Someone will slip inside you and release your imprisoned heart. And you will love like you have never loved before."

"You allow Zeena to fill your idle brain with foolish romantic notions."

"No one *allows* Zeena anything. She does as she pleases," Santos reminded him with a laugh.

Lucian smiled recalling Zeena, who had been his house-keeper since soon after he had landed on his island three years ago. Her silky black hair hung to her waist and her bearing was proud and regal. She demanded respect and gave the same to man or woman. And she had fallen deeply in love with Santos.

Love. A fool's notion, Lucian thought, and he was no fool. "You and Zeena share something rare and special."

"Your tongue won't fall from your mouth if you say the word."

Lucian shot Santos an intimidating glare.

Santos ignored it. "Love. It's called love, and some-day—"

"Enough!" Lucian shouted. His powerful voice reverber-ated off the walls, sending the scarred wood to creaking. "I'll not hear another word about it."

"About love?" Santos asked in feigned innocence.

"So help me, Santos," Lucian warned.

"Exactly," Santos declared, banging his tankard down on the table. "That's exactly what I'm trying to do. Help you. You should lay the past to rest. Look to the future. You've made yourself a fortune. Find a woman and settle down on your island and raise little ones."

"When my revenge is complete, perhaps then I will consider your suggestion."

"With Catherine Abelard's beauty, she would certainly bear beautiful babies."

An angry response rushed to Lucian's mouth, but it was quelled by the deadly smile that captured his words. "The only problem would be that her husband would not know if the babe was truly his."

Santos shook his head slowly. "I still can't believe her a whore. She looks too much like an angel."

"An angel who has spread her wings once too often."

Santos laughed. "I bet the angel awaits Lucifer's return."

Lucian stood. "She waits for naught. I'll not satisfy her blasted lust."

"She could tempt."

"She'd be wasting her time." Lucian walked to the door.

"If she is as skilled as you believe she is, she could succeed in seducing you," Santos warned.

Lucian looked back around at his friend. "An angel is no match for the devil himself."

Santos watched the door close behind Lucian. "An angel has been known to save many a lost soul, perhaps this angel will help you find yours."

Catherine dried her eyes with the back of her hands. Tears would not help her now. Sound reasoning would. With her emotions so distraught she would need to calm herself and attempt to be rational about her situation.

Her first thought was to dress. She slipped cautiously to the edge of the bed, fearing at any minute the captain would burst into the room. The long strand of pearls rolled along her bare flesh and sent a tickling sensation running over her warm skin.

You mustn't dress yet! The warning thought halted her. She cast an uncertain glance at her clothes neatly folded on the chest and considered the consequences of her intended actions.

Would a woman, an experienced, worldly woman, hurry to dress or would she remain abed relaxing in her nakedness?

She gently shut her eyes against the drumming pain that began in her temples and against the worrisome decision.

She was far from a worldly woman and far from a whore. She was a virtuous young lady who wanted desperately to save her father from a heinous and wrongful death. And for that she was willing to pay dearly.

Catherine shivered to the tips of her toes thinking of the consequences of becoming Captain Lucifer's wife. Her eyes widened with her thoughts. He was so large, so overbearing, so powerful and so terribly frightening.

She had thought for certain she would have fainted when he had grabbed her and held her so close. The angry look in his eyes, the smell of the sea on his hard chest, the blood red color of his long wet hair and his starkly handsome features all served to frighten her beyond reason. She had not been sure if he meant to kiss her or strangle her.

Catherine slipped beneath the linen sheet, her body chilled though the morning sun had toasted the cabin to a pleasant temperature.

The idea that as his wife his control over her was limitless made her tremble even more. She should be grateful that she would not suffer such a horrid fate. As long as she kept her wits about her and continued to act as an experienced woman, he would leave her alone. He would not kiss her, touch her, or—

Catherine turned several shades of red. She could not fathom herself laying naked beneath Captain Lucifer, her legs spread wide while he had his way with her. He would certainly cause her pain, perhaps even crush her with his mighty strength or force her to do unspeakable things.

A sudden thought rushed a short startled cry to her lips. Certainly, as a woman who had lain with so many men, she would be expected to know of such unspeakable acts. She knew only bits and pieces of the intimate act shared by a man and a woman. And that information she had learned in a most unladylike fashion. She had eavesdropped on the housemaids' conversations. She would need to make a mental note of the things she had heard and hopefully she would make reference to them correctly.

She turned to her side, the pearls rolling off her flesh to rest comfortably beside her. She caressed the shiny beads, relaxing in the solace they brought her. They were her armor, her protection, her symbol of faith in herself. Wearing the pearls she would never feel naked no matter the circumstances. She had to hold on to that belief, her survival depended on it.

She returned her thoughts to her present and foremost problem. Captain Lucifer had to be constantly reminded of her intimate dalliances so he'd refrain from touching her. She in turn would need to search for the documents that would prove her father's innocence.

The pain in her temple was like a thousand drums beating a horrendous cadence. She applied pressure to the pulsating veins, her fingers attempting to force the pain away. Her rhythmic suffering continued and with difficulty she focused on her ultimate goal, finding the documents that would prove her father's innocence. She prayed that the papers were somewhere on this ship, preferably in this very cabin and not in the captain's island home.

She feared that if she set food on his island, she would never leave it.

The dreadful pain in her head lulled her into a fitful slumber. Her dreams vividly reminded her of the bargain Captain Lucifer and she had struck. She tossed and turned and whimpered as she found herself becoming the devil's own bride.

Lucian entered the cabin reluctantly. He would have much preferred to remain topside with the heat of the afternoon sun beating down upon him and the sea breeze refreshing his heated skin.

He wondered whether, if he viewed Catherine Abelard spread out so invitingly for him, he would either strangle her or ravish her, he just wasn't certain which.

God's blood, but he wouldn't mind having a taste of her. She was truly a tempting morsel. *Who had been sampled by many.* He could not—would not—give her the satisfaction of adding him to her list of conquests.

Besides he intended to learn more about Randolph Abelard from his daughter's own lips and in so doing discover an alternate way of bringing about the man's destruction.

A strange whimper caught his attention and he walked further into the room after shutting the door behind him. He approached the bed with hesitation, hearing her soft sensuous whimper. He didn't care to admit just how much her passionate moans affected him though his breeches strained with the proof of his response.

He stopped near the side of the bed and cast a curious and reluctant glance down at Catherine.

Passion, hot and ardent, filled her dreams. Her hands fondled her bare breasts frantically, her breathing was heavy, her body thrashed about the bed and her legs locked tightly together as though capturing her dream lover solidly within her.

"Please, oh, please," she begged softly and with just the right amount of proper reluctance for enjoying herself while innocently enticing her lover.

Lucian found the heat rushing to his loins and his hand racing out, without thought of consequence, to touch her. With a sudden and anxious roughness, he cupped her breast. Her intake of breath was sharp, the moan that followed seductive.

"Please," she whispered again with barely a quiver, almost as though she feared instead of desired her lover.

His fingers complied, playing with her rosy nipple, exciting it to hardness while his hand squeezed the fullness of her. His lips ached to take the pebble-hard orb into his mouth and suckle its sweet taste.

She doesn't dream of you, his thoughts reminded him. An angry smiled curved his lips. "Which lover do you dream of?"

A whisperingly sensuous plea tumbled almost incoherently from her lips, but her pleading words were enough to send Lucian near to bursting. He released her with the suddenness of one who had just been burned by a red-hot flame.

Abruptly, he turned away from her and stormed out of the room, shutting the door violently and hastily throwing the latch that locked Catherine Abelard in and locked him out.

❧ 5 ❧

"LADY CATHERINE, PUT some clothes on!" Lucian demanded forcefully, rising from the large chair behind an equally large desk that sat before the row of windows in his cabin.

Catherine slowly uncrossed her legs and retreated from her perch on the bed to a chair by the unlit stove near a corner of the room. Her innocent expression and casual tone bespoke confidence though fear prickled her fair skin. "Sir, I have clothes on."

Lucian's voice rose in agitation. "You have *my* linen shirt on and *nothing* else."

Her head went up defiantly. "I have my pearls."

"Excuse me," he said sarcastically, and executed a hasty bow. "A lady must wear her pearls."

For a brief second Catherine felt exposed. She had thought he understood the significance of her pearls and that her armor would be breached. But over the past two days she had become aware of the fact that the longer he remained in the cabin with her and the more she elaborated on her intimate exploits, the more sharp and biting were his barbs. Equally surprising was her discovery that if her verbal defense was casual it raised his ire even more and caused him to storm from the room not to return for hours or until morning.

She settled herself comfortably in the chair, folding her legs beneath her and tucking his shirt that gracefully fell to her knees over her slim limbs. "How charming. You actually understand the dictates of polite society."

Lucian stood and walked around to the front of his desk. He braced his backside against it and folded his arms across his broad chest. "Polite society be hanged. *You,* madam, shall behave as I dictate."

Catherine presented a calm exterior, not even raising a brow in response, though her skin crawled with gooseflesh. She still feared his intimidating manner and his size. Lord, his size alone could bend a person to his will. Add to that his arrogant swagger of self-confidence, his ability to command those around him with a single word and his eyes that penetrated so deeply that she thought he could capture a person's most profound secrets with a mere look. All of this only served to heighten her own inadequacies and make her fear him all the more and doubt, doubt so very much, her ability to find, and hold on to, the courage and wisdom to carry out this charade.

Catherine forced a smile and made her response before she could doubt herself. "As I've offered before, I'm at your disposal."

Lucian lunged forward and was upon her in three quick strides. His large hands latched on to the arms of the chair, locking her into her seat. His face hovered a mere inch from hers. She could smell the spicy scent of his clean-shaven face, see the spark of anger in his blue eyes, and catch the tensing of his jaw muscles.

She shivered.

His voice questioned without emotion. "Cold?"

The truth ran from her lips. "No, you frightened me."

He looked at her strangely, his eyes searching for an answer that appeared to puzzle him. "I didn't think any man frightened you."

She had allowed her guard to slip. She had stepped out of character and had responded foolishly and without thought.

He waited patiently for his answer. His eyes had lost their

anger, but not their intensity. His jaw muscles had relaxed and his lips parted slightly almost as though they waited to capture—

A kiss. The thought struck her suddenly. An experienced woman would have recognized the fact immediately. A harlot would have stolen one from him by now. But she was neither and her response was her own.

Her hand grabbed hold of the pearls and her other hand moved upward to his face. Her fingers glided in feathery softness over his smooth, warm cheek.

He tensed, every muscle tightening like a taut rope secured to the mast.

Her hand stilled, but only for an instant. She moved with precise slowness to his lips, running her fingers over his exquisitely shaped mouth. Her fingers tingled strangely, the sensation rushing up her arm.

He shot her a glaring look.

Her fingers remained on his lips as she gathered all the courage she possessed to calmly announce, "I won't hurt you, Captain Lucifer."

He moved away from her in a flash. His eyes cast her a venomous look and his tone was just as lethal. "But I have yet to determine if I shall hurt you, Catherine."

Think, Catherine, think. The little voice in her head warned her. You mustn't show your fear. You must remain strong and conquer this giant with your wit. *What wit?* her own senses argued.

Feeling smug that his retort had rendered her speechless, he said, "No response, Catherine?"

Catherine placed her finger to her mouth and chewed softly on it in contemplation. Her thoughts raced to recall anything that would help her to respond wisely, or in this case unwisely, to this situation. Unintentionally a slow sensuous smile spread across her face. "I was thinking, Captain. Pain sometimes can bring pleasure."

Lucian released a low frustrated growl.

Catherine decided to take her response one step further, hoping it would send him out of the cabin for the entire night as had been the case since she had boarded his ship.

She stretched her arms out to him and in an aching whisper said, "Let me pleasure you with pain, Captain."

Lucian's angry roar bellowed through the entire ship before he stalked out of the cabin, slamming the door behind him, causing not only Catherine to tremble but the room as well.

Catherine slumped in the chair. Her hands shook so badly she had to release the pearls she held. How much longer could she continue to play this game? Her nerves were near to shattering. Each time she offered herself to him, she feared his response. What if he accepted? Then what?

She shook her worries away. She couldn't waste time pondering the consequences of her actions now. She had to take the time to search the cabin for the papers that would prove her father's innocence. The faster she located the papers, the faster she could attempt an escape.

Catherine had methodically searched a section of the cabin each time she was alone. She had begun her search in the captain's desk, but had found it locked. Not wanting to waste precious time she had moved to the opposite side of the cabin and had searched the trunks and various nooks that could possibly be used to conceal papers.

It was during her first exploration that she had decided to wear one of the captain's shirts. Her decision was actually a pragmatic one. It had nothing to do with her charade. The hem on her dress was torn and she didn't possess the needle and thread to repair it, and she didn't want the captain even remotely aware of the fact that she had purposely removed her pearls from her dress to wear. So she had grabbed his shirt from the chair and slipped into it. She had worn it ever since. She had even slept in it.

It had taken time to grow accustomed to his smell on her. The mixture of fresh sea air, gunpowder, and male flesh was potent—as potent as the man who had worn it.

She chased her strange thoughts away and hurried over to the desk. In the captain's haste he may have forgotten to lock it and she would have a chance to search it and hopefully find the papers.

Catherine pulled at the drawer on the side. It creaked open. She smiled and dropped to her knees, her hands already busy rifling through the papers.

Charts, maps, and other sailing papers occupied the drawer. She shut it in disappointment and pulled open the one beneath. Her eyes scanned the writing quickly and she shook her head. She was reading too fast and not comprehending the words.

She leaned back on her haunches and slowly read over the document. She frowned, shook her head, and read the paper again.

On the last page she studied the official seal in the lower right corner and the royal signature. If she understood this document correctly Captain Lucifer was a privateer for England. If that was the case then he would have had knowledge of her father's merchant ship routes, to make certain he didn't attack English ships, and he would have known full well those ships carried only cargo for the Crown and not supplies for the enemy.

She shook her head again. This didn't make sense, unless . . .

The chilling realization that rushed over Catherine sent the shivers through her. Captain Lucifer himself had fabricated the evidence of her father's guilt. And he alone held the key to freeing him. Catherine shut her eyes against the tears that threatened to spill. Why? Why did the captain hate her father with so much vengeance that he would go to such lengths to see him destroyed?

A scurry of feet outside the cabin door sent her into action. She returned the papers to where they belonged and rushed over to the bed. Her bottom hit the middle of the wide bed as the door opened and Santos stumbled in, attempting to balance the tray he held in his hands.

Catherine smiled. She liked the short, robust man. He spoke kindly to her and brought her water to wash with and food to fill her belly as he declared each time he brought her a meal.

"I brought you extra wine and cheese tonight to fill your belly," he said setting the tray on the bed. "You don't eat enough."

"I don't always have an appetite."

Santos handed her a large chunk of cheese. "Tonight you eat."

Catherine took the offered cheese and nibbled at it, though her churning stomach protested. Jokingly she asked, "Does everyone on this ship give orders?"

Santos shook his head while he filled her tankard with wine. "Only Captain Lucifer."

She swallowed, with difficulty, the small piece of cheese in her mouth. "Then it is his order that I eat?"

"He sees your tray returned to the galley with barely a nibble taken from it. He tells me to make certain you eat tonight or else."

"Or else what?" Catherine attempted to keep the tremor from her voice.

Santos caught her nervousness but showed no signs of his detection. "There's no telling what he would do."

Unpredictable. That was one frightening aspect of the

captain's manner. She couldn't judge with accuracy his reaction to any given situation.

Her father's involvement in politics had afforded her the privilege of meeting all manner and types of men. Her father would caution her to study the men and watch their reactions to various situations. He had explained that within a short time one could predict one's opponent's reaction to any given situation.

Captain Lucifer defied this principle, but then so did her father.

Even now she worried that the captain would find a reason to return to the cabin and decide he no longer wished to reject her advances. Then what?

The piece of cheese suddenly felt heavy in her hand. "I find myself hungry tonight, Santos."

"This is good," he said, and walked to the door. "I will return for the empty tray later."

She smiled, nodded, and wondered how she would dispose of the food since her stomach revolted at the thought of swallowing it.

Lucian gripped the mighty ship's wheel firmly. He lifted his face to the warm night breeze and drank deeply of the rich salty air. He felt in command when he was at the wheel and free. Free to travel what course he chose, free of restraints, and almost free of the past.

The ship dipped and rose gracefully riding the endless sea with dignity. He braced his feet more firmly on the deck and held his head high. It had taken time and patience to regain his dignity, having been treated far worse than the lowliest animal for what seemed like countless years. And through all that time he had recalled over and over the name of the man who had condemned him to suffer the tortures of hell. Abelard. Abelard. Abelard.

Catherine. Her name rushed to his lips and in a soft whisper he released it, the night breeze catching it from his tongue and carrying it away.

She presented an obstacle to his plan, a serious obstacle. He had intended to seduce, now he was the one being seduced, and with great skill. When she had caressed his cheek and had so sumptuously informed him that she wouldn't hurt him, he had thought his control would snap and that he would rip his shirt and those damn pearls off her and give her exactly what she had ached for from the first day in his cabin. But he had managed to control the fiery passion that had raced through his veins.

He took a deep, fortifying breath of sea air, lifting his face to the heavens and locking his eyes on the star-studded night sky.

"An angel," he whispered, and as though the heavens agreed, a spray of sea mist sprinkled his face.

He shook his head as if in disagreement, recalling how she had offered to pleasure him with pain. The sensuous suggestion alone was enough to rush his manhood to stiff erection and his anger to boiling. She may look like an angel, but she possessed a harlot's soul.

But that he would deal with, he had no choice, if he was to accomplish what he had set out to do—ruin the Marquis of Devonshire.

"She obeys you well."

Lucian showed no surprise at Santos's approach. He was attuned to every movement on the ship and was surprised by none, except from the woman below in his cabin. Her every movement surprised him. "I'm her master and she knows it."

"Then perhaps you should master the one below," Santos suggested, placing his hand on the wheel to transfer command.

Lucian gave it up freely. "You know my thoughts well."

Santos shrugged while holding the huge wheel steady. "I assumed in time you would realize what must be done and do it. I grow tired of the sea and I miss Zeena. Finish this business and quickly so we may return home."

"It may be necessary to take her to the island."

Santos shrugged again. "So take her and be done with it. Use whatever is necessary. Command her as you command this ship and see that once and for all you quench that vengeance that eats at you."

Lucian stepped in front of the wheel to look his friend straight in the eye. "Are you suggesting that Catherine Abelard commands me?"

Santos met his friend's stare straight on. "I don't suggest. I tell you what I see with my own eyes and I see that you *don't* see the truth."

His voice was low and demanding. "Then tell me truth as *you* see it, Santos."

The short man shook his head. "I can tell you nothing. You must discover it for yourself or it will hold no meaning for you."

"You talk in riddles like Zeena."

Santos laughed. "She taught me well. Now you must learn your lessons as I have learned mine."

"What lessons?" Lucian asked irritably.

"About life, my friend."

"I learned my lessons the hard way," Lucian said, "or have you forgotten?"

"No, I haven't forgotten, but I have learned from them and let them go. You have held steadfast and still seek revenge. Be careful what you seek doesn't come back to seek you."

"Again riddles," Lucian said in disgust.

"There are no riddles when you see the truth. Do what

you must, Lucian, but keep your eyes open wide as you go."

"My eyes are wide and my path is clear. I'll have my revenge." He turned and walked away, the night swallowing him up.

Catherine had just settled herself in bed for the night, content that once again the captain would spend the evening elsewhere and leave her alone.

The opening of the cabin door startled her and without thinking she sat up in bed, bracing her hands behind her.

Captain Lucifer stepped quickly into the room. He captured her shocked expression with his confident one. He gave the door a hard shove behind him.

The click of the latch sent a shiver through her, but she moved not a muscle. She just continued to watch him.

He walked to the end of the bed and with deft hands he stripped himself of his clothes in only minutes, resigning them to a heap on the floor.

Catherine kept her eyes on his face, not daring to glance lower though her warning voice told her she should. She just couldn't. Lord, she couldn't bring herself to view his private parts. The scope of his broad chest, the fullness of his muscled arms were enough for her to speculate on how large the rest of him actually was.

His slow steps brought him to the side of the bed.

Catherine craned her neck back to keep his face and chest alone in her view.

His red hair hung over his shoulders, falling onto his bare chest. His damp flesh smelled of salty sea air and he stood with his hands at his sides in relaxed arrogance.

"Tonight, Catherine, we sleep together."

❧ 6 ❧

CATHERINE FROZE, KEEPING her steadfast gaze on the captain's eyes. Aware that her response must not be hesitant, her thoughts raced and her inner voice cautioned her actions.

She smiled, buying herself precious time and realized that she should not shy away from inspecting his body. He probably expected her to look. He probably assumed she wanted to view all of him, and all things considered, it would give her extra time to think through her dilemma.

She sat straight up, her fingers going to the pearls hanging down around her neck and coiling part of the long strand around one finger. With a soft blink of her eyes she drew her gaze away from his.

She had never observed a naked man before and suddenly her mind focused on a sobering thought and her smile blossomed. This was her chance to learn about the male anatomy. She could study him at leisure in hope of procuring more knowledge. If she kept that thought in mind and viewed his nakedness as a learning experience, perhaps, just perhaps, she would succeed in keeping him from her bed.

The captain remained silent and still. He didn't even blink an eye. He undoubtedly had expected this reaction from her and stood prepared.

Courage in hand, her gaze wandered to his chest. She was familiar with the breadth of his taut, hard muscles and his sun-drenched skin. His midriff was tight and flat, not a bit of fat marred his waistline unlike so many men. More slowly, her gaze descended lower. She held it steady for a moment, her well-bred nature warning her that her actions were not at all proper. But then what choice did she really have? To admit her innocence would surely mean the end of her innocence. With a soft blink of her eyes and a forceful breath of courage, she allowed herself to look. Her eyes widened and her mouth dropped opened. He was large *all* over.

"I can safely assume from your surprised reaction that your lovers were not generously endowed?"

Catherine struggled to find her voice and a response. With speech impossible, she leisurely licked her dry lips not realizing how her innocent reaction resembled sensual hunger.

The captain released that low growl that Catherine had become so familiar with. She had agitated him and if she could continue to do so he would leave her alone. The more aggressive her actions, the more he avoided her.

Determination kept her eyes focused on his manhood, which she thought looked bigger than when she had first set her eyes upon it. She dismissed the thought as nonsense, anxious to be rid of him.

She lazily shifted her gaze up to his and casually reclined back to rest on her side. She drew back the white linen sheet covering her, careful to keep her own body concealed, and in a whisper, afraid if she spoke any higher her nervous voice would betray her doubt, she said, "Do join me. I've *never* enjoyed a man of your ample size."

Lucian took an angry step forward, then stopped himself. He stood poised in thought for a brief moment . . . then he moved. He braced one knee on the bed and descended slowly over Catherine, forcing her onto her back. He braced his hands beside her head as his mouth rushed down on hers.

Shock made her mouth drop open and he took her reaction as an invitation. His lips captured hers and his tongue glided smoothly into her mouth.

She responded out of innocence and surprise, her tongue darting around his. Her hands ran urgently over his chest in thought of pushing him away only to realize his strength wouldn't allow her an escape. With no choice left to her she hesitantly settled her warm palms against his hard chest muscles.

Lucian cursed his impulsive actions. She teased him like a consummate harlot, her tongue forcing a chase that heated his loins. And her small hands had wasted no time in seeking out his flesh. They rested comfortably against his nipples, causing them to harden against her touch. He couldn't help but wonder how her small, delicate hands would make him feel if she explored his body further.

His thought shocked him back to reality and he pulled away from her, his teeth tugging at her bottom lip as he left her.

Catherine arched up afraid he would bite her lip clear off.

His hand swiftly moved to her chest and he shoved her back down on to the bed. "No more!" he shouted, and threw himself on his back beside her.

The bed bounced and the ropes squeaked from his weight and Catherine released a grateful sigh of relief.

To Lucian's ears it sounded more like disappointment. "I will not satisfy your lust, madam."

Catherine gave no thought to a response. She was too busy attempting to calm her racing heart. She had thought for sure that he intended to have his way with her and thus discover her lies.

"Too breathless to speak?" he mocked with satisfaction.

Too breathless with worry, she thought, and sighed heavily, her racing heart having finally slowed.

His manly pride assumed her response meant one thing. "Never experienced a satisfying kiss, have you?"

Catherine felt herself bristle. He had the nerve to believe her a harlot and the gall to assume she was an unsatisfied one.

Lucian rested his arm over his eyes and smiled. "Perhaps that's why you've gone through a string of lovers, none have ever fulfilled you."

The words rushed from her mouth before she gave thought to the consequences or to the sarcastic tone in which she delivered her remark. "And naturally you think you could *fulfill* me."

With his first movement she realized her mistake, but to move a mere fraction from him would show her concern, so she remained still.

Lucian turned on his side, bracing himself on his elbow and resting his head in his hand. His other hand casually reached out and his fingers played with the pearls that lay directly over her breast.

"Yes, Catherine, I could easily fulfill you, *but* I wouldn't give you the satisfaction."

Catherine kept herself from tensing as his fingers brushed over the shirt where it covered her nipple and especially when he carelessly, but she assumed deliberately, dragged the pearls across her breast. She needed a response that would annoy him enough to at least move him away from her. He was close, much too close, and his nearness was causing her stomach to flutter nervously.

"But think, Captain, you could be the talk of London. I would sing your praises, or is it prowess, to the aristocracy."

Her remark hit bull's-eye. His fingers released the pearls, tossing them away to fall to her side. He once again fell onto his back.

"I don't like repeating myself, Catherine, though I will remind you one more time. I don't plan on giving you the satisfaction. I will leave you—"

Relief ran through her. He would leave her alone once again.

"—to imagine what you have missed in having me as a lover."

Catherine hid her smile beneath a practiced frown. "You upset me, Captain, I surely shall not sleep tonight."

"If sleep escapes you this night it is your own fault. Just don't toss and turn and keep me awake, *and* stay to your side of the bed."

Catherine couldn't believe her ears. He actually planned on sleeping in the bed with her. She wondered if she attempted to agitate him just a wee bit more if it would be enough to chase him from the cabin, or enough to—

She didn't want to think about the repercussions, and she didn't want him sleeping with her. She spoke before she lost her nerve. "Very well, Captain, though—" She paused just enough for a dramatic effect, then continued on a sigh. "You overestimate your kissing talent. I *have* experienced better."

Lucian had had enough. He turned on her so swiftly that she rolled away from him startled. He rolled her right back and right beneath him and then he proceeded to demonstrate just how exceptionally talented he was at kissing.

He took her breath away. She didn't even have a second to think about what was happening and in only seconds she couldn't think. His tongue and his mouth took command of her and saturated her with such drowsing sensuality that she lost all focus on time and reality.

As he feasted on her, he caused her to hunger. A hunger she had never experienced. And a hunger that only he seemed capable of satisfying.

He dragged his mouth from hers and trailed wet kisses down along her neck then up to her ear. "Tell me," he whispered almost breathless himself. "Tell me you've been kissed like this."

His powerful kisses had stolen her ability to speak and if she could she would not be able to tell him anything but the truth. With only the experience of a few stolen kisses from some ardent suitors, Catherine had never had a man claim a kiss such as the one the captain had just demonstrated.

Too long in her response, Lucian once again urged one

from her. "Tell me or I will test my skills on you again and this time I will pleasure myself until *you* cannot stand it any longer."

She could hardly bear the breathlessness she experienced now. She couldn't imagine it being worse. She shook her head and whispered the truth. "I've never been kissed like that."

Lucian rolled off her, giving her a persuasive shove to her side of the bed. "Now go to sleep . . . *if* you can."

He turned, reached out, and extinguished the oil lamp, bathing the room in darkness.

Catherine could think of no appropriate response, nor did she wish to give one. She turned quietly on her side, tucking her hands beneath the side of her head and pulling her legs up almost to her chest.

Lord, what had she gotten herself into? She didn't have near enough knowledge of the intimacy between men and women to succeed with her plan. She was playacting like a child at adult games and she was bound to get caught. It was only a matter of time.

Again the result of her discovery reared its ugly head and she pictured the captain in all his strength and size looming over her. Yet this time his kisses didn't frighten her and that thought scared her senseless.

Her thoughts continued to race, setting plans, planning escapes, thinking of home and her father. She twisted and turned with each fresh thought until finally . . .

Lucian's hand shot out and grabbed her around her waist, dragging her back up against him. "Now stay put," he growled in her ear.

She felt the hard strength of his large body braced against hers, felt her breath catch from the tug of his arm around her middle where it remained, and she instantly stilled.

"Go to sleep," he ordered in a tone that expected immediate obedience.

Catherine said not a word. His warm breath had fanned her cheek and sent gooseflesh rushing over her skin. She had no intentions of moving and no intentions of sleeping. She would remain still and hope that he would fall asleep quickly, then she would slip away from him, to the chair, and find her sleep there, alone.

She closed her eyes against her worry, against her strange plight and against her thoughts, and drifted peaceably into a dreamless state, her body following until sleep crept up and unsuspectingly claimed her.

The leather lash struck Lucian for the fourth time and still he made no sound or movement. His body stiffened, his mind closed off the torture he suffered. The lash sang through the air again and caught his already raw flesh. His teeth clamped down, imprisoning the scream that lodged in his mouth, forcing it back to lock deep in his throat. He would not give the captain the satisfaction of hearing him scream. The captain enjoyed the whipping so much more when the men screamed and cried for mercy. He received no pleasure, no excitement, from a victim who remained silent.

The whip hit his back again and again and with each lash he heard the captain scream, "I'll have my satisfaction. I'll have my satisfaction."

"Never!" Lucian yelled, and bolted up in bed and out of his dream.

Catherine jumped up with him, frightened and startled by his scream and by the darkness that surrounded her. Her hand reached out searching for him and ironically for protection. "Captain?"

Lucian felt her nervous touch to his chest. He needed her closeness and protection as much as she needed him. He covered her hand with his, pressing her warm flesh against his chest. "It's all right, Catherine."

His thudding heart and damp flesh spoke otherwise and strangely she found herself concerned for his welfare. "Are you sure?"

Her voice was soothingly soft and he ached to lose himself in her comforting tone. He wanted to take her in his arms and lose himself within her, make her lose herself within him and shut the ugly world outside away.

Then the ugly world interfered, he recalled her true nature and his years of torment and plans for revenge.

"Captain?" she asked once again.

Her sincere voice lulled his senses, or perhaps once, just once, he wanted to believe someone actually cared about him. He slipped his arm around her, tugging her against him, and eased her back on the bed with him. He cradled her against his chest, wrapping his large leg around her small one. She didn't object. She snuggled against him. He gratefully hugged her to him.

"You had a bad dream, Captain?" she all but whispered, doubtful that she should attempt to comfort him and wondering why she should feel compelled to do so.

"Yes, Catherine, I had a bad dream."

"Would you like to tell me about it?"

"Why would I want to do that?" He felt her shrug against him.

"It might help you to speak about it."

"I never speak about it."

"You've had this dream before?"

"Often," he murmured.

"Then you should talk about it. Talking about it will help you feel better," she advised.

"I don't think you would want to hear about it."

"I don't mind listening."

"It's not fit for your ears."

"My ears have heard many things."

"I forget how experienced you are. At times you remind me of an innocent angel," he found himself admitting.

"I'm no angel, Captain." She cringed against the lie that followed. "And I'm no innocent."

The thought angered him. He had fooled himself into believing briefly that the young beauty he held in his arms was naive and pure. But she wasn't naive and her stepfather was the reason his dream plagued him. It was time for her to discover her stepfather's true nature.

"I dream of the whipping I received while I was a forced crew member of the merchant ship I sailed on."

"Forced?" she asked, then added, "And whipped? The captain whipped you?"

"Often, and enjoyed doing so."

"I've heard such cruelty existed on some ships and I've heard how some men must crew the merchant ships to settle their unpaid debts."

"I owed no debts, though it was made to look otherwise," he informed her with a coolness to his tone.

"You were unfairly sold into service?"

"Exactly."

"That's horrible," she stated angrily. "Who would do such a thing?"

Lucian had waited for this moment and calmly he told her. "Your stepfather."

Answers to so many questions suddenly became clear and her response was swift. "You're mistaken."

His arms fell away from her and she rolled away from him. "I am not mistaken."

She moved to the edge of the bed. "My *father*," she emphasized, "would never sell a man into servitude for an unpaid debt."

Captain Lucifer's response was so calmly and forcibly delivered that she shivered.

"He did."

"Never," she corrected.

"You have no idea what your *stepfather* is truly capable of."

Catherine felt her anger rise. Her hands began to shake and she had no doubt that when she spoke her voice would tremble. "You know nothing of my father, Captain Lucifer. I know him better than anyone."

He laughed before he responded. "You know him *that* well? Then tell me, Catherine, how are his kisses?"

It took a moment for his nasty insinuation to thoroughly sink in. Her response was swift. She turned on him and swung her hand full force at his face.

The stinging blow reverberated through the darkness. Silence followed for a brief second and then he reacted. He reached out, grabbed her by the back of her head and yanked her face down to a mere inch from his.

She felt his warm breath, smelled the fruity wine scent and sensed his deep-rooted anger.

His grip on her tightened with each word he spoke. "You ever raise your hand to me again and I shall tie you to the mast and whip you myself." He shoved her away from him, to her side of the bed.

Catherine huddled to the edge of the bed, hugging the side so as not to fall out. She hadn't known the reason behind his revenge and now that she did it made her task all the more difficult. No wonder he hated her father so much. To Captain Lucifer the Marquis of Devonshire had been the reason for all the ills that had befallen him. He now planned to have the marquis suffer as he had suffered. The captain was so blinded by anger and revenge that he couldn't see the truth, the truth about her father or the truth about herself.

❧ 7 ❧

CATHERINE CHOSE TO remain silent when she woke the following morning. Her somber mood seemed in keeping with the weather. The sky outside the row of four windows was overcast, promising rain or perhaps a storm.

She felt her own mood brewing beneath the surface. She was upset with her actions last night. She had lost her temper when she shouldn't have. After all, she had taken great pains to paint herself a harlot, and if the captain thought poorly of her, it was her own doing. His obscene response meant she had succeeded in convincing him of her promiscuous nature. Oddly, she thought, she should be proud of herself.

She wasn't. Her difficult task had just begun and already another burden had been added to her load. Not only was she determined to find the documents proving her father's innocence, she intended to make certain Captain Lucifer was made aware of his mistaken notions of her father.

She sat up in bed, adjusting the covers across her lap before running her fingers through her tangled hair. She glanced casually around the cabin, aware that the captain sat at his desk, but attempted to appear indifferent to his presence.

A grimace of pain forced her to cease her attempts at combing her hair with her fingers. The pulls and tugs were just too uncomfortable and actually served little benefit in making her hair appear presentable.

"If you wish your comb, ask for it," Lucian commented

with annoyance, and shoved the quill pen into the inkwell in front of him.

"My comb," she repeated, "is on the other ship."

Lucian pushed his chair back and stood. "Your belongings were brought upon my ship along with you."

Catherine smiled joyously and clapped her hands together like a child delighted with receiving a gift. "How wonderful! Where are they? May I have them brought to me?"

Lucian felt a sudden stab to his belly that raced with lightning speed through his body and struck his throat, nearly taking his breath away. Good Lord, she was even more beautiful when she smiled. He wouldn't have believed her angelic looks could improve if he hadn't witnessed the transformation with his own eyes.

Her deep green eyes brightened, her cheeks flushed to the palest of pinks, her lips widened with her considerable smile and looked all the more appealing and ready to kiss. Even her hair, tangled and unkempt as it appeared, added to her allure.

Lucian stepped around his desk and was about to advance on Catherine when he caught his own actions, brought an abrupt halt to his firm strides and turned, heading straight for the decanter of wine in the cabinet.

He was about to pour himself a generous portion and drink heartily of it when he realized the control of the situation had slipped away from him, forcing him to seek comfort from stronger spirits. He had never allowed a woman to have such power over him and he wasn't about to start now.

His body lusted after her, but his mind was his to control and his body would have no choice but to follow his dictates. He was in command. He gave the orders. He demanded obedience. She would learn.

Her beauty made no difference, but her gentle voice? He

laughed beneath his breath. Her tender voice was nothing more than a mere subterfuge to conceal her wanton nature. She was a master at the art of luring men into her web of deceit. He would not be drawn in by her honeyed ways.

He turned, his face expressionless, his voice in calm control. "You demonstrate such joy over a minor matter, I would have imagined it took expensive gifts to gain such a notable reaction."

Apprehension caused her smile to falter, but her strong-willed nature forced her to retain her composure. She had forgotten how foolishly most aristocratic women reacted to gifts their husbands lavished on them.

"You hesitate. Don't tell me you never demanded *trinkets* from your lovers?"

His tone, so full of scorn, irritated Catherine and her defenses emerged for battle. She sat up straighter, her shoulders going back, her chest out and her chin up. Her hands immediately sought her pearls. "I *don't* accept trinkets."

Lucian gave her a slight bow. "Excuse me, m'lady, for the insult. I suppose gems and gold are more to your taste. Like that strand of pearls you seem to favor. A gift from a satisfied lover?"

Catherine surprised herself with her hasty response, especially since she had no idea where it came from. "An earl presented me with this lovely strand in gratitude for a brief affair that he insisted gave him pleasure beyond his wildest fantasies."

Lucian felt his skin prickle. Damn, but her little barb frustrated him. *Fantasies.* That was a dangerous word for her to mention. It was a rare woman willing to fulfill a man's fantasies and he wondered just how rare Catherine Abelard was.

Catherine once again felt the need to force him into leaving the cabin. She required time alone, to see to her needs and to think. Lord, how she needed to think things over. "If you would like to see various other pieces of fine jewelry presented to me by grateful gentlemen, then bring my traveling case to me and I'll be glad to detail each gift. Of course I can detail the affair if you prefer."

Catherine held her breath for his answer. She could no more detail an affair than she could swim. She had a strange feeling that she might just drown in her own words.

His retort was biting. "Your affairs hold no interest for me. And I will *bring* you nothing. You, Lady Catherine, are in no position to give orders."

One look at him reminded her just how precarious her position was. She just couldn't get over the size and muscled bulk of him. She had never imagined a man structured so superbly and powerfully. She could understand how women would find him appealing, but strangely enough it was his eyes and hair that Catherine found her glances returning to.

"Don't play your games with me, Catherine," he nearly shouted. "That innocently yearning look will not work on me. You may yearn, but you're far from innocent."

Catherine had no idea what he was referring to and thought when in doubt it was best to agree. "You're right, Captain. I do apologize if I caused you *discomfort*."

Damn, but she was good with those cunning barbs. It was time to take his leave before he lost his temper and did something he would regret.

He moved to the door.

"Captain," she called out to him, halting him in his tracks.

He turned once again and with annoyance asked, "What now?"

"My comb."

He looked at her oddly.

She clarified. "I would like my comb if you could possibly have it sent to me."

"Sweetness," he said with a strange laugh. "It doesn't fit you, Catherine." He left the room, slamming the door and causing Catherine to jump.

Her shoulders slumped and she sighed heavily and then as though throwing off her cloak of despair, she bounced out of bed. She had no time to feel sorry for herself. There was work to be done. A lazy mind or body would get her nowhere and she ached desperately to return home.

While having a quick wash from the white ceramic water basin in the wooden-and-brass stand near the stove, she gave more thought to her father. She wondered about his condition. Had he improved? Would his condition worsen when he learned of her fate? Would he attempt to search for her?

The marquis had been the perfect father, loving her unconditionally. She recalled when she was young, about ten perhaps, he had caught her in a small lie. He had taken the time to discuss with her the importance of honesty and the honor of one's word. She had promised that she would never, not ever, lie to him again. He had pledged the same.

That single memory was the reason she knew her father was not guilty of Captain Lucifer's accusations. He was a fair and honest man. His merchant ships were of the few who did not brutalize their crew members. He fought for the less fortunate even though his ideals made him less popular with his own kind. He was truly a man of strong convictions and that was why these treason charges were so ludicrous.

Catherine was sitting in the wooden chair next to the stove deep in thought, drying her hands on a white cotton towel when a rustle outside the door caught her attention.

A loud thud was followed by a painful "Ouch," followed

by argumentative voices. One voice she recognized and it brought a smile to her face.

"You clumsy idiot, I should have had one of the other men, one with more brains, help me," Santos complained as he limped in, pushing the door wide open.

"It's heavier than it looks, Santos. Honest," Bones declared, dragging the polished oak traveling trunk into the cabin.

Catherine discreetly draped the towel she held over her bare legs and smiled her greeting.

Bones beamed from ear to ear his toothless grin, causing Catherine's own smile to widen. "I can't tell you how thankful I am to you for carrying my trunk here. You are very kind and thoughtful."

Santos snorted a laugh and Bones blushed, fumbling to find the right words. "Thanks, my pleasure, pleased to help—"

"Enough," Santos ordered. "He was following the captain's orders and doesn't need any thanks."

"That's right, that's right," Bones agreed, bobbing his head. "The captain told me to get your trunk and bring it right quick. And I always do what the captain tells me no matter what it is."

"Why?" Catherine asked.

Both men looked at her as if she were daft.

"I should explain my interest in your reason for following the captain's orders?" Catherine asked.

Both shook their heads.

"I've heard tales of pirates, especially about Captain Lucifer, and I wondered if perhaps he was as vicious to his crew as the stories make him out to be."

"Who's spreading such bloody lies? Why, me and the crew will find the bastard and—"

"Bones!" Santos shouted. "Watch your mouth in front of the lady."

"Beggin' your pardon, mum," Bones said with a nod.

Catherine acknowledged his apology with her own nod, too dumbfounded to speak. She had not expected to find the crew loyal to the captain, especially not to the point of physically defending him against a verbal accusation. And foremost she had not at all expected Santos to refer to her as a lady. It worried and touched her simultaneously. She could not afford to have her charade uncovered, but it was nice to have someone to think of her as such.

"Move the trunk to the end of the bed and be gone with you," Santos ordered gruffly.

"Right you be. I'll just take it—"

"Ouch!" Santos yelped when Bones hit his other foot while he attempted to drag it where Santos had ordered. "Get your useless ass out of here."

"The lady," Bones said with a whispered reminder and a blush to his already ruddy cheeks.

"Out, out," Santos shouted, shooing him out of the room like an irritating pest.

Catherine couldn't contain her laughter. When the door closed her giggles burst free.

Santos turned an angry scowl on her, but it vanished quickly when he caught sight of her bright face. "I don't know why I put up with him."

"There must be a reason," Catherine said, feeling comfortable enough with Santos to probe for answers to questions. Questions that would help her plan succeed.

"Aye, there is," Santos said a bit sadly, easily moving the trunk to rest at the end of the bed.

Catherine remained silent, having learned over the last few days that with a simple question and only a minimum of prodding Santos spoke freely.

"Lucian saved Bones from a mean one, he did." The memories caused the lines on Santos's face to crease more deeply with his frown.

Lucian. The name drifted in Catherine's head. Could it be the captain's given name? She listened closely, intending to learn as much as possible.

"The details aren't fit for your ears. All you need to know is that Bones is safe and the pirate is rotting in hell where he belongs."

"Lucian killed him?" She used the captain's name without thought.

"Lucian does what is necessary to survive." Santos returned. "And how is it that you know his name?"

"Whose name?" Catherine asked.

"The captain's. You called him Lucian."

"That's his name?"

"I called him by his name." Santos shook his head, answering his own question. "He's going to have me flogged."

"He'd never do that!" Catherine said, stunned.

Santos glared at her oddly. "How do you know Lucian never flogs his men?"

"Simple," Catherine said. "The barbaric punishment was inflicted on him repeatedly. He wouldn't make another suffer such abuse."

"You begin to understand him."

She hoped to understand Lucian even better thanks to Santos. "Those forced years on the merchant ship must have been difficult."

Santos's attention drifted far away, though his eyes remained on her. "I still can hear his screams, though he learned quickly enough that the captain enjoyed when the men screamed. Then he silenced his pain even when the salty seawater hit his open wounds. He didn't respond. He remained silent. Dead silent. Then there were his recoveries when the insects would swarm around his festering wounds. I spent many sleepless nights keeping the bugs from feasting on his raw flesh."

Catherine shuddered. The horrible picture Santos painted turned her stomach. Her father would never have employed such a captain. Never. The cruelty Lucian had endured was inconceivable. No wonder he hated her father. But how did he come to think her father responsible for his plight? Who had provided him with false information and why?

"Our situation didn't improve much when our ship was captured by pirates," Santos said, and waved his hand in disgust. "But those tales are best left untold."

"You spent many years with him?"

"Over ten, and it wasn't until Lucian took command of the pirate ship did our lot improve." Santos moved toward the door.

Catherine wished to hear more, but Santos had his way about him. He spoke in bits and pieces and with each piece Catherine planned on solving her puzzle.

"He's not what he appears," Santos said softly. So softly that Catherine barely understood him.

Her response was just as soft and spoken as the cabin door closed. "Neither am I."

❧ 8 ❧

THE RAIN BEGAN early in the afternoon. It was a steady and heavy downpour, but lacked the strong wind that would have made it a raging storm.

Surprisingly, Catherine hadn't noticed when the rain had begun. She had been too occupied rummaging through her trunk and reflecting on her situation to take note.

She considered dressing, but after examining her wardrobe she felt the garments were too cumbersome for her confined quarters. She required light, unrestricting clothing so she could move about quickly and quietly. She decided upon her pale pink linen shift trimmed at the low neckline with a row of embroided roses. It was one of her favorite garments and she wore it often beneath her dresses. It was sleeveless and fell down along her body, curving slightly over her hips to rest at her ankles.

She draped her pearls over the shift, breathing easier when they fell protectively against her. She spied the captain's white silk shirt on the bed where she had discarded it.

With a spark of delightful mischief in her eyes, she reached for the garment. "I shall continue to wear your shirt, Lucian."

Her use of his given name startled her and she hesitated a moment in picking up his shirt.

"Lucian," she whispered, testing the name once again on her lips. She slipped his shirt on, rubbing the soft material against her cheek.

"Who are you, Lucian?" That question had plagued her often of late. His speech was refined as were his manners when he ate. He kept himself clean-shaven and his body was always damp at night when he returned to the cabin as though he had just washed. And his long dark red hair always shone and smelled of the sun and sea.

He was not, Catherine decided, a commoner. Could he be of noble birth? But that didn't make sense. A nobleman would never be sold into service to a merchant ship. Perhaps he was an illegitimate offspring of a nobleman who didn't wish his secret known. She shook her head. She would talk with Santos more and learn what she could. Eventually all the pieces would fit.

She liked talking with Santos. He treated her not only like a lady, but like a friend. And she got the distinct feeling that although he would follow Lucian's dictates, he did not always agree with him.

Catherine yawned and looked to the windows. The rain pounded against the glass. The sky was a dreary gray and would darken early tonight because of the foul weather.

She closed the lid on her trunk and looked around her on the floor. Several of her personal articles surrounded her and she smiled. She planned on accenting the cabin with her own things to irritate Lucian all the more and hopefully force him to flee from the cabin as often as possible. She would then be free to safely search for the documents and also be safe from his close scrutiny.

She placed her silver comb set on the small chest next to the side of the bed where Lucian slept. She added her bottle of rose water and her skin lotion especially blended for her by a local herbalist.

She draped her assortment of silk ribbons over the brass bar on the washstand and placed her blue-and-white china soap dish on the shelf beneath the brass bar, adding a bar of rose-scented soap to it.

A rumble in her stomach alerted her to her hunger and the fact that supper would soon be arriving. She decided to arrange the table a bit more formally this evening. Lucian had joined her for the evening meal these last couple of nights and she had felt intimidated by his presence and silence. Not tonight. Tonight she would play the harlot so well, he would storm from the room never to return.

She laughed at her own daydreams and set about to work. She took a white lace scarf from her trunk and arranged it to run down the middle of the scarred table. She fetched the crystal goblets and mother-of-pearl-handled utensils from the cabinet that housed Lucian's liquor and placed them appropriately on the table. She chose a bottle of red wine from the lower shelf of the cabinet and moved the oil lamp to the center of the table.

The flickering light reflecting off the crystal and the setting for only two suggested that it was an intimate interlude for lovers.

Catherine smiled, slipped out of Lucian's shirt, and sat at the table to wait.

The rain had soaked Lucian. His clothes clung to him, his hair dripped with water. He could have retreated below, his men wouldn't have minded. But he would have. He had promised himself when he took over the ship that he wouldn't expect his crew to do anything he wouldn't do himself. He had earned their respect and their faithfulness and he had no intentions of abusing those privileges.

He took the steps down to his cabin, tired and worn out from the physical duties he had performed. He was in no mood to spar with Catherine this evening. It was the comfort of his cabin, a good meal, and his bed that he sought, and no more.

He reluctantly opened the door and entered. He stopped abruptly only a few feet into the cabin.

"Good evening, Lucian," Catherine said, attempting to hide her nervous tremble. The sight of him glistening wet caused her heart to thunder. His features appeared more handsome, his body more powerful. He gave the appearance of a mighty god who had just risen from the sea. "Santos promised our meal would be here soon. Are you hungry?"

He was hungry all right. But it was a lusty hunger that gripped him seeing her standing there with her body so exquisitely outlined in that pale pink shift. The garment hinted at what lay beneath and knowing what it concealed only heightened his passion.

"I'm hungry and tired," he snapped. "And in no mood to be seduced."

Catherine couldn't hide her smile. She was becoming talented at playing the harlot and with so little experience. She felt proud of herself.

"I was thinking only of your comfort, Lucian," she said sweetly.

"I'm sure you were, Cath—" His eyes suddenly grew heated with anger. "Blast it all, woman, how did you find out my name?"

Catherine was about to answer him when he waved her response away with his hand. "Forget it. Santos could have been the only one to tell you."

"Completely by accident," she said, defending Santos.

"It was no accident," Lucian said, walking over to the washstand to grab a towel. His glance took in the colorful ribbons and the soap, its rose scent drifting up to tempt his nostrils.

He was about to bellow in rage when he realized her intentions. She planned to torment him into making love to her. She'd be relentless in her pursuit of him. He would be her prize, her trophy to discreetly display before her intimate friends upon her return. Whispered gossip would spread like wildfire and soon her string of lovers would grow and multiply.

But not if he had his way. He'd give her a sample, a small

taste of what she ached for, but—she would never know fulfillment in his arms. He wouldn't give her the satisfaction.

Lucian stripped out of his wet clothes, discarding them to lie in a heap at his feet. He snapped the towel off the brass bar and roughly dried himself. He took his time, running the white towel over his chest and down around his flat belly.

He turned, offering Catherine a better view, and propped his foot up on the nearby chair while he vigorously dried his leg. He treated his other leg likewise, then dropped the towel down over his back, grabbing the other end at his waist and running it back and forth diagonally across his back. With that finished he tossed it aside, stretched his arms up to relieve his sore muscles and give Catherine more time to devour him with her eyes. He then stepped behind the washstand and reached for his moss green silk robe hanging from a peg and slipped into it, tying the belt loosely around his waist.

Catherine watched in amazement. At first glance she hadn't thought too highly of a man's anatomy. She had actually thought the male physique odd. The odd part being the one that jutted out like a prideful peacock. Naturally the intimate act required such a protrusion, from what she had heard.

But at the moment he didn't protrude and he reminded her of a sleek, muscled panther, long in limbs, graceful in movement, and confident in his abilities. He could stalk, he could capture, and he could devour with ease. Her thoughts chilled her, but she hid the shiver that ran up her spine and warned herself to remember well the predator she had so richly compared him to.

Lucian took a smaller towel from the stack of towels that sat on a narrow cabinet next to the washstand and vigorously dried his hair. Satisfied that only a dampness remained, he tossed the towel to the floor to join his wet clothes and ran his fingers through his hair. He focused his eyes on Catherine. Surprisingly, she was staring right back at him and with the most enthralled look.

She spoke honestly and without forethought, a habit her father often warned her needed correcting. "You are quite a specimen of a man."

"A compliment?"

"A fact."

Lucian finished combing his hair with his fingers as he spoke. "Then I assume you are comparing me to your previous lovers and find them sadly lacking in manly attributes."

Catherine smiled. "And I thought women were vain with their constant need for attention. Is it a compliment you are fishing for, Captain? Do you wish to hear that I find you more appealing than any man I have ever known? That you and you alone send my heart to fluttering? Easy enough words to utter, Captain."

Her voice dropped to a whisper. "Tell me, Lucian. Tell me what you want to hear."

Damn, but she made him sound like a petulant little boy needing praise and stroking, and her seductive whisper promised just that.

Catherine tempted fate further by stretching her arms out to him. "Come, Captain, come to me."

Lucian advanced on her in quick strides.

Catherine froze and attempted not to show her fear. Had she gone too far this time? Why in heaven's name had she so blatantly summoned him? Her breath caught in her throat as he neared her.

Lucian stopped short of her and casually walked around the table until he was close enough to reach out for the bottle of wine. He picked it up and poured himself and Catherine a glass.

"I'm curious, Catherine," he said, handing her a glass of red wine. "Who introduced you to sex?"

His obtrusive question startled her. Sex was never mentioned, much less discussed, with the opposite sex. Ladies followed their husbands' dictates where the primal act was concerned and never questioned the matter.

Time had rapidly caught up with her and she had barely the slightest notion about *sex*. She was aware that she shouldn't be discussing the subject with the infamous Captain Lucifer, but then he didn't consider her a lady. And she intended to see that his opinion of her remained so.

"Have there been so many lovers since your first that you can't recall the man, or was it a disappointing experience you prefer to forget?" Lucian asked, having taken the seat opposite her at the table.

"I was but thinking of the pleasant memories," she said, and sipped at her wine, hoping the soft dry flavor would help relax her.

"Pleasant, not memorable?"

Catherine took another sip of wine. A tiny drop of wine lingered on her bottom lip and she hastily licked the drop away with the tip of her small tongue before she spoke. "Pleasantly memorable," she corrected.

Memorable. Lord, but he'd have a hard time chasing away the memory of her tiny tongue skillfully scooping up that drop of wine. He wondered what other tantalizing feats her tongue could perform.

He reached for the wine bottle and poured himself another glass. "Tell me about him."

Catherine looked puzzled. "Who?"

Lucian raised his glass in a salute to the unknown man. "Your first lover."

"Benjamin," she said with such a genuinely happy smile that it irritated Lucian so much that he fussed in his seat as though prickled by a thousand pins.

"I was positively mad about him," she continued, her eyes sparkling with delight as she recalled to mind Ben-

jamin Bristle, Earl of Combstock. He had been a friend of
her father's and she had been all of fourteen and in the
throes of a hopeless crush. He had been a perfect gentleman,
never once hurting her feelings by reminding her of their
considerable age difference. He had been tolerant and
patient with her youth and therefore received even more of
her adoration. "He was several years my senior."

"Why am I not surprised?" Lucian muttered, and swallowed a generous portion of wine.

She hadn't quite heard his remark. "What was that you
said, Captain?"

"Why, I wondered what qualities endeared him to you."

The truth spilled from Catherine's lips. "He thought me
intelligent."

Lucian almost choked on his wine. He sprang forward in
his chair and glared at her. "I never thought of intelligence
as a requisite to sex."

Catherine didn't falter in her response, her knowledge had
been too hard gained to brush it off in amusement. "You do
yourself an injustice if you feel sex involves no intelligence."

Lucian relaxed back in his chair. "Explain your theory."

Catherine held her empty wineglass out to him. She spoke
while he filled it. "It isn't a theory. It's a logical, intelligent
conclusion."

"Go on."

She paused to sip her wine and gather her thoughts. She
had never made love, so she had to go on the assumption of
what she would expect from a man before, during, and after
such an intimate act. And she recalled to mind how
Benjamin had made her feel so special simply by listening
and sharing in conversation with her. Wouldn't an act so
intimate require the same details, to listen to each other and
share, for one to give as much as the other? To equally

satisfy and please simply because one cared or perhaps loved enough to do so.

"When two intelligent people make love they take into consideration each other's feelings. They share in the act, without dominating it. So together they can both find satisfaction and pleasure."

"Benjamin taught you this?"

She nodded. "He treated me with respect."

Lucian's look was caustic. "He took your virginity, but treated you with respect?"

Catherine didn't hesitate to correct him. "I gave him my virginity. He never would have taken it otherwise. He taught me what to expect from a relationship and to accept nothing less."

"So it's respect you demand from your lovers."

"A mutual respect."

"Then I take it you don't like to be fu—"

Catherine's angry glare cut him off. "I don't like verbal vulgarity."

"Or physical vulgarity?"

"No!" she said, color rising to stain her cheeks. "I don't—don't—"

"Rut," he said with a laugh.

"Rutting is for animals," she snapped.

His grin was carnal. "I don't know, rutting can have its moments."

"I'm sure you would know about that."

"I suppose only the less intelligent rut while the aristocrat makes love."

"You twist my words, Captain. One doesn't require wealth to possess intelligence. And if more women used their intelligence they would find themselves not having to rut."

Lucian's expression grew dark. "Some women have no choice. It's called survival, not intelligence."

Catherine sighed and nodded in agreement. "You're right about that. Too many women have no choice."

"And then there are women like you who do." He once again raised his glass in a salute, only this time it was to Catherine.

At that moment Catherine felt like a whore. His remarks set in and she realized the significance of his statement. The women of the street didn't choose to become whores, she had.

How ironic, she chose to portray a harlot to survive, just like the women of the streets. Despair washed over her thinking how those women must feel, thinking how she felt at this very moment.

She chose her words carefully feeling as though she defended more than just herself. "We all make choices for a reason, Captain. The most basic being for survival."

"Excuse my laughter," he said with what sounded more like a sardonic growl than a laugh. "Are you telling me that you chose to have a multitude of lovers because it was necessary to your survival?"

The truth of his statement stung her nerves and she felt a tremor rush up her spine. "With knowledge comes a degree of protection. I chose to seek that protection."

Lucian shook his head wondering if it was the wine that befuddled his brain or if Catherine actually was more intelligent than him. "Protection from whom?"

"Men," came her sharp retort.

"Ahh," he said with an understanding shake of his head. "Now I see. You're one of those women who prefer to control."

Catherine considered his remark. "Do you like to be controlled, Lucian?"

His expression darkened, his finely shaped brows arching and his eyes narrowing as they concentrated on her face. "No one will ever control me again, Catherine."

"Then we understand each other."

"Was he a good lover?"

She looked at him oddly, the change of subject confusing her.

"Benjamin," he said, his stare steadfast on her as he waited for an answer.

Her answer expressed her hopes and dreams for the future. "He was kind and gentle and concerned for my feelings. He made our time together a memory I shall cherish forever."

"Benjamin sounds like a real gentleman. And you do prefer *gentle men,* don't you Catherine?"

Catherine didn't care for his emphatic tone. The captain was far from a gentle man. She had experienced that firsthand. He was a man bent on revenge and she was the instrument of his revenge. If there ever was a gentleness to his soul, it was probably whipped out of him with each stroke of the lash he had suffered.

She studied his hardened stare, ignoring his question. His eyes looked weary and strangely enough lonely. She experienced an overwhelming sense of loneliness looking into their depths. He almost seemed to drown in it, fighting against it, tearing at it like a frightened child needing to be loved. Her heart went out to his suffering and she wished at that moment that she could put her arms around him and chase his loneliness away if only for a short time.

"Do you often get lost in your thoughts, Catherine, or is it a ruse so you don't have to answer a question you don't wish to?"

Catherine was saved from answering once again by a knock at the door.

"Supper, Captain," Bones called out.

"Come in," he ordered.

"Right fine supper tonight," Bones commented, his skinny frame struggling with the heavily laden silver tray.

"Don't dare drop that, Bones," Lucian warned.

"Don't you worry, Captain, I have everything under control."

"Good, because you're in a room with people who respect control." He shot Catherine a sharp glare.

"Let me help you," Catherine offered, rising and ignoring Lucian's intimidating tactic.

"Sit down!" Lucian bellowed, causing Bones to jump and the dishes to rattle on the swaying tray. "Don't dare touch that tray, Catherine."

"I've got it. Everything's fine, just fine," Bones said, lowering the tray to the table with shaking hands. "Cook outdid himself," Bones rattled on nervously. "Fresh-caught fish, potatoes, biscuits, and cheese."

"That will be all, Bones," Lucian said, his eyes focused on Catherine as she returned to her seat.

"Sure thing, Captain. Enjoy the meal," the skinny man said, bobbing his head, his toothless grin wide as he backed out of the cabin.

"Let's get one thing straight, Lady Catherine," Lucian said as the door clicked shut. "I'm in control here and you *will* obey me."

"Or?" She heard her own audacity and couldn't believe her own ears.

"Or you'll suffer the punishment," he said calmly, too calmly to her way of thinking.

"And the punishment?" My Lord, but she was being willful tonight. She wondered where the devil it came from.

"I'll think of something appropriate. After all," he said with a nasty grin, "I am a pirate."

✎ 9 ✎

A PIRATE. SHE was sharing a bed with a pirate. The
evening meal had been partaken in relative silence. His
casual remark had reminded her of his felonious trade and
had stirred an uneasiness in the pit of her stomach. After-
ward she had quietly taken herself off to bed without so
much as a by-your-leave.

Now she lay on her back, her arms crossed, hugging her
middle with her eyes opened wide staring at the planked
ceiling. The gentle sway of the ship and the soft steady
rhythm of the rain against the windows provided little help
in her quest for a blissful sleep.

Her thoughts ran rampant. Mental images of Dulcie's
pirate tales danced in her head. And the question tormenting
her to the brink of insomnia was . . . were they truths or
tales?

The only way for her to have peace of mind and blessed
sleep was to ask the captain himself.

A soft, almost undetectable, sigh slipped from her lips
and she hugged her middle more tightly.

Courage. It would take a strong amount of courage to
even discover if he was still awake. It had been at least thirty
minutes or more since he had climbed into bed. And she
mustn't forget that he lay completely naked next to her. If
she probed for answers now while in such close proximity
to his nakedness would she find herself in a precarious
situation?

But if she didn't at least attempt to settle her concerns
they would grow out of control. Then of course there was

that chance that the answer she received might prove more upsetting than settling.

You're wasting your time, Catherine, she silently warned herself. *Either ask or spend the remainder of the night listening to the rain and the creaks of the ship.*

She took courage in hand, squeezed her eyes shut for a brief moment, then opened them wide as she softly said, "Lucian."

His sharp response attested to his alertness. "I'm not in the mood, madam."

Her thoughts centered on her immediate concerns, leaving her confused by his statement. "In the mood for what?"

Lucian reluctantly admitted she was talented. Always playing the innocent while she spun her seductive web drawing her victim in closer and closer. Like a spider she waited patiently to snag her prize. Waited until he was so caught up in her sweet web he had no alternative but to surrender.

His anger got the better of him. "To ravish you," he shouted.

Startled by his unexpected outburst Catherine spoke candidly. "I'm not interested in your body tonight, Captain."

"Then why disturb me at this hour and while in my bed?"

She took objection to his reply. "I have no choice in my sleeping arrangements, but—"

She took a deep, fortifying breath and surged on. "I was thinking that since I shared my exploits with you, it is only fair that you share yours with me."

"You wish me to detail my sexual exploits?" he asked incredulously.

Catherine almost choked on her quick response. "Good heavens, no. Your pirate tales are what strike my fancy."

Lucian turned, bracing his head on his hand to stare down at her in the dark. Her eyes were open wide, their dark green color sparkling like emeralds. "You fancy to hear pirate tales?"

"Yes," she answered with the excitement of a little girl impatient to hear a bedtime story.

He gave his head a quick shake. "Such stories aren't fit for your ears."

Catherine decided to remind him of their unusual topic of conversation just before supper. "Really, Captain, earlier this evening we discussed sex. Surely a few plundering tales wouldn't be improper."

"Make up your mind, Catherine," he said irritably. Her remarks were well aimed and, he was certain, intentional. "Is it plundering or pirating tales you wish to hear?"

His response confused her. Evidently she had spoken out of turn and her wisest choice was to return a simple answer. "Pirating."

Lucian dropped onto his back, the feather pillow cushioning his head. If he didn't keep his wits about him she would drive him insane. One minute her voice was sultry and full of confidence, the next it was soft and accented with a slight tremor. Sometimes he wondered if his own mind was playing games on him. He had to keep his mind focused on the fact that she was his instrument of revenge and that he would use her to achieve his goal. How, he wasn't certain, but in the end he would succeed.

Perhaps a pirate tale or two was just what she needed to hear at the moment. His tone was brisk while the darkness concealed his smile. "Remind yourself, madam, that *you* asked to hear these tales."

"I'm most anxious to hear them," she assured him, and folded her hands on her stomach and closed her eyes ready to pay close attention to every detail of his stories.

"I'll start with Dirty Dunbar—"

"Dirty Dunbar, my, what an interesting name," Catherine

commented as she attempted to visualize a man tagged with such a name.

"Madame, do you intend to frequently interrupt me?"

"Certainly not."

"Then kindly keep your remarks to yourself until the conclusion of my story, then and only then may you comment."

"It was because I found his name amusing that I related my opinion."

"The reason he was given such a name is far from amusing."

Anxious for Lucian to continue his tale, Catherine turned on her side to face him. "You mean Dirty Dunbar was actually dirty."

"Filthy. So filthy that neither man nor beast could stand next to him."

"He was a pirate?"

"I thought you weren't going to interrupt," he said, amused by her eager question.

"But I needed to know if he was a pirate or a captive."

"This tale is about a pirate. I will tell you a captive tale next."

"All right," she agreed quickly, wanting to hear more.

"Now, where was I? Yes, I was telling you about filthy Dunbar—"

"Dirty Dunbar," Catherine corrected hastily.

Lucian turned on her in a flash, the tip of his nose coming to rest against her own. "Madam, if you don't cease interrupting me I shall sew your lips shut."

Catherine felt her breath catch in her throat and there it stayed locked in fear. She recalled the story Dulcie had told her about a pirate captive having his prisoner's lips sewn shut and here she was rattling off at her mouth without thought to the consequences.

Lucian instantly regretted his idle threat, though it had served its purpose. It had silenced her, but at a price. Her childish enthusiasm had vanished instantly, replaced in a flash by fear. Her eyes had widened, her lower lip trembled, and she fought to control the breath that appeared caught in her throat.

He could have booted himself for his rash threat. Though he had seen such cruelty performed on captives by other pirates he himself would never inflict such a harsh and barbaric punishment.

Frightened that she would faint from holding her breath, he tugged at her chin, forcing her mouth to open. Her breath whooshed out, the faint scent of wine fanning his face.

Feeling his senseless remark was best laid to rest, he asked, "Do you wish me to continue?"

She nodded, her eyes not quite so wide as they were only moments ago.

His hand fell away from her chin to rest near her cheek. "Do you know why he was called Dirty Dunbar?" he asked in a considerably gentler tone, hoping she would respond.

Again she shook her head.

He certainly had silenced her, which hadn't been his intention. Strangely enough he had found their conversation intriguing and oddly entertaining. He couldn't fathom the idea that she would remain silent, that he wouldn't hear her lively tales or soft quivering replies. The notion disturbed him. "Aren't you going to cast your opinion?"

Catherine shook her head again.

"Why not"

She shrugged.

He'd had enough. "Are you afraid of me?"

Catherine was about to shake her head, though her answer demanded a nod, when his hands grasped hold of the sides of her face and prevented her response.

"You will give me a verbal answer, madam."

Catherine's long eyelashes fluttered several times as her eye drifted open with a look of uncertainty. His hands covered her cheeks and locked under her chin. Her foremost thought was that he could squash her easily.

"I'm waiting," he reminded her.

She cast him a doubtful look.

"I haven't sewn your lips shut yet, Catherine, you can still speak."

She spoke with a more steady voice than she thought possible.

"Would you?"

It was his turn to look at her doubtfully. "Would I what?"

Catherine whispered her answer. "Sew my lips shut."

His thoughtless remark *had* disturbed her. He released her face and tenderly ran his finger over her velvety lips. "Though you sorely tempt me at times I would never inflict such a barbaric punishment on you."

"You would on others?" She surprised herself with her question and how easily she had asked him.

His finger continued to caress her lips while he spoke. "No, Catherine, I would never deliver such brutal treatment to a captive."

Her inquisitiveness wasn't satisfied. "But such treatment has been utilized by other pirates?"

"The more demented ones."

Catherine attempted another question but Lucian pressed his finger to her lips forcing her silence. "Enough. I would much rather discuss Dirty Dunbar."

Catherine smiled and Lucian reluctantly dropped his finger from her lips.

"He smelled?" she asked, anxious to hear the tale.

"Atrocious."

"He never bathed?"

"Not since the day he was born."

Catherine laughed at his answer. "You're fibbing."

"I'm relating the tale as it was told to me."

"Many an old tale has been embellished."

"Are you insinuating that I'm a liar?" he asked with a sly smile.

"No," she laughed softly, "though you are a gifted tale teller."

"Thank you," he said with a slight nod of his head. "Now if I may, I'd like to finish this tale before dawn breaks."

"By all means," Catherine agreed and snuggled her head into her pillow to comfortably listen to the story.

"Dirty Dunbar was short, round, and possessed a robust aroma."

Catherine giggled and kept her excited stare on Lucian.

He could almost feel the intensity of her deep green eyes, feel her thrill, her passion to hear his every word. And he gladly fulfilled her whim. "Men gave Dirty Dunbar a wide berth when he walked the streets and when he entered a room." Lucian shook his head, adding a grave expression to dramatize the tale. "The men scurried out like panicked rats."

Catherine was captivated by his every word.

"Dirty Dunbar took to the sea and was captured by pirates. He was given the choice of joining the motley crew or death. He chose to join the pirates. The pirates, none too familiar with soap and water themselves, gave Dirty Dunbar a warning. 'Wash up or else.' Dunbar didn't heed their caution. The grumbling crew issued him another warning and another and another until . . ."

Catherine waited anxiously to hear the man's fate.

"The sky was on the verge of a storm that fateful morning the crew took matters into their own hands. They pounced on him as soon as he showed himself on deck. It took ten men to hold him down and ten men to tie him up."

Catherine was beginning to feel sorry for Dirty Dunbar.

"And each of those men had plugged up their noses just so they could get near him."

Catherine laughed and her sympathy swayed to the crew.

"Once they had him all tied up tightly they took him to the plank stretched out from the deck of the ship over the sea. They told him to walk the plank or be pushed."

Catherine gulped, having heard of captives being forced to walk the plank and wondered now if those tales had been true.

"Dirty Dunbar chose to be a man about it and walked to the end of the plank, turned and smiled at the crew, then jumped. The men ran to the balustrades and peered over whooping and yelling in satisfaction. Then it happened." Lucian said quietly, almost in a whisper, as though he shouldn't have uttered a word.

"What happened?" Catherine asked just as softly.

"The sea churned and roared and rocked the ship until suddenly the water heaved like a sickened belly and in one loud belch it spit Dirty Dunbar right back on the deck of the ship."

Catherine burst out laughing and playfully poked Lucian's bare chest. "You're teasing me."

Lucian grabbed hold of her finger. "Madam, you asked for a tale and I related one to you. And might I add, a favorite tale among pirates."

"And why would that be their favorite tale?"

He gently turned her own finger on her, giving her chest a poke before releasing it. "Any pirate that accuses his fellow mate of smelling is put to the test."

"What test?"

"The accused must jump in the sea and if the sea doesn't

spit him back then he doesn't smell bad enough that the crew can't live with him."

Catherine stared at him wide-eyed. "You are fooling with me, aren't you?"

"No, Catherine, I'm not," he assured her, though his eyes danced with merriment in recalling the tale he had heard often enough himself.

She shook her head and laughed.

Lucian responded to the pleasurable sound. It tingled his flesh and hardened his loins. His unexpected reaction annoyed the devil out of him. And set the devil inside him to work.

"Now that I've told you a tale, answer me a question."

"But I've answered questions, this tale was to reciprocate for our earlier exchange. And besides, you promised me a captive tale next." She had grown tired and sleep was tempting her eyes and jumbling her thoughts.

He didn't ask again. He demanded. "You'll answer my question."

Catherine felt too weary to argue. "As you wish."

"Did you like the way Ben kissed you?"

Catherine had to think a minute before she recalled what she had told him about Ben earlier. "Yes, he was most skillful."

"And gentle?"

Catherine gave pause before answering. She had described his kissing as gentle if she remembered correctly. "Yes, and gentle."

"Ben never took you beyond gentle?" he asked, annoyed that he found the uncontrollable need to question her on the matter.

She wasn't even aware there was a step beyond gentle. Her experience with kissing had been a few pecks on the cheek and a brush across the lips. And then there was

Lucian's kisses, delivered with an edge of anger and revenge, not desire or love. "He was my first and most gentle lover."

"You've had ones that demanded more?" The thought infuriated him for it reminded him of her many lovers.

"I gave only what I wish to give, Captain," she said, and rolled on her back with a yawn.

Lucian felt like a small child being chastised by a tutor for not having learned his lessons properly and then dismissed without consideration. It was his turn to teach her a lesson.

"Demonstrate this gentleness Ben taught you."

Catherine felt a jolt to her stomach and suddenly sleep was the furthest thought from her mind. She decided to pretend otherwise, not having the slightest idea how to handle the situation except to run, and being on a ship in the middle of the sea vastly limited her possibility of escape.

She yawned extra widely, covering her mouth to hide her pretense. "Another time, Captain, I'm so very tired."

Lucian rolled over next to her, grabbed her hand that lay on her stomach and her hand that covered her mouth and held them, locked by her wrists, above her head. "Catherine, you must listen and learn."

She stared at him, a sense of captivity descending over her as he continued to hold her imprisoned. Her fear escalating, she studied the perfectly formed lines and angles of his face. Lord, but he was handsome. Too handsome. Handsome as Lucifer himself and just as dangerous.

"Are you listening, Catherine?"

His voice was strong and even in tone just like his hold on her. His hand held her firmly, the forceful pressure evenly distributed, not hurting her, but reminding her of her capture. Catherine responded with a nod, too fearful to speak.

"Now for your first lesson, Catherine." He paused a moment, stared down at her, then lowered his face to hers with each word spoken. "I never make a request twice. I'm always obeyed the first time."

His lips were suspended a mere breath away from hers waiting. He intended for her to demonstrate the kiss Ben and she had supposedly shared. He had no intention of repeating himself and this she would understand if she had learned her lesson. She had learned her lesson, all right. She had learned it was best to keep quiet upon entering his bed and not ask any stupid questions.

Now she had to kiss him. Kiss him as she had convinced him Ben had kissed her. Gentle. A gentle kiss should be easy to give. She could close her eyes, pretend it was Ben, and give him a simple kiss.

He breathed not a word, he just hovered over her waiting.

She lifted her head a fraction preparing to hastily deposit a kiss on his lips when her senses were assaulted. He smelled of the sea, fresh and salty and temptingly lickable. His long hair hung down around his face, tickling her bare shoulders, and the warmth of his flesh penetrated the cotton of her shift until his heat actually caused the shivers to race through her.

Without thought or reason she slowly lifted her head and captured his frowning lips. Gently, almost worshipfully she brushed across them, testing, feeling their velvet smoothness.

She instantly became addicted and drew her lips back and forth, slowly, sensually, succulently. Wanting to savor more of his exotic taste, her small tongue sneaked out and stole a hasty lick of his lips. Her sigh confirmed her satisfaction.

Lucian hadn't expected this slow and tortuous assault on his senses. His passion flared like a roaring fire. Heat cursed through his veins, his blood boiled, his body soared to life.

He had intended to teach her a lesson and she had taught him one. She had taught him just how erotic a gentle kiss could be. If he didn't bring a halt to it soon, he'd find himself added to her string of lovers and his plans for revenge destroyed.

He snatched his mouth away from hers, released her arms, and jumped from the bed, grabbing his clothes as he walked toward the door. Without a word, and stark naked, he stormed out of the cabin, slamming the door behind him.

Catherine collected her rapid breath while she rubbed her tingling lips with her fingers. She hadn't expected to feel so highly sensitive, so completely alive.

She felt edgy, highly agitated, and her eyes immediately looked to the closed door. Had she overstepped her boundaries and teetered on the threshold of unbridled passion? Had she actually lost control of her emotions? Had she wanted Captain Lucifer to kiss her?

Catherine shivered at the disturbing thought and pulled the sheet up to her neck. Searching for a sensible reason for her odd actions she decided after several minutes of deliberation that sleepiness had been the culprit that had caused her momentary lack of control.

She would need to be more vigilant, more aware of her predicament, and tread wisely. But most of all she had better make certain that she never, ever, kissed Captain Lucifer again.

❧ 10 ❧

"SHE NEEDS SOME sunshine," Santos insisted, standing beside Lucian on the quarterdeck of the ship.

Lucian appeared not to have heard. His eyes were focused on the endless sea, his hands clasped behind his back, and his legs spread just enough distance to allow him a steady stance.

Santos persisted. "I said she—"

"I heard you the first time," he said curtly.

"Then give me an answer."

Only Santos was allowed to speak to him with such bluntness and he had paid a high price for that privilege. "You didn't ask a question."

"Don't play games with me, Lucian. You know what I'm suggesting. You're annoyed with yourself so you punish others with your black mood."

"I have a right to my moods," he snapped.

"You have a right to feel the pain of the past, but you should have the wisdom to bury it."

Lucian turned his head to look down at Santos. His eyes snapped with fury, though he contained his hostility when he responded. "Your tongue is sharp today, Santos. Beware."

"I speak the truth, my friend," he said with a sad smile.

Lucian shut his eyes against a look he had become all too familiar with. He had seen that expression many times over the last few years and every time he had it had been when Santos had shared Lucian's pain and sorrow. "Let me be today, Santos. I have much on my mind."

"She still needs—"

"Why does Catherine need the damn sunshine? She gets plenty of it through the windows."

Santos shook his head in disgust. "It's not the same. She needs the sun on her skin, the fresh air to fill her lungs, she needs to get out of that cabin if only for a short time."

"Fine," Lucian begrudgingly agreed. "Have it your way. Allow her out for thirty minutes and no more. And you're responsible for her."

"Fine with me," Santos said with a nod. "She'll give me no trouble. We get along just fine."

Lucian grumbled beneath his breath and turned his attention back to the sea. "She gets along with all men. She has you wrapped around her finger. Bones can't do enough for her, bringing her this and that from her stored trunks. And Jolly? He's so besotted by her that all he does is smile when her name is mentioned."

"You forgot Gumble, the cook."

Lucian turned a quick glance on Santos. "Gumble?"

"Makes her something special every day."

Lucian cast his eyes to the heavens. "Give me strength with this motley crew."

Santos laughed. "You wouldn't trade us for anything."

"No, but I would her, if I could get the price I wanted." Lucian felt a catch in his belly. An ache that gave him pause. Why should his own words disturb him?

"Revenge has a high price and is not always as rewarding as one thinks."

"You begin to philosophize like Zeena."

"Zeena is a wise woman, if I sound like her then you should heed my words."

Lucian's stare once again took on a faraway look. "I heed my own words. No others. Go and see to Catherine and remember, she is your responsibility while out on deck."

"I'll take good care of her," Santos said before walking off.

"See that you do." Lucian's words followed him and sounded more like a stern warning than an order.

Lucian's glance returned to the vast sea stretched out endlessly before him. His thoughts returned to matters at hand. His plans for revenge had been completely destroyed. He could think of no way possible that Catherine's capture could benefit him. He had given serious consideration to allowing the evidence against the Marquis of Devonshire to stand and watch him hanged for treason. But then Abelard would not suffer the endless pain and sorrow that he had. And he wanted Abelard to suffer.

He had thought of returning Catherine to her home, but decided against such action. He had not questioned her about her father, had not sought to use her knowledge of him against him. Tonight he would seek information and find another way to have his revenge.

He brought his hands to his neck and rubbed at the stiff muscles, tender and sore from standing at the ship's wheel a good portion of the night. He had piloted the ship until exhausted and then returned to his cabin, falling into bed and into an instant slumber.

He had not anticipated his reaction to her kiss. He had not expected such a kiss. He had not thought her such a consummate lover. The notion disturbed him. The idea that she had shared her body with so many men irritated him. The fact that he should care one way or another infuriated him.

A delightfully teasing peal of feminine laughter drifted on the sea breeze around him. He stiffened knowing Catherine was on deck. He would ignore her presence. She was Santos's responsibility. When male laughter joined hers he grew angry. She was probably using her womanly charm to wrap his crew around her finger. When their combined robust laughter escalated his control snapped like a dry twig ready for kindling. He swung around and marched straight for her.

Catherine had not felt this relaxed and content since leaving England. When Santos suggested a breath of fresh air she had almost screamed with delight. She had rushed into a peach silk dress, the design simple. No bows or trims adorned it, except of course her pearls. It was a frock for relaxation and not to entertain in, and she had fastened the garment with a smile of satisfaction.

Her hair had been hastily combed and secured with a yellow ribbon, wanting it drawn away from her face so she could catch the warmth of the sun upon her skin. In no time she had finished dressing and had pulled Santos out the door of the cabin and up onto the deck.

The afternoon sun felt glorious against her skin and she breathed deeply of the fresh salty air, filling her lungs with the vibrant scent. She laughed with wonder and delight at the seabirds overhead circling the ship and squawking loudly as they attempted to claim their meal from the sea.

Bones had hurried off in search of her shawl, insisting she needed it and that he had seen it packed in one of her trunks. Cook had ambled his ample bulk on deck and handed her a spiced muffin fresh from the galley and Jolly stood close by smiling at her.

Santos stayed beside her, making certain no one bothered her. Not that his presence mattered. Soon the crew found reason to pass by her way and each one sent her a nod or called out a friendly greeting. When Bones returned with her shawl, she accepted it with a heartwarming smile that brought the crew to swarm around her like a pack of bees hovering near the queen bee.

Catherine laughed and joked with the crew, sharing news of England with them and sensing many of them missed family that they had been forced to leave behind. She felt a kinship with them and relaxed as they exchanged conversation.

Lucian charged down on the peaceful scene like a raging bull bent on slaughter. The fire in his eyes and the fury in his expression sent the men scurrying and bumping into one another to get out of his path of destruction.

Catherine even took a step back though it did no good since she was his target and he was heading for a bull's-eye. He converged on her in one swooping motion, lifting her up into his arms and heading straight for his quarters below.

"Get back to work," he bellowed to the crew before disappearing below with Catherine safely in his arms.

She grasped hold of his neck afraid if he lost his balance he'd drop her. But he wasn't even breathless from carrying her or the rapid strides he took.

He kicked the cabin door open and deposited her on her feet just inside the room. "I allow you some fresh air and you have every man sniffing after you."

She gasped at his audacious remark. "They were doing no such thing. We were talking and I was enjoying the sea air. You had no right to take that pleasure from me."

Lucian loomed over her, his hands planted firmly on his hips. "I have every right to do as I wish. You, madam, have no rights. You do as I dictate or else."

Upset that her short taste of freedom had been unfairly snatched away from her, she swung her hands to her hips and stuck her chest out and her chin up as she challenged, "Or else what? You'll punish me?"

Lucian's nostrils flared, his eyes glared red and his chest heaved with controlled anger. He turned, slammed the door shut, then turned on her once more. "You, madam, have no idea what punishment is."

Catherine's own temper sparked into a flame. "No idea? You call stealing me, keeping me captive against my will all for the sake of revenge no form of punishment?"

Lucian had had enough. It was time she heard the stark truth about life and about her father. He delivered his tirade slowly, emphasizing each word harshly. "Punishment, Catherine, is having your hand cut off for being accused of stealing whether you committed the crime or not. Punishment is having your teeth broken off with a metal bolt because you ate when the captain hadn't given permission. Punishment is being forced to eat cockroaches because the captain insisted that bugs provided nourishment. Punishment is being sold into servitude to a barbaric captain for debts you never incurred, by a man you never met."

"My father would never condone such savage treatment, and especially not on his ships. You have been misinformed and harbor resentment against the wrong man," she insisted, strongly moved by his horrifying experiences and equally moved by his false accusations against her father.

"You prefer tales instead of truths?" he asked, angry that she defended Abelard with such decisiveness.

"You," she said, pointing an accusing finger at him, "accept the tale, not bothering to search out the truth."

He advanced on her so quickly that she barely had time to drop her hand.

He hovered over her, his size engulfing her. "After discovering Abelard's name, I searched long and hard making certain no mistake was made." He paused and held her wide-eyed look with his own heated one. "*Your* father signed my sentence to hell."

A chill ran through Catherine at the bitter belief that filled his every word. His mind had condemned her father, his heart sought revenge. How would she ever make him realize his mistake?

As usual she chose a simple response. "You're wrong."

Her unwavering defense of her father annoyed him. "You don't know your father."

She shook her head adamantly, the yellow ribbon falling loose, her hair spilling free to wave over her shoulders. "I do know my father. I know him far better than anyone."

Swiftly he reached out and grabbed her by the shoulders, pulling her up against him. "Randolph Abelard lies, cheats, and steals. Do you know that about him?"

Catherine struggled against him. "You know nothing about my father, nothing. You lie to feed your thirst for revenge against an innocent man."

He pushed her away disgusted by her unyielding defense of Abelard. "Innocent?" He laughed and walked toward the door.

He grabbed the door latch, swinging it open, and turned, pointing a finger directly at Catherine. "He is as innocent as you are a virgin."

The door slammed so hard behind him that the metal hinges squeaked and the frame trembled.

Catherine sank to the floor where she stood, her legs too weak to hold her up any longer. She sat on the cabin floor hugging her pearls tightly and sadly shook her head. "He finally speaks the truth and doesn't know it."

The day drifted lazily into evening. Lucian kept his distance from everyone, his black mood growing darker. He sat on the quarterdeck, his back braced against a rain barrel, his legs stretched out before him. He discarded his shirt, his skin still thirsty for the warmth of the sun.

He stared out at the endless seascape. Once, not long ago, he had hated the sea. It had represented a prison that held him captive. Escape was impossible. Existence was intolerable.

Now after years of struggle, the never-ending sea meant freedom. He could sail forever and never feel imprisoned. He had one last shackle to free himself of and then he would finally, truly feel free.

Lucian ran his hands through his dark red hair drawing every strand back tightly into his hand at the back of his neck. He closed his eyes and gave in to his thoughts.

Abelard. Somehow he had to destroy Abelard. He couldn't let Catherine interfere with his plan. If he must he would destroy her too. She was no different from her father. Where her father used his ships to get what he wanted, Catherine used her body. She was no innocent and he had better remember that or else he'd be taken in by her honeyed tongue and curvaceous body.

Lucian gave the matter further consideration. His plan had been waylaid, therefore an alternative one was necessary. Where, he thought, was the best area to attack one's opponent?

His eyes drifted open and he looked to the sea for strength and wisdom. A seabird squawked and swooped down on the surface of the sea several times before capturing his meal.

Lucian watched the bird's actions intently and smiled at his victory. "From within," he whispered. "From within your own home, Abelard. And Catherine, your own sweet stepdaughter, shall be the pawn in your downfall."

He stood, stretched slowly, easing his shoulder muscles back. He felt better, but then decisiveness always lightened his sour moods. Discovering Catherine's promiscuous nature had hindered his plans, but since he couldn't use her that way he would use her another.

Catherine loved her father, believed in his innocence. What would she do when she discovered the truth? What would she do when he showed her the documents that proved Abelard sold him into servitude? She would turn against him, the stepdaughter he loved beyond reason would detest him. She would choose not to return to him. He would suffer humiliation and pain. Then he would go after Abelard's business ventures until he had nothing, absolutely nothing, left.

A smile as wicked as the devil's own crossed his face as he headed to his cabin.

Catherine sat with her legs crossed in the middle of the bed chewing on a piece of sweet plump date she held between two fingers. Her other hand turned the pages of a book full of charted maps. The charts appeared specific with odd markings on each one and written in different languages. She was familiar with Spanish and understood those charts.

She had decided a couple of hours ago that her time was best spent searching for the documents proving her father's innocence rather than trembling like a frightened child. The maps had been left on his desk and hoping they would provide useful information she had gathered them up to carefully decipher them.

She took another bite of the date and continued to view the Spanish chart when the cabin door opened. She remained with her legs crossed, bent over, her finger running along the lines, her heart racing as Lucian walked into the room.

"Entertaining yourself with drawings?" he asked, stopping at the foot of the bed.

She raised her head, smiled and popped the last of the date into her mouth before nodding.

"If they entertain you by all means look at as many as you like. There is a whole chest of them," he said, and pointed to a medium-sized brass chest beside his desk. "I'll leave it unlocked for you."

She smiled like a child delighted with a gift. "Thank you. I love to follow all the lines with my finger and see where they take me."

"Where they take you?"

"Of course," she said excitedly. "Sometimes they take me to other lines and then on to another and another while other lines end abruptly."

Lucian shook his head. "If you enjoy tracing lines with your finger I see no harm in your viewing my charts. But be careful of your sticky fingers. I don't want my charts ruined."

Catherine licked her fingers slowly like a cat savoring sweet milk. "Dates. Cook brought me some. They're delicious. Want one?" she asked, scooping a fat date out of the small bowl resting beside her and offering the fruit to him.

"No," he snapped, and snatched away the chart that lay in her lap.

"I wasn't finished tracing the lines," she complained, annoyed since she had determined that the chart outlined a specific Spanish route and wanting to investigate further.

"It's the chart or the date," he ordered.

Not wanting to appear anxious about viewing the chart and having secured his permission to do so anytime she wished, she took a bite of the date.

Catherine found chewing difficult and felt certain she'd never swallow the piece. Not after Lucian turned his back to her and she once again viewed his scarred flesh. The scars had healed, leaving long, thin lash marks. The sun had darkened his skin hiding a few, but some couldn't be hidden. They stood as a testimony to his endurance.

He turned back around and she quickly popped the date

into her mouth, holding onto the end and sucking on it like a licorice stick. She didn't want him to know she had been staring at his back so she purposefully concentrated on the date, sucking it slowly, succulently, insatiably.

Lucian focused on her mouth and the date. Her small tongue rode up the sides of the plump date skillfully. He could almost feel her pink flesh slither sensuously along the meaty fruit. His skin quivered and he hardened in an instant.

"Are you sure you don't want a taste?" she offered, the juice sticky on her lips.

Lucian, don't, his inner voice warned.

He smiled recalling the name his crew had bestowed on him. *Lucifer.* He could handle the results of a sampling of the forbidden fruit. Could Catherine?

"I'll have a taste," he said, walking over to the bed, dropping down over her and forcing her to scramble out of her awkward position as he descended upon her and feasted directly on her mouth.

🕉 11 🕉

She tasted sticky and sweet and his tongue eagerly sought to sample all of her. He roamed her mouth slowly, savoring her unique flavor, drinking his full of her.

Her tongue danced with his, initiating their pace. She picked up the tempo, darting, fencing, hiding, making him pursue her. She moved beneath him with the same gusto, pushing up against him, obviously anxious and impatient for him to touch her.

He pressed against her, running his hand behind her neck and forcing her head up. He drank deeply of her rich taste and the urge to sample more of her overwhelmed him and sent his hand roaming.

Catherine's head dropped back on the pillow and she moaned, her breath short and rapid.

"Delicious, but I want more," he said firmly, rising up over her and bringing his legs to rest on either side of her belly, straddling her.

Catherine bit at her bottom lip and shook her head slowly.

"Much more," he emphasized, "my tongue is going to taste every delectable inch of you."

Her eyes flew open as though she had been pricked by a pin. Surely he was jesting with her. She had strained against him trying not to fight him, but fearful none the less. She ran her tongue across her puffy lips attempting to control her nervous tremors before speaking.

He misread her actions. "Tonight I feast on you. Perhaps I shall allow you to feast on me another night."

Catherine's eyes couldn't have grown any wider, and they

didn't. They slammed tightly shut against his sinful remark. She felt his hands at her shoulders, felt him free the fastenings of her dress, felt him ease the silk down along her shoulders slowly inch by inch, exposing her breasts to him.

"You are lovely," he whispered, "but then I suppose you've been told that often enough." He took the strand of pearls in his hand and ran the cool beads over her breasts and across her nipples.

Catherine focused on his words, fighting against the tingling sensations racing over her flesh. Fighting the heat that raged inside her. Fighting the thought that she could conceivably enjoy the captain's touch. She had to concentrate on the seriousness of the situation and find a solution, a way out.

His fingers brushed her nipple, skimmed the tip, circled the rosy bud before he took the hard peak between his fingers and teased it unmercifully.

"Damn, but you feel good," he said, his voice a deep husky whisper. "Let's see how you taste."

Her eyes popped open again as his head descended to her breast. She gasped and sighed, so unexpected was the jolt of pleasure that shot through her when he took her nipple into his warm wet mouth and gently suckled the hard tip.

Catherine think, she warned herself. *Think of a way to stop him before it's too late.* But all her thoughts could center on was his mouth and the magic it worked on her.

He stretched out over her, his mouth seeking her other nipple and delivering the same sweet torment to it.

Catherine. The sharp voice in her head called. *Think. Think of the consequences of his actions. If he discovers you are a virgin, his plan will succeed. You will fail. He treats you as he does other women. You mean nothing to him. Nothing.*

His mouth moved down to her belly leaving a trail of

sensual kisses across her midriff and around her navel. He
raised his head, smiled at her and asked, "Is your fruit as
sweet as the plump, succulent date, Catherine?"

Catherine stared at him, attempting to comprehend his
remark. When his mouth began to descend between her legs
she realized what he had meant.

Good Lord, he wouldn't! He couldn't. She had to stop
him. She couldn't allow him to invade her so intimately, not
like this, not for the purpose of revenge.

Her mind raced. His head descended. She released a low
rumbling moan and he looked up at her with a wicked smirk
on his handsome face.

At that precise moment, seeing the satisfaction, the
overwhelming sense of victory written on his stark features
she knew what she must do.

"Yes, Lucian, yes. Taste me. Taste deeply of me. I miss
it so," she cried in feigned passion and with courage she
didn't think she possessed she spread her legs wider.
"Philbert often took his pleasure this way with me. Night
after night he would cradle his head between my legs
and—" She paused, searching for the right words. Her mind
worked quickly and she felt proud of herself when she said,
"favor me with the talents of his tongue."

Shocked, Lucian stared in wide-eyed stupor at her.

Seeing her remark had affected him much more than she
had hoped gave her courage to continue. And as she did
she heavily dramatized each word. "His tongue would
pleasure me for hours. Will you do the same, Lucian? Will
you pleasure me as skillfully as Philbert did?" She paused
again and lowered her voice to a whisper as though about to
tell a naughty tale and used his earlier, salacious suggestion
on him. "Then I could pleasure you, Lucian, as I pleased
Philbert. He insisted my mouth worked *magic*."

Lucian flew off the bed as if he'd been doused with a

bucket of ice water. "Blast all, woman, have you no morals?"

He turned his back on her and stormed over to the cabinet that held his liquor. He needed whiskey and he needed to bring the hard bulge in his breeches under control. He certainly didn't need her to see his reaction to her lascivious remarks.

Feeling drained from her performance, she relied once again on a simple answer. "No."

He turned his head and looked at her over his shoulder. She lay naked, her peach dress crumpled at her ankles, her pale, unblemished skin shimmering with a fine sweat, her hair tumbling over her shoulders, teasing her breasts. She looked precisely as a woman in the throes of passion would look, wild, willing, and wet.

He turned back around, grabbed a whiskey bottle from the cabinet and swallowed a mouthful straight from the bottle.

Lord, but she had tasted sweet, he thought as the fiery liquid scalded his throat all the way down to his stomach. Her skin had felt silky soft, her nipples pert and hard, her . . .

He severed his erotic thoughts and took another swig from the bottle. She was a harlot, he reminded himself, that she resembled an angel made no difference. She had slept with dozens of men, had satisfied their lusty whims as well as her own. She used men for her own selfish reasons. She was an Abelard. Randolph Abelard's daughter.

More in control of his emotions, he returned the bottle to the cabinet and turned around. Catherine had discarded her dress and had slipped into her cotton shift. She sat in the middle of the bed combing her hair as though she had not a care in the world.

"You know, Lucian," she began with what sounded like a

voice that was about to chastise. "You shouldn't condemn another person where morals are concerned, after all you are a pirate. A man of dubious character."

Lucian couldn't believe his ears. The woman had the blasted audacity to scold him. "My character is not in question here, madam."

Catherine shrugged. "Neither is mine. I made it perfectly clear to you from the onset that I had enjoyed frequent liaisons. I kept nothing hidden from you."

Lucian took advantage of the moment. "Then tell me of your father."

A knot twisted in her stomach. "You know of mine, tell me of yours." She dropped her hands with the comb grasped tightly in them to her lap.

"He's dead," he answered bluntly, and walked over to the bed, dropping down beside her and stretching out. "Now tell me of yours."

She cast a hasty glance at him out of the corner of her eye and licked her lips nervously. Dare she trust him this close?

"Temper your passion, madam. You shall not feast on me tonight."

Relief that he had no intentions of continuing from where he had so abruptly left off overwhelmed her. Her hasty and brazen reply surprised her completely. "Your loss, Captain."

Lucian reached out like a striking snake coiling his fingers painfully around her arm, drawing her down across his chest to stare directly into her eyes. "Someday, Catherine, we'll discover if that is so."

He released her, pushing her back up away from him. "Your father," he reminded her, and pillowed his arms beneath his head.

Catherine rubbed her aching arm as she spoke. "My father is a patient and gentle—"

Lucian interrupted with an unpleasant grunt.

She turned her head, her brow raised in annoyance. "Do you intend to interrupt my every word?"

He smiled wickedly as he asked, "Why, do you intend to sew my lips shut?"

"I am skillful with a needle." She grinned, pleased at the suggestion.

"Your countless skills amaze me."

"You have yet to learn them all, Captain." Her grin grew.

"We have time, Catherine, for me to discover *all* of your talents."

Catherine instantly read his implied message. He intended to keep her captive for some time. Why? What good would her continued captivity do? And how long could she carry on this charade?

"As I was saying," she said, returning to safer conversation.

"By all means," Lucian interrupted again, "tell me of your *gentle* father."

Catherine ignored his sarcastic remark and proceeded. "I was four when my mother married the marquis. From the moment I entered his home, he treated me like his own daughter. He took me for walks, read to me—"

"Pampered and spoiled you," Lucian added with disgust, annoyed by her description of an attentive and loving father.

"He most certainly did not," Catherine said indignantly. "He expected proper behavior from me."

"Proper?" he asked with a quirk of his brow. "And proper is hoisting your skirts for any man who sniffs at them?"

Catherine felt the hot tears gather in her eyes. They begged for release, begged to ease the ache in her heart. She would never embarrass her father by behaving so indecently. Yet her pretense of indecency would be her father's saving grace. How ironic, she thought sadly, and locked her tears away to shed when she was alone.

She raised her chin in courage, not in arrogance, though she was certain Lucian would assume otherwise. "I keep my affairs discreet."

"Discreet affairs are proper?"

"The aristocracy insist on being discreet for propriety's sake," she explained, having learned at an early age that the nobility made their own rules to cover their own indiscretions.

"Ah, yes, the aristocracy, the ruling class who rule themselves. And give not a damn for the common folk."

"My father cares."

"Don't make me laugh," Lucian said contemptuously. "The marquis cares for his own and no one else."

Catherine took offense at his disparaging remark. "My father has been a proponent of the less fortunate for many years. He has established several orphanages, hoping to provide a home for the children that are forced to beg on the streets. He has arranged for educational funds for the needy. He does what he can though he considers it not near enough."

Lucian stretched his arms up grabbing the top of the intricately carved headboard secured to the wall and pulled himself up. He rested comfortably against a stack of white pillows and regarded her with a scornful look. "And where does he get the money for these charitable works?"

Catherine chose her words carefully, feeling distrustful of him. "He possesses centuries-old family wealth and continues to invest it wisely."

"Like an investment in merchant ships?"

A response seemed senseless. Lucian appeared intent on faulting her father regardless of anyone else's opinion.

"What, no answer, madam? And here I thought you would jump to your father's defense."

"Why? You won't bother to listen to reason. Your head is filled with nonsense and your heart is bitter with hate."

"And for good reason," he argued.

She shook her head sadly. "What reason? Because someone spoke the name Abelard?"

"His signature condemned me to hell."

"Show me this document with my father's signature, prove to me his guilt."

"When I'm ready," he answered calmly.

Much too calmly to Catherine's way of thinking. A shiver ran down her spine and she took it as an omen of things to come.

"Had you been in debt to my father?" she asked, attempting to solve the misunderstanding that had existed for years.

"I was in debt to no man. My finances were above reproach, my family is known for their integrity."

Catherine glared at him and spoke the sudden thought that popped into her head. "Nobility! You were of noble birth."

He shifted uncomfortably against the pillows.

"I knew it," she continued, pleased that she had solved one piece of the puzzle. "Your speech and manners are too refined for that of a pirate or a common man."

"Being of noble birth did little good for me when I discovered myself on the merchant ship as part of the crew."

Catherine paused at this remark, then commented, "Do you know of anyone who harbored resentment against you, or your family?"

Lucian shrugged, having briefly considered the possibility years ago and having found no validity to it. "I thought about it, but could think of few if any who held grudges against the Darcmoors."

"Darcmoor?" Catherine repeated in surprise. "You're a Darcmoor?"

"Lucian Darcmoor, the Earl of Brynwood, to be exact, my lady." He executed a short mocking bow of his head.

Catherine stared incredulously at him. "The Darcmoor estate called Brynwood that lies next to my father's in north Yorkshire?"

"Correct."

She shook her head as if confused. "I don't recall seeing you there over the years. And I've met the earl that is in residence now. Charles is his name. He has become a friend of my father's and has dined often with us. But I do recall some rumors . . ."

"That I was dead," he finished.

"An accident I believe was mentioned, concerning the son of the earl."

Lucian nodded. "How that rumor came about I'll never know. Charles is my cousin, next in line to inherit after me, which he has successfully done. He now possesses all the Darcmoor holdings."

He paused considering the plan he had implemented to regain his title and possessions. He had shared his intentions with no one but Santos. He didn't know why he wanted to reclaim his holdings, perhaps it was a matter of honor, or revenge. Whatever the reason he knew it was necessary.

"I had never cared for the country estate and spent little time there. I much preferred the active social life London had to offer. I was young and pompous like so many of the gentry. I learned quickly and harshly how life was for the other half."

Catherine sat listening, gaining a better understanding about the infamous Captain Lucifer.

"I wrongly and ignorantly assumed my social position would free me from mistaken debts. The captain laughed in my face when I told him *who* I was. He informed me that he didn't give a rat's ass as to my title. He had a paper that said my ass belonged to him for three years and he intended to see that I worked off every minute of every day of my debt."

He raked his hands through his hair, briefly closing his eyes on his past. Then he opened them and held her concerned gaze once again while he continued the story. "I never knew such misery existed. I never realized how harsh life could be. I never knew the gnawing pains of hunger, but I learned fast enough. I learned that when you're hungry you'll eat just about anything, even food laced with weevils."

Catherine cringed at the thought of bugs in her food and shivered at the cruelty that necessitated such an act.

"I swore as each day passed that I would find the man who wronged me and make him pay."

"This captain on the merchant ship," Catherine asked. "Is he the one who gave you my father's name?"

"With his dying breath."

"Dying breath?" Catherine repeated.

Lucian once again relived that fateful day. "The ship was attacked by bloodthirsty pirates. They boarded and raided the vessel in minutes, killing any crew member who refused to join them. I took up a sword immediately, foolishly assuming freedom was close at hand. The captain lay on the deck of the ship bleeding to death. I went to him and asked him for the name of the man who claimed the debts that sold me into servitude. The name spilled from his bleeding lips. *Abelard.*"

Catherine began to protest.

"Don't bother to look for an excuse. A dying man isn't about to lie. Why should he?"

"He could have harbored a grudge against my father."

"Catherine." He sighed her name. "When will you finally accept the fact that your father is capable of cruelty?"

She answered swiftly. "Never."

Lucian smiled, a stark unfriendly smile. "Not even when I show you the papers with your father's signature?"

"Show me them," she challenged, "and we shall see."

"Yes, Catherine, eventually the truth will be obvious to you."

"And the documents that prove my father innocent of treason?" she asked. "Will you give me those papers as you had promised?"

"We had a bargain," he said, his smile still indifferent.

"You broke the bargain, not I."

Lucian stared at her strangely. "You really would have married me?"

She tossed her chin up. "To save my father I would have married the devil himself."

Lucian laughed deeply and glared at her with eyes as hard as stone. "And it's the devil you would have taken your vows with."

Slowly her skin crawled as the truth of his statement settled in. His years of forced labor and subjugation had worn on his body, mind, and soul. He needed to heal, to forgive himself before he could find it in his heart to forgive others.

Catherine felt a sudden need to comfort him and strangely enough she gave no thought to her actions. She did as she felt she must.

She moved over beside him, leaned down across his chest, kissed him gently on the lips and said, "You are no devil, Lucian." Then she cuddled against his naked chest, yawned, and went directly to sleep.

Lucian sat there stunned by her actions. He glanced down at the top of her head and her arm draped across his waist.

What in the hell was he to do with her? She confused him. Just when he thought he understood her, she stepped out of character.

She stirred as though troubled by a bad dream. His hands instinctively sought to comfort her, wrapping around her and soothingly rubbing her back.

She responded, settling in an instant.

He sighed and shut his eyes. Damn, but she could play with his emotions. He admired her fortitude and her strong belief in those she loved. He wished someone had loved him with such intensity, perhaps then he would not have found himself on that merchant ship, sold into service.

His heart ached with memories of his mother. He had thought that she of all people would have fought endlessly for his release. He couldn't remember a day that had gone by that she hadn't reminded him of how much she cared for him and always would. He had been devastated when he heard nothing from her and then he had heard of her death. He had never felt so alone in his life, so abandoned.

He stared down at Catherine protectively wrapped in his arms. With every word she spoke, she had defended her father. She believed in his innocence, never once doubting it, fiercely defending his honor.

Never in his life had he experienced a love that strong. He envied and hated Abelard and was more determined than ever to seek his revenge through Catherine somehow.

❧ 12 ❧

CATHERINE STOOD ON the deck of the ship full of anticipation and excitement. She wished the crew would hurry
and drop anchor. She couldn't wait another minute to touch
solid land and an island at that. And not just any island, the
island of Tortuga.

She had read stories of Tortuga and its lawlessness. One
story had called it "the pirates' spawning ground," another
had labeled it "worse than Hades," yet another referred to its
location as "the end of the earth." All Catherine cared about
at the moment was that she had the opportunity to see it with
her own eyes and not through stories and books.

Lucian had only this morning informed her that they
would be dropping anchor there shortly and staying for a
day or two. He had tossed her a bundle of clothes and told
her if she wished to join him on the island that she must
dress in the clothes he provided and she must keep herself
by his side and obey his every word.

She hastily agreed. She now waited impatiently for them
to disembark. She had followed Lucian's instructions,
changing into the bright blue skirt and white linen blouse
and leather sandals. She had braided her hair and fastened
the sides back with ivory combs so no strands would fall
free.

She turned her attention away from the island in the near
distance and searched the ship for Lucian. The sight of him
standing on the fo'c'sle deck startled her. He fit a romanti-
cized image of a pirate perfectly. Large and strong and
breathtakingly handsome, he stood arms akimbo, feet braced

apart, dressed in tight black breeches and high black polished boots. His white shirt billowed in the breeze and hung open almost clear to his waist, showing off his sizable muscular chest.

And his long dark red hair? Catherine shook her head. Lord, but he had gorgeous hair for a man. Long, shiny and . . .

She smiled noticing the braid he had fashioned on one side behind his ear running down over his shoulder. It labeled him dangerous. Dangerously alluring.

She easily understood why women would be attracted to him. He had an air of mystery and risk about him. A woman took a chance when she became involved with him. A chance with her heart and soul.

Catherine shivered, thinking of the captain's soul. She sensed a dark side, full of hate and contempt. And buried, locked deep away, a part existed that needed not only to be loved, but to give love as well. Lucian was a complex man, Catherine was only beginning to understand.

He shouted orders to the crew, walked a few feet, jumped over the wooden rail to the deck below and headed straight for her.

She smiled at his approach, clapping her hands together, demonstrating as usual her little-girl excitement. "I can't wait to see the island."

Lucian stopped in front of her, grabbing her clasped hands in his. "You will obey my every word once on the island. You will not question my commands, you will do as I bid. Is that perfectly clear, Catherine?"

"Perfectly," she agreed.

He pressed the point. "This island is like no place you have ever been. Men are shot dead in the street. Women ply their trade wherever they wish. Liquor flows like water. Weapons are carried by everyone."

"May I carry a weapon?" she asked, the thought thrilling her.

"No, you may not," he answered sternly, annoyed that she had not paid attention to his all-too-accurate description of Tortuga.

Catherine stuck her chest out proudly. "I know how to shoot a pistol."

Lucian fixed his gaze directly on her. "You know how to shoot a pistol at a target set up at an appropriate distance for practice. But have you ever shot at a moving target?"

Catherine answered honestly. "No."

Lucian admired her forthright manner and strangely enough he sensed he could trust her. An odd feeling for him to accept since he rarely trusted anyone.

He raised his leg and brought his boot down to rest on the edge of the barrel next to Catherine. He reached down inside his boot and withdrew a small knife sheathed in a leather pouch.

"For you," he said, handing it to Catherine.

She accepted it with surprise.

He answered the question that he assumed was on her lips. "You may need to protect yourself."

Catherine looked perplexed. "You'll be with me."

Pleased by her confidence in him to protect her, he explained, "Always be prepared, Catherine. You never know what dangers may befall you."

Catherine nodded, agreeing with his remark, and proceeded to unwrap the strings from around the pouch. "Where do I fasten it?"

Lucian moved his boot off the barrel and with a gracious wave of his hand extended an invitation. "Your leg, madam."

Excitement raced through her and she hoisted her skirt and plopped her foot down on the barrel's edge.

Lucian pushed her skirt back, but as he raised it clear to her thigh, her hand shot out stopping him.

He looked at her questioningly. "I've seen every inch of you."

Catherine felt her cheeks heat up. "But your crew hasn't, nor do I wish them to."

Lucian thought it odd that a woman who had known so many men should be embarrassed by the show of her limb. But catching the crew's sudden interest in their actions, he bowed to her wish.

"Then allow me to secure it for you," he offered, slipping his hands out from under her petticoats and taking the pouch from her hands.

His hands once again disappeared beneath her skirt, his fingers riding intimately up her leg to the inside of her thigh.

She shuddered against his gentle touch. It flamed her belly and tingled her flesh.

"A sensitive spot. I must remember that," he teased, feeling gooseflesh ripple beneath his hand. He caressed her thigh more thoroughly, relishing her response.

"I would enjoy your lips much better there, Captain. Perhaps tonight when we're alone?" she said, realizing that only an outrageous remark would make him stop.

He looked up at her, a dangerous smile curling his lips. "Hold your lustful tongue once on the island, madam, or you may get more than you bargained for. The men of Tortuga are far from mannered or gentle."

His fingers deftly secured the leather ties to her thigh before roughly pulling her petticoats and skirt completely down over her leg.

Catherine detested the charade she played. The character she portrayed was foreign to her, her morals alien. The idea that he thought her capable of seducing a stranger on an island known for its sinful pursuits disturbed her. She was a lady, and Lord, how she wished she could behave like one.

Instead, she yanked her foot off the barrel, shook out her skirt, fluffing it as if concerned with how it looked, and raised her chin up. "I have no intentions of searching for a—"

She interrupted herself with a pause, hastily exploring her thoughts for the right phrase.

"A quick toss of the skirt?" Lucian finished her curtly.

She turned her head to the gentle breeze that billowed the lowering sails, begging for the fresh wind to cool her heated cheeks. He could embarrass her so easily with his crude remarks. And only a lady would blush appropriately. She couldn't have her secret discovered for he would make certain she didn't remain a lady for long.

She turned her head back, her eyes narrowing as her scrabbling thoughts provided her with a fitting response. "I hoped for an hour of exotic lovemaking."

Lucian grabbed her in a flash, flattening her up against him. She bent her head back to look in his face and guarded her gaze and tongue well against the angry blackness she saw boiling in the depths of his blue eyes.

His every word was punctuated with contained fury. "You, *madam,* will keep your skirt down and your legs closed. I'll not have you bringing back a disease from a flea-ridden, stinking pirate."

His hands squeezed urgently at her arms, hurting her delicate skin. His expression glowered with repressed rage, highlighting every handsome feature. In an instant she understood why he had been given the name of Lucifer, the handsomest of angels and the most sinful. Wisdom born of instinct warned her to tread lightly. "As you wish."

His hand squeezed her arms harder. "This is no jest, Catherine. I mean every word."

Her breath caught for a moment in her throat and she

cleared it quickly not wanting him to see her fear. "I understand. I will obey you."

He shoved her away from him. "See that you do."

He strode away, the sheer size and strength of him sending the shivers through her. Catherine shook her head and rubbed her arms. She watched him give orders to the crew and saw the men scurry to obey.

A fleeting thought flashed through her mind. *How would he treat a wife?* Would he order her about? Would he expect obedience of his every command? Would his powerful hands bring pleasure or pain?

She blushed and turned away embarrassed by her own wonderings. She had on one or two occasions glimpsed a thoughtful side of him, though he hid it well. Was the title Captain Lucifer a protective mask for Lucian Darcmoor? Perhaps he wasn't what he appeared to be at all.

"Catherine!"

His shout startled her and she swerved around. He stood steady on the deck, the ship rocking beneath him, his hand thrust out to her. He spoke not a word, but commanded her with a fierce look.

She went to him without hesitation. Why shouldn't she? she thought, rushing up to take his outstretched hand. If she didn't, he would just come after her, swing her over his shoulder, and cart her off.

"Remember my warning, madam," he said curtly, and took her hand in his.

She nodded with a smile.

He walked to the ship's railing with her in tow and tossed one leg over to straddle it. "You will follow me over the side. I will stay beneath you guiding your step. The rope ladder can be tricky, be careful."

"I'll manage," she assured him.

He released her hand and went over the side with ease. He

waited a few rungs down, his one hand hooked to the ladder, the other outstretched to assist her.

"I can manage," she insisted, casting a glance over the side past Lucian to the waiting longboat below. Santos stood in the middle looking up at her with a smile while Bones and Jolly occupied opposite ends of the boat and were busy keeping the slim vessel steady.

Catherine with only a modicum of difficulty and no assistance from Lucian made it over the railing and onto the rope ladder.

"Take easy steps," Lucian warned her, and descended down the ladder to give her room.

A sense of exhilaration filled Catherine and she took each rung with renewed confidence. She had learned much and conquered many fears in the last several weeks. She had survived this hardship and she would succeed in her mission of proving her father's innocence.

With a broad smile she cast her foot to the next rung just as the rope steadying the ladder to the longboat snapped from Bones's hand. The ladder broke free and smacked the side of the ship, causing Catherine to lose her balance.

Lucian had only set foot in the longboat when he felt the jerk beneath his feet. Years of sailing temperamental vessels and coping with unexpected storms allowed him to keep his footing steady. He looked up at Catherine and his stomach knotted as her small hands grasped tightly to the ladder and her dangling feet frantically searched for a rung. One slip of her hands and she would come crashing down.

"Secure that blasted rope, Bones, or I'll have your miserable hide," he shouted, reaching for the swaying rope ladder.

Santos aided him, holding it steady as Lucian easily raced up the ladder to Catherine.

His body braced hers from behind in an instant. His one

arm circled her waist, his other hand slipped over hers. "Steady, angel, you're all right."

She sagged against him, though she retained her grip on the rung. His large body offered safety, his formidable strength security from harm. He wouldn't let any harm befall her. She knew it as certainly as she knew she would breathe her next breath.

"Lucian," she whispered with relief.

His arm tightened around her waist more firmly and he felt the last tremor of fear race through her before she completely relaxed against him. "Are you in any pain?" he asked, recalling the way the ladder had collided with the side of the ship.

Surprisingly she realized her knee pained her, but not unbearably. "My knee hurts a little."

"Nothing else pains you?"

She laughed, a surprising response to Lucian. "Only my pride."

He smiled at her ability to find humor in an accident that most certainly could have been fatal. "Fear not, madam, your pride is intact. You did a most splendid job of saving yourself from an accident that was by no means your fault."

"Wonderful," she said, "my confidence is restored."

"Enough to finish the climb down the ladder?"

A nervous flutter attacked Catherine's stomach. "With your assistance?"

"Most definitely," he assured her.

"Then I'm ready," she said, her quivering voice betraying her fear.

"Put your arms around my neck and trust me. I'll not let any harm come to you, angel," he whispered near her ear.

A shiver raced through her and not from fear. He spoke with gentle concern. He had even called her angel. Was it possible that Captain Lucifer did possess a soul? And had she touched it?

She carefully transferred her grip from the rung to around Lucian's neck and with it went her trust. She buried her head against his chest and closed her eyes, willing herself not to foolishly believe that the captain actually cared about her. She was still his instrument of revenge and therefore extremely valuable to him. How could he let anything happen to her?

"Good, Catherine," he praised. "Now hold on tight."

She did and he took the rungs slowly so as not to frighten her. He deposited her on a seat in the longboat, leaning over her as she dropped her arms from around her neck.

He caught her chin and raised her face to him. "You're full of spirit, Catherine." And with that he kissed her. It was meant as a light congratulatory kiss, but once their lips touched . . .

His hand wrapped around the back of her neck, his tongue delved into her mouth. He tasted her, shared her breath, her fresh scent, and then as quickly as he had plundered her mouth, he released her.

He stood straight, towering over her, his voice echoing on the warm sea air. "Get this boat under way, Bones, and one more accident and you'll find yourself *accidentally* swimming to Tortuga."

Lucian stared at her, looking oddly confused, and then turned, retreating to the bow of the boat.

Catherine felt quite drained by the incident and her rambling thoughts ignored his strange reaction and attended to her injured knee.

Lucian glared out at the island in the near distance. He focused on it and the business he needed to attend to while there. His hands balled into fists at his sides, his eyes narrowed and his jaw tightened.

Bones, taking note of his captain's mounting anger, leaned to the side and out of his range of fire if one of his fists should shoot out.

Lucian called himself a million kinds of fools. What in the bloody hell had come over him? He had tasted fear and near death in battle, yet when he had witnessed Catherine precariously dangling above him, he had known such deep-rooted fear it had frightened him to his very bones.

Had she slipped beneath his skin to prick him without his realizing it? Had she woven her wanton web so skillfully around him that he had lost control of his senses?

It was a willing woman he needed naked beneath him to appease the ache Catherine Abelard had inflicted upon him. He would find one in Tortuga. He would fill himself to bursting with her ten times over and be done with it.

He grimaced.

"You all right, Cap?" Bones asked, never having seen the captain display such emotions.

"Shut up, Bones," Lucian snapped.

Bones inched a bit further away from the captain's still-balled fists.

Lucian admonished himself for his foolishness, this time calling himself names not fit for any but a pirate's ears. How could he? How could he call Catherine Abelard an angel? How victorious she must feel at this moment.

He turned expecting to see her gloating but instead he caught her wincing against the pain as she probed the large bruise on her knee.

"God's blood," he groaned, and headed straight for her, forgetful of his own warnings.

Catherine counted herself lucky for only receiving the bruise to her knee. She could have suffered much more severe injuries if Lucian hadn't come so quickly to her aid.

The bruise would fade as would her fear of the incident, but Lucian calling her angel would remain forever inscribed in her thoughts.

A shadow fell over her and she looked up.

"Does it pain you?" Lucian asked.

Her knee barely caused her discomfort. The pain that filled her was from Lucian's sharp tone. Captain Lucifer had returned.

"Answer me, madam," he snapped, annoyed with her brief hesitation and annoyed with himself for needing to hear from her own lips that she did not suffer.

Catherine tossed her petticoats and skirt over her injury. "I've suffered worse."

"That's not what I asked you. Do you suffer now?"

A sigh proceeded Catherine's response. "No, Captain. I suffer no pain, only a mere discomfort." She had thought to argue with him, but that would only spoil the rest of her day and she refused to allow him to ruin her adventure.

"If it should bother you—"

She finished for him. "I shall most certainly tell you immediately."

"Landin' ahead. Landin' ahead." Bones called out.

"Remember," Lucian warned. "You stay by my side and obey my every command."

She nodded, attempting to peek around him at the island's approach.

"Believe me, Catherine," he said with a dangerous smile. "It's not what you expect."

∞ 13 ∞

CATHERINE CHOKED ON the stench. She covered her nose and mouth with her hand while rushing to keep up with Lucian's powerful gait.

He had been right. Tortuga was like nothing she had ever expected. Men lay in a stupor in the street and in doorways. Women bartered their bodies for naught but a few pence, brazenly displaying a breast or hoisting a skirt to show the buyer her wares.

Spanish, French, Portuguese, and languages foreign to her abounded. Weapons were bought and sold openly, fists were thrown and women tumbled in the street screeching and fighting over God only knew what.

And smells? Catherine pressed her hand closer to her nose, sniffing the salty sea scent of her palm. She couldn't determine if it was rotting fish, days-old body odor, or the garbage cast along the dirt streets that stank the worst. Moreover it was probably a combination of all three and then some.

What shocked her the most, though insignificant in contrast, was the lush foliage and beautiful flowers that flourished amongst the filth and rabble of the island. It stunned the eye and presumably favored the nose.

"A short distance and you'll find a marked change," Lucian said, grabbing hold of her arm as they moved along past two burly and exceptionally drunk men.

"She for sale, Captain Lucifer?" one man daringly called out.

To Catherine's surprise Lucian stopped right in front of

the large man. His hands were meaty, his girth equally so, and his head as bald as a baby's bottom. And the smell?

Catherine stepped behind Lucian and planted her face against his shirt. Fresh sea air, warm sun, and Lucian's own distinctly pleasant odor rewarded her nostrils. She breathed deeply relishing his rich and breathable scent.

An icy tone marked Lucian's every word. "Big John, have you ever known me to sell a woman?"

Catherine peeked around Lucian's arm, her nose still plastered to his shirt. The heavy man rubbed his bald head and attempted to take a step back away from the feared Captain Lucifer. But he had difficulty performing two tasks at once. So he stopped rubbing his head and took a stumbling step back.

He looked at Lucian for a mere second, rubbing his bulbous nose, then casting his glance down at his scuffed boots. "Nope. Sorry, Captain Lucifer."

"Go sleep off your stupor before you find yourself gutted and left for dead," Lucian warned.

Big John's eyes widened three-fold. He dropped his whiskey bottle and hurried off in a stumble. The smaller man beside him stared at Lucian briefly, threw his bottle down and ran after Big John.

Catherine giggled as Lucian reached behind himself and yanked her around in front of him.

"You find my shirt comforting, madam?"

She smiled, and surprising herself and Lucian, she buried her face against his shirt at his chest. "I love the scent of you," she whispered, and snuggled her nose against the white linen.

Lucian yanked her away. "Behave," he warned with a shake. "I want no man knowing you a harlot."

Catherine stiffened and retaliated so incensed was she by his crude remark. "I do not give myself to just any man."

His lips curled in a sardonic smile. "Only the gentry?"

Catherine returned his smile with a disdainful one of her own. "Only a man of *my* choosing, Captain. Or did you forget the stable boy?"

Lucian roughly dragged her alongside him as he moved on and beneath his breath, barely audible to Catherine's ears he said, "Thank you for reminding me that you're a whore."

Her heart shattered upon hearing his vulgar remark.

It is necessary, Catherine, the small voice reminded her. *You do this to save your father. Do you think he would do any less for you? In the end it will all work out for the best.*

The latter was a favorite phrase of her father's and one whose prophecy she hoped would prove true.

They turned a corner and remarkably the scene before her changed. Not to a great degree, but enough to demonstrate that civilization did exist on the island. The street was lined on either side with narrow houses and shops, some attached to each other and some set a distance apart. Smells of richly roasted food spiked the warm air and mingled with the unmistakable odor of fresh ale.

The wares peddled on the street were colorful and interesting. Necklaces and bracelets fashioned from shells, bright-colored ribbons of burning yellow, glorious reds, and shocking pinks, and scarves varied in color and design, like none she had ever seen, strange herbs and exotic incenses, all served to excite Catherine.

She took a step opposite Lucian and found herself halted in midstride. She turned a pleading look on him. "The items the peddlers have to offer are different from those in England, I would love to look them over."

He shook his head. "Another time. I have business to tend to." With that he pulled her along, entering an establishment whose sign claimed it to be Heaven's Fare.

Catherine smiled over the name, though upon entering had second thoughts.

The large room was clean, the patrons loud but not boisterous. The food smelled eatable and looked appetizing. Platters were stacked with thick meat stew and hot stone-baked bread and of course there was a never-ending flow of ale.

Lucian chose a table in the corner, his back planted to the wall and her bottom planted directly beside him in a chair.

A buxom woman with hair the color and texture of straw weaved her way around the tables, her platter held high above her head, her smile bright and her cheeks flushed cherry red.

She brought the platter down to the center of the table with ease and with equal ease and familiarity caressed Lucian's cheek. "It's grand to lay eyes on you again, you handsome devil."

Lucian wrapped his arm beneath her backside and pulled her toward him. "Bonnie, my fair girl. I've been missing you."

"Go on with you, Captain." She laughed and playfully swatted his shoulder. "A man that has the devil's own good looks doesn't miss any woman."

Lucian winked at her. "But you're not any woman, Bonnie."

Bonnie's cheeks flamed brighter and she backed out of his grasp that fell away to release her. "What can I be getting you, Captain Lucifer?"

"Some food to start," he said, his eyes devouring her full breasts.

"Whatever pleases you," she said with a catchy smile.

"I'll let you know what pleases me later on."

Bonnie nodded, her smile like that of a cat that had just

been stroked lovingly by its master and walked off without so much as an acknowledgment of Catherine's presence.

Catherine made a serious pretense of inspecting her surroundings, purposely ignoring the woman and Lucian's exchange though catching every word. He sniffed after her skirts like a rutting animal and he had had the audacity to warn her of men sniffing after her. Indignant with his actions, she kept her attention diverted from him.

"Jealous?" he asked, filling each of their tankards with ale.

Her head snapped around and her eyes narrowed. "Jealous? Jealous of that brazen hussy? Captain, if you prefer vinegar to wine then you most certainly don't deserve me."

"No, Catherine, I don't deserve you," he said, and raised his tankard in a mocking salute.

"A shame," she retorted sharply. "I think you would have enjoyed the rich and satisfying fare I had to offer."

"Rarely does a fare satisfy me, madam." His words challenged, his eyes attempted to convince.

Catherine, having established appropriate replies to act out her charade, leaned closer to him and whispered with more conviction then any response she had ever delivered. "I would satisfy you, Lucian."

He stared at her lips, pouting with sensuality while aching for a kiss. Her wintergreen eyes stirred with restrained passion and her body . . .

His heart raced, heat rushed through his veins, and he hardened instantly. He cursed his uncontrollable response.

He caught her chin in a pinching grip. "When matters are settled, Catherine, I'll test the truth of your words."

Panic rushed through Catherine. Good Lord, what had she been thinking? Why had she responded like a jealous woman in love? She didn't care for Lucian. She feared his size, strength, and arrogance at times. Yet those same traits that induced fear in her provided protection and safety at other times.

She pulled away from him, dropping back against her seat, silent and weary. This charade had turned difficult and hazardous. She trod on dangerous ground. She spoke like a wanton woman and yet barely possessed knowledge of one. And worse, she was beginning to believe her own act.

Did she actually think she could satisfy a man as lusty and experienced as Captain Lucifer? And why would she even think such a foolish thought? He cared nothing for her. He would use her, then discard her.

He hides a tender side.

She flushed at her thought, her hands rushed to cover her cheeks. Lucian had displayed a tender side. She recalled a few mornings she had stirred to near waking and had felt him ease the covers over her. He had seen that she received a daily recess on deck, warm wash water, plenty of tasty food, and a gentle arm protectively wrapped around her as she drifted into sleep. These actions were not the actions of a bloodthirsty pirate.

But then Captain Lucifer differed from Lucian Darcmoor. The captain was moody, argumentative, demanding, and brazen in his remarks. And it was Captain Lucifer she needed to protect herself from.

How? How could she gain the necessary knowledge to continue a believable charade?

"Catherine," Lucian said, dragging her attention back to him.

She looked his way, a faraway gaze in her eyes.

"Pay attention, madam, this is important."

Catherine sat up straight and fixed wide eyes on him.

Satisfied she was listening, Lucian continued. "I must meet with someone privately. You will stay put until my return. Bones and Jolly will be nearby if need be."

His eyes searched the room, Catherine's followed spying Bones and Jolly two tables away, quaffing ale and shoveling stew into their mouths.

Lucian shook his head. "They don't resemble men who can offer protection, but they're both swift with a blade and their fists. They will let no harm come to you—or they will have me to answer to."

Catherine didn't doubt the two men would defend her courageously, yet the thought of Lucian leaving her filled her with dread. "Will you be gone long?"

"No." He stood.

Catherine reached out, grabbing his hand.

He cast an uncertain glance down at her. "What's wrong, Catherine?"

She shrugged, produced a weak smile, and spoke with honesty. "I fear your absence."

Her sincere response returned him to his seat. "Why?"

Another shrug followed a fading smile. "A strange island with strange people, I much prefer your presence while here. And you *had* warned me about leaving your side."

Lucian smiled the devil's own smile, wicked and sensual and definitely heart stopping. "I would allow no danger to touch you. You're as safe from harm with members of my crew as you are with me."

Catherine found herself responding before giving consideration to her remark. "How safe am I with you, Lucian?"

He caressed her cheek, tempted her lips with a light kiss, and whispered, "Since your virtue is no longer intact, your safety is guaranteed."

The color drained from Catherine's face.

"Something ails you, that you're suddenly pale?" he asked concerned.

Catherine placed her hand to her stomach. "I'm hungry."

He nodded, searched the room, and catching Bonnie's eye he waved her over. "Bonnie will make certain you—"

He stared at her strangely, his sudden silence disturbing.

Catherine said nothing, feeling it a wise choice. He looked perturbed and she had no intentions of increasing his ire.

"You pale even more, what troubles you?"

"Hunger," she repeated softly.

His eyes narrowed and his icy tone sent shivers through her. "I want the truth, Catherine."

She opened her mouth to confirm her earlier answer when he interrupted. "Do you carry a lover's child?"

His question shocked Catherine speechless, her mouth fell open but no words slipped forth.

"I'll have an answer now, Catherine." His low raspy voice warned her of his anger.

The truth rolled easily from her lips. "I carry no child."

Bonnie reached the table, depositing the silver tray heavy with food in the center. "I brought extra bread and some fresh cheese."

Lucian ripped off a hunk of bread and grabbed several slices of hard cheese. He focused angry eyes on Bonnie. "See that she eats and make certain she stays put till I return."

With his orders issued he stormed off, Santos rushing to finish his tankard of ale at a nearby table before dutifully following behind him.

Bonnie shook her head and plopped down next to Catherine. "Eat while the food is hot and fresh."

Catherine for all she had been through found herself surprisingly famished. She helped herself to a large bowl of stew, a fat piece of bread, and a portion of cheese.

"Had a lovers' spat?" Bonnie asked.

Catherine chewed on the delicious warm bread while she shook her head.

"Aren't you Captain Lucifer's lady?" Bonnie queried, slicing a piece of cheese.

Her remark amused Catherine. Bonnie tagged her perfectly, a lady. "I'm a thorn in his side."

"A rose is more like it, your beauty is such."

Her compliment caused Catherine to blush.

Seeking chatter and gossip since several patrons had left and calm had descended over the establishment, Bonnie continued. "I've not known the captain to worry over a female eating."

That bit of information sparked interest in Catherine.

"The captain usually enjoys a woman and then takes himself off, not concerning himself further with her, at least around these parts, that is."

Catherine ached to ask Bonnie if she had learned that from experience, but being a lady she hesitated.

Bonnie smiled pleasantly and cut herself another piece of cheese. "The captain, he teases me all the time, but he's never taken me to bed. Not that I wouldn't mind, him being as handsome and strong as he is."

Catherine relaxed listening to Bonnie's easy chatter. She had missed female companionship. The fact that Lucian hadn't bedded Bonnie also proved a relief, though she fought to understand the meaning of that.

Bonnie leaned in closer so the nearby tables couldn't hear. "Tell me, is he as good in bed as the women say he is?"

Lacking experience, Catherine hadn't the slightest notion how to rate him. She decided honesty was best. Before she could answer a sudden idea popped into her head. Instead of the smile that pinched her mouth she wore a frown. "The captain hasn't bedded me."

Bonnie seemed surprised. "He looks as if he aches to devour you."

Catherine continued. "I fear I haven't the skills necessary to please him."

Bonnie laughed and waved the silly remark away. "That's easily remedied."

Her heart jumped with excitement. "How?"

"I can give you some tips that are sure to please the likes of Captain Lucifer."

Elated Catherine smiled. "You don't mind?"

Bonnie shook her head. "Us independent girls need to stick together. If you please the captain, maybe he'll keep you. You're too beautiful and nice to be passed around like a common whore. Me, I pick and choose. I like it better that way."

Catherine liked Bonnie, she spoke from her heart and not many people possessed that quality. "I appreciate your help."

"Let's get busy before he returns. There's a lot to discuss." Bonnie blushed a faint pink. "My favorite is tongues. There's so much pleasure a man and woman can give each other with their tongues."

Catherine refused to display her shock. She kept a straight face and listened. She intended to learn all she could to help her succeed in her charade. Then as soon as she found the documents she planned to escape.

"Let's start from the beginning. When you first have an itch for a man and you want to let him know you need him to scratch it," Bonnie joked.

"I'm listening," Catherine said, pushing her partially eaten stew aside and resting her elbows on the table.

Bonnie leaned in closer and began to whisper.

Catherine soon found her cheeks blushing three shades of red. In only minutes the blush deepened and spread over her entire face. Catherine had had no idea what skills she had been missing.

Thirty minutes later, Bonnie sat back in her chair and smiled. "So how about a test?"

Catherine didn't comprehend. "Test?"

Bonnie nodded. "Your newly acquired skills."

"Here?" Catherine asked incredulously.

"You want to wait for the captain?"

Catherine shook her head. "No, but I really don't know about testing my newfound knowledge on anyone but the captain," she lied, intending that all the information she learned would benefit her charade.

"Just a simple test. An innocent smile, a suggestive sway of the hips, a nonchalant lick of your lips, a few little tempts to stir a man."

"I suppose a sampling wouldn't hurt." At least she hoped it wouldn't. It sounded harmless enough.

"Don't worry, I'll keep an eye on you," Bonnie said. "If it looks like you're having trouble, I'll step in."

Encouraged by her offer of help, Catherine agreed with a reluctant nod. She had her doubts. She had played her part well around Lucian, but a stranger? Revenge blinded the captain's senses, allowing her pretense to succeed. The tavern patrons possessed no blinders. Would they see the truth?

Bonnie cast a studious eye around the tavern. "See a man that strikes your fancy?"

Catherine pondered her choices carefully. None looked appealing. All the men appeared more interested in their food and drink than in women. And none came close to comparing to Lucian in looks, size, or manner. They were all truly a disappointment.

"The fare is better at night," Bonnie said, sensing her discouragement. "Why don't you take a walk around the room, sway your hips a few times and lick those lips and we'll see what happens?"

Catherine decided a quick spin around the room wouldn't hurt. Hopefully no one would pay attention to her and then she could return to her seat.

"Go on, now," Bonnie said, easing her away from the table with a gentle nudge.

When an unpopular chore needed attending, Catherine had always dug her heels in and finished it one, two, three. This chore topped the list of least desirable. She would put her mind to it and get it over with as fast and painlessly as possible.

Her mind spun with countless pieces of information on seducing a man. Bonnie had stressed that the simplest action could pique a man's interest in no time.

She sighed heavily. If she was lucky she'd fail. With that thought in mind she weaved her way around the tables with a gentle provocative sway of her hips, produced more from nerves than on purpose.

Heads instantly turned, including Bones's and Jolly's.

Her eyes flashed wide and bright as she fought to control her nervous jitters. Her lips dried from fright and she ran a slow tongue over them, round and round attempting to force moisture into them. All her innocent actions made her appear a woman on the prowl.

Several smiles and winks were sent her way and she turned an anxious glance to Bonnie.

Bonnie rewarded her with a huge smile and a brief nod, quietly acknowledging her success.

A grand smile whisked across Catherine's face and she turned back around, intending to circle back to Bonnie. She caught sight of Bones and Jolly, their faces pale, their mouths open wide, staring at her.

Her smile faded and forgotten were her attempts to

seduce as she hurried over toward them wondering how she would ever explain her improper actions.

"Where are you going, little lady?" the deep voice asked, seconds before a thick hand reached out and grabbed her wrist.

Catherine stared down in horror at the hand that gripped her tightly. "Let go," she said, putting as much strength into her voice as possible.

He yanked her hard, forcing her to sit on his beefy lap. His height was several inches short of Lucian's, but his weight easily tripled the captain's. His brown hair fell to his shoulders in knots and his face wore a rough stubbly beard and several vicious-looking scars. His soiled clothes smelled of fish and sweat. And his bloodshot eyes and the liquor on his breath attested to his inebriated state.

She was definitely in trouble. Her glance shot straight to Bones and Jolly in a silent plea for help.

Both men stepped forward ready for battle. A pistol pointed at them stopped them dead.

"Leave Handsome Harry be," said the large black man sitting at the table to Harry's right.

Bonnie skirted around the pistol and the table to stand in front of Harry. Her blouse hung off one shoulder, offering a good portion of her plump breast. "She's too small for the likes of your handsome size, Harry. Let her go and I'll show you a good time."

"I have a taste for a wee one this time, especially her lips. They look to fit me just fine."

Bonnie paled and so did Catherine. Having learned well from Bonnie she realized exactly what Harry intended.

"Come on, gal, let's have a taste," he said, and hoisted her up with him as he stood.

His meaty arm was so strong around her waist that she

could barely breathe. Even her attempted shouts for help fell short of their projection.

Her bottom smacked the top of the table while his hand pushed her back to stretch out full-length across it. "Now I'll have me a fine taste of those lips before those lips pleasure me."

He dropped down over her, his weight crushing her, his mouth reaching for hers. With a mixture of fear and determination she fought, swinging her fists, hitting solid flesh and bouncing off, causing Harry no harm.

"I like a woman that gives me a good fight." Harry laughed and moved in closer, using his weight to pin her hands beneath his sizable belly while his own beefy hands grabbed her face.

Horrorfying fear gripped Catherine. The smell of rotting fish, the stench of body odor, and the strong scent of ale assaulted her nostrils. Fate closed in on her. She had played the whore well and it would cost her. Her charade would matter no longer, for it would no longer be a charade.

Tears pooled in her eyes and an odd notion captured her thoughts. If she had to lose her virginity why couldn't it have been to Lucian?

Her chest felt heavy, her fear grew and panic engulfed her. She screamed for the one person who strangely enough had once threatened, but since protected, her.

"Lucian!"

Handsome Harry laughed in her face and lowered his mouth to hers.

🙟 14 🙝

A BONE-CHILLING YELL split the air and froze every person in the tavern, except Handsome Harry.

He was plucked off Catherine like a feather from a chicken. He bounced against the nearby wall, sank to the floor and shook his head to clear his senses, then stood and received a fist to his big belly and then another fist to his chin. The blows sent him slamming back against the wall, where he sank to the floor unconscious.

Lucian stood glaring over Catherine, his red knuckles still firmly molded into fists. "Bloody hell, woman, you've gone too far this time."

"I—"

Catherine had no time to explain her actions. In a flash she was yanked off the table and flung over Lucian's broad shoulder. He turned and headed for the stairs off in the corner that led to the second floor.

He stopped abruptly, swung back around, causing Catherine's head to spin and in a tone that made one want to beg for mercy, for he surely sounded as though he wanted to kill, he said, "Bones. Jolly. You both have explaining to do."

With that threat issued he mounted the stairs two at a time. He walked down the short hall to the end, kicked the door open, sending it crashing against the wall, walked in, kicked the door shut, and then walked over to the generous-sized bed and dropped Catherine down on it.

The bed ropes groaned beneath the mattress and Catherine lost her breath from fright or relief, she had yet to determine.

"Good God, madam, do you possess any brains?" he asked, his voice raised enough to demonstrate his ire, but not enough to share their argument with the patrons below.

Catherine took several deep breaths to fill her lungs and to give her sufficient time to form a reasonable explanation.

"Answer me now!"

Catherine had no doubt the whole tavern had heard his demand.

"I did nothing wrong," she said calmly, which irritated him all the more.

"Nothing? Nothing?" he repeated with an unbelieving shake of his head. "You expect me to believe that Handsome Harry strolled over to you, dragged you back to his table, and decided to ravish you in front of the entire tavern?"

"That isn't how it happened."

"Then pray tell, madam, how did it happen?"

Sprawled on her back, Catherine lacked the confidence to speak with conviction. She hastily slipped off the bed and stood. "I needed to stretch my legs, so I simply walked around a few tables."

Lucian stood a few feet away from her attempting to control his anger. His fury was on the edge of erupting into gale proportions, its strength growing every time he recalled Handsome Harry stretched over her. "Simply?" he asked.

She hated that chilling serenity in his voice. It frightened her. "Bonnie suggested—" She paused for a plausible excuse.

Lucian wouldn't allow her to finish. "Don't blame Bonnie for your own stupidity."

His cruel remark stunned her, especially since it brought back memories. Memories she had thought long buried and forgotten. "I am not stupid," she said, her chin raised, but not nearly as high as usual.

Lucian continued his attack. Angry with himself for

leaving her and angry with her for being a harlot. "When you brazenly offer your wares in a tavern, you are most definitely stupid."

Catherine detested her intelligence being humiliated and retaliated with the only weapon she possessed, her questionable virtue. "Captain, do you honestly think I would offer myself to the likes of a stinking pirate?"

Fury widened Lucian's eyes and flared his nostrils. He stormed to the door, yanked it open and yelled loud enough for the while island to hear. "Bones! Jolly! Get your useless asses up here."

Catherine remained composed while her mind frantically searched for answers to the inevitable questions that would follow.

Bones and Jolly nearly tripped over each other hurrying into the room.

"Yes, sir, Captain," Bones said, appearing to speak for both of them as they stood shivering nervously before Captain Lucifer.

Lucian was blunt. "Did she entice Handsome Harry?"

Both men stared wide-eyed at her.

She sent them a weak smile, feeling guilty that they should suffer because of her lack of common sense.

Bones answered. "No, sir."

Relief rushed through Catherine, turning her legs weak.

Lucian walked over to the two men and planted himself right in front of them. His size alone could intimidate, but his look sent the devil's own chill through them both. "What did she do?"

Both men peeked around him casting sympathetic glances at her.

"Stop looking at her and answer me," Lucian shouted, irritated that both men appeared more concerned with Catherine's feelings than with his command.

"She was coming over to our table, Captain, when Handsome Harry grabbed her," Jolly said quickly.

Catherine had rarely heard Jolly say two words, so his defense stunned her.

Lucian looked to her and then back to the two men. He obviously didn't believe anyone from the black expression crossing his face.

"Get out!" he shouted at them, and once again Bones and Jolly nearly tripped over each other while rushing out the door.

He slammed the door shut and bolted the iron lock. Then he turned on Catherine, his anger still raging. "What took you to their table?"

Catherine hesitated a moment before anxiously answering, "I was wondering when you would return and thought perhaps they would know."

"Your wit is quick, madam."

Catherine almost laughed nervously. In one breath he insulted her and in the next, unwittingly, he praised her.

Tense silence followed and then in the next instant he descended on her, grasping her slim arms in his powerful hands. "I'll have the truth, Catherine."

His voice warned, his manner promised, that she would answer or else.

Her father had taught her that when in a contest of wills and an impasse seemed likely, turn the opponent's own questions back on him. She braced herself for a confrontation when she asked, "What do you think is the truth, Captain?"

His fingers dug into her soft flesh. Catherine refused to respond to the pain he caused her. Instead she sent him a glaring challenge.

Lucian shoved her away from him in disgust. "I think,

madam, that you offer lame excuses and that you sought to satisfy your lusty hunger."

"If that is what you choose to believe then so be it."

Lucian exploded. "What I choose to believe? You flaunt yourself at me, begging me to appease your passion, telling me it has been too long since you have had pleasure, and you expect me to believe you didn't seek to find what I refused to give you? Don't insult my intelligence with such stupidity."

Her own temper flared hot. "Don't impugn my intelligence."

"You have none to impugn. If you had you would have followed my instructions and behaved."

"Like a good little girl," she said sarcastically, recalling the times her tutor would instruct her to be a good little girl and play with her dolls.

"I doubt you were ever a good little girl."

Catherine stiffened against his insult. She had always been an extra-good girl, trying to please, trying to learn, *trying, trying, trying* until she had cried with frustration and fear. Then Randolph Abelard had entered her life and changed it completely.

A smile lit her lips. "I was daddy's little girl."

Her sweet smile and sincere words ignited a second fuse in Lucian and once again he blew up. "I should have remembered you're Abelard's daughter and, like your father, a liar and cheat."

"I refuse to debate my father's character. He is a good man no matter your opinion." She turned her back on him, her intent obvious, she would argue with him no more.

Lucian still ached for a fight. "Don't turn your back on me."

"I have nothing more to say to you," Catherine said without turning to look at him.

Lucian advanced on her with each word he spoke. "I have plenty to say to you, madam."

Catherine listened to his steady approach and prepared herself for further combat.

Bloody hell, but he was outraged. He wanted to shake her senseless and then kiss her breathless. She was playing havoc with his emotions, and what was worse, he was succumbing to her talents. He struck out at her with his words. "If you need a man, Catherine, I'll find one for you."

Catherine swerved around, her eyes rounded, her lips partially open and dewy with moisture.

Lucian felt his loins tighten and cursed his inability to control his reactions to her.

Fearing her words might be true, her response was a bare whisper. "I want no man but you, Lucian."

Her sensual confession fired his own hot passion. He fought against his emotions, fought like a man fighting for his next breath.

"Lucian," Catherine whispered again, softly, innocently, achingly.

Lucian groaned and reached out for her, circling her neck and drawing her to him. His mouth reached down and covered hers.

She pressed against him, opened to him, returned his passion with wild sensuality. His hand roamed her arching back, urging her closer against him. Her full breasts thrust against his chest, her small hand dipped into his open shirt, splaying her hand on his warm, muscular chest.

He anchored his leg between hers and she moaned moving against him. He felt the swell of her heat. It matched his own and he wondered why they both didn't burst into flames so torrid was their passion.

He wrapped his hand in her silky blond hair and pulled her head back slowly.

She whimpered her disappointment, he sought to appease her.

He bent his head to her breast and took her nipple into his mouth wetting the material with his tongue. She hardened against him and he teased the peaked nipple through the material, nipping, sucking, circling until he could tolerate no more.

His teeth deftly tugged and pulled at her low neckline until it slipped down off her breast and her rosy pink nipple popped into view. His mouth gratefully captured it and feasted.

She moaned again, low and erotic. He was reminded of a purring cat who needed petting. And he certainly wanted to pet her.

His mouth remained at her breast toying and teasing. His hand moved down her back to her backside. He cupped her firm cheeks and pushed her into him as he slid his leg from between hers and planted her firmly against his hardness.

"Feel the need I have for you, angel?" he asked almost contemptuously, rubbing rhythmically against her.

She nodded, her breath lost, her senses soaring.

"Do you need me, angel?" His breath was a hoarse whisper, rough and sensual.

"I—I—" She paused, searching for words. "I need—"

"Me, angel, you need me," he finished, stealing a kiss from her.

Her lips ached, her body begged, and she surrendered to the new and strange emotions that controlled her completely.

He hoisted her up to fit her against him. She slipped her legs around him. "You're ready for me, aren't you, angel?" He bit teasingly at her bottom lip.

"Yes," her answer slipped out in a ragged breath.

His fingers found their way beneath her skirt, her skin

soft and warm and welcoming to his touch. He probed intimately along the inside of her thigh, feeling her heat, knowing he rested mere inches from her womanhood. His fingers moved with skill, brushing over her sensitive bud, gently separating her moist lips, breaching her slowly, pleasurably, deeply. Sinking into her tight nest and slipping into complete and utter sensual madness.

She cried out his name and dropped her head on his shoulder.

"Have you ever felt such pleasure?" he asked softly against her ear. His finger inched out and when he invaded her intimately again it was two fingers that sent her breath to catch in her throat. "Tell me, angel, tell me now," he urged with words and movement, needing to hear, needing to know that no one brought her to this pitch of passion.

Speech escaped Catherine. Reason escaped Catherine. Consequences escaped Catherine. She was irrevocably lost to his touch.

"Tell me," he urged, his voice sharp.

She shook her head, her face buried in the collar of his shirt.

"No one, angel, let me hear you say there is no one but *me* who could make you ache with want, make you hot, make you wet with pleasure."

No one, Catherine thought. There was no one. She was a virgin. The thought stunned her. What in the name of holy heaven what she doing? Had she completely—

She moaned involuntarily when his fingers buried so snugly inside her began an infuriatingly slow and tender rhythm.

Lost. If she didn't put an end to this madness immediately she'd be lost and lose more than her virginity. She would lose her father's life.

Why? Why did life play such dirty tricks? Why couldn't

Lucian have remained in England and become the Earl of Brynwood. Why couldn't she have met him at a party? Why couldn't he have fallen in love with her? Why couldn't he have seduced her, then married her? Why was this situation completely impossible?

Brushing her confused thoughts and wishes aside she resumed the role that would win her what was necessary, her father's freedom and her escape.

She turned her lips to his ear and whispered. "Captain, don't torture me so. It has been so long since a man has filled me."

Lucian stilled all movement. Then abruptly and with haste he released her, casting her aside, turning away from her. He walked to the door and without facing her said, "Stay put, madam, or this time you will be sorry you disobeyed me."

The cold contempt in his voice warned. Catherine didn't need to see the icy sharpness in his eyes to confirm his fury.

He slammed the door behind him and Catherine collapsed on the bed, her legs too weak to sustain her.

Lord, Catherine, whatever is the matter with you? She had no answer for the silent voice that questioned her. She didn't understand her own actions. Had the confines of their journey produced a dependency on him? Did she feel him necessary to her survival? Did she feel unsafe with him not near? Did she need him? Did she want him? Did she love him?

Her hand flew to cover her mouth as though afraid her silent thoughts would be voiced. She couldn't love him. He was a pirate, cruel and uncaring.

Not so. She closed her eyes against her private war. He possessed a soul, she was certain of it. Without a soul he could not feel such pain, such hurt, such suffering from memories from the past. He cared for his men, his ship, his revenge, and in a strange way, for her. If not she would have long since been killed or cast off. Buried beneath his pirate veneer still lurked the Earl of Brynwood, Lucian Darcmoor. And Lucian was capable of love, strong, deep, and vibrant.

As vibrant as her need—she paused in her thought wondering if it was love instead of need for him. Her body still ached for his hands to touch her, for his lips to taste her, for his voice that urged and promised unspeakable pleasures.

If only. If only circumstances and fate had not been so cruel.

Catherine sat on the ledge by the open window, hugging her knees and staring at the night sky. A strong breeze fanned her face and rattled the outside shutters that braced the sides of the window.

She sniffed deeply of the rich air and mumbled, "Rain."

"What was that you said, madam?"

Catherine turned her head sharply, not having heard Lucian enter the room. He filled the doorway with his size. His eyes no longer raged with anger. And his handsome face appeared free of concern. She relaxed. "Rain. It seems like rain."

"Some tonight," he agreed, and pulled his shirt from his breeches and over his head, tossing it to land on a threadbare tapestry-covered chair. "Sunshine will see us off in the morning."

"We're leaving Tortuga?" she asked anxiously, and wondered with further anxiety of their next destination.

"My business is complete," he said, and added sternly, "No more questions. Go to bed. We rise early tomorrow."

Sleep was the furthest thing from Catherine's mind. "I'm not tired."

Lucian sat on his shirt on the chair, yanking off his boots. "Did I ask you if you were tired?"

She didn't favor another altercation so she answered simply, "No."

"Then get into bed," he ordered, and stood to strip off his breeches.

Catherine had seen him naked often enough, but tonight his nakedness disturbed her. His broad shoulders promised protection, his full chest thick with muscles offered comfort for her weary head, and his large manhood—

She cast her glance out the window away from what his body could offer her.

"Catherine," he called out to her softly.

She turned reluctantly and he stood closer, though not too close. She kept her eyes focused on his face.

"You need your sleep. It has been a long and tiring day."

"I'm not tired," she insisted, fearing to share a bed with him while feeling so emotionally uncertain.

"Catherine," he tried again.

A strong shake of her head stopped him as he advanced on her and her urgent plea struck his heart. "Please, Lucian."

He understood her reluctance for he experienced the same misgivings. If he crawled in bed with her this night, his plans would be ruined, his revenge unattainable.

"As you wish, madam," he relented, and walked over to the bed and climbed beneath the covers. He turned on his side away from her and forced himself to sleep.

Catherine kept her attention diverted from him. She required a clear, precise mind to calculate her next step.

Stupid.

"I am not," she whispered to her herself. Old memories haunted her and she questioned her ability to succeed in rescuing her father from hanging. Too often when she was young she was made to feel intellectually inadequate. Incapable of the smallest chore or lesson.

Her mother had insisted she was lazy, repeating over and

over the story of how Catherine caused her mother a long and laborious birth simply because she was too lazy to be born.

When she couldn't tie her ribbons quickly and prettily, her mother accused her of laziness. When she made mistakes on her cross-stitch samplers she was again accused of laziness. Even when she showed interest in books she was scolded for idling her time away looking at pictures.

Catherine had thought herself foolish and worse, unlovable. She assumed no one would love someone so stupid. Until Randolph Abelard married her mother.

At first she was shy and frightened around him. She feared if he learned of her stupidity he wouldn't love her as a father loved a daughter, so she tried extra hard at her lessons.

Still after all these years she found it difficult to believe how he gallantly defended her against the tutor and then dismissed him. And when she remembered how he began teaching her himself, Catherine smiled and was filled with warm thoughts and pleasant memories.

Her father had taken time out of each day to sit with her and discuss all sorts of subjects. When she had excitedly dragged a book from the shelf and pointed to pictures, attempting to relate a story to him, he had smiled broadly and announced that he would teach her to read and write.

It had been difficult at first and she had cried often, feeling a failure. Her father had wiped her tears away and had offered encouragement. He sat her on his knee and explained that her mind worked at a slower pace when learning her lessons, but that she possessed a spark for knowledge that few people did. All that was necessary was for her to take her time and think things over.

When he began to teach her how to write. She often became confused and messed up her letters and numbers.

Again he cautioned her to take her time and proved his point by questioning her orally on math. She answered his every question correctly and without hesitation. And whenever she doubted herself she would take pen to paper and practice her letters and numbers as she did as a child.

She glanced about the room, stopping briefly to make certain Lucian was asleep. He didn't stir and his breathing seemed steady. She continued on until she spotted an inkwell and pen on top of the chest on the far wall.

She slipped off the wide sill and quietly hurried over to the chest. Stepping on tiptoes, she reached up and grabbed the inkwell and pen, and finding a sheet of parchment paper, she took that as well, returning to her perch by the window.

Rain fell heavily outside sending the inhabitants of Tortuga indoors. Gone was the raucous laughter, singing of songs, and argumentative exchanges. Silence filled the night, to Catherine's relief.

She placed the items she had collected on the sill and carefully moved the oil lamp from the bureau to the small narrow table next to the sill, providing her with sufficient light to write.

She climbed back on her perch, brought her knees up to rest the parchment on, and dipped the pen in the inkwell, slowly she began to write her name.

Tired from the long eventful day Catherine had difficulty concentrating. Her vision blurred. Every attempt at completing her name failed and she grew more frustrated and doubtful. If she couldn't write her name, a simple enough task, how could she hope to succeed in clearing her father's name?

She bit at her lower lip and concentrated. She had to write her name correctly, she just had to. She tried again and then again, but each time the letters appeared more scrambled.

Finally she began to cry in frustration softly and steadily while her hand fought to write her name correctly.

Lucian stirred in his sleep, a sense that something was amiss rousing him. He heard Catherine's soft whimpers as his eyes drifted open. He wasted no time, he climbed from the bed and went to her, his heart racing in concern.

She looked up at him, her eyes red and filled with tears. He looked down at her and the paper resting against her bent legs. His look appeared puzzled and he reached for the paper.

"Bloody hell, Catherine, weren't you properly taught how to read and write. Look at the mess you've made."

All the years of struggling to learn, all the years of keeping it a secret, all her fears surfaced at once and she lashed out at him, grabbing back the paper. "I was taught to read and write."

She put her pen to paper and once again attempted her name, slowly, carefully, concentrating on every line and curve of the letters. Her fingers grasped the pen tightly as she worked diligently on proving her intelligence. But her mind had suffered enough badgering for one day and failed to cooperate.

She cried out in frustration when she made an error and sought to correct her mistake.

Lucian stood beside her stunned. Obviously she had been tutored in reading and writing, but perhaps the lessons were never finished. Even if that was so, she had learned remarkably well for a woman. She was far more intelligent then he had given her credit for. And he respected and admired her determination and her courage.

He bent down beside her and slipped his hand over hers. "Let me help you."

Catherine froze in shock, her tears running down her cheeks.

He smiled at her, a soft, encouraging smile and Catherine's fear suddenly melted away. His large hand covered hers and together they wrote Catherine's name perfectly.

"Thank you," she whispered, and smiled. "You truly are a gentleman."

Lucian stared at her. She looked vulnerable and innocent with her silver blond hair tumbling wildly over her shoulders and around her pale face. And her green eyes had grown deep in color from her crying, her cheeks flushed pink and her bottom lip reddened from her biting nervously at it. She resembled a little girl, innocent of life.

But she was no innocent and he was no gentleman. He was a pirate, the infamous pirate Lucifer, with tales of his plunder and savage escapades crossing oceans and continents. And she was Randolph Aberlard's daughter and a harlot.

He ran his finger down the side of her cheek tenderly as if touching her for the first time. "If only," he whispered, then stood and took himself off to bed, turning his back on her and his emotions once again.

❧ 15 ❧

CATHERINE GRIPPED THE wooden rail and watched Tortuga fade in the distance. Where would Lucian take her now? What were his intentions? How long would she remain his prisoner? How long could she continue this charade?

A shudder ran through her and arms wrapped around her.

"Have you a chill?" Lucian asked, drawing her back against him and crossing his arms to rest beneath her breasts.

Catherine released the railing along with a soft sigh. She ran her hands over his large ones, her tension fading as she felt his strength locked around her. He was offering her protection, comfort. For how long? She didn't know and she didn't care. She gratefully accepted his offer of peace.

She decided upon an honest answer. "My thoughts chill me."

"Why is this?" His voice held no icy contempt. It rang warm with concern.

"My fate has yet to be decided."

He hooked his fingers over hers. "Your fate still remains in my hands, nothing has changed."

"Our destination has."

"You need only to ask, madam, and I shall be pleased to tell you."

"Where is it you take me, Lucian?"

"To Heaven," he said with a gentle laugh.

"Heaven?"

"My island," Lucian explained. "I named it Heaven since it is the closest thing to paradise."

Afraid to ask, but knowing she must, she took a deep breath and said, "How long is my stay in Heaven?"

He hugged her closer to him, leaned down near her ear and whispered, "Don't you know Heaven is for eternity."

Another shudder raced through her.

"Do you fear eternity with me, Catherine? You had agreed to marry me. Marriage is a lifetime commitment. Would you have honored your vows? Would you have given yourself to me for a lifetime?"

"If we had exchanged wedding vows, I would belong to you at this moment. It was not I who broke the agreement."

Lucian brushed his lips over the rim of her ear. "But you played me false, madam."

Thinking was difficult with him nibbling at her ear. "I did no such thing. I came to you—"

"With your lost virginity."

Catherine attempted to ignore his warm breath, his teasing lips, and his hard body pressing into her. "You did not specify virginity as a prerequisite to the marriage."

"I did not think it necessary. I assumed you were a lady."

Catherine closed her eyes against her own response. "You assumed wrong."

He retaliated swiftly. "And you sealed your own fate."

"What is my fate, Lucian?" she asked, her desperation to know haunting her.

He turned her around to look at him. "Once again, madam, I think you will be the one to seal your fate." He kissed her gently, released her, and walked away.

Catherine watched him saunter off to the opposite end of the ship. Why did he speak in riddles? What could she possibly do to seal her own fate?

Allow him to make love to you, her own silent voice answered.

Either way he would win. If he made love to her and

discovered her virginity, his revenge would be sweet. And if he returned her untouched society would still assume the opposite. She would lose, seal her own fate, no matter her choice. Her only hope was that at least she would be able to prove her father's innocence, otherwise this whole charade would be for naught.

She needed to keep him at a distance. She needed to keep her wits about her. She needed to find those papers and escape. She needed to ignore Lucian's gentle side and remember who he was and why he held her captive. He was the infamous Captain Lucifer and he sought revenge.

Don't forget, Catherine. Don't forget, she silently warned herself while a single tear trickled down her cheek.

"You informed Abelard, didn't you?" Santos asked as Lucian joined him at the wheel.

Lucian leaned against the huge rain barrel strapped to the mast. "I did."

"The man you spoke to on Tortuga?"

"Will take my message to Abelard."

"And the message?"

"I have his daughter."

Santos heard the cold calculation in Lucian's voice and dreaded the outcome of this venture. "What do you expect Abelard to do?"

"Offer me money in return for his daughter's safety."

"And will you take it?" Santos asked, though he knew well the answer.

"No," he said curtly.

"Then how—"

"Catherine," Lucian finished. "I will still have my revenge through Catherine. She sees her father as a hero. A good and decent man incapable of hurting anyone. When the time is right I will show her the papers proving her father's guilt. Then she will see the truth."

"And?" Santos waited.

"She will hate her father and seek solace with me."

"You intend to keep her? Make her your mistress?"

"I intend to allow her to chose her fate."

Santos shook his head. "She will not stay with you."

"Her body tells me otherwise."

Santos gripped the wheel. "You've touched her?"

Lucian laughed. "You act as if I had offended a virgin."

"Are you sure you haven't?"

"You're a blind fool," Lucian snapped, springing away from the rain barrel and raking his fingers through his long hair. "Catherine Abelard is no virgin."

"You're more the fool if you believe that," Santos said. "Open your eyes, Lucian, before it's too late."

Lucian cast him a sad smile. "It is already too late, my friend."

Catherine once again wore a cotton shift, this one trimmed with yellow flowers. Her pearls hung down around her neck past her belly while she vigorously combed her hair before retiring.

"The viscount bored me," she said, having entertained Lucian with tales of her sexual exploits since he had entered the cabin an hour ago. She intended that he keep his distance and she could almost guarantee he would if she constantly chattered about her naughty liaisons.

Lucian sat in bed, his expression blank, his hands clenched at his sides. The white sheet rode low across his flat, hard belly and his long red hair fell over his shoulders still damp from the washing he had given it before retiring to his cabin.

Catherine kept her eyes averted from him, looking at him could prove fatal. He reminded her of a mighty warrior, strikingly handsome and ready for battle. His opponent didn't stand a chance, especially a woman.

She hung her head down between her legs and repeatedly combed her hair over her head.

"Are you going to tell me why the viscount bored you," Lucian asked irritably. Annoyed with himself for having asked the question and even more annoyed that he found an answer necessary.

Grateful that her long hair hid her blush she continued. "He always wanted me beneath him. He had no adventure in his soul. It was always the same position. He completely bored me."

Catherine blessed Bonnie every time she fabricated a story. She had had no idea that men found different positions exciting or that there even were different positions to enjoy when making love.

Lucian's question startled her. "Which position do you prefer?"

She brushed her hair harder. Recalling Bonnie's favorite she chose it as her own as well. "I prefer being on top. I can feel so much more and move more freely."

Lucian cursed his curiosity. Now all he could think of was her riding some damn viscount, her head tossed back, her breasts pushed out, her moans of pleasure filling the room.

"Blast all, woman, you're going to comb every hair out of your head. Put the damn comb down and come to bed."

Catherine tossed her head back, her silver blond hair flying around her, her cheeks flushed a vivid pink and her eyes aglow with surprise. "My hair tending annoys you?"

"Yes," he snapped, though in truth he found pleasure in watching her comb her silky mane. He loved the strange blond color of her hair and often itched to run his fingers through it. He just couldn't stand hearing another lover's tale. He had had enough.

Not wishing for an argument Catherine put her comb away and climbed into bed. "Lucian—"

He turned, capturing her chin harshly between his fingers. "No more. I will hear no more about favorite positions, boring positions, any positions except the one you intend to fall asleep in."

"My side," she said with difficulty, his fingers still gripping her face.

He released her. "Good, go to sleep on your side."

"I will, but, Lucian?"

"Yes," he said, settling himself against his pillows.

"I've never made love side by side. I've heard it is possible, but I have never known a man skilled at that position." Why she continued to chatter on about sexual positions, she couldn't say. Unless it was Lucian's skills that interested her.

"Go to sleep," he shouted angrily, and reached out to extinguish the lamp on the table beside the bed.

Quiet descended on the cabin. The sea could be heard slapping the sides of the ship while it rocked it gently. Catherine found peace in the simple sound and motion and listened allowing the sway to ease her into sleep.

"Catherine," Lucian called softly.

"Mmmm," she answered, too tired for words.

"Side by side is indeed pleasurable."

Catherine's eyes burst wide open.

"Perhaps one day I shall show you."

It was an hour before Catherine was able to sleep or breathe easily.

The lash struck his back over and over and over. The leather thongs tore at his flesh, ripping it apart. The pain was excruciating, blinding him, tearing at him, searing his very soul.

He pressed his cheek against the mast he was strapped to, willing himself to block out the pain, to survive, to have his revenge.

The lash struck him again, his back feeling like the fires of Hades. Then the voice followed.

"How dare you touch my daughter? How dare you defile her innocence? How dare you steal her love from me?"

Lucian turned his head, looking over his shoulder, fighting the pain it caused him until his eyes connected with his abuser . . . Randolph Abelard.

He stood holding Catherine in his arms. She cried on his shoulder. He shook his head sadly.

"You fool," he whispered, and turned away, taking Catherine with him.

He tried desperately to see who swung the lash, he craned his neck, stretching, looking, searching and then he saw him. . . .

Lucian almost jumped from the bed screaming. Sweat poured from his brow and his breath was short and rapid. His eyes bulged wide, afraid to close, afraid of what he might see.

Catherine woke in terror, turning and tumbling from the bed so fearful was she of his scream. She got to her knees and peered over the edge of the bed. "Lucian?" she asked softly, wondering if he remained in the throes of his nightmare or if he had awakened.

He shook his head and looked beside him. "Catherine?"

She scrambled back into the bed. "I'm here," she said, offering her hand to him.

He grasped onto her, pulling her into his lap and hugging her almost breathless. "I frightened you?"

"A wrenching scream tearing through one's sleep would have that effect."

He squeezed her to him again and laughed. "Oh, angel, you do save my sanity at times."

Catherine snuggled against his chest, her small fingers rubbing his taut warm muscles. "And cause you madness at other times."

His voice was a bare whisper. "I cause my own madness."

Catherine could only imagine the horrors he had endured while captive to a madman. She wished she could make him forget just for the moment.

She gave no thought to her action. He needed her, she felt it in his tense muscles, in his rapid heartbeat, in his heavy breathing. And she could not deny him.

She kissed his chest lightly, her lips barely brushing his flesh.

"Catherine." Her name was issued after a sudden intake of breath.

An answer wasn't necessary. She continued, her lips gently pressing kisses against his warm flesh until she found his nipple and took it between her teeth.

"God's blood, woman, this is madness," he said in uneven breaths.

Her tongue circled his nipple while her teeth held him captive. The hard orb tasted as she thought, warm and salty like the sea. She moved to his other nipple to treat it likewise, pushing him back aggressively until they both lay stretched out on the bed.

His hands found her bottom and hoisted her over him, her nightdress the only thing between her and his nakedness.

Catherine spread herself over him, feeling the rough kneading of his hands on her buttocks, feeling the strength of him anxious beneath her, feeling her very center burn with desire.

"Catherine," he moaned again, pressing her against him, urging himself into her and cursing soundly her night dress that separated them.

She continued to pleasure him with her tongue, losing all reason, all sanity.

"I need to feel your flesh in my hands," he moaned, and ripped at the bodice of her shift, tearing the fine material away.

The long strand of pearls fell free and tumbled on his face. He cursed them. And lifted them to slip over her head. "Off with these, I'm sick of seeing them."

Catherine froze, staring at him wide-eyed.

He stared back as if for the first time realizing the consequences of their actions. "Second thoughts, madam?"

Her voice failed her. Her limbs failed her. Her senses failed her.

Lucian regained his senses for them both and, grabbing her shoulders, eased her off him. He swiftly drew the covers over himself, hiding away his need for her.

"Go to sleep, Catherine," he said coldly.

Catherine turned on her side, hugging her pearls and her torn night dress. Silent tears ran down her cheeks. Tears of regret for it was just a matter of time before her own passion destroyed all her plans and sentenced her father to death.

Lucian lay still, his arms pillowed beneath his head, his eyes staring into the darkness. He was still hot, still hard, and still heavy with passion from Catherine's innocent assault.

Innocent.

He laughed silently. She was no innocent.

Fool.

A fine sweat broke out across his brow as his nightmare returned and he glimpsed once again the face of the man who swung the lash.

It was himself.

❧ 16 ❧

Lucian had kept his distance from Catherine for three days. He took his meals alone and slept on the deck. His back pained him. His neck pained him. And he pained the crew with his curt temper.

The weather even appeared to mimic his mood. Dark clouds raced overhead while mild thunder rumbled in the distance. Lucian wasn't worried about a severe storm— some thunder, some rain, but nothing worse.

He had more of a problem with the crew. Several of the men walked around grumbling about sick stomachs and blamed the cook.

Serving on a ship from hell, he had learned to steel his stomach against the worst food and still survive. But there had been times the food had been so rancid that nothing helped but to rid yourself of it.

He had lacked an appetite last night and had eaten nothing but a few pieces of cheese and bread, electing to forgo the fresh fish. The fish was more than likely the culprit and he had quickly ordered the cook to prepare simple meals for the next few days.

Now his problem consisted of securing the deck with a limited crew. Santos hadn't shown his face all day and he had assumed he also enjoyed last night's fish and was now regretting it.

Jolly, possessing an ironclad stomach, worked diligently fastening everything in sight, while his friend Bones moaned in agony in his hammock below.

"No fish for you last night?" Lucian asked, checking the knot on the water casket.

"My stomach protested last night, but not much. I'm feeling right fine and ready for another meal."

"Noontime is near, though I doubt the fare will be generous. I hear cook isn't feeling too well himself," Lucian said. He caught sight of Santos on deck. Catherine was hooked to his arm.

"If cook isn't up to it, I can tend to the meals until he is," Jolly offered.

Lucian nodded his approval, his interest fixed on Santos and Catherine. She appeared to cling to him. And worse, Santos seemed attentive to her. His arm circled her waist, her head dropped every now and then to rest on his shoulder.

Had Santos lost his mind? The ship needed attending before the storm hit. Catherine could damn well entertain herself. He marched across the deck straight for the unsuspecting couple.

"Bloody hell, Santos, the ships needs—" He stopped abruptly when Catherine raised her head from Santos's shoulder. Her complexion was deathly pale, her lips dry, dark half circles beneath her eyes and she looked to have lost weight.

"What's wrong?" he asked, jealous of the way she clung to his friend.

"I think the fish," Santos explained. "She hasn't kept down any food nor drink since last night. I found her this morning on the cabin floor, heaving into the chamber pot."

Lucian blanched at the thought of her alone with no one to help her, reduced to tending herself over a chamber pot. If he had stayed with her or at the most seen to her care this would not have happened.

"I thought some fresh air might help," Santos said, but shook his head at Lucian.

"You're still not feeling well, Catherine?" Lucian asked, the answer obvious. He ached to scoop her frail body up and cart her down to the cabin and tend to her himself. But she appeared content with Santos and he would not force his help on her.

She shook her head, leaving it on Santos's shoulder.

"Would you like Santos to take you back to the cabin?"

She hesitated, then nodded.

"See to her care," he instructed his friend, and turned to walk away blaming himself for her suffering.

"Lucian."

His name pleaded so softly barely reached his ears and he turned unsure if he had heard the summons.

Catherine stood crying, her hand at her stomach.

He rushed to her side, slipping his arm around her waist and practically carried her to the railing. His arm cushioned her stomach as he bent her over the railing while she attempted to retch into the sea. But her stomach had already been purged and she suffered dry heaves and no more.

"Nothing stays down," Santos said anxiously.

Lucian caught his worried look. They had seen men die from such constant and useless retching.

Catherine moaned and dropped back against Lucian. Her hand sought his and weakly she grasped hold of him. "Please stay with me."

His heart almost broke from her soft, aching request. He scooped her up into his arms and her head immediately sought the comfort of his chest. "Don't worry, angel, I won't leave you."

She sighed her relief. She was with Lucian now. She would be safe. Everything would be all right. Her stomach cramped again and she moaned.

"Get cook to fix chamomile tea," he instructed before hurrying off to his cabin.

He cursed himself a million times over for not tending to her properly, for ignoring her and for realizing how much he missed being with her.

He entered his cabin and blessed Santos for seeing to its cleaning, the strong scent of lye soap filling his nostrils. The sheets also had been seen to, freshly scented and drawn back for her return.

With care he lowered her to the bed. "Your shift would prove more comfortable than this silk dress," he suggested.

"I would love so to wear one of my shifts, but I soiled them in my feeble attempts to make it to the chamber pot to retch. That is why Santos found me on the floor. I had no strength left to move."

And she had no strength after her explanation. His anger with himself grew, thinking of her alone and suffering, unable to move or help herself.

Reluctantly he stepped away from the bed and hurriedly searched his chest in the far corner for a silk shirt, discarding garment after garment until he located the soft white one, a favorite of his. He returned to her, sitting on the bed beside her.

"This garment should prove more comfortable." He didn't wait for permission to assist her, his hands were already easing the silk dress off her.

His eyes narrowed when he stripped her completely and saw that in one day's time she had indeed lost weight. Her rib cage showed beneath her translucent skin and her stomach sank in instead of curving seductively as it did before.

And then there were her pearls, white and creamy against her skin. Always around her neck. Always hanging down past her belly. Always feeling cool against his skin when she cuddled beside him during the night. He had never seen her without them. They lay pooled in the curve of her belly.

Concern gripped him. He had seen men lose ten pounds in one day, twenty in two and dead by the third. He had to get something, even if only liquid, into her stomach and force it to stay down. He slipped his shirt over her head and worked it down her body gently.

Her eyes had closed minutes ago, and not wanting to disturb her needed rest, he stood and carefully placed her legs beneath the sheet, then tucked it around her waist.

He returned to her side on the bed and watched her take each breath. Her chest rose and fell normally, no hampered breathing plagued her. Thank God.

What was it about the silver-haired beauty that haunted him so? His passion for her seemed unnatural. He ached to possess her, to taste her forbidden fruit and see if the price he paid would be worth it.

But his thirst for revenge interfered and the fact that she was Abelard's daughter and a harlot tormented him.

He could hear Santos's warning. He shook his head against his strange thoughts. He had felt cheated, denied, furious when he had discovered she was no innocent. Her pure beauty and caring nature belied her true character. She could fool the devil himself.

The thought startled him. How many times had people thought him the devil, hence the name Lucifer.

Men argued that he possessed no soul.

Cruel and heartless he was, women had cried.

Other pirates gave him a wide berth whether it was on land or sea. He was feared. He was hated. He was the infamous Lucifer. And he owed it all to Abelard. His hatred of the man had fostered a resolve, a promise to stop at nothing to see his destruction.

"Lucian," Catherine moaned, and his hand covered hers.

"Do you feel sick again?" he asked.

She nodded and he left her to return with the ceramic

washbowl. He slipped his arm beneath her and hoisted her up.

She began to choke and gag.

"Easy, angel," he warned. "There is nothing left in your stomach to eliminate, it but protests."

The dry heaves racked her body once again and Lucian cursed soundly beneath his breath as he held her through the useless heaving.

He had settled her comfortably and once again she slept.

Santos entered the cabin. "Cook is feeling better. He sent the chamomile tea and bread and his regards that she's well soon."

"She won't be if I don't get something to stay in her stomach," he said seriously, his growing worry evident in his bleak expression.

"Do you need help?" Santos offered.

"I need your help on deck, making certain everything is attended to before the storm hits. I don't expect a serious gale, but I prefer safety over assumption."

Santos nodded. "I'll see to it." He hurried to the door, the clouds outside the window having grown darker and more menacing.

"Santos."

Lucian's voice halted him and he looked to him for further instructions.

"Am I really blind?"

Santos spoke seriously. "Only you can answer that question, my friend."

His question was answered several days later as Catherine, fit and healthy from Lucian's gentle care, related a compelling and titillating tale of a particularly talented earl.

"Danford possessed the most wicked tongue," Catherine said, running her silver comb through her hair in preparation for bed. "It danced and twirled, Lord, but he could do the most imaginative things with it."

Lucian had only entered the cabin twenty minutes before, having purposely kept himself from her presence. He no longer doubted her innocence. She didn't possess an ounce. As soon as she was well she talked endlessly of her many lovers.

When he had tended her she seemed different, almost as if she were another person. She spoke of no other men. There was only him. She wanted only him, needed only him, relied on only him. She hadn't even whispered her father's name—only his—Lucian.

"Lucian, did you hear me?" Catherine asked.

He stood in front of his desk shirtless, having discarded it when he entered the cabin. He tossed the chart he held down on the desk and shook his head at her in answer.

He didn't want to hear any more talks of tongues, kisses, naked bodies, beds, positions, whatever. He didn't want to think of her having sex with so many men in so many positions with so many tongues licking and probing and—

"Then I shall repeat myself. And, Lucian, you should really take care to listen. After all, if you do surrender to our passion you would know exactly what pleasures me," she scolded.

What would pleasure him at this very moment was to gag her mouth with a cloth and tie her to the main mast.

"So this earl started on my lips and inch by inch worked his way down my body, treating my quivering flesh to the most delightful licks."

Lucian attempted to shut her out, close his mind to her chatter. He sat on the chair by the stove and worked his boots off, concentrating on every tug and pull. But bits of her tale interfered.

"Warm and wet—"

He yanked one boot completely off and sat it beside the chair.

"Belly and thighs tingled—"

The other boot proved a worthy adversary, giving him difficulty in coming off. He focused on the challenge it presented, tugging and pulling and—

"And long, why I never felt—"

Fury raged through him as he looked at his boot and demanded his mind focus on the stubborn black leather and to hell with the earl's long tongue.

He gripped the scuffed leather, reminding himself it needed polishing, a good, *long*—

"Damn," he muttered, and viciously yanked the boot from his foot. Instead of placing it next to its mate, he tossed it clear across the room.

"Whatever is the matter?" Catherine asked innocently, knowing full well how her stories affected him. Bonnie had been a godsend. With Bonnie's many sexual exploits Catherine was able to entertain Lucian daily, and daily he would leave the cabin to return late or not return at all.

Guilt had almost caused her to cease her chatter. He had been so good, so caring, so tender to her when she had taken ill. She had wanted to confess everything to him and pray that there would be a way they could work things out and perhaps, like in fairy tales, fall in love forever and ever.

She had realized before it was too late that only fairy tales had happy endings. This was real life and he was a real pirate and not just any pirate. He was Captain Lucifer.

"Well?" she said, pushing for an answer.

"Nothing," he mumbled, and stood unfastening his breeches.

Catherine averted her eyes, toying with the pearls around her neck. Lord, but they had saved her time and time again. She has grasped them often when fearful of discovery and the smooth white beads had calmed her, protected her, saved her. They were her shield, her armor, her salvation.

She resumed her tale. "The earl also favored strange places when making love."

Lucian growled beneath his breath and shrugged out of his breeches. He turned his back on her and walked to the washstand, pouring water from the pitcher into the bowl.

"It's cold," Catherine warned, admiring his firm derriere, narrow waist, and broad shoulders. The scars no longer disturbed her. His pain and suffering were in the past and there they would stay. His flesh had healed nicely, now if only his mind could.

"I know," Lucian said, and splashed the cold water on his face, cursing Catherine Abelard to hell for his suffering.

"I found the huge dining table a most desirable and satisfying object to make love on," she continued.

Lucian splashed his face again and again, attempting with great restraint not to strangle her. He thought of the sea, the wind, the sway of the ship beneath his feet, the sway of Catherine's hips beneath the earl's.

He growled again though not so unnoticeably.

"Did you say something, Lucian?"

"No!" he snapped, and grabbed the towel from the brass bar on the wall.

Catherine shrugged indifferently while inwardly she suffered from her own suggestive remarks. The earl she spoke so intimately of was Lucian. She had fantasized the pleasure they could share, using Bonnie's many stories to detail each and every time she had pictured them making love.

"The earl favored the garden, in the warm weather of course. The scent of the flowers in full bloom still stings my nostrils," she sighed.

Lucian held the towel to his face, trapping the rage that threatened to spill from his mouth. He had thought often of

Catherine naked in the lush tropical paradise of Heaven. The sweet scent of the island flowers surrounding them as they made slow, passionate love.

"The earl would pluck a rose, a blood red one," she said, thinking of Lucian's hair. "Deep and dark in color and rich with its sweet scent. He would gently crush the flower in his hand and sprinkle the velvet soft petals over my breasts and then—"

"Stop it, Catherine," Lucian ordered, and turned to face her with fury in his eyes. "Don't say another word."

But she did, she had to for she was fearful if he stayed this night with her all would be lost. "I was but sharing—"

"Sharing?" He threw back his head and laughed. "You were bragging, madam. Bragging about your bloody lover, and I daresay a favorite of yours."

Catherine stood and held her chin high. "The earl was my favorite. My very most favorite. He made me feel things no other man could. He touched me like no other man touched me, kissed me like no other man kissed me." Catherine took a breath to deliver the final blow. "And forced pleasurable cries from me like no other man could."

Lucian lost all control. He advanced on her.

She stepped back, his size, his anger making him look like Lucifer himself rising from the depths of hell.

He grabbed her by her shoulders and shook her. "You are nothing but a whore."

His words pierced her heart painfully. "And are you any better, Captain Lucifer?"

Grim lines framed his narrowed eyes. "I do what I must to survive. You spread your legs for any man just for the pleasure."

Catherine felt the hurt of his words clear to her soul. She thrust her chin up higher and attacked. "You're right, Captain. Any man that pleasures me I gladly welcome between my legs."

Fury raged through Lucian like a blazing inferno. "You have no morals." He released her in disgust, stepping back from her.

"Morals? I do as I please and I please myself numerous times with whoever strikes my fancy. And that earl, my favorite, struck my fancy over and over and—"

Lucian released a savage scream. "Enough! Enough, I tell you. Enough of those damn stories—" He stopped abruptly and stared at her chest. "And enough of those damn bloody pearls!"

His hands reached out for the long strand.

Catherine screeched, jumped back, her hand flying to protect her only salvation.

She was too late.

Lucian's large hand grasped the pearls and swiftly tore them from around her neck.

One by one the pearls dropped from the broken strand, bouncing around her feet and scattering in fright.

Catherine's painful scream pierced the cabin and with wide horrified eyes she dropped to her knees. Frantically she gathered what fallen pearls were in her reach, locking them in her one hand while the other chased the beads around her. Reaching, picking, capturing her armor.

Lucian stood in shock watching her. Watching her frantic attempts to capture each round precious pearl that rolled from her reach. She appeared mad, crazed that her strand of pearls had broken. They were only pearls, mere baubles that could be replaced. Good God, it wasn't as though she was a lady who had lost her—

And in that second as he watched her hand capture pearl after pearl and tightly grasp them protectively in her hand, he knew. . . .

He knew that Catherine Abelard was a virgin.

❧ 17 ❧

Lucian dropped to his knees beside her.

"My pearls, Lucian, my pearls," she cried.

"Let me help you, angel." Her tears streaming down her cheeks tore at his heart.

She looked at him bewildered.

His hand reached out and plucked a pearl from the floor. He took her hand that tightly grasped the collected pearls and tucked it between her fingers to join its mates.

She smiled hesitantly in thanks.

He couldn't smile, his heart ached so badly from the pain he had caused her. Instead, he turned and proceeded to pick up the rest of the pearls from the floor.

Catherine stared at him several seconds before joining him in gathering the remaining scattered pearls.

Silent minutes passed while all the pearls were gathered.

Lucian remained on his knees, his shoulders back, his chest out full and in his hand he gripped the pearls.

Catherine remained on her knees as well, her shoulders bravely drawn back while in her hand she gripped her pearls.

They stared for long hard minutes at one another, then Lucian fed her hand his pearls, covering her overflowing hand with his to hold them captive.

His other hand lifted her chin gently. "I know, angel."

Catherine's whole body turned weak.

"I know you're a virgin."

She closed her eyes against his discovery.

He studied her face, her creamy complexion, her long

blond lashes, her sleek lips he ached to kiss for too long and he understood why he wanted her to badly. It wasn't her virginity. It was her innocence of life and of love.

She had chosen to sacrifice both for her father. She had chosen to accept Lucifer as her husband no matter his character and to love him, unconditionally.

She was pure and innocent of heart.

"Look at me, angel," he said softly.

She opened her tear-filled eyes. "What now?" she asked bravely.

"Now I make love to you."

"Lucian, please—"

He pressed his finger to her lips and silenced her plea. "Tonight we forget who we are. There is only you and me. Only now. Only us. Only the love we will share."

Confused, she shook her head. "But your revenge—"

His finger once again prevented further talk. "Only you and me, angel. Not the past. Not the future. Not revenge. Simply desire."

Catherine couldn't believe his words. Her breath caught. Her mind whirled. Her passion flared.

"I will not touch you unless you want it as much as I do," he whispered. "And I want you so badly I ache to the depths of my soul."

Catherine smiled shyly. He did possess a soul.

"Do you want me as badly as I want you, angel?" His voice was rough with constrained desire.

Speech locked in her throat. Dare she trust him? Dare she give herself to him?

"Answer me, angel. Answer me now or I'll prove that your want equals mine."

Still her voice wouldn't oblige her. Or was it that she wanted the choice taken from her?

Lucian growled like a hungry animal. "No more chances."

He lowered his head and lifted Catherine's chin. Their lips met and touched briefly. He moaned. "You taste like paradise, angel."

He stroked her lips with his, aching to introduce her to all the pleasures she had spoken of so knowledgeably but never experienced.

His tongue slowly swept the thin line that prevented entrance to the sweet haven he longed to explore.

He groaned against her mouth. "Let me in, angel, I want you to taste paradise."

Her lips separated reluctantly, uncertain of her decision, and before she could change her mind Lucian slipped with skill inside.

The thrill of her taste, warm and wet, fired his passion. He circled her waist and drew her closer, both still clinging to the handful of pearls.

Her tongue touched his shyly and retreated. He chased after her easing her to mate with him and share the thrill of their union. Gently he sparred with her until she relaxed and enjoyed his intimate invasion.

Lucian had kissed scores of women, but none—none—had compared to the magic he experienced with Catherine. It was almost as though when he kissed her she reached down into the very depths of his lost soul and freed him to love.

He tore his mouth away from hers. "Damn, angel, but I can't get enough of you. I want to taste every delicious inch of you. Tell me you want me to taste you. Tell me," he urged, biting with a soft hunger at her bottom lip.

She drifted lost, unaware of reality, only knowing she needed Lucian. Her eyes fluttered, she attempted to focus on his face and tell him that tonight—she belonged to him and him alone.

Concerned with her hesitation, he captured her lips and

kissed her breathless. He didn't want her to doubt for a second that he made love to her this night out of desire and not revenge.

He kissed her cheek, her chin, her mouth.

"Lucian," she whispered barely able to speak.

"I need an answer, angel. Give me an answer or I'll let you go."

Catherine tensed against the thought. He gave her a choice. The decision was hers. Her voice caught in her throat. Speech seemed impossible. She delivered her answer the only way possible. She released the pearls clutched in her hand.

Lucian felt her fingers spread and he swept his hand away. He kept his eyes on hers and she on him, and together they listened to the pearls bounce and scatter around them.

He had heard of broken hearts and had frowned at the absurdity of the expression, but at this moment his heart ached with such love that he thought surely it would tear in two. Her actions had demonstrated so much more than words could have ever said.

He stood, his hands around her waist, bringing her to her feet with him and then swiftly scooped her up into his arms. "You won't be sorry, angel."

"Promise me," she murmured.

"You have my word."

She smiled and kissed his lips like a young pupil intent on impressing her tutor. "I'll see that you keep it, Captain Lucifer."

"And I'll see that you cry with pleasure—numerous times tonight."

She hugged his neck and rubbed her cheek to his. "What are you waiting for?"

He answered with a kiss that left her hungry for more as

he lowered her to the bed. He sat beside her, her hand reaching for him to join her.

He locked her hand in his, bringing her fingers to his mouth to nibble on. "Not yet, angel. The night is young and you have much to learn."

Shivers raced over her from the thought. Bonnie had given explicit lessons, now Lucian would personally instruct.

"First," he said, releasing her hand and easing his own hand down over her flat tummy, slipping lower to stroke faintly between her legs, moving across her thigh and down her leg to slide ever so slowly beneath her shift. "We must rid you of this intrusive garment."

Shyness assaulted Catherine. She had stood naked often enough in front of him, but always with her pearls on. Now when he rid her of her night shift she would lay completely naked before him. The thought sent a fearful shudder through her.

Lucian felt her tremble beneath his hand and cast her a questioning glance. "This isn't fear I feel, is it?"

Catherine chewed thoughtfully at her lip.

Lucian kept his hand where it rested, beneath her shift on the inside of her thigh just above her knee. Her skin was petal soft and warm as though kissed by the morning sun. He ached to peel the shift from her and touch all of her, every last blessed inch. But he didn't want hesitation from her. He didn't want her to doubt.

"Catherine," he said softly but firmly. "Do you fear me?"

She shook her head.

His hand inched farther up. The shift caught on his wrist and moved along with him. "Then tell me what troubles you."

Seeing the sincere concern in his eyes helped her to answer. "I'll be naked."

He smiled. A small laugh followed. "Madam, I've seen you naked before."

She shook her head slowly, a serious expression filling her face. "I had my pearls on."

Lucian glanced to the floor where the pearls lay quiet and still as if in respect to the two lovers. He turned back to her. His own expression as equally serious as hers. "Then tonight, angel, I see you for the first time, innocent and fair of heart."

That he did not laugh at her concern made her at that very moment lose her heart to him. She only prayed he wouldn't break it.

Lucian eased the shift up and off her, tossing it to the floor. He devoured her with his eyes slowly, meticulously, lovingly. "You are more beautiful than the fairest rose in full bloom."

His sincere compliment stunned her speechless.

Softly he warned her of his intentions, "I'm going to taste you." He leaned over her, his hand cupping her breast. "All of you." His lips settled on her rosy pink nipple.

He loved the flavor of her hard little bud rolling around his tongue, the feel of her breast spilling over in his hand and her soft moans of pleasure.

He drew his mouth away briefly as he stretched out beside her. She turned and arched enough to offer him her other breast, he accepted it greedily.

Slowly his hand explored her body. Soft and warm, her silky skin quivered with passion beneath his touch. He splayed his hand on her belly, reveling in her rich softness. He dipped with teasing playfulness between her legs and then withdrew again.

His fingers drove her wild, taunting and then rushing away to leave her hungry like a starving woman in need of sustenance.

"Lucian," she whispered.

He paid her no heed, his mouth intent on enjoying her breasts. His fingers still magically teased her. She dug her fingers into his long hair and pulled until his mouth released her nipple and he looked up at her.

Words failed her and she stared at him helplessly.

"Tell me what you want." He breathed roughly, her interruption of his enjoyment costing him desirous pain.

Catherine thought. So many things she wanted to experience with him, but what? What did she tell him? What did she want at this moment?

"What?" He ceased all movement and waited.

Her hands dropped from his hair, she moaned and shut her eyes, giving voice to her desire. "Touch me, Lucian. Lord, but I need you to touch me."

He eased her legs apart, stroking her flesh, stoking the fire that he had kindled with each teasing touch.

He brushed his mouth over hers and felt the spark of passion so intense that it stilled him for a moment. Then he resumed, intending to make this night, their first, last forever.

"I'm going to enter you, angel, slow and sweet. Wrap yourself around me. Let me know that you want me."

His words fired her soul and his touch—

Her deep, erotic moan filled the cabin.

"That's it, angel," he encouraged. "Feel me. Enjoy me."

Insane. His touch drove her to near insanity. Nothing had prepared her for such exquisite torment.

"Tighten around me. Let me know you want me inside you." He felt her warm moistness wrap around him, engulf him, and he almost cried out at the thought of burying himself so snugly within her.

Catherine felt breathless and on fire, her flesh sensitive and quivering, alive and aching. "I never thought—" She stopped, her breath and Lucian's intimate strokes making it difficult to continue.

"You haven't tasted it all yet, angel. Wait," he whispered, and lowered his head to her belly, his tongue painting intricate swirls and paths as he descended to where his fingers teased her.

In her innocence she had learned much and knew exactly what he intended. She braced herself, but nothing prepared her for the jolt of sheer pleasure when his tongue caressed the tiny bud that flamed her soul.

She cried out, grasping the edge of the pillows, biting her lower lip, curling her toes against the strange and beautiful sensation that consumed her body.

"Come on, angel," he urged. "I want to feel your first climax against my lips."

His words were the devil's own. She should have been embarrassed. Should have blushed at his audacity. But instead she surrendered to his talents and felt herself rise, soar, fly higher than the sun itself and then burst like a radiating star and scatter in sparks back to the earth.

Lucian felt her convulse against his lips. The mere thought that this was her first climactic experience hardened his loins beyond pain, beyond agony.

Time. Patience. He warned himself. Tonight she would be his. Over and over and over.

He moved to rest full-length beside her, taking her in his arms while her breathing eased and her body relaxed. He caressed her arm, kissed her forehead. "You taste like the sea, fresh, tangy, and delicious."

Catherine snuggled against him to hide her embarrassment, tucking her head beneath his chin so he couldn't see her heated cheeks. Wondering why he had stopped from satisfying himself, blessing Bonnie for having described so explicitly the joys of lovemaking. And praying Lucian intended to continue.

Her prayer was soon answered.

His hands roamed past her arm to her naked bottom. He stroked, he squeezed, he patted her soft flesh. "I want more of you, angel."

She bravely lifted her head to look at him. "And I of you, Lucian."

He needed no more encouragement, his mouth dropped to hers. Where before he had been gentle, introducing her to new delights, now he kissed her savagely. He demanded and took from her, but in return he ignited a passion that this time would not be easily extinguished.

His one hand caught in her hair, tightening around the silver strands, his other hand slipped around her waist and in an instant she lay flat beneath him. His powerful, muscled body covered hers.

He pulled away from her mouth. "Damn, but I love the taste of you."

He settled his mouth over her nipple and Catherine threaded her fingers in his hair. She never wanted him to stop tasting her. She wanted him to feast and enjoy. She wanted this pleasurable torment to last forever.

He attempted to give her her wish. Wherever his lips touched he lingered, treating her to the most exquisite tortures. She moaned, cried out, begged, and still he lingered.

She moved impatiently beneath him, against him, her hands roaming his body exulting in his strength and power. She was beyond reason, beyond insanity, she had sunk into the very depths of madness.

"Do you want me, angel?" His voice was ragged, his breathing heavy. He gave her no chance to respond, he continued on. "*Me*. Do you want *me*?"

She understood his urgency. Understood what he needed to hear. What she needed to say. "I want you, *Lucian,* only you."

He held himself above her and stared down at her, his eyes narrowed, his thoughts serious. "There is only you and me at this moment. *Only you and me.*"

Her arms reached up and circled his neck, pulling his mouth down to hers to steal a much-needed kiss.

He rested his forehead against hers, kissed her nose, her cheek while his hand reached down and gently eased her legs apart. "Bloody hell, but I hate the thought of hurting you."

Catherine attempted to reassure him. "It's all right. Bonnie explained it all to me and warned me to pay it no mind."

"Bonnie?" he questioned, and lost all reason when he slipped a finger inside her. Finding her more than ready his body responded with an unbearable ache. Sanity eluded him.

He lifted himself to his knees and eased his shaft to her entrance, gently he probed her, gently urged inward, her liquid heat closing around him, encompassing him, cradling him.

Catherine grasped the edge of the pillows, tossed her head, moaned, and closed her eyes.

"Not this time, angel. This time I want you looking at me."

Her eyes widened. She couldn't. She just couldn't.

"Don't dare," he commanded. "Keep your eyes open and focused on me."

"I—"

"Will obey me." He smiled and slid farther inside her. Her eyes fluttered.

He warned, "Keep them open. Look at me. Feel me."

In deeper he drove, steeling himself against the urge to rush into her. He wanted her to remember. He wanted to remember this night together.

"Lucian," she cried, his size filling her to near bursting.

"It's all right," he soothed. "Soon it will be—"

"Over?" she finished anxiously.

He shook his head and dropped down over her. "Just beginning."

He took her completely then, tearing through her maidenhead, the small obstruction that had begun this whole charade.

She cried out at the piercing pain and dug her fingers into Lucian's broad shoulders.

"Easy, angel, easy," he comforted.

His words relaxed her and his movement, though a discomfort at first, quickly turned to pleasure and forgotten was the moment's pain and knowledge of the importance of what she had forfeited to him.

Lucian eased with grace and skill within her, his movement growing, gaining intensity, gaining a rhythm that couldn't be denied.

Catherine wrapped her arms around his back and held on, her soaring passion climbing to the stars.

Lucian felt her tighten around him, hot and hard. Wild and wicked. Sensual and *satisfying*. His jolting thought took him over the edge into oblivion where Catherine soon joined him.

She lay silent, her body exhausted, her mind unable to focus. Her only thought was to calm her racing heart and breathe.

Lucian trembled from the aftermath, unwilling to move, feeling fulfilled and satisfied.

Satisfied.

The thought that Catherine satisfied him so thoroughly

disturbed him. He had come to accept that such euphoria was out of his reach. Yet . . .

"Lucian," Catherine said softly.

He lifted his head.

"Are you all right?"

Laughter rumbled in his chest. "That is a question I should be addressing to you."

"I'm fine," she said, her smile hesitant.

Lucian eased his weight from her and wrapped her in his solid arms. "The truth, angel."

She attempted to shrug her answer, but his firm hug made it difficult. "I feel odd."

"How so?"

"As if I—I—"

"Don't turn shy on me now. Tell me," he urged, curious.

"I feel that perhaps I enjoyed myself too much."

"You can never enjoy lovemaking too much," he teased, and kissed her forehead.

"But Bonnie said that ladies didn't enjoy lovemaking, that they found it bothersome, a chore they tolerated."

Lucian eased Catherine away from him and raised a brow as he asked, "What did you discuss with Bonnie?"

Catherine squirmed uneasily in his arms.

"I'll have an answer, now," he insisted. He sat up, bracing himself against the pillows and lifting Catherine to sit across his lap.

Stunned when her bare derriere met his naked leg, her mouth dropped open.

"Think of yourself as nesting, madam. If you keep him warm, he'll grow to delight you," he teased outrageously.

Catherine buried her red face against his chest.

He wouldn't hear of her hiding. He yanked her away. "Forget about your perch for the moment and answer me."

The idea of changing the subject appealed to Catherine. "I

asked Bonnie to enlighten me about lovemaking. And she did a most wonderful job of it. She detailed everything."

"Hence the tales you entertained me with?"

"Each and every one."

"Handsome Harry?" he asked, wanting an explanation.

Catherine sighed. "I allowed Bonnie to talk me into seeing if what she had taught me would work. A quick trip around the tables," she had suggested. Everything seemed all right until I caught sight of Bones's and Jolly's faces. I realized how foolish I had been and intended to speak with them."

"Handsome Harry stopped you on the way over," he said, finishing her explanation.

She nodded.

"Anything else I should know about what Bonnie discussed with you or your tales of delight?"

A deep blush rushed to stain Catherine's cheeks.

"A blushing response," he taunted. "What is it you hide this time?" He caressed her arm, needing to touch her again.

"It's nothing," she said, attempting to brush it off as inconsequential.

"No so," he protested. "A blush suggests that the matter is important or—embarrassing. Are you too embarrassed to speak to me about it, Catherine?"

His fingers drifted to her lips and he traced and toyed with them, his finger slipping inside her lower lip for her to taste. "With what we've just shared and what we will share again how can there be anything that flusters you?"

Catherine stirred in his lap, enjoying his teasing play with her lips. "My imagination."

"Embarrasses you?" He stroked her neck slowly.

She nodded with a sigh. "Remember my favorite earl?"

"Explicitly," Lucian answered, recalling how he had detested the imaginary fellow.

Her head dropped back, giving him room to continue to

stroke her. His strokes extended farther down to her breasts. "You know him well," she teased for a change.

Lucian stopped stroking. "I do?"

She nodded again. "He's you."

Lucian cast her an odd look.

"I—" She paused, uncertain if she should tell him.

He encouraged, his hand resuming his caressing strokes. "I'm curious, share this tale with me."

She did before she lost her nerve and her voice. "I fantasized that you were the earl that I had such a devilishly good time with."

"You thought of us making love on a dining table?"

"Yes," she said, relieved he remembered that part and not the other.

He thought a moment and she felt him shift her on his lap. And felt him rise beneath her. She looked at him wide-eyed.

"I thought of how long the earl's tongue was and how he pleased you."

Catherine shuddered against him. She raised her hand to his cheek and stroked his clean-shaven face softly. "You pleased me well, my earl."

"I wish to please you again, m'lady."

"And I you, m'lord."

Their lips met and forgotten was all but the pleasures they sought from each other.

Hours later, wrapped in each other's arms, Lucian and Catherine slept, having loved time and time again. And having tried to make the night last forever.

❧ 18 ❧

CATHERINE WOKE ALONE in bed. She sat up and glanced around the cabin. She was its sole occupant. She collapsed back, pulling the covers up to her chin and shaking her head, her tangled mass of silver hair splaying over her pillow.

Good Lord, what had she done? She peeked beneath the sheet at her nakedness, shutting her eyes when she recalled all the exquisitely titillating things Lucian had done to her and how she had responded with such abandonment.

A warmth spread along her lower belly down between her legs until it turned into a tingle. Not an inch of her flesh had gone untouched by his hands, lips, or tongue. Repeatedly he had brought her pleasure and repeatedly she had brought him his.

She smiled, thinking that although his body was large, it had been extremely accommodating. He fit her perfectly and he made her feel . . .

Her body shivered from sensuous remembrances.

Their only thoughts had been of each other and the passion they had hungrily shared. They had loved deeply and fulfillingly. They had made memories and now the night was over.

Whatever would she do now?

Nothing. She warned herself. There was nothing she could do. The choice was up to Captain Lucifer.

She still hadn't found the papers providing her father's innocence. She had searched long and hard through his cabin but found nothing. With the situation changed, she wondered if he would offer the documents to her. She had paid a high enough price for them.

Tears stung her eyes. Who was she fooling? She knew why she surrendered to Lucian last night. Simply put . . . she loved him. She wasn't certain when it had happened, or even why she loved him. It confused her. He wasn't always lovable. He was fearfully large and domineering and yet strangely enough those very traits offered comfort and protection.

Lord, she loved the devil himself. Surely she had lost her mind. He lusted for her, but love? She wondered if his hate and need for revenge consumed so much of his emotions that he was incapable of loving.

She shook her head. He might think that of himself, but it was far from the truth. Deep inside he possessed strong, passionate emotions he kept locked away, fearful of being deserted and hurt once again. He felt alone and betrayed and he lashed out, wanting others to suffer as he had suffered.

He needed to heal, to let go, to allow himself to love freely without fear or guilt, to lay his past to rest. Catherine realized that the only way he could heal completely was for him to face his accused . . . Randolph Abelard.

The cabin door opened and she instantly sank farther beneath the covers, her thoughts fleeing.

"You hide from me, madam?" he asked sternly. His steps sounded heavy as he crossed the room. "Was my performance last night that unsatisfying?"

She held the covers beneath her chin and stared wide-eyed waiting for him to come into view. Her breath caught in her throat at the sight of him.

His black breeches molded to muscular thighs she was all too familiar with and hugged a waist she had hugged repeatedly last night. His white linen shirt hung open exposing his broad chest she had lain against, and Lord how she had kissed those hard muscles. And his lips . . .

She moaned.

He laughed and yanked the cover from her hands, stripping it completely off her.

She cried out and scrambled up, rushing down the bed to retrieve her protection.

"Oh, no you don't." He laughed and grabbed her about the waist, twirling her around to anchor her against his chest.

Her breath caught at the feel of his warmth against her cool flesh. "Lucian," she cried, her hands rushing to his chest to shove at him, fearful more of her own reaction than his.

"You haven't answered me," he warned, his voice low, but far from menacing.

"Answer?" She couldn't even recall the question. He held her too close, he felt too good, his lips looked too inviting. He was too damn tempting.

He repeated it for her, his mouth a mere inch from hers. "Was my performance last eve unsatisfying?"

"No," she whispered, fearful of moving.

"Good." He captured a kiss, fleeting yet sensuous. "Neither was yours. You—" He paused abruptly about to describe her performance as satisfying. The significance of the word disturbed him and he altered his response. "You pleased me."

"Now what?" she asked courageously, her body willing to capitulate, but her mind prepared to defend.

"Now we strip off our clothes and feed the passion that fires our souls." His mouth came down on hers again.

Her mind faltered, listening to her body's cries for surrender, feeling his hand cup her breast and squeeze gently, knowing in seconds she would be completely lost to his masterful touch.

Somewhere deep inside reason doused her flame and fought to surface. She shoved at his chest and ripped her mouth from his. "Lucian, we must talk."

He released her, stripped off his shirt, tossing it to the floor, and sent her a nasty sensual smile as he advanced on her. "I don't want to talk."

Catherine scrambled backward. "We must," she pleaded, her outstretched hand warding him off.

He laughed at her puny defense and caught her small wrist in his large hand. "No."

His response reverberated with finality, sending a shiver to ripple all the way down to the tips of her toes.

She saw his intention in his eyes. They smoldered with desire. In seconds she would be beneath his powerful body and all would be lost.

She searched for the words that would halt his actions, her thoughts tumbling for choices. Her answer surfaced and escaped her lips with the speed of a fired arrow, surprising herself. "Do you intend to seek your revenge?"

He released her wrist.

She hurried to draw the cover around her.

He didn't stop her. He turned away, walking to stand by the row of windows and staring out at the endless sea.

She debated repeating the question. If he found it too difficult to respond then perhaps she had her answer.

"Catherine, come here," he summoned gently.

She dropped the cover and stepped from the bed, retrieving his shirt from the floor and slipping into it as she crossed the room to him, the thought of denying his request never having entered her head.

His hand stretched out at her approach and she reached for it, hooking her fingers with his.

He drew her in front of him and tucked her back against his chest, wrapping his arms around her waist. He spoke with concern and Catherine listened intently to his every word.

"Last night when I discovered you were a virgin, my only thought was of you. Your fears, your concerns, your needs. And I would be remiss if I failed to mention my own desire. I wanted you. My need for you overwhelmed me, consumed me, entrapped me. There was nothing I wouldn't give to have you. And I gave it." He paused.

She waited sensing he hadn't finished.

"Look at the sea, Catherine. It's vast and endless, going on and on and on. Sometimes it feels as though it has no beginning and no end."

He paused again and Catherine clearly understood that he gathered his thoughts as she often did. She studied the sea as he suggested and a bittersweet feeling washed over her.

"Day after day I would watch the never-ending sea. I cursed it. I spit on it. I hated it. The dark waters became my nemesis. It surrounded me keeping me captive, never letting go, constantly reminding me I was a prisoner.

"Then miraculously the sea granted me what I most desired, my freedom. But those years of tormenting hell still lingered and I promised myself I would have my revenge."

Catherine went rigid. He would tell her now. He would make his plans clear.

His arms hugged her more closely and he spoke with a gentle strength. "Last night I gave that revenge no thought. No consideration. Only you and I existed."

She took a breath to speak.

He squeezed her. "Let me finish," he urged, and continued. "I have known many women and enjoyed their talents, but I have never experienced the all-consuming pleasure I did with you last night. I strongly suspect, angel, that you robbed me of my soul."

She said not a word, but fought back the tears, for he had robbed her as well. Only he had robbed her of her heart.

"We need time. Time to make sense of this situation. Time to learn more about each other. Time to share more intimate moments. Time to decide the future."

And time for him to heal and forgive, she thought, slipping her hands over his arms.

"Let me love you. Come to Heaven with me, angel, and let me show you paradise."

He turned her in his arms, lifted her chin, and stole a kiss.

She breathlessly and hopelessly surrendered. All thoughts vanished except . . .

Time. She had only so much time to prove her father's innocence and heal Lucian's heart to love again.

Hours later Catherine lay in Lucian's arms yawning.

"I tired you, madam?" he asked with concern.

"You pleased me, sir." She laughed and rubbed her cheek against his chest. "Most wonderfully."

His tone turned serious and his hand ceased caressing her backside. "Has my insatiable appetite left you tender?"

Catherine thought of the slight soreness between her legs and recalled the delightfully wicked things he had done to her to cause it and smiled.

"Madam, I'll have an answer." He attempted to sound stern, but Catherine heard his concern.

"A minor discomfort," she said.

He turned her on her back and loomed over her. His long hair fell over his shoulders to rest on her breasts. "I'm sorry, angel, I never meant to cause you any suffering. I just couldn't seem to get my fill of you. The more I tasted, the more I thirsted."

Catherine caressed his cheek. "My hunger was as greedy as yours."

He smiled. "But I have more experience and should have considered that the loss of your virginity would leave you tender."

She blushed at his reminder.

He turned his lips into her palm and kissed it. "Thank you for giving me that precious gift. I shall cherish that memory forever."

Words failed Catherine. His response had touched her heart deeply and just as deeply she feared the outcome of their precarious situation. But for now she would savor this time with him.

She twisted her fingers in his hair and tugged, bringing his mouth down to hers. "Thank you for being my first. I would have wanted no other," she whispered against his lips before kissing him.

Another yawn attacked her as their lips parted.

"You," he said, pressing his finger to her lips to ensure silence, "will rest while I see to the running of this ship."

She pouted and spoke against his finger. "Must you?"

"Yes," he insisted, and hurried off the bed. He retrieved his clothes from the floor where they had been hastily discarded.

"Rest with me," she suggested, bracing herself on her elbow to watch him. She wanted him to stay with her, to hold her, to sleep safely tucked in his arms.

He threw his shirt over his head, pulling it down to tuck in his breeches. "You will find no rest if I stay with you."

Her pout turned petulant. "Perhaps I have no desire to rest."

He laughed, tugging his boots on. "I didn't ask you if you wanted to rest. I said you will rest."

"A command?"

"Precisely," he said, standing tall and looking ever so like the dashingly handsome pirate that he was.

Intent on arguing the point, she said, "And if I don't?"

He sprang to the spot on the bed beside her, capturing her hands and forcing her onto her back. His face drew close to hers. "You will rest or I won't do this. . . ."

His words trailed off as his head lowered to her nipple and licked it ever so teasingly slowly.

Delivering identical treatment to her other nipple he then moved lower until he rested in the valley of her legs. "And I won't do this. . . ."

His mouth found her sensitive flesh and harassed it near to bursting. He then moved back up along her quivering flesh, kissing her belly, her midriff, her breast, her neck, until he reached her lips once again. "And you do want me to do those wicked things to you, don't you, angel?"

A response proved difficult. Breathing proved difficult. Thinking proved difficult. She nodded her head.

"You will rest?"

She nodded again, doubting rest would be possible now.

He smiled and brushed a kiss across her lips. "I will make certain sleep comes easily for you."

With that he lowered his head and claimed her intimately.

Later that night when most of the crew slept and the sea slumbered and the night sky sparkled with hundreds of stars Lucian and Catherine stole up onto the deck.

Lucian wearing only his breeches and Catherine snug in his shirt and a quilt cuddled comfortably on the deck.

"Will we reach Heaven soon?" she asked, anxious to see his home, but nervous that this special time they shared would end all too soon.

"Two or three days at the most."

"Tell me about your home."

"It's like no place on earth," he said. "The island welcomes all regardless of wealth or manner. Rules are set forth and everyone obeys for each islander respects their freedom too much to jeopardize it. Food is plentiful. Fresh fruit grows profusely. Fresh fish is available with a simple drop of a baited line into the sea. Shelter is but a day's work of constructing a hut until a more permanent structure can be constructed."

"It sounds like paradise, this Heaven."

"It is, and created by people who spent most of their lives in hell."

Catherine remained silent, well aware that Lucian would continue. She had come to understand him well. He often paused to give an important subject thought before proceeding.

"Outcasts, they are. Accused of thievery, murder, and whatever else the Crown decided was their crime."

He paused once again and Catherine understood that his concern for these people weighed heavily on him.

He continued, his voice deep with emotion. "Many stole to feed their children. Some murdered out of self-defense and some never murdered at all, but were accused nonetheless since the aristocrats could suffer no blame. England's unwanted and longsuffering wash up regularly on my shore. Some survive, some don't. But Heaven welcomes them regardless. I turn none away. The island was deserted when I came upon it. So all who live there now come from foreign shores. Even the island people there are from other islands where they found living intolerable. It's a haven for those willing to work and keep the island flourishing. Everyone does their part in maintaining Heaven as the perfect paradise."

"Then your island is most appropriately named." She

relaxed when she felt the rumble of laughter deep in his chest.

"Heaven is exactly as I imagined it. Thick with foliage and flowers so colorful and beautiful they take one's breath away. And beaches of white warm sand to stretch out upon and soak in the sun while a crystal blue sea beckons one to swim."

"Swim?" Catherine asked cautiously. "You swim often?"

"Every day," he answered. "We'll swim together. I promise you'll enjoy it."

Catherine shook her head. "I don't think so."

"You don't think you'll enjoy it?"

"No." She shook her head again. "I can't swim."

Lucian lifted her chin. "You can't swim?"

"Where I lived the skill wasn't necessary."

"Where you live now, the skill is extremely necessary," he insisted. "I will teach you."

"But—"

"I will teach you," he repeated sternly, warning her the matter was settled.

Catherine refused to argue the point. When the time came she would decide if swimming was a skill she wished to acquire. A yawn raced to rush free and try as she might Catherine couldn't hide its escape.

"It's time to retire," Lucian said.

"I only yawned once," she protested, enjoying their late-night interlude.

Lucian ignored her objection, setting her aside to stand, then reaching down to scoop her up into his arms. He carted her off to his cabin and placed her on the bed.

She unwrapped herself from the quilt and slipped out of his shirt. Arranging the covers as Lucian undressed, she shook the quilt to span out upon the bed and settled across the length.

She heard a small *ping* and looked about to see the cause of the faint noise.

Lucian joined her in the bed, beneath the covers. "I found the culprit who puzzles you." He raised his hand and between his fingers he held a pearl.

She took it from him. "I thought I had found all of them."

He heard sorrow in her voice and felt her loss. "I will replace your pearl necklace."

Catherine turned and leaned on his chest, rolling the pearl between her fingers. "It isn't necessary."

"Why?" he asked, watching her caress the small pearl.

"The strand of pearls was my protection, my armor against you."

"And you don't wish this protection replaced?" he asked, reaching up to caress her cheek.

She shook her head. "It's no longer necessary."

"Why?" His whispered query sounded anxious.

Her eyes held his. "You're my protection now, Lucian. I shall never fear anything as long as you're near, or as long as I hold your strength in my heart."

Her words cut deep, touching his heart, caressing his soul. He captured her mouth instantly, needing to show her how he felt, needing to lock away the surprising words that had almost tumbled from his lips.

He wouldn't. He couldn't admit that he could possibly be in love with Catherine Abelard. The thought was ridiculous, impossible. He was Lucifer the pirate. He possessed no soul or heart. He cared for nothing. Nothing but . . .

The soft ping reached his ears. She had released the final pearl. She lay bare before him. His to do with as he wished.

He wrapped his arms around her and settled her beneath him. "Tonight, angel, I'm going to take us to the very depths of madness."

"I'll go anywhere with you, Lucian."

"They don't allow angels in hell," he said sadly, and moved to claim her lips.

Catherine pressed a finger to his seeking lips. "The devil isn't welcome in Heaven, but he resides there anyway. Anything is possible, Lucian. *Anything.*"

He smiled. "Like a strand of pearls that defended your honor?"

"And like a man who took my virginity with desire instead of revenge."

They stared briefly at one another and then reached out to once again make memories.

✧ 19 ✧

CATHERINE SPIED THE small speck in the distance. She leaned on the railing squinting against the bright sunlight to get a better look. Her bare feet hugged the deck of the ship as it cut with speed through the water, the sails having caught a high wind. She wore a pair of Bones's Sunday-best breeches rolled up to her ankles and Lucian's white linen shirt that fell past her knees. The sleeves were rolled up numerous times and still hung to her wrists. Her hair she had tied back with a black ribbon, though the wind freed several silver strands to whip about her face.

The crew bustled around her in excitement. Their tension ran high, but not from an impending battle. They were going home.

"Be in Heaven by morning," Bones said, his grin wide as he rushed past her.

She returned his smile and continued to study the tiny spot that was Lucian's home. The last few days had been blissful. They hadn't been able to get enough of each other. Even now her flesh anticipated his touch.

Would all be the same once they reached his island? Would he be the same? And when? When would his revenge that lay so silent beneath the surface emerge and shatter their paradise?

"A pertinent name for the place," Santos said, walking up to stand beside her.

"Why do you say that?" He had piqued her curiosity, especially since Santos told the most marvelous stories.

"Didn't Lucian tell you how the island got its name?"

Catherine shook her head and smiled.

Santos rested against the wooden rail to comfortably relate the tale.

Catherine settled herself as well and listened.

"Lucian, myself, and a few crew members had just taken over the pirate ship that had freed us from the merchant ship years before. The pirate captain had been a vile sort and detested by his crew. It was fairly easy to lead a mutiny."

"What happened to the captain?"

Santos wore a wide grin. "Lucian made certain his punishment was worthy of his crimes."

Catherine didn't request a more detailed explanation.

"We were tired, hungry, and in dire need of a cleansing. Lucian instructed the crew to anchor at the first island we spotted."

"Heaven?" she asked excitedly.

Warm, powerful arms slid around from behind her to lock at her waist.

Catherine leaned back against hard muscles, fully aware of who would dare be so familiar with her.

"Her mouth never ceases with questions long enough for you to complete a story," Lucian teased.

Tilting her head back, she childishly stuck her tongue out at him.

"Careful, madam, your suggestive action sorely tempts me."

Catherine blushed three shades of red before scolding him. "You are positively the most sinful man."

"And you love my sinfulness, don't you, angel?"

"Lucian!" she scolded again, and turned ten shades of red.

He laughed and gave her a playful squeeze. "Finish your story, Santos. I think I have managed to silence her for the moment."

Santos nodded with a pleased smile. "As I was saying, Lucian instructed that we anchor at the first island sighted. By the time we arrived, our thirst was great, our hunger gnawing, and our bodies protesting the bugs."

"Bugs?" Catherine repeated.

"Hush," Lucian warned.

"Bugs are common on pirate ships," Santos explained.

"I haven't noticed any—"

"I insist on a clean ship, madam. Now let Santos finish."

Santos hurried the story along. "We dropped anchor and rowed a longboat to shore. Fresh fruit hung so thick and heavy from the trees and on vines that the branches bent with the weight. The men feasted until full. A pool of cool clear water was found and our thirst quenched, then our bodies bathed."

"So you named—"

A hand slipped over her mouth silencing her.

"Finish quickly," Lucian warned.

Santos laughed, shaking his head. "It will take much to silence this woman."

Lucian responded to him in Spanish.

Santos laughed.

Catherine turned twenty shades of red having been taught to speak fluent Spanish and having understood perfectly Lucian's boastful remark that his mouth and hands usually silenced her in seconds.

Santos continued. "Lucian and I sat by the campfire that night, his only words being, 'we just escaped from hell, this must be Heaven.'"

Lucian released her mouth when he felt her smile against his palm.

"You must tell me more stories of Lucian and yourself," Catherine urged.

"No," Lucian said coldly.

Santos patted her arm. "Another time." He walked away grinning.

"Why won't you—"

He interrupted curtly. "Let the past be for now, Catherine."

Catherine didn't argue. The past would surface fast enough to haunt her. "Will you show me how to pick fruit from the vines?"

"That and more. We'll swim the blue waters of the sea and the cool waters of the lagoon naked. We'll make love on the warm sand and in the garden where I can sprinkle your bare flesh with flower petals."

"Lucian," she cried softly, and teasingly added, "you sorely tempt me."

"Can I tempt you down into my cabin now?" he whispered near her ear.

"It is but late morning," she said, properly shocked, yet pleased by his suggestive invitation.

"Good, then it gives us the remainder of the day to enjoy each other." He turned her in his arms. "And I warn you, madam, it will take me that long and then some to get enough of you."

Catherine read the fiery passion in his eyes and decided to enflame it. "Love me like you never have, Lucian?" she whispered for his ears alone, and dropped her face to rest against his chest.

"Are you prepared for the consequences of such a request?"

She wasn't prepared for anything. Not this intimacy between them, not this passion that ran rampant through her, and certainly not this love she was feeling. She draped her arm around his neck. "I'm prepared to trust you."

He lifted her chin and warned sternly, "Never trust the devil."

Catherine smiled and shook her head. "Don't you know, Captain Lucifer, that an angel can tame the wickedest soul?"

Lucian ran his finger over her lips. "Don't you know, angel, that the devil doesn't possess a soul?" With that he scooped her up, stepped over coiled ropes, marched past cheering men, and carried her beneath to his cabin.

After kicking the door shut he lowered her to the floor, pressing his body to hers until she was forced up against the closed door.

His mouth sought hers, hungry and thirsting, while his hands roamed beneath his shirt meeting the warm flesh of her full breast.

"I'm going to take you right here, angel. Against this door with your legs wrapped tightly around me."

Catherine looked at him strangely. "Is that—"

"No questions," he ordered, and swiftly rid her of her shirt.

Warm and wet, his tongue circled her nipple. "I love when your nipple hardens in my mouth."

Catherine blushed, shutting her eyes against his descriptive words and actions.

"Your taste excites me," he said, and licked the hard bud, sending gooseflesh straight down to the tips of Catherine's toes and rushing back up again.

He freed himself of his shirt and unfastened his breeches. His tongue returned to delight her while his hand worked at freeing her of her breeches.

"Are you ready for me, angel?" he asked, tucking his fingers in her breeches and sliding them slowly down her hips. "Are you?" he repeated, his teeth tugging at her nipple.

Rational thought escaped Catherine. Her nipple tingled with every lick and tug he treated it to and his remarks— Lord, but his bold remarks could spark the most dwindling flame, fanning it to full blaze.

"Shall I discover for myself, angel?" he asked, and didn't bother to wait for an answer. His finger dipped into her and she closed around him. He explored deeper and deeper, feeling her warm wetness, feeling her muscles convulse, feeling her desire grow.

Catherine groaned and grabbed hold of his shoulders for support.

"I think," he said, easing her garment down her legs, "that you need some *wicked* tempting." He bent down, hastily removing the breeches past her feet and casting them off to the side. His mouth then found her and took her with a gentle intimacy.

Her head dropped back against the door, her eyes fluttered closed, and her moans filled the cabin.

Good Lord, she had never imagined, never thought—

Thought escaped her as his tongue skillfully toyed with her and his fingers worked magic. She tingled, she ached, she never wanted him to stop loving her.

But he stopped and a protesting sigh ran from her lips.

He stood, took her hand, and whispered against her mouth before kissing her. "Free me." He guided her hand down inside his breeches to his swollen shaft.

Nervous, her fingers faltered as she wrapped around him. Hot and hard, he pulsated in her hand.

"Do you want him inside you?" he asked, his breathing labored.

Large but accommodating, she thought, and nodded, words failing her.

"Then free him, angel. Free him so he can bring you pleasure." His speech was strained and broken by heavy breaths.

Catherine realized his need was as close to bursting as hers. She gently eased him out of his breeches, stroking the long length of him as she did. He felt so good, so wickedly right to her touch that guilt swept over her. And her hand slipped off him.

He captured her retreating hand and replaced it around him. "Don't, angel, don't ever think that it's wrong to touch me so intimately."

Surprised and encouraged by his understanding of her feelings she stroked him again and again and again. Until he moaned and removed her hand.

"Enough, or I'll burst in your palm."

Her own passion near to bursting, she thrust her hips forward.

He smiled and kissed her. "Do as I tell you. I don't want this to hurt you."

"You could never—"

"I could easily hurt you, angel, and I have no desire to cause you pain—only pleasure."

He grasped her beneath her buttocks and hoisted her up. "Wrap your arms around my neck and your legs around my waist."

She did as he instructed, resting her forehead against his. "I once feared your size."

He eyed her strangely.

Realizing his misunderstanding, she corrected, "The height, the breath, the width of you. You took my breath away."

He adjusted her against him, bracing her back against the door. "Then my size no longer frightens you?"

She smiled and brushed her lips across his as he had done so many times to her. "Your generous size offers me protection and safety."

"And pleasure," he teased, kissing her soundly.

Catherine whimpered when he tore his mouth from hers.

"Hold tight to me, angel," he said, settling her around him. "And if you feel the slightest discomfort—"

She gasped as he entered her, his smooth entrance startling.

He halted his progress, though it pained him to do so. "Are you all right?"

Her honesty spoke. "I thought you but teased me about this position."

He laughed and allowed more of himself to slide into her welcoming nest. "Angel, this position is just one among many you'll learn is possible."

She closed her eyes and kept her forehead rested on his as he filled her slowly and smoothly. He paused when she had accepted all of him thick and wide inside her. Then he moved. Lord, did he move. And he forced her to move with him, harder and harder and harder.

"Paradise or madness, angel," he whispered, "which one do you want to feel?"

Catherine as usual lost her speech. He stole her senses and drove her wild. She could form no sensible thoughts or phrases. She could barely think and a response was completely impossible.

He pounded into her, her body's impact causing the door to creak. "I think," he said between heavy breaths, "I prefer madness."

His tempo increased. Catherine clasped her arms more firmly around his neck and buried her head against his shoulder.

"Lost," he murmured. "I could lose myself forever inside you."

His words were enough to explode her into a thousand sparkling lights, their tingling warmth cascading like rain over her sensitive flesh until fading away and leaving her utterly replete.

Lucian felt her shatter and his own body responded. He

burst hot and wet, spilling himself within her again and again, shuddering when his final burst faded to a sweet numbness.

He continued to hold her. He needed to hold her, needed to feel her damp, satisfied flesh against his. Hear her uneven breathing, know without a doubt that he had brought her to complete satisfaction.

Why? His thought urged. Why was his need to possess her so overwhelming? Why couldn't he get enough of her? Why did he always need to touch her, feel her silky flesh, wrap himself around her and within her? *Why?*

She satisfies you like no other.

The thought jolted him and he eased her off him. Her legs trembled when she attempted to stand and his arm circled her waist to steady her. She rested against him, seeking his strength, trusting him.

He lifted her into his arms, receiving no protest from her, he carried her to the bed and settled her upon the clean white sheets.

Her arms dropped from around his neck to her side and her eyes drifted closed.

His glance strayed over her naked body. Her lips were puffy from his hungry kisses, her nipples red from his playful bites, her woman's bud swollen with pleasure.

He had marked her well and she belonged to him, no other . . . not even her stepfather, Randolph Abelard. She was his and his alone.

He ran his fingers through his long hair and silently cursed his strange emotions. This need to possess her, to love . . .

He stood, glaring down at her sleeping comfortably. Love had nothing to do with his feelings. Passion and lust were the emotions that drove him to behave so insanely.

Pure lust was the culprit. And once he filled himself, once he drank too often of her taste he would—

Love.

The word echoed in his mind, threatening his sanity.

"No," he said quietly, and shook his head while he settled himself over her, thirsty once again.

◈ 20 ◈

CATHERINE STOOD ON the balcony outside of Lucian's bedroom, contentedly glancing out over the island. She had been here two weeks and those weeks had been blissful. From the moment he had lifted her out of the longboat and placed her on the shore, she had realized why Heaven felt like home to so many interesting and diverse people.

The island reached out and welcomed you regardless of age, manner, or station in life. The white sand felt warm and comfortable beneath her feet, the trees so strange in shape and size swayed in a balmy greeting, and the inhabitants themselves smiled and reached out with open arms.

Catherine smiled and hugged herself, the blue silk robe cool against her naked flesh, the extreme opposite of Lucian's hands, hot and demanding only thirty minutes before.

Life had been good these last two weeks, too good. She had met many of the residents of Heaven, each having a horror story of their own and each thanking the Lord above for Lucian's generosity.

One man, short, brawny, and fixed with a permanent smile, couldn't say enough about Lucian's kindness. On a visit to the local market square, where the islanders bartered their produce and wares, he had captured Catherine's ear. He had held her attention and caught her sympathy when he explained that he had lost three fingers as his punishment for pickpocketing back in England. He had been near to death when he had landed on the island and if it hadn't been for Lucian's orders that he be taken care of, he would have died.

Lucian saw to it that he had shelter and food until he could care for himself, then he was told that thievery wasn't necessary for survival on the island, nor was it acceptable behavior. If he was caught stealing he would be put off the island. The man had smiled broadly and winked at Catherine, informing her that he had been smart enough to realize he had found paradise and had no intention of ever leaving. He then had handed her a small, strange fuzzy fruit and told her to enjoy and God bless.

Catherine had learned much from her visit to the market. Heaven was paradise to its inhabitants and Lucian was the man responsible for creating it. And he had created beauty in a lush jungle.

The size and magnificence of his home had surprised her. An open carriage, highly polished and well maintained, had driven them from the market square up a winding hill road to emerge at the most beautiful home Catherine had ever seen.

A circular crushed-shell driveway with a spouting fountain in the middle greeted visitors as the driveway wrapped around to the entrance of his home. Gleaming white and two stories tall, it stood proudly with full-length windows whose shutters were thrown wide open allowing the island breeze to drift through the entire house. A balcony ran the full length of the second floor. Bamboo chairs with bright print cushions and tables with pots of flowering plants decorated it tastefully. On the front veranda numerous pots overflowed in a riot of colors and wide-back bamboo chairs begged visitors to sit and relax.

And that was only the outside. Inside had been equally shocking. Lucian had blended native comfort with English charm. The outcome was simply breathtaking.

Rosewood furnishings with bold native prints at the windows, ceramic vases and plates from foreign ports, highly polished ceramic tile floors of intricate design, brass fixtures, paintings with gilt frames, and numerous windows open wide to welcome the sun and the warm island breeze.

Lucian had taken care to create his home strictly for his taste and comfort. He had accomplished that most successfully.

"I have brought breakfast for you, Catherine."

Catherine turned with a warm smile to greet Zeena, Lucian's housekeeper, though the term seemed inapplicable when used in reference to the attractive woman.

"Thank you, but I would have joined Lucian shortly."

Zeena placed the silver serving tray on the bamboo table out on the balcony. "Lucian is occupied and requested that you not wait to eat."

Catherine had come to know and respect Zeena in the short time since their acquaintance. She had learned Zeena was a woman of few words and offered only that information which she felt necessary or that she felt concerned you. So evidently she assumed that whatever occupied Lucian at the moment was of no concern to Catherine.

"There is fruit, tea, and hot biscuits. Sit and eat."

Catherine didn't argue. She was hungry and Zeena's size and elegant poise was intimidating. She slid in the chair sinking into the comfort of the bold green-and-yellow print pillow that cushioned the bamboo seat. She reached for the silver teapot and stopped as Zeena's hand grasped the handle.

Her fingers were slim and graceful. But then everything about Zeena was graceful. She carried her five-foot-ten-inch frame with confidence. Her rich dark complexion was flawless, her beauty unmistakable. Her shiny black hair was kept braided and pinned like a thick rope up along the back of her head and secured at the top with a lovely ivory comb. She wore the rich colors of the island in a sarong that wrapped around her body, detailing every perfect curve and slipping over her shoulder before knotting around her waist.

Her speech was articulate, her manners impeccable, her bearing regal. Catherine swore nobility ran through her blood. And the very best part of her appearance was the obvious love that she and Santos shared.

"You spend much time daydreaming," Zeena said, and lowered herself gracefully in the chair opposite Catherine.

Catherine had learned that Zeena was never invited to join anyone, if she wished to favor someone with her company, she did. The decision was hers and no one else's. One was honored if she joined one and accepted it as such. "I have much on my mind."

"It is obvious that your thoughts weigh heavily." Zeena relaxed back in the chair, crossing her long slim legs. "What troubles you?"

Catherine shrugged, spearing a juicy piece of melon. "Many things I have no control of."

"Intelligent women control their lives," Zeena stated. "You are intelligent, therefore it must be your heart that rules at the moment, causing confusion and uncertainty."

Intelligent. Zeena believed her intelligent.

A smile spread across Zeena's face. "When I found love all rational thought vanished. I was not accustomed to such contrary emotions. It seemed I opposed myself. It was most puzzling and delightful."

With her pleasure in Zeena's compliment banished to the back of her thoughts, she anxiously sought to appease her own concern on the subject of love. "How did you know you were in love?"

Zeena laughed. "A hard question even for the most intelligent person to answer." But Zeena attempted to offer her opinion. "Love is an elusive emotion, much sought after and hard to maintain. But then, how can one hold onto something so fragile without causing pain?"

Catherine felt the truth of her words.

"Don't look so sad," Zeena scolded. "Pain brings understanding and growth and all things must grow and mature. Even love."

Catherine shook her head, the challenge of Zeena's words confusing.

Zeena reached across the table, covering Catherine's hand with hers. "You are young, like the love you feel. Let yourself mature with that love and you will gain much. I did."

Catherine smiled and squeezed Zeena's hand. "Your love for Santos shines in your eyes."

Zeena laughed gaily. "Santos is impossible, wonderful, infuriating, enriching—" She stopped abruptly, her laughter settled, her voice soft. "He is the love of my life. His breath is mine, mine is his. I love him to the depths of my soul."

Her declaration moved Catherine to near tears. "Will you marry him?"

"If he wishes. If not . . ." She shrugged and stood, her long body stretching to a confident stance. "We are married in our hearts. I need no paper to tell me what we both know. Our life and love we will share forever. But this is acceptable to me. It may not be enough for you."

Catherine pretended ignorance, for she had on occasion fantasized of marriage to Lucian. "Why would I think of marriage?"

Zeena smiled gently. "Love also shines in your eyes."

Lucian read the letter again and then stared across his massive desk at Santos. "He wants her returned."

The coldness in Lucian's voice made Santos shiver. "What does he offer?"

"A handsome sum." He dropped the letter on the desk and leaned back in his chair, steepling his fingers as he thought.

"He has no knowledge of your wealth or he would not have extended such an offer."

"Which means he knows nothing about me."

Santos nodded. "Unless—"

"Unless what?" Lucian snapped. He didn't care for surprises. He had trained himself to always be prepared.

"Unless a political friend makes him aware of your involvement with the Crown and your petition."

"My petition concerns Lucian Darcmoor and is no way connected with Captain Lucifer. The court has been petitioned to return the Darcmoor lands to me since I was mistakenly pronounced dead. Having survived my ordeal on foreign shores I wish to return and resume my duties as the Earl of Brynwood. No one is aware that most of those years were spent as the pirate Captain Lucifer."

Santos disagreed. "A man with political power can uncover many hidden secrets."

"Or bury many of his own," Lucian countered, and stood, walking to the doorway that opened onto the veranda from his study.

Santos moved to join him. "What will you do?"

"Abelard's name still isn't completely cleared and will remain blemished until I provide the documentation proving otherwise."

"And will you?"

Lucian folded his arms across his chest and leaned against the door frame. "When I am ready."

"And Catherine? Will you return her as he requested?"

Lucian narrowed his eyes. "He did not request. He

demanded that I return his daughter safe and sound, and promptly."

"A mistake," Santos said, shaking his head.

"A big mistake. He is in no position to give orders. He may make a request or better yet beg for her return, but demand?" Lucian shook his head slowly.

Santos attempted to calm his captain's mounting anger. "He's upset and most likely frightened for his daughter. He isn't thinking as rationally as he should."

"Defending the enemy?" Lucian asked, his stance rigid.

"Justifying his actions. What would you do if you discovered Catherine was being held by a pirate?"

His response was instantaneous. "I'd go out and hunt the bastard down, then kill him."

Santos was surprised by his vehement tone. "Then you can empathize with him. He seems to care deeply for Catherine and love can often—"

Lucian turned on Santos like a rabid animal. "Love? Abelard doesn't know the meaning of the word." He stepped out onto the veranda, pacing back and forth, raking his hair with his fingers. "He cares for no one but his precious self. At the moment he is probably more concerned by the problems this *inconvenience* represents. If he cared at all for his stepdaughter he would have acted calmly, thought the matter over, approached me with respect. Instead he remands I return her or else. Or else!" He repeated with fury.

"Lucian," Santos attempted, but Lucian ranted on, ignoring his friend.

"Abelard is a fool if he thinks I'll return her to him. He's a bigger fool for not attending to his fatherly duties and seeing that his daughter was protected and safe from harm." He stopped his pacing and shook a finger at Santos. "Well, she's safe here and here is where she will stay until I say otherwise."

"Is she safe here?" Santos asked.

Lucian threw his hands up in the air. "You sound like Zeena. Her questions always have an underlying meaning. Say what you will, Santos."

Santos glanced about, intending his question for no one but Lucian. "Catherine is no longer innocent, is she?"

Lucian dropped into a nearby chair, the soft cushion collapsing from the weight of him. "I should tell you to mind your own damn business."

"But you won't," Santos said, sitting in the chair next to him.

"You were right," Lucian said, turning to look him directly in the eye and admit his mistake. "She was a virgin."

"So your plan is in motion. You will destroy Abelard emotionally, politically, and then financially."

"Perhaps, I'm not certain, though one decision is clear."

"What's that?"

"Catherine will remain here with me . . . indefinitely."

"Abelard will never agree to that."

"I don't recall seeking his permission on the matter."

"He will protest."

"It will do no good."

"Will you inform Catherine of her father's demand?" Santos asked, although the answer appeared clear.

"No." Lucian stood and leaned his hand on the white veranda railing, looking out across his land that seemed to stretch on forever. "Catherine and I have matters to settle."

"Be careful, Lucian," Santos warned.

"Don't worry, my friend, I will not be as foolish as Abelard and allow my emotions to rule."

Santos shook his head as he walked to the open door.

"What I worry is that you will foolishly not listen to your emotions and instead allow revenge to guide you."

Lucian swerved around, holding his hand out. "I have waited years to have Abelard in the palm of my hand."

"You have something much more fragile and important in the palm of your hand. Be careful you don't crush it."

Lucian turned his back on the sound of the door closing. He held his hand out over the railing and stared down into his empty palm.

Catherine fit comfortably in his palm, her breast full and heavy to his touch. He loved the feel of her, so warm and responsive. Her nipple would pucker, she would moan and arch against him and beg to be stroked.

And he would stroke her. Bloody hell, how he stroked her silky flesh, every blasted inch of her. He charted her body as he did the sea, noting every welcoming channel and depth and the extent to which he could sail her.

"Lucian."

His name anxiously spoken brought a smile to his lips and he turned, holding his hand out to Catherine.

She took it, fitting perfectly in his palm, and Santos's warning rang clearly in his thoughts.

"What is it you want, angel?" he asked, drawing her up against him, needing her body pressed to his. She looked exotic in the pink-and-red sarong that wrapped snugly around her body, outlining every curve and mound. The simple garment excited him beyond control.

Catherine blushed, making her response unnecessary.

He laughed low and wickedly. "I did not fill you enough this morning?"

"You cannot ask me what I want?" she said, her face buried in his shirt, hiding from him.

"Why?" he asked, attempting to catch her chin and force

her to look at him, but she eluded his grasp, burying herself against him.

Her reply muffled, he grew irritated and gripped her shoulders, pulling her back away from him. "What the devil did you say?"

Her blush barely faded before another tinge painted her cheeks.

Lucian held her firmly. "You may turn as many shades of red as you wish, but you *will* answer me."

Catherine bravely raised her head and blurted out, "I always want you."

"Always?" he asked, wanting to hear her say it again.

"Always," she agreed softly, and reaffirmed it with a nod.

"Does your body ache now for me?" He needed to hear that she did, for he bloody well ached and throbbed and hungered for her.

"As soon as you turned and smiled at me, I ached for you."

"And you searched me out?"

She smiled and he released her, taking her hand in his but keeping a safe distance between them.

"I searched you out," she agreed, "but it was to see that you kept your promise to me."

"Promise?"

She nodded. "You said you would teach me to swim and I have decided I would like to learn."

"And I know the perfect spot where I can teach you," he said, reeling her slowly toward him. "The beach is private, the water warm and clear. It's a perfect little paradise for lovers."

"Swimming lessons," she corrected with a catch to her breath. "You will give me swimming lessons."

He leaned down and took her lips, separating them with

his tongue slowly before slipping inside to tease and tantalize.

"I want to give you more, so much more," he whispered between erotic kisses. "Will you let me give you more, angel?"

He didn't wait for an answer, he tore his mouth from hers, grabbed her hand, and hurried down the veranda steps with her in tow.

↠ 21 ↞

"STRIP?" CATHERINE REPEATED, watching while Lucian cast off each of his garments and tossed them to the sand.

He was gorgeous. And once he peeled those breeches off she would be hard-pressed to keep her hands off him.

She spoke sternly. "You promised to teach me how to swim."

He discarded his breeches.

Catherine captured the traitorous moan that rushed to escape her lips. She intended to learn to swim first, later they could roll playfully in the sand.

Lucian walked up to her, reaching for her sarong. "Aye, madam, I did. And you can't learn to swim properly fully clothed."

His fingers deftly plucked the end of the sarong from where it sat tucked just above Catherine's left breast and began to unwrap her.

A ripple of sensual pleasure attacked her lower belly. "Is this a good idea, Lucian?"

He wore a teasing grin. "Most definitely. Living on an island surrounded by water, one should definitely learn to swim."

She caught his hand, preventing him from releasing her sarong. "That's not what I meant and you know it."

His strength was no match for her, he let fall the last layer of her sarong, her hand seeming to assist him. His eyes appreciatively followed his hand as he cupped her breast and tenderly squeezed her full flesh.

His one whispered word promised heaven on earth. "Later."

Her body shivered in anticipation.

He laughed, grabbed her hand, and ran with her toward the rolling waves gently rushing to shore.

Catherine tugged at his hand, halting him as the water rushed up encircling her ankles. "Wait," she cried fearfully.

He stopped, turned, and swung her up into his arms, carrying her the rest of the way into the warm clear water until he stood waist high in it.

"Lucian!" she protested loudly, and locked her arms around his neck.

"Hush, angel, I'll allow no harm to come to you." He kissed her forehead and slowly lowered them both until the water covered nearly up to their necks.

She stiffened as the warm water engulfed her naked flesh. She had not thought that her lesson would begin with her bare skinned and immersed in the sea, in Lucian's arms.

"Relax," his voice soothed. "You'll be swimming in no time."

She had her doubts. "Are you certain this is the proper way to learn how to swim?"

"Proper?" He paused and studied her before claiming her lips demandingly. Hot and heavy, his tongue assaulted her and she surrendered. When she finally lay limp in his arms, he spoke. "I never do anything proper."

That, he didn't have to tell Catherine. She was well aware of his penchant for impropriety.

"Now for your first lesson," he said with a sense of impatience.

She smiled with satisfaction. He was as hot and bothered as she.

"You must learn to breathe through your nose correctly in

order to swim. It is important since there may be times you find yourself submerged longer than usual."

Catherine objected. "I have no plans of submerging myself for any great periods of time."

"Fine. But you will learn anyway."

Catherine meant to protest. Lucian stopped her.

"I am the instructor, you are the pupil. We will do things my way."

His tone left no room for argument. He meant to be obeyed and he would brook no interference. She assumed silence and attentiveness was the best course of action at the moment.

"Now," he began again, expecting and receiving no objections from Catherine. "Breathe down through your nose like this." He demonstrated, his nostrils flaring as he expelled the air. "Try it."

She did and smiled, pleased by her success.

"Good," he praised. "Now you're going to breathe exactly that way as we dip our heads beneath the water."

"No!" she protested loudly, and anchored her arms more tightly around his neck.

"Yes," he corrected her and submerged them both.

Catherine barely had time to inhale as he had ordered and shut her eyes before she felt the sea swallow her whole.

He surfaced them quickly.

Catherine opened her eyes surprised. "I did it," she announced proudly.

"And that's just the beginning," he smiled.

Excited by her achievement, she laughed, announced she was ready for lesson two, and kissed Lucian soundly.

He was caught off guard, a tendency he thought he had broken years ago, so his lack of attention shocked him. So did her kiss. It was quick, but artfully sensual. Her tongue shot in his mouth, fenced a brief and excited moment with his, and then departed, leaving him excited and hungry.

"Lesson two," she repeated, unaware of how she had raised his temperature considerably.

He became astutely aware of their nakedness and the buoyancy of the water surrounding them. Bloody hell, but he'd enjoy taking her here in the sea. And here he could take her roughly, the water softening his urgent thrusts. He hardened at the idea.

"Lucian?" Her voice questioned gently.

He shook himself from his reverie. "Lesson two," he heard himself say, and wondered which lesson he'd demonstrate lovemaking in the sea.

"My arms ache," Catherine protested an hour later.

Lucian sounded annoyed when he spoke. "You insisted on practicing too long."

"I wanted to learn."

"It wasn't necessary to learn in an hour's time," he said curtly, surprised by how quickly she had mastered the skill.

Catherine continued to bob beneath the water, her feet prodding the sea's soft floor to add to her bounce. She wondered over his snappish remark. "I hadn't known swimming could be so enjoyable."

"It has its moments," he said, standing. The water fell to his waist, his well-muscled torso dripping, his hair wet and glistening.

Catherine caught the ragged gasp that rushed to her lips. It wouldn't do to let him see how he affected her. To let him know that with a simple look, her blood could race hot with passion for him and her body could tingle with the anticipation of him filling her to the brink.

She stood as well, assuming their lesson over. "I suppose

you've had enough instructing for one day." She turned her bare backside to him and headed toward the beach.

One step, two steps, three steps. He watched her walk away. She thought her lessons over, complete, finished. The hell they were finished. If she thought that he touched her wet naked flesh for the last hour with no intention of making love to her, she was a damn fool.

He intended to touch, stroke, kiss, and bloody well ease this damnable ache that started as soon as she had entered his arms on the veranda.

His eyes devoured the way her round backside swayed, rivulets of water running off her firm flesh. The sea fell away from her nakedness almost reluctantly as she emerged farther and farther.

Lucian watched with steady and hungry eyes. Watched as the water released her and exposed her legs and the haven where he knew he'd find paradise.

She raised her arms, squeezing the saltwater from her long silver hair. She turned slowly, gracefully, and for an instant stared at him. Her breasts jutted out full and invitingly, her belly was soft and flat, and the silver triangle of curls beckoned most sinfully.

Gracefully she turned once again, only this time she rushed to the shore . . . away from him.

Her anxious flight angered him and like a mighty god emerging with wrath from the sea he descended on her.

Her feet barely touched the warm sand when she was swept up into Lucian's arms.

"I want you."

Catherine shivered though warm, his voice ran like icy fingers down her spine.

"That's right, angel, fear me, for at this moment I want to take you like I've never done before."

"Lucian." His name spilled in a soft plea from her lips.

He ran his mouth roughly over hers. "No amount of pleading will help. I plan on taking you here. Now. My way."

His own words enraged him with passion. He wanted desperately to possess her, to love her so thoroughly that she would never forget him, never want another man, never want to love again. He wanted her to be his and his alone.

He dropped slowly to his knees with her still cradled in his arms. "Lesson number ten," he said, placing her on the warm sand, moving down over her and savagely capturing her mouth.

Bloody hell, but she tasted like the sea, salty, fresh, and wet. So damn wet that he could think of nothing but her warm, slick sheath that waited for him.

"Lucian." Her voice attempted sanity, but the tremors that racked her clearly declared her on the threshold of madness.

Lucian pulled back away from her, kneading her breasts as his knees nudged her legs apart.

"I'm going to take you beyond paradise, beyond passion, into the deep dark recesses of insanity," he said, his hand stroking her silver mound roughly. "You want to go with me, don't you angel?"

Her eyes fluttered. She could barely gather a cohesive thought much less manage a sensible response. The warm sand burned into her back, his touch fired her body beyond reality, beyond any emotion she had ever experienced. He dominated, he controlled, he brought her unspeakable pleasure. The devil himself possessed her very soul.

She shook her head, for a brief moment fearing where he might take her.

He laughed, slipped his arms beneath her legs and drew her up against him, his hardened shaft bidding entrance to her. "Liar," he said, and plunged into her.

She arched her back and cried out from his thrusting

impact. Her hands clawed the sand, her breath locked in her throat and she thought she would surely die if he ceased his forceful invasion.

He didn't stop. He delivered exactly what he had promised, he took them into the depths of insanity.

His movements were wild, full of savage need, and she responded with equal abandonment. Nothing existed but their unholy desire to be consumed by each other. To touch the very core of their beings, to unite and become one. To love as they had never loved before.

They splintered together like a thousand shards of glass bursting beneath the hot sun. Painfully satisfying and emotionally frightening.

Lucian collapsed on Catherine, his breathing heavy, his heart beating out of control. Catherine fared no better. Her heart beat erratically as though searching for a steady rhythm, but too crazed to find one.

Several silent minutes drifted by before Lucian regained control and rolled off Catherine. He lay on his back, his eyes squinting up at the sun. "Are you all right?"

Catherine still hadn't regained control. Her breathing was labored, her heart pounded, and her body felt ravaged with pleasure.

"Catherine?" he questioned, his strength returning.

She still was unable to answer him.

He sat up and looked down at her. "Catherine?"

Her eyes resembled large round coins and she gasped for breath.

Lucian had her in his arms in seconds. "Easy, angel, easy," he soothed, and stroked her back. "Take slow breaths. Slow."

His reassuring voice calmed her, his powerful arms protected her. She belonged here with him as surely as night turned to day. They were part of a whole and could never be completely one unless together. She loved him. Loved him beyond reason, beyond reality, beyond madness. She loved the devil himself.

She sighed heavily, her breathing finally normal, her heart pierced by the truth. What in heaven's name was she to do?

"Feeling better?" His hand caressed her arm.

She spoke honestly. "I feel like I've never felt before."

He lifted her chin. "And shall never feel again . . . unless it is with me." His words dripped with icy warning.

She let him know his caution wasn't necessary. "I want no other man." Her finger traced a slow path down his cheek to his mouth. Her words came simply and were spoken from her heart. "I love you."

Lucian stared in disbelief at Catherine. Words escaped him, rational thought disappeared. His heart urged him to respond in kind, declare the love he had tried so hard to ignore and kept buried in his heart.

But old hurts and wounds surfaced to oppose and prevented him from admitting just how very much he loved Catherine Abelard.

Catherine grew uncomfortable with his silence. She had foolishly acknowledged her feelings. Would she ever learn to think wisely before she spoke? What now? Did she expect the infamous Lucifer to admit his love for her? Did she think they would or could live happily ever after?

Words rushed to her mouth though this time she attempted to save herself from further embarrassment. "The sand is irritating my skin. I must rinse it off."

She squirmed out of his arms and hurried off into the gentle rolling surf.

Lucian watched her retreat and cursed himself. Why? Why couldn't he forget the past, bury the hurt, and go on with his life?

But he knew the answers to his questions. He had suffered and he wanted Abelard to suffer. And he wanted, wanted desperately to learn why—why Abelard had lied and condemned him to hell.

Catherine's actions caught his attention and he watched as she stooped to grab at something in the water.

He stood and walked to the water's edge. "What buried treasures do you look for?"

She almost cried out "Your love," but caught herself and held up a grooved seashell.

"Would you like me to help you collect more?" he asked, already entering the water.

I want to collect more, so much more from you. She nodded, smiling briefly before she returned to her hunt.

The silence hovered heavily over them. The sun seemed to grow hotter, the air thicker. Catherine edged away from him, distancing herself, fighting to ease the ache in her heart and the emptiness in her soul.

Lucian noticed her retreat and grew angry. He didn't like her attempting to detach from him. They had grown closer since their arrival on the island, much closer, and he refused to lose that strong emotional bond they had forged.

Damn it, but she belonged to him. Love or no love, she was his.

"Catherine!" he yelled, tossing the shells back into the sea.

She jumped, startled, and looked at him with wide, questioning eyes.

"Come here," he said, holding out his hand to her.

Deny him. Her voice warned. *Turn and run. Save yourself from the pain and hurt he surely will cause you. Run, Catherine, run.*

She did—right into his arms.

❦ 22 ❧

CATHERINE RUSHED DOWN the staircase, her hand sliding along the polished teakwood banister. She cast a hasty glance about the entrance foyer. Spying no one about, she hurried down the last few steps and peered into the large receiving room to her right.

Heavenly blues and lush tropical greens blended perfectly to fill the airy room with the sense of the outdoors. Satisfied the room was empty she gave a quick look across the foyer into the dining room, shook her head at the huge dining table, wondering when Lucian would have the opportunity to entertain so many people, and hurried along down the wide hall.

She stopped near the end on the right in front of a closed door. She cast another curious glance to both sides of her. When she was certain no one watched her she turned the handle gently, nudged it open, and slipped inside, carefully shutting the door behind her.

"I've waited far too long. I must find those documents," she murmured to herself. She had allowed Lucian to consume her days and nights. It had been close to a month since they had arrived on Lucian's island. And a good part of each of those days had been spent with Lucian. The nights as well, but then the nights always belonged to him. They never retired without each other. Always they made love in his large bed upstairs and always they fell asleep wrapped in each other's arms.

Catherine had guarded her feelings and words carefully since that day on the beach when she had declared her love for him. They had swum often after that day, her skill improving and every inch of her body tanning gradually from the combination of wet, salty sea and hot sun that beat down on her daily.

She had laughed with him, picked fruit with him, hunted shells with him, and made love repeatedly with him. But she never again mentioned her love for him.

Now the time had come for her to face reality and recall why she was here, a prisoner on his island. She had come to save her father's life.

Undoubtedly her father or Charles had been in contact with Lucian, though he refused to speak of it to her. No matter how many times she questioned him, almost begged him, he denied her all information.

Her choice was obvious. Search for the papers herself. Then what? She wasn't certain. She only knew she could no longer sit by and do nothing. She would search and when she found them? Their relationship would be sorely tested.

Catherine had investigated Lucian's office once before, but she had been interrupted and had never found another opportunity to continue her hunt. Today Lucian and Santos had gone off to see to matters concerning the *Black Skull*. He had informed her he would be gone most of the morning. And with Zeena off to the market square that gave her a few hours and she planned on using every precious minute.

His study reflected him. Solid, strong, and massive in size from desk, to chairs, to tables, to paintings. But the colors, gentle blues and soft whites, reflected that part of him that he attempted to keep hidden. The part of him that cared, cared more deeply about others than he would ever admit.

Catherine shook her straying thoughts aside. She had work to do and little time to squander. She advanced on his desk, hurrying around its bulky size to squat down in front of three rows of drawers.

The bottom, she decided, eyeing the three drawers decisively. She eased it open, her arms straining against its weight.

Papers stacked to the top occupied the entire drawer. She sighed. This was going to take time. And it did.

A full hour later she laid the last paper aside and gazed out the window. She failed to notice the clouds that hovered outside promising an afternoon rain. She was steeped in thought.

Lucian privateered for England and had provided handsomely for the Crown. He had been supplied with maps and charts of every English ship that left English shores and foreign ports. He would know her father's shipping routes and the cargo they carried. He would have no trouble falsifying documents to show that the Marquis Randolph Aberlard had traded with the enemy. Lucian had skillfully fashioned documentation that proved her father guilty of treason.

Catherine sighed heavily and shook her head. Bitterness consumed him like a starving animal scavenging for food. Until he quenched that unsatiable hunger he would not rest.

She replaced the papers as she had found them. If there were false papers proving her father's guilt then there were also papers proving his innocence. Lucian had said that he intended to present the papers to Catherine when he returned her to her father, so that proved their existence. But where would he hide such important documents?

A hasty check of the other drawers determined that the papers didn't occupy the desk. She glanced about the room. Where? Where would she hide important papers she would want no one to discover?

Wrong, her mind argued. Where would Captain Lucifer hide papers *he* wanted no one to discover?

The room was a virtual cubbyhole of hiding spots.

Everywhere Catherine looked tempted her eyes to peek. Shelves upon shelves of books, chests made from bamboo or bright red lacquer and cabinets with locks, where in heaven would she start?

"Looking for something?"

Catherine jumped, startled by Zeena's voice. She was relieved it wasn't Lucian who had found her prying in his office, though Zeena's discovery of her could border on a problem.

Quickly her mind grasped a reasonable answer. "I was searching for something to read. Something entertaining."

Zeena raised her brow. "You read?"

Catherine smiled. "Yes, all women in my country and of my social status read."

"This is a remarkable accomplishment," Zeena said skeptically. "The native women here possess no such skill."

Catherine sensed the woman didn't believe her and wasn't surprised by her question.

"Demonstrate for me." Zeena walked to a bookshelf and ran her hand down the row of books, stopping at a slim volume and slipping it out. She held it out to Catherine.

Catherine took it, opened the book and shook her head. "This is in Latin. I can't read Latin."

A sly smile tempted Zeena's lips.

Catherine didn't care for the innuendo her smirk represented. She returned the book to its place on the shelf and searched for another one. Happy with her selection, she drew the book out, opened it, and began to read, " 'In the year of our Lord . . .' "

Zeena stared in awe as Catherine continued to read the passage from the holy book. "I have never heard a woman read," Zeena admitted when Catherine finished the passage.

"My father taught me." She felt a stab of regret. She had failed her father. She had fallen in love with a man who despised him, and she had given that man a forceful weapon to help defeat her father.

"Your father must be a special man to offer you such riches." Zeena possessed an astute nature and it pleased Catherine immensely that she so easily recognized the marquis's attributes. "He is very special to me. He encouraged me to learn and helped me when I thought I would never succeed."

"Few men have tolerance for females. They think us unintelligent creatures whose sole purpose is to please them and give them children."

"Our choices are limited. Marriage and motherhood."

"Guidance and nurture," Zeena corrected with a smile. "Wise women like ourselves are far too superior to simply accept marriage and motherhood. We take our life tasks seriously and use our wisdom to guide our men and nurture our children. No easy tasks, but worthy ones."

The idea that Zeena viewed her as wise astounded Catherine and she voiced her surprise. "I never thought of myself as wise."

Zeena shrugged. "Most women don't recognize their own worth. You have accomplished much for one so young. Your wisdom will mature as you do. You are destined to become a very wise woman."

Catherine sighed. "I could use a little of that wisdom now."

"Do not hide from the truth, face it," Zeena cautioned.

"How do I know the truth?"

"Your heart will provide the answer."

"It isn't my heart I question," Catherine said with a sad shake of her head.

Zeena nodded knowingly. "Some hearts must heal before they can trust and love again."

"What if a heart remains bitter and scarred?"

"Then the love was not true. Remember, seek the truth. Always seek the truth . . . for him as well as yourself."

Catherine considered Zeena's words later that afternoon. She had gone for a walk in the garden. A spectacular garden designed by a horticulturist named James Bartlow, who had fled England just before his debts would have condemned him to the workhouse.

His work was sheer artistry. He had lovingly combined the island flowers with flowers Lucian must have brought back from foreign shores. The blend of color, the variety of flowers and foliage, and the intricate pathways leading to small gardens within gardens gave the impression of paradise.

Catherine favored the rose garden. It sat tucked away from prying eyes, offering solitude and beauty. The roses stole one's breath away. Every single rose in the garden was blood red.

She wandered among the rosebushes, every so often reaching out to delicately touch a fragile bloom while she allowed herself to speculate.

The truth, wherever would she find it? Many questions perplexed her. An important one being why would her father's name spill from a dying man's lips? And if there was truth to the accusation then why would a man who abhorred forced labor condemn someone to suffer it?

She shook her head, confused. Where would she more than likely find the answer?

Your father.

The thought prickled her skin. Could her father put an end to Lucian's torment?

"Lost in your thoughts, madam?"

Catherine swerved around at the sound of Lucian's voice. He resembled a sun-drenched god standing there in nothing but his breeches. And the beauty of the roses that surrounded him warred for attention with his stunning red hair, silky and shining in the afternoon sunlight.

Your father, her silent voice warned.

She guiltily cast her glance away from him. The issue of the documents, her reason for being here, must be addressed. She could no longer ignore it, pretend it didn't exist.

"Something weighs heavy on your mind," Lucian said, approaching her from behind to gently span her waist with his hands and turn her to face him.

She took courage in hand and lifted her chin. "We must talk."

"I had a different purpose in following you here."

There was no mistaking the sensuality in his voice. And suddenly she recalled her fantasy of rose petals on bare flesh when making love. The notion of velvet-soft petals teasing her skin sent gooseflesh running up her arms and a flutter to her stomach.

"Please, Lucian," she whispered, the strength of denying him and herself such pleasure fading with a glance at the flaming roses surrounding them.

"This is important to you?" he asked, stroking her slim neck.

"Extremely," she managed to answer.

His hand dropped away. "Then we will talk, but . . ." His words drifted off and his lips found hers. He stole a breathless kiss. "It will be a short discussion."

Her breath quickened even more, and not from passion. She feared his reaction to her questions, she feared his unwillingness to cooperate, and inevitably, if the conflict was not resolved, her father's demise.

She took a step away from him, needing distance between them. "My father," she said, not certain where to start.

He stiffened, his shoulders appearing broader, his chest wider.

She continued. "My father is in grave danger, as you well know."

His hands tightened into fists but he remained silent.

Tears threatened, but she held firm to her emotions. She loved Lucian. Loved him more deeply then she had thought possible. But his bitterness and anger consumed him beyond reason. She had no choice. She had to confront him.

"You falsified documents that ensured my father would be accused of treason."

Fury swept across his face and he took a step toward her. She backed away from him, his anger tangible and frightening.

He stopped. "You searched my desk?"

Her hand instinctively flew to her chest, protectively reaching for her pearls. She felt only the simple white cotton dress she wore. "You gave me no choice."

"I gave you much more," he said gravely.

It wasn't necessary for her to gather her thoughts to answer him. She smiled sadly and shook her head. "You gave me your protection, kept me from harm, but in turn . . ."

She paused and took a deep breath. "In turn you have made me your prisoner, kept me as your mistress, and refused me any information concerning my father's dire situation."

He took another step toward her. "Your father's situation is not as yet critical. I supplied documentation that has eased his problems for the moment. And only because you kept your word and came to me."

A wave of relief settled over Catherine. Her father, though momentarily, was safe. "He has been in touch with you."

"Repeatedly he has demanded your return."

"And you have denied him."

Lucian advanced on her again, his steps sure and steady, almost like that of a mighty predator playing cat-and-mouse with his prey. "I will not bargain for your return. You are mine until I decide otherwise."

"My father—"

His hand shot up in an angry wave cutting her off. "Will find no peace from the problems that plague him as of yet."

"He is not well," Catherine implored.

"I do not care if he suffers."

"I care, and that is the reason that brought me to you."

Another step brought Lucian to stand directly in front of her. Behind her spread several rows of fiery rosebushes, their blooms open wide, their thorns thick and sharp.

"What do you want from me, Catherine?"

His voice was emotionless, but his eyes . . .

They were cold, as cold as the ice that covered the pond back home in winter. She shivered even though the hot island sun drenched her with its heat.

Courage, Catherine, courage.

She addressed him with the emotions of a woman deeply in love. "I want happiness for us, but I want my father's safety secured. Please, send the documents clearing his name."

A harsh challenge gleamed from his eyes. "And if I don't?"

Catherine accepted his challenge and used her only weapon, the truth. "I have nothing left to bargain with. Please—"

She paused and then whispered. "Do this for me."

He raised his hand waiting for her to take it.

Lord, how could she love a man who wronged her father? How could her body flare to life by the simple summons of his hand? How could she crave him so unabashedly that nothing mattered at the moment . . . not even her father.

She felt ashamed, not of her need for him and not of her failure to her father. She felt ashamed that she had failed Lucian himself. She had hoped to heal his heart and soul with her love. A love so strong that not bitterness, hurt, or anger could stand in its way.

Don't give up. Never give up. Her father's voice challenged her.

Catherine shoved his hand aside and threw her arms around his waist, hugging her face to his bare chest, resting her warm cheek near his heart.

Lucian wrapped his arms around her and spoke softly. "I can promise you nothing, angel." And with those words spoken his hands moved along her white dress and slowly dragged it up her trembling flesh until he yanked it completely off her, leaving her naked and vulnerable.

He then stepped back and out of his breeches and once again summoned her to him. "Come to me."

The scent of roses grew heavy around her, heat rushed through her body, she trembled and stepped toward him . . . collapsing in a dead faint.

❦ 23 ❧

CATHERINE WOKE FROM her faint in Lucian's bed upstairs. A linen sheet covered her naked body and Lucian sat beside her on the bed, his breeches back on.

He patted her forehead with a cool cloth. "Feeling better?"

She nodded though her stomach felt queasy.

"I didn't mean to upset you, angel."

"It was the heat," she attempted to reassure him.

"Possibly," he said, and returned the cloth to the ceramic bowl on the table beside the bed.

She sighed and moved uncomfortably beneath the covers, her stomach rumbling.

"You aren't feeling well, are you?" His voice held concern and sympathy.

"I feel tired and my stomach is upset," she admitted, realizing she wanted nothing more than to slip into a peaceful slumber and forget all her problems and her troublesome stomach. She wanted to get away from the world if only for a couple of hours.

Lucian smoothed the covers over her, then stood. "Rest. I will send Zeena up with some mint tea to soothe your stomach." He turned to go.

She weakly called out his name. "Lucian."

He returned to her and took her outstretched hand.

She pulled him to her and kissed his cheek softly.

"Rest," he ordered sternly, and hastily left the room.

After seeing that Zeena would look after Catherine, he walked to the beach, stripped off his breeches, and dove into the sea. He swam like a drowning man attempting to save himself.

His hard-muscled arms sliced the water with the strength of a mighty oar and his legs propelled him with the speed of a ship that caught a gusty wind.

He needed this exercise, this draining of his strength, this punishment of his body. With every stroke, with every aching muscle, he thought of Catherine and the pain he had caused her.

She asked only for her father's safety. She asked nothing for herself, instead she gave freely of her love to him. She loved him, Captain Lucifer, without any restrictions. And what did he offer in return?

Lucian dragged himself out of the sea to collapse on the warm sand. He closed his eyes against the glaring sun that beat down on him, and gave freedom to his troubled thoughts.

He offered only anger and bitter resentment to Catherine, and why? Simple because she was Abelard's stepdaughter.

Santos had been right. He had allowed his hatred for the man to consume his life and in so doing he blinded himself to all things but his revengeful need.

He had been unable to see Catherine's purity, her innocence of heart, her ability to love so unconditionally. He had even failed to note her intelligence and courage when faced with such a monumental task of protecting herself against the infamous Lucifer.

He recalled her strand of pearls, her protection. And how she had released them that evening from her hand, presenting him with the precious gift of her trust and her virginity. And what had he managed to do? Cause her more pain and worry.

Was the revenge he craved that necessary to his future? Or was Catherine his future? Could he forget? Could he allow himself to love her without regret, or would the past always surface to haunt him?

Since his return home with Catherine his nightmares had disappeared. He found himself forgetting this bitterness and looking forward to his days while yearning for the nights. He loved waking up in the morning with Catherine cuddled against him or wrapped around him. He enjoyed their daily swims, their shell-hunting expeditions, their trips to the market square where she easily made friends with the islanders. And where she laughed and excitedly inspected the island jewelry and bright printed material and tried every fruit available.

She belonged here with him on his island, and every message from Abelard had been a warning that eventually Catherine would leave here. Leave him unless . . .

He sat up staring at the deep blue sea, the brilliant yellow sun that hovered in the clear sky and the seabirds that squawked before diving into the water to claim their food.

This was home and he loved it. He wanted to live out his life here, raise a family here, marry Catherine here.

He stood, his decision made. It was time to bury the past and move on. He would clear her father's name and then offer Catherine marriage. His proposal would be made without restrictions. Except one.

He would hear Catherine once again saying "I love you." He smiled and walked to the water's edge eager to wash the sand from his body and shed the last remnant of his past.

Lucian returned to the house to find another letter from Abelard waiting for him.

Santos followed him into his study after handing it to him.

"Catherine?" he asked, breaking the seal on the letter.

"Zeena has seen to her. She gave her a special blend of

teas that will help ease her stomach and allow her to sleep comfortably."

Lucian nodded. "Good, I was concerned she was taking ill."

"Zeena thinks it's just a mild upset stomach."

Lucian's expression changed from concern to anger. His lips tightened, his jaw grew rigid and his eyelids flared with fury. "Abelard has discovered that I privateer for England. He correctly assumes that was how I was able to provide false evidence to the Crown concerning his so-called illegal activities. He suggests that for whatever reason I seek to destroy him, to do so and be done with it. But he implores me to spare Catherine. He writes eloquently of her innocence, her love for people, for life, for simple pleasures. He begs that I don't rob her of her innocence."

"He's willing to give his life for hers, and Catherine for him. They appear to care deeply for each other," Santos said, watching the play of mixed emotions cross Lucian's face.

Lucian dropped the letter to his desk. "He emphasizes that there isn't anything he wouldn't give to have his daughter returned safely."

"This is a man who loves his child deeply and is suffering over her absence," Santos said sadly.

Lucian pounded his fist on his desk, startling Santos. "You think he speaks the truth?"

"He's offered you his life for his daughter's," Santos argued.

Lucian rubbed his head, the thought disturbing him. Abelard would willing trade his life for Catherine's, this he didn't understand. He had thought Abelard a cold, hard man who thought only of himself and his position in society. He had never expected such an unselfish offer like this from him, the man who had condemned him to rot in hell.

"What will you do?" Santos asked.

He answered swiftly. "I'll not return Catherine."

"Abelard has no recourse if you don't unless . . ."

Lucian moved to the bright red liquor cabinet, throwing open the doors and snatching a crystal decanter and two matching goblets off the shelf. "Explain 'unless,'" he ordered, and placed the two goblets on the desk, filling them with rum.

"Unless Abelard approaches the Crown for help."

Lucian shook his head. "Unlikely. His credibility is damaged and until repaired no one would dare side with him. Besides I don't think he wants Catherine's capture made common knowledge. He'll deal discreetly with me for now."

Santos took the goblet Lucian offered him. "And what of Catherine?"

"What of her?"

"She must wonder if her father has contacted you."

"She knows her father has, but I have refused her any information."

"And she has accepted this?"

Lucian shrugged negligently. "She has no choice."

"She may not remain agreeable with your decision for long."

"She may not have to," Lucian said, and raised his goblet in a salute. "Wish me luck, I intend to ask Catherine to be my wife."

Sleep evaded Catherine while Lucian slumbered soundly beside her. Her jumbled thoughts kept her from a peaceful night's sleep. She worried over what course of action to pursue. All alternatives to her problems appeared, in the end, unacceptable.

She couldn't neglect her father's safety and well-being.

She couldn't leave Lucian alone and full of bitterness. And she certainly couldn't ignore the love she shared for both men.

She shifted to her side attempting to find a more comfortable position. Her thoughts plagued her even more. Lord, but she loved her father. In all the years growing up she had never once thought of him as her stepfather. When she was young she had imagined him her real father who had come to rescue her from a wicked family. And he truly had rescued her. Rescued her from people who had made her feel inferior and worthless. He was her knight in shining armor who did battle for her whenever she required defending.

Now it was her turn to battle for him and she couldn't fail him. She just couldn't.

Troubled by her emotions she shifted again, turning on her other side. She faced Lucian. He lay on his back, one arm beneath his head, the other at his side. She had come to realize after so many nights of sharing his bed that it was a position he had acquired out of necessity.

His arm acted as a pillow, his other hand rested at his side where a weapon would normally lie, and he lay rigid as though if he turned either way he would tread on another's sleeping space.

Of course by morning she would be wrapped around him or snuggled next to him and more often than not he would have himself wrapped around her. Her presence in his bed had helped ease his tense sleeping pattern. And if she continued to sleep with him? He would find peace beside her.

You can't leave him.

She agreed with her silent voice. She had once thought that when she had found the document she would plan an escape. But she had decided of late that escape was impossible. Her heart would break if she ever had to leave him. She loved him beyond reason, beyond madness. She couldn't live without him.

So what were her alternatives? No answers materialized. No voice in her head cried out to solve her problem. She was alone, confused, and frightened. Lately her strength and courage had waned and she found herself fearful and close to tears. She did not like this change in herself.

She shifted again, this time onto her back. She had attempted to talk to Lucian when he had returned to their room later in the evening. But he had insisted she rest and that they would talk tomorrow when she felt better.

Restless and worried she would wake Lucian, she slipped from the bed, reaching for her blue silk robe on the chair near the window. She left the room quietly, leaving the door ajar for her return.

She padded softly down the stairs, making her way in the dark to Lucian's study. She slipped inside, leaving the door partially open. In barely a minute she had lit the oil lamp that sat on the end of Lucian's desk. She raised the lamp and casually walked alongside the shelves of books searching for something to read. She needed to lose herself in words. Words that would ease her troubled thoughts.

Her fingers drifted along the bindings of various books, but none seemed appropriate to ease a weary soul. A smile flashed across her face and she turned, returning the lamp to the desk. She hurried behind Lucian's desk to the floor-to-ceiling shelves flanked by two tall windows. She dropped to her knees and allowed her hand to guide her in the dark along the bindings of the books that occupied the bottom shelf. When her fingers connected with a thick volume, she pulled it out and hefted it up into her arms.

Catherine clutched the heavy book to her chest and

plopped herself down in Lucian's chair before depositing her treasure on the desk in front of her.

She lovingly ran her hand across the book. The book she had turned to often when troubled and needed encouragement . . . the Bible.

Opening it slowly, she carefully turned the pages. What passage would settle her emotions tonight?

Lucifer.

The thought startled her and she found herself searching his passage out. Page after page she turned until . . .

Catherine stared down wide-eyed at the papers that lay between the pages. Slowly and with some reluctance she reached for the sheets of hastily scrawled print. Aware of their significance, she drank a deep breath, preparing herself.

She read carefully, concentrating on every word. When she finished she read them again and then again. Finally she shook her head and rubbed at her weary eyes.

"Catherine."

She jumped, startled by Lucian's voice and by the tenderness with which he had said her name.

He walked farther into the room, dressed in only his breeches that hung partially unfastened. His hair looked as though he had hastily run his fingers through the long strands, but his eyes were bright and alert to his surroundings and to the significance of the situation they now faced.

"I'm sorry you found them."

She stood, remaining behind the desk, the papers clutched in her hand. "I don't understand."

Lucian approached her slowly and spoke to her with the sympathy of one who had just suffered a loss. "I know how this must hurt you."

"No," she argued, another shake of her head confirming her denial.

Lucian continued, attempting to ease her pain. "I know how dearly you love your father."

"No, he couldn't have done this," she protested strenuously.

"But he did, Catherine. He signed the papers, condemning me to servitude on the merchant ship." He stood in front of his desk bathed in the faint glow of the oil lamp.

"You don't understand," she pleaded, hurrying around to stand beside him with the evidence of her father's guilt crumpled in her hand.

He lovingly ran the back of his hand along her cheek. "I understand this is a shock for you and in time—"

She brushed his hand away. "No, you misunderstand. My father couldn't have signed these papers."

He stiffened hearing her defend Abelard. "You have the indisputable evidence in your hand."

She vehemently denied the obvious, shaking the papers in his face. "My father would *never* do this."

Lucian felt his temper mounting. She actually stood in front of him, papers in hand, denying her father had signed the documents. Documents that carried his neatly scripted signature.

"You are holding the proof of your father's guilt." His voice rang with cold malice.

She spoke with conviction. "If my father truly signed these papers then he must have had good cause."

Her words struck him like a harsh blow to the face. If she loved him as she had claimed that day on the beach, how could she stand here and hurt him so?

"You must understand my—"

His sharp words cut her off. "You defend him even with such blatant evidence?"

"You don't know my father. He could never condemn a man to suffer as you did."

"But he did."

Still she argued. "No, Lucian. Something is wrong, terribly wrong. My father is a good man."

He stood stunned, not believing the tenaciousness with which she defended Abelard. Her love for her father far outweighed her hastily expressed love for him. And he wanted her to love *him* with that unwavering tenacity.

"You still believe your father innocent?"

"I believe this matter needs further investigation."

"That isn't what I asked," he said curtly, and repeated his question. "Do you believe your father innocent?"

"Yes."

Simple and direct. She had announced exactly how she felt and sealed her fate.

Lucian walked around his desk and reached beneath the desktop.

Catherine heard a click. Her heart caught in her throat.

Lucian drew his hand out from beneath the desk and dropped several papers to scatter over the top. "Your freedom, madam."

Catherine understood the papers that lay in front of her proved her father innocent of treason. She didn't understand what he meant by her freedom.

"You gave me what I sought. Now take what I promised in return."

An icy chill ran up Catherine's spine and a shiver touched her soul. "Lucian." His name ran like a gentle plea from her lips.

He stood tall, his shoulders back, his demeanor that of the pirate Lucifer and not the Lucian Darcmoor she had come to know and love.

"You will sail the day after tomorrow for England."

"Lucian," she cried, feeling her heart painfully break.

He ignored her as if he hadn't heard her plea or cared. He walked around the desk and straight out the door without a backward glance. Catherine clutched the papers to her chest and sank to the floor. Her father's freedom had cost her dearly. She had lost Lucian forever.

❧ 24 ❧

CATHERINE HADN'T SEEN Lucian since the night before in his study. After having cried for an hour she had returned to their room. He hadn't been there, nor had he been at breakfast this morning. He had purposely kept his distance from her.

He had left orders for her to pack and ready herself for her return to England on the morrow. A ship was being prepared for her journey, not the *Black Skull,* but one that could take her directly to English shores.

She dropped down to sit on the edge of the bed and sighed heavily while staring down at the sarong she held in her hand. The meager garment would be considered scandalous back in England. But not here in Heaven.

A regretful frown marred her lovely features as she cast a sorrowful glance around the bedroom. She would miss this house, this island, and the friends she had made. She had come to think of it as her home. She had come to believe that in time Lucian would grow to love her as much as she loved him. She had convinced herself that fairy tales did indeed come true.

She had been a fool.

A single tear spilled from her eye and fell on her cheek. She roughly brushed it away. What good would tears do her? Lucian was determined to have his revenge. He would let nothing stop him. Not even love.

"He is a fool." Santos said, standing in the open doorway.

Catherine wiped at her teary eyes and forced a smile. "His hurt won't allow him to forget or forgive."

"Do not make excuses for his poor behavior," Santos ordered, entering the room. "He is a grown man and should behave like one. Not like some little boy who pouts over ridiculous things."

Catherine looked up at Santos when he stopped in front of her. She nervously twisted the sarong in her hand and her lips quivered, fading her smile to a mournful frown. "I never knew love could hurt so much," she admitted, and began to cry.

Santos opened his arms and heart to her.

She tossed the wrinkled sarong to the side and hurried into his arms.

"Cry," he told her, and wrapped her snugly in his fatherly embrace.

"I can't bear the hurt," she cried, her voice barely coherent with her face buried in his chest.

"He doesn't deserve you. You are much too good for him," Santos defended. "He is ten times a fool. No, a hundred times a fool to treat you so."

Catherine eased away from him and looked up into his eyes. "Then why do I hurt for him as much as for myself?"

Santos smiled sadly. "Because you love without restrictions."

"And he can't?"

He shook his head slowly. "Not yet. He must free himself of his past before he can look to his future."

"Then it is too late for us." Catherine stepped out of his arms.

"No," Santos insisted strongly. "It is never too late. Don't give up. Don't ever give up."

"But isn't that what Lucian is doing? Never giving up. Never forgetting the past. Seeking his revenge at all cost."

"It is what one seeks and the reason for it that matters. Follow your instincts and your heart."

Catherine's lip quivered. "I have, and love hurts. It hurts badly."

Santos offered her his comforting arms once again and Catherine gratefully drifted into them.

By late afternoon Lucian still hadn't returned to the house. Catherine had finished packing her things and Santos had secured her traveling cases and had them sent on to the ship. She had kept one small traveling case for herself as she had done when leaving England over four months ago.

She had attempted to eat the noon meal, but her stomach had protested and she had only been able to eat a few slices of melon.

Afternoon had drifted into early evening and Catherine found herself wandering from room to room lost in her thoughts and her sorrows.

Her heart ached unbearably. She thought of seeking Lucian out and begging him to reconsider his hasty decision. But she recalled last night and his expression when he had dumped the proof of her father's innocence on his desk. At that moment he had resembled the pirate Lucifer when he had stepped through the shattered cabin door on the ship and so calmly ordered her to drop the pistol she held.

His threatening stare had frightened her then and that same stare had managed to frighten the devil out of her last night, but this time for a different reason. The first time she had feared for her life, his look had been so fierce and menacing. Last evening his look was just as fierce and menacing . . . and determined. Nothing would stop him from seeking his revenge, not even love.

A teardrop spilled on her cheek and she brushed it away while walking toward the rear of the house. She abhorred her penchant of late for tears. She had never taken to crying easily. She had learned young to hide her hurt feelings, so these frequent tears annoyed her.

When a problem needed facing, tears only blinded one's vision and emotions. She needed clarity of thought, her emotions . . .

Were totally out of control.

She wandered out the back of the house, past the cookhouse and toward the garden, deciding to take one last glance at the lush flowers and plants, embedding them in her memory to retrieve on a cold winter's night in England.

"Love is painful."

Zeena's familiar voice caused Catherine to turn around. "No one ever warned me of that."

Zeena walked toward Catherine after issuing orders to the young girl beside her at the entrance to the cookhouse. "Would it have made a difference?"

Catherine pondered her question briefly and shook her head. "No. I wouldn't trade this love I feel for Lucian for anything in the world. And I will never regret the time I spent with him."

Zeena raised her brow and smiled strangely as if just receiving news that left her wondering. "You truly love him."

"Of course," Catherine said, stunned. "Did you doubt that I did?"

She shrugged. "I thought perhaps you suffered a young girl's whimsy. And that the island and its beauty would soon weigh on your nerves. I assumed you would miss England and your grand parties and the life you are accustomed to."

Catherine sighed. "I miss my father. I never cared for the lavish parties and balls, or the manner of people. I lived a quiet and partially secluded life, and I preferred it that way. I will miss Heaven."

Zeena held out her hand to Catherine. "And Heaven will miss you."

Catherine took her offered hand, squeezing it. "Your friendship means much to me. I wish—" Tears filled her eyes and her throat tightened. "I wish I—" She couldn't finish. She couldn't openly admit that she was leaving Heaven never to return.

Zeena in return squeezed Catherine's hand. "Do not lose hope. Love can often work magic."

Catherine sniffed back her tears. "Magic would be the only possible ingredient powerful enough to rectify this situation."

Zeena winked. "Love is more powerful. Watch and see for yourself."

The two women hugged and Catherine took herself off to the gardens. She hadn't wanted to disagree with Zeena about love being more powerful than magic. Her love could survive the worst gale, cross a continent, travel through time, and still remain as strong as it was at this moment. Lucian's love was the one in question and obviously he did not possess as deep a love for her as she did for him.

She had been a foolish as a young schoolgirl in her first throes of puppy love. She had laid her heart bare and he had broken it. She had no one to blame but herself.

How could she have possibly thought that the infamous Captain Lucifer would love her? She was, after all, the stepdaughter of the Marquis of Devonshire, the man he had sworn revenge against.

After an hour of senseless and warring thoughts she returned to the house. Lucian was still noplace to be seen. Weary and heartbroken, she climbed the stairs, having refused any supper.

She entered the bedroom she and Lucian shared. She took one glance around the familiar room, so barren now with the removal of her personal articles. She turned around, walked out, and closed the door behind her.

She found a guest bedroom down the corridor on the right. She closed the door quietly, slipped out of her dress, and climbed naked between the covers of the bed.

Peaceful sleep was what she prayed for, her thoughts having pained her far too long. She only wanted tomorrow to hurry and arrive so she could sail away, so afraid that when it was time to say good-bye to Lucian she would break down and cry and beg him to let her stay.

Lucian stood on the veranda outside his study. The late-night air had dropped the temperature to a comfortable level and the cool breeze caressed his warm skin.

He had thought of drowning his pain in liquor, but had decided against it. He wanted a clear head when he bid Catherine good-bye in the morning. He wanted to remember her face, her expression, her words when she said her good-bye.

He had purposely avoided her all day. He hadn't wanted to hear her excuses, her defense of her father, attempting to reason with him that Abelard was a good man.

Abelard was far from good and it was time Catherine realized that people weren't always what they seemed to be, like her. She had claimed she loved him, yet she had defended her father against him when he was the one who had been wronged and hurt.

He hadn't expected to feel such a strong emotional reaction to his decisions. The idea that she would sail tomorrow and he would never see her again weighed heavily on his mind. The thought of her not sharing his bed, of swimming alone, of never hunting for shells again, of never seeing her smile, of—

"Stop!" he cried out to the emptiness of the night. *Stop tormenting yourself,* he silently warned.

He ran his hand through his hair. It fell over his shoulders onto his chest. He recalled how Catherine would sometimes wrap her hand in the long strands and tug at it when they made love.

His thoughts strayed to her naked in the bed upstairs. She never wore nightclothes, simply because he had removed them every time she had climbed into bed. He enjoyed her sleeping beside him. She cuddled against him nightly, often initiating foreplay with her innocent touches and soft words.

He thought of her penchant for wrapping her leg around his and lightly rubbing herself against him. She thought nothing of it, she teased him with sexual innocence and it drove him absolutely crazy.

With a quick step back and a sudden turn he headed toward the door. He had one last night with her. One night that he had planned to spend alone, but now . . .

Lucian headed up the staircase, taking two steps at a time. He hurried down the hall, paused briefly, debating the wisdom of his decision, then opened the door and walked in.

The room lay bathed in heavy silence, candles flickered from the gentle breeze drifting through the window and the bed lay ready, waiting . . . and empty.

Lucian panicked at first, thinking something had happened to her. Then he realized she purposely had not come to his bed tonight. His eyes widened. His hand clamped into tight fists. His nostrils flared and he whirled around as if a mighty gale had spun him about and he left the room.

In the distance Catherine heard her name screamed, followed by several loud crashing sounds. She drifted slowly out of her heavy sleep, opening her eyes just as the door crashed against the wall and sent the room atremble.

She pulled herself up, grabbing the sheet to cover her naked breasts and he stormed over to the bed.

He stood with his hands on his hips, his chest naked, his hair wild, his eyes wide and menacing as though having found his intended prey and ready for the capture.

He spoke not a word. He reached down, tore the cover from her hands, slipped his arms beneath her, and lifted her up against his chest.

"Will you deny me, angel?"

Though his tone was stern Catherine heard an unbearable ache beneath the surface and her heart went out to him.

"Never," she whispered, needing him to love her one last time.

She laid her head on his chest, listening to the thunderous beating of his heart, relishing the warmth of his hard flesh, smelling the sea and fresh air that was so much a part of him. All these things she stored away in her memory for lonely winter nights and endless days to come.

He carried her to his bedroom and gently deposited her in the middle of his bed. He stepped back, stripped what clothes he wore, and returned to her.

He covered her with the length of him. He needed to feel all of her, every inch of her naked flesh stretched out beneath him. He needed to know she belonged to him this one last time.

Her green eyes betrayed her hurt and pain and he ached for her. He hadn't wanted to hurt her and he hadn't wanted to be hurt. He had wanted to love her and have her love him, only him.

But inside where his hurt ran deep, where scars still lay open and sore, he yearned for relief. Relief from the pain of the past and the fear of the future.

When he had landed on this island he had finally been free. He had found Heaven and he had hoped against hope that someday he would find an angel to make his home complete.

Catherine had entered his life, an angel with a strand of pearls. An angel with the name Abelard. How could he trust the very daughter of the man who had sentenced him to hell? How could he love her as much as he did? How could he let her go?

"Lucian," she whispered in a soft plea.

He understood her need. He had satisfied her and himself night after night. He brushed his lips across hers, tasted her passion, her fire.

"Love me, angle. Love me," he murmured, and captured her mouth, but not before she answered.

"Always."

Catherine reached out to him with the same hunger, the same need to share, to become one.

His hand roamed her body, familiar with every valley and mound, aware of every erotic spot she possessed and creating new ones with his masterful touch.

Breathless and seeking air, she pulled away from his mouth. His lips sought her nipple, still hungry for her taste. While he teased her unmercifully, flicking his tongue across her hard little orb and taking playful bites, his hand roamed.

He nestled his fingers in the valley between her legs, cupping her mound with the palm of his hand and gently massaging her.

She moaned, feeling the tingling sensation run to the tips of her toes. Her second moan sounded his name, though incoherently. And her third was a simple plea for him to ease her torment.

"I can't get enough of you," he whispered between bites to her nipple. "You're a fire in my soul and an ache in my heart. And still I—"

He stopped himself and looked into her passion-filled

eyes. He couldn't bring himself to say the words. He couldn't tell her he loved her. But slowly and thoroughly he demonstrated the strength of his love.

She moaned and writhed under his touch, begged him for release, begged him to love her.

And he did. He took her beyond reality, beyond madness. He took her to the realm of pure ecstasy. She cried out, trembled, and nearly fainted from the exquisite pleasure.

He followed along with her, climaxing with a strength he had never thought possible.

They lay quiet and still, their labored breathing the only sound in the room. When he finally eased off her, he pulled her into his arms and held her.

After several silent minutes passed he spoke, his voice strong and determined. "I'm going to make love to you all night, angel."

She blinked away a tear and prayed that morning would never come.

Catherine woke alone in bed. She hurried to wash and dress and find Lucian. Surely after last night and the closeness they had shared he had second thoughts as to his decision on her return to England.

She hastily tied her hair in a lavender ribbon to match the lavender traveling dress she wore, though she assured herself that in no time she would change into her sarong as soon as Lucian and she had settled things.

Her slippered feet took her quickly down the staircase only to stop short when she caught sight of Santos. His expression looked grave and he appeared upset.

"Are you ready, Catherine?" he asked.

Her heart caught in her throat, her flesh turned hot, her stomach quivered. He wouldn't. He couldn't return her, not after last night.

"Lucian?" She almost choked on his name.

Santos answered gruffly. "He's on the beach, by the longboat, waiting for you."

She reached out for the banister, feeling faint.

Santos hurried to her side, wrapping his arm around her waist. "Easy, Catherine, it will be over soon."

"It will never be over," she cried, and wrenched herself free to run upstairs.

Catherine held her head up high as Santos escorted her along the beach to the longboat. The sand seeped into her slippers, but she continued walking, holding her dress above her ankles so it wouldn't trail in the sand.

Lucian stood beside the boat with his back to her. He wore his breeches, his boots, and his shirt. He was dressed entirely in black, an appropriate color for the infamous Lucifer.

He turned at her approach and as she drew closer he held out rolled papers tied with a purple ribbon.

"Your payment, madam."

Catherine felt as if he had struck her in the face. She almost raised her hand to her chest in search of her pearls and the feeling of protection they had offered her. But she had no protection, only herself to rely on. She raised her hand and took the papers from him.

Not a spark of regret, not a quiver of emotion. Nothing. He planned to send her off without a word.

Anger and hurt warred within her and she turned to go, then stopped, recalling the courage and determination of the young woman she had become when held captive on his ship.

She turned around with a smile and a flourish, walked up to him, leaned on her toes, kissed his cheek, and said,

"Thank you. You have taught me much and I will put it to good use."

His eyes and nostrils flared suddenly, but his lips remained stubbornly locked.

She drank in one last look at him and hurried off. Santos helped her into the longboat and she sat watching Lucian grow smaller and smaller as the boat rowed out to the ship.

Shortly, she stood on the deck of the ship, the crew weighing anchor, the sails unfurling, the ship swaying, and still Lucian stood in the distance.

She had hoped, prayed, begged the Lord above to let her stay in Heaven with Lucian. But he hadn't answered her prayer.

Don't give up!

"Never," she whispered, needing to hold on to her courage and strength. She sent the Lord a silent prayer that one day she would return to Heaven and all would be different.

She repeated the prayer over and over, blinking back her tears as she watched Lucian standing on the shore while the ship sailed farther and farther away from him.

❦ 25 ❦

"Love me, angel," Lucian demanded staunchly, and kissed her with a hot, sweet passion that sent the shivers racing through her. She returned his kiss, ached for it, hungered over it. It had been too long, much too long, since she had tasted his lips, felt his naked flesh against hers, felt his hands roam over her and ignite her flesh with passion.

Lord, but she needed him.

"You belong to me, angel," he said, lowering her to the bed in his cabin and covering her with his fevered flesh.

"Yes, Lucian," she cried softly.

"Love me," he repeated, kissing her with a fierce frenzy.

She threw her arms around him holding tight, returning his kisses. "I love you." She cried through her tears.

"Never stop. Never give up loving me. Never," he urged as he faded from her arms.

"Lucian!" Her scream filled the darkness of her bedroom as she bolted up in bed crying his name repeatedly.

Her door burst open and her father, oil lamp in hand, hurried into her room. He rushed to her side, placing the lamp on the bedside table before joining her on the bed and taking her in his arms.

"Another dream?" he asked, cradling her against him as he had often done when she was a small child and needed comforting.

"Yes," she sobbed, relieved that he held her, relieved that his health had returned and he was once again the strong, imposing man she remembered. His hair was completely white now, but he had gained back the lost weight. His features, though marked by age and stress, were as handsome as ever. This ordeal had at least been kind and aged him gracefully.

"I thought by now . . ." His words faded and he shook his head. "You've been back two months. I thought time would heal your hurt."

"I'll never forget him. I can't," she said softly. "But it would help if you—"

Her father released her abruptly and stood. "We've been through this before. I will not discuss it."

Catherine had seen her father adamant about an issue before, but this stern refusal to speak to her about the papers he had signed condemning Lucian to servitude was unlike him and gave her cause to wonder what he had to hide. "Your explanation of your signature—"

He interrupted her again. "Would serve no purpose. It was many years ago and there is no point in going into the details. You only need to know I made the wisest choice possible then."

Catherine slipped to the end of the bed, holding her hand out to her father for her rose-colored robe that lay across her vanity bench. "I don't understand why the choice was necessary and perhaps giving me the reason for your choice would make a difference."

He handed her the robe. "Catherine, dredging up the past will do no good."

Catherine hurried into it, tying the belt around her waist and slipping her feet into the slippers beside the bed. "I need to know. For myself, if for nothing else, I need to know."

Her father shook his head sadly. "You have been through a tragic ordeal. It is over. Why Captain Lucifer is disturbed about papers I signed concerning another man doesn't matter. Forget it and go on with your life. You will never see this Captain Lucifer again. I made certain he will never privateer for England again. He will never cross your path, or hurt you again. I will not allow it!"

Catherine felt her breath catch. Her father's words had hurt her more than he could ever understand. The thought of never seeing Lucian again hit her full force and she collapsed to the bed.

"Catherine," Randolph Abelard cried, and hurried to his daughter's side.

She once again accepted the comfort of his embrace. She purposely hadn't informed him that Captain Lucifer was Lucian Darcmoor. Santos had requested on her return voyage home that she keep that information to herself. He had explained that Lucian sought to reclaim his father's estate and if it was known that he was the pirate Lucifer his lands would never be returned to him.

Catherine honored his request, having had no intention of telling anyone of his true identity, not even her father.

"You must put these memories behind you and get on with your life," her father urged. "It is time we found you a husband."

"No, Papa," she said, and pulled out of his embrace with a sigh.

"Now, Catherine, I am your father and if I feel it is time that you marry then you must trust my judgment."

Catherine stood, shaking her head while running her fingers through her tangled hair. "Will you buy me a husband, Papa?"

Her father grew cross over her question. "I will offer a generous dowry, which is normal with your social status."

"The dowry would indeed need to be generous, or no man would accept it."

Her father attempted to argue, but she again shook her head. "It is time we both faced the facts, Papa. My reputation is ruined. As hard as you tried to keep my capture silent, it just didn't work. Gossip spread like wildfire upon my return. Men have propositioned me—"

Her father jumped to his feet. "Who? Who dared to insult you so?"

"Papa, don't," she said sadly, recalling the few men who had brazenly told her they wanted to taste a sample of Lucifer's private stock. "Don't make this any more difficult than it already is. I am being openly gossiped about by men and women alike. No respectable man would accept me in marriage and I refuse to create even more gossip. It is time I go home."

"You can't run away," he insisted. "We must stay here in London and fight this injustice."

Injustice. Lucian had often spoken of the injustice he had suffered. Now she suffered along with her father. She wondered if Lucian's revenge tasted sweet to him.

"I want to go home to Yorkshire where I belong."

"You're going home to hide," he argued. "You must stay and fight back. In time the gossip will wane. The social set will find fresh gossip to entertain them and yours will have been forgotten. But if you run off and hide, they will forever hound you with their spiteful tongues."

"I'm going home," she said. "Tomorrow I will attend the Trentons' dinner party with Aunt Lilith. I promised her I would go and I don't wish to disappoint her since Gwen Trenton is her close friend. Naturally the two have been scheming in hopes that this small intimate gathering might help my social status."

"It might," her father added optimistically. "Lilith tells me Gwen has invited a few recent visitors from outside London to attend."

Catherine shook her head. "I have no doubt that by tomorrow evening the new arrivals will have heard all about me. And besides, it doesn't matter, I leave for Yorkshire at the end of the week."

"You can't. I forbid it," her father said sternly.

Catherine sighed and dropped down on the vanity bench. "Oh, Papa, you don't understand. I must go home."

"You are strong and courageous, stay and battle for your future. I will help you. We will face these fiends together," he offered.

"I can't, Papa." She took a deep breath and delivered the news that she had been aware of just before she left Heaven. "I carry Captain Lucifer's child."

Her father turned pale and dropped to the bed. "Good Lord, Catherine."

Bravely she announced what she felt she must. "I love Captain Lucifer, Papa. I love him with all my heart."

He stared at her for what seemed like eternity and she wondered if this would be the first time in her life he would turn away from her and not offer her comfort or help.

"Catherine," he said, standing and opening his arms to her.

She went to him and released her tears as she had done when she had been a small child.

He hugged her to him and stroked her hair. "I had no idea. I am so sorry. You must hurt terribly. We will go home at the end of the week. I don't wish to see you suffer any more grief and pain."

"Thank you," she sobbed, having thought she couldn't hurt any more than she had the day she left the island. But knowing she carried Lucian's child and that she would never share the joy of raising their son or daughter with him broke her heart.

"Don't worry, Catherine," her father comforted. "I will take care of everything. No one will ever hurt you again.

You'll be safe in Yorkshire and together we will face this crisis. You'll see, everything will be fine. Just fine."

Everything wasn't fine and would never be again, Catherine thought, looking at the dozen or more calling cards on the entrance hall table.

Men had been stopping by the Abelard town house all morning, leaving their cards, requesting a visit and sending flowers with suggestive notes.

Dunwith had handled each one appropriately, accepting their card and closing the door in their startled faces. After the first vase of flowers had been delivered and Catherine turned pale reading the note, she had seen him disposing of the flowers that followed and sparing her the hurt.

"My lady," Dunwith said, entering the entrance hall. "Dulcie has tea prepared for you in the drawing room."

She smiled, holding back a tear. At least now she understood the reason for her teary state. Her pregnancy had heightened her emotions, causing her to cry all too frequently. "Thank you, Dunwith. I don't know what I would do without your support."

Dunwith nodded in his usual expressionless manner and waited to escort her to the drawing room. She hurried off with him, afraid that another caller would knock and request to see her.

Dulcie waited for her in the blue drawing room. The heavy drapes and dark furnishings seemed so drab compared to the bright, fresh colors of Lucian's island home.

"Sit, my lady, the tea is hot and cook prepared fresh scones with cream for you," Dulcie instructed having fussed like a mother hen over her since her return.

Catherine obliged her, sitting in the comfortable wing chair near the empty hearth.

"If you're cold I could have a small fire started. The late

spring rain has brought a chill with it," Dulcie said, moving the tapestry stool in front of Catherine and lifting her feet up on it.

"That isn't necessary. I'm comfortable," she said, though she now found the clothing she once wore restrictive. She had omitted several undergarments when dressing, particularly her boned corset, since her clothes had begun to fit snugly due to her expanding waistline. She missed the sarong she had often worn and thought how comfortable it would be as her pregnancy advanced.

Dulcie prepared her tea, handing her the china cup. Catherine glanced up as she took the cup and caught a sorrowful look in the young woman's eyes. "You know, don't you, Dulcie?"

Dulcie dropped her stare to the carpet. "I'm sorry, my lady. I promised your father I wouldn't let on, but . . ."

"It's all right, Dulcie. I'm glad you know I'm going to have Captain Lucifer's baby. I'll need all the help and support I can get. I fear I have no knowledge of the birth process."

"Don't you worry, my lady," Dulcie ordered. "I know all there is to know and I'll be by you every step of the way. I'll take care of you. No one will hurt you. *No-good, wretched pirate.*"

Catherine smiled. "He wasn't that wretched."

Dulcie looked at her with surprise. "Truly, my lady?"

"Truly, Dulcie, and one rainy day in Yorkshire we'll share tea and I'll tell you a few pirate tales I've learned."

Dunwith entered the drawing room as Dulcie bobbed her head in excitement.

"My lady, a visitor to see you and he is most insistent."

Catherine sighed. "Who is it?"

"The Earl of Brynwood—"

The cup fell from Catherine's trembling hand before Dunwith could finish.

Dulcie blotted her mistress's hand and her rose-colored day dress where the tea had spilled and stained her skirt.

"I shall tell Lord Brynwood that you are indisposed."

Catherine released her held breath. "No, Dunwith, send Charles in. I wish to see him."

Dunwith nodded and left, returning in a moment with Charles.

"Catherine." Charles greeted her with a generous smile, walking over to her and taking her hand to kiss the back. "It is so good to see you again."

"It is nice of you to call, Charles." She couldn't help but stare at him, curious to see if there was any resemblance to Lucian. She could find none.

He perched on the end of the chair opposite her. "I have heard all the dreadful rumors about you since my arrival yesterday and I had to stop by to extend my support during this trying time."

"Thank you, Charles. You are a true friend," she said, noticing his eyes. They were dark brown like many men, but they appeared cold, almost as if his look belied his words.

"As you and your father have been to me since my arrival at the Brynwood estate. You both made me feel accepted into the small but prominent social circle of north Yorkshire."

"Nonsense, Charles. We were glad for your company and for your support of my father during his troubled time."

Charles dismissed her appreciation with a casual wave. "I never believed a word of that rubbish. Your father is too fine a man to even think of treason."

"Yes, he is a good man," she said, wishing Lucian had believed in her father's fine character as easily as Charles.

"Your father has offered his help to me in a most pressing matter and I immensely appreciate his assistance."

Catherine's interest was piqued. "What does my father help you with?"

Charles gladly related his troubles to Catherine. "My cousin, Lucian Darcmoor, has appeared to have returned from the grave and has laid claim to the Darcmoor estates and title. Your father is helping me in my attempt to secure the properties."

Catherine hid her shock behind a forced smile. "Have you seen your cousin Lucian?" His name trembled from her lips.

"No, he has arranged for a solicitor in London to handle all of his financial matters. I heard he doesn't even plan to live on the estate, but stay on the south sea island he has made his home these past many years."

"I'm sure my father will do everything he can to see that you retain the property," she said, though in her heart she wished Lucian victory. He had been robbed unfairly of his family's estate and he deserved to have his lands and title returned to him. She only hoped his decision to remain on his island never changed. She wouldn't want him to travel to Yorkshire and possibly catch a glimpse of his child.

"I have a hearing to attend tomorrow. That is when I shall learn what the courts have decided," Charles said nervously.

"I wish you well, Charles."

"Charles," her father said, entering the room. "Glad you stopped by. I have a few matters to discuss with you."

Charles stood. "I was visiting with Catherine. She looks well."

"Yes, she does. You must come and visit with us when you return to Yorkshire," he insisted. "We leave at the end of the week for home."

Charles laughed. "You have confidence in my victory tomorrow."

"Of course I do," he said. "No doubt in my mind."

Catherine stirred in her seat unable to listen to a conversation about matters that, if they turned out as her father predicted, would cause Lucian more pain. "I'll leave you two to talk."

"Nonsense, Charles and I shall take tea with you and then go off to my study to talk," her father said.

"That sounds delightful. I would love to have tea with Catherine," Charles agreed.

Catherine forced another smile, not caring for the gleam in her father's eyes.

Aunt Lilith waltzed into the town house in mounds of purple flounce announcing they were late and Catherine must hurry.

Catherine shook her head at her aunt. The woman didn't look nearly her more than fifty years, nor did she act it. Short and round and full of life, she defied polite society yet was accepted cheerfully by them. While most women wore modest wigs her aunt refused to cover her own hair, insisting it was her best asset. Her shiny brown hair bore not a trace of gray and was piled artfully on the top of her head unlike any style Catherine had ever seen, yet on her aunt it looked stylish.

"Come, Catherine, don't dawdle. Gwen and her guests are waiting," she said, and waved a commanding hand at Dunwith. "Fetch her cape so we can be off."

Catherine had taken pains to wear a dress that would conceal her expanding waistline. She couldn't wait to leave London so she could alter some of her clothes to more comfortably accommodate her changing shape.

Tonight she had, with the help of Dulcie, managed to alter the shape of her gown enough that no one would notice the slight bulge of her stomach. Besides, she had chosen a dark green gown with a matching shawl that would help conceal her shape. Though becoming to her fair features and silver hair color, it was bland in design and wouldn't draw attention to her.

"Are you sure you want to wear that dress, Catherine?" her aunt remarked, eyeing her from top to toe.

"Yes, Aunt Lilith. I'm quite comfortable and we are late," she reminded.

"Oh, dear, you're right. We must be off or Gwen will have a fit." She hurried Catherine into her long cape and out the door.

"Tell Father I'll be home early," she called to Dunwith as she was rushed down the front steps.

"Tell my brother she will be home late," her aunt corrected as she hustled her into the carriage and ordered the driver to make haste.

They arrived only moments before supper was to be served and with only moments for a fast introduction to the other guests.

Catherine stood beside her aunt and smiled pleasantly as William Bacon and his wife, Margaret, the Earl and Countess of Sheffield, were presented. Then a young man named Benjamin Bond greeted her with a lopsided smile while the Baron and Baroness Harthington bid her a warm welcome. After that she lost track of the various names until . . .

"And lastly, Catherine, I am pleased to introduce a newly arrived gentleman, Lucian Darcmoor."

Lucian stepped out of the shadows from the corner of the room and approached her. Her heart hammered violently in her chest, her breath caught in her throat, her knees turned to rubber and she thought for certain she would faint. No resemblance to the pirate Lucifer existed. He wore mostly black evening clothes, from his black stockings to his breeches to his coat, but his shirt was stark white. His hair was neatly tied back, and though it was still long, its fiery color was lost in the drab confines of the house. He needed the sun and sea to bring it to life.

"My lady," he said, and took her hand to place a gentle kiss on the back.

"Dinner is ready, my lady," the servant announced.

"Lucian, as long as you have Lady Catherine's hand will you be so kind as to escort her to dinner?" Gwen asked, and sent Lilith a conspiratorial wink.

"I would be delighted," he said, and hooked Catherine's arm over his. He leaned over as they walked out of the room and whispered, "Easy, angel, you wouldn't want to faint and cause a scene."

◠ 26 ◠

Lucian watched Catherine through the entire meal. Being seated across the table from her, he could easily study her. He didn't care for her pale complexion or the dark half circles so evident beneath her eyes. He had thought her skin paled at the shock of seeing him, but as the meal progressed her face still retained a pallid color.

He hadn't been in London long, a mere day, when he had heard the rumors of her capture and return by the legendary pirate, Lucifer. His plan had worked well, too well. He had realized too late that he had made a mistake in returning her to her father. She belonged to him. He loved her.

Minutes after sending her off he had reached that conclusion. He had gone mad waiting for Santos to return, gone mad without her beside him, without her to love. If the *Black Skull* hadn't been in the midst of repair he would have sailed after her, attacking his own ship if need be to get her back.

Revenge no longer mattered. Catherine did. He had made a dreadful mistake. He had made her suffer for her father's sin. His fight was with Abelard, not her. He couldn't blame her for loving her father as strongly as she did, the man had been good to her when others hadn't been. She had offered him her love, a love he had realized was just as strong as the love she felt for her father and he, like a fool, had denied it. Denied the love simply because he was selfish and wanted every ounce of love she had to give.

And yet she had given freely of her love over and over again to him and he had ignored it, abused it, tossed it aside as though it hadn't existed. His anger for Abelard had fueled his ignorance and in the end he had lost the most precious love of all.

Now he was back to claim Catherine and her love, to take her back to the island with him, marry her, raise a family and live out their lives together in Heaven.

"Catherine, you can't be serious," Gwen said, sitting at the head of the table with Catherine to her right and Lucian to her left.

"I miss my home," she said softly.

"But you can't leave London now," Gwen insisted.

"I've told her the same thing myself," Lilith argued. "But she's adamant."

"You're going back to Yorkshire?" Lucian asked.

"Yes," she said, casting a brief glance at him and then turning to Gwen. "The country is lovely this time of the year. The flowers are bursting in full bloom, the fields are ripe for planting, everything seems more alive and potent."

"I don't understand how a niece of mine can love a simple life," Lilith complained. "I had hoped she would have some adventure in her soul. Be daring and not predictable. I'm afraid Catherine will marry, have a ton of children and grow old without ever experiencing the excitement of life."

Catherine raised her head and met Lucian's full brooding stare. Only they knew she had experienced an adventure of a lifetime. And only she knew that she would not have had it any other way.

"You look pale, Lady Catherine, perhaps you would like a breath of fresh air," Lucian said, and stood, giving her no opportunity to refuse.

Her aunt turned to her. "Are you all right, my dear?" She gasped. "My goodness, you do look pale. By all means, Lucian, do take her outside for a spot of fresh air."

Lucian stood behind her and assisted her out of her chair.

He offered her his arm. She had no recourse but to accept it. They walked to the terrace doors running the full length of the dining room wall. He opened one, followed her through, and then shut the door soundly behind them.

They were finally alone.

The rain had stopped earlier in the evening and had left the city doused with a spring chill.

Catherine rubbed her arms.

"Are you cold?" he asked, stepping closer to her.

"No," she answered softly, her nervousness having produced the chill, not the weather.

"We need to talk, Catherine."

She turned around, still hugging her arms. "We have nothing to discuss. Your victory is complete. You have caused my father and me great suffering just as you wished. Now please go away and leave us in peace."

"Catherine," he whispered, and reached out, the need to touch her so painfully sharp that if he didn't he thought he would surely perish. His hand stroked her pale cheek. Soft and smooth she felt to his touch, just as he had remembered.

She sighed, released a small alarmed cry and backed away from him. "Please, Lucian, please leave me be." With her pitiful plea spoken she dashed around him and back into the dining room.

Lucian returned to find the room in turmoil, servants running about and Gwen shaking her head, charging past him in a frenzy.

"She's ill, must get her home immediately."

"Who?" he asked as she passed by him.

"Catherine."

Lucian followed her to find Catherine looking paler and appearing as though she were about to faint. He pushed his way through the women who fluttered about her and bent down in front of her where she sat on a chair in the drawing room.

"What's wrong?" he asked, alarmed by her ashen complexion.

"I'm not feeling well," she said, and looked to her aunt. "Is the carriage ready?"

"Soon, dear. The driver was summoned to take your father out," Lilith worriedly informed her.

Catherine didn't think she could last five more minutes. She felt nauseous and light-headed and had no doubt that the upset of seeing Lucian had affected her condition.

"I'll take you home in my carriage," Lucian said, and stood. "Gwen, please see that my driver brings the carriage around front."

"It isn't necessary," Catherine protested, and stood; an unwise move. The room spun before her eyes and blurred.

"Catherine?"

She heard Lucian call her name and fear ran through her. Fear that he would fade away forever and that she would wake to find their meeting a mere dream. She called out to him. "Lucian."

He reached out to her, catching her as she fainted and scooping her up in his arms.

"Good gracious," Lilith said. "We must get her home. I feel positively guilty insisting that she come tonight. She had complained about not feeling well and I thought it an excuse to stay home."

"Follow me," he ordered the older woman, who continued to babble on.

He ignored his hostess as she bid him good night, his only thought of Catherine and seeing her home safely to bed.

Santos jumped down from the driver's seat atop the carriage when he spotted Lucian walking out of the house with Catherine in his arms. He rushed up to him. "What happened?"

"She fainted," he informed him. "I need to get her home immediately."

"The ship?" Santos asked.

Lucian paused in thought then shook his head. "As much as I would like nothing more than to abduct her at this moment I don't wish to cause her any more hurt. I'll talk with her when she's feeling better. If she doesn't listen to reason, then . . ."

"We'll abduct her and take her back to the island," Santos finished.

"Island? No, no, driver," Lilith fussed coming up behind Lucian. We don't live on Island Way, come, I'll give you directions to the Abelard town house while the earl tends to my niece."

Santos smiled. "As you say, madam."

Lucian climbed easily into the carriage with Catherine in his arms. She was coming to and stirring when Santos assisted Lilith into the carriage.

Catherine moaned softly and pressed her face against the familiar hard chest, relishing in her stupor the protection she always felt when in Lucian's arms.

Arms. Good Lord, she was in Lucian's arms. All he had to do was slip his hand over her waist and he would feel the small bulge of her stomach where his child nestled safely.

She opened her eyes and looked up at him.

"You're safe, madam."

She couldn't help but smile, his words comforted her so.

"Are you feeling better, Catherine?" her aunt asked, leaning over to her.

"Yes, much," she said, and attempted to squirm out of Lucian's arms.

"Stay put," he ordered sternly, causing Catherine to still immediately and her aunt's eyes to widen in surprise.

Not caring what either woman thought of his brazen demand he continued. "You will settle yourself in my arms and I will see you safely to your room. Tomorrow I will call on you and we will talk, then I will speak with your father."

Lilith smiled approvingly. "Randolph will be happy to receive you."

Catherine shut her eyes against the thought. Why did he want to speak with her father? Hadn't he caused them both enough pain?

The carriage stopped and Catherine attempted to scramble off his lap, placing her hands across her stomach protectively.

"Sit still," he warned with a whisper near her ear.

"Please let me go, Lucian," she begged softly. The outline of his handsome features in the moonlight stole her breath away and sent her heart to racing.

Her aunt was already out of the carriage, rushing up the front steps for assistance from the servants. Santos stood discreetly away from the open carriage door.

"Promise me you will see me tomorrow," Lucian said, running his hand slowly up her neck.

"I promise," she nearly shouted, needing to run from him, far from him. His touch had ignited her passion, and it flared to a hot flame. She ached for his hands to touch more of her heated flesh and if she didn't move away from him soon she would surely beg him to love her.

"You want me, angel, don't you?" he asked, his lips following where his hand had been and kissing the slim column of her neck, licking gently, lovingly, where her pulse throbbed rapidly at the vein in her neck.

She moaned, biting back the need to tell him not only how much she wanted him but how much she loved him.

"I can taste the passion that rushes through you," he whispered harshly, his hand moving to cup her breast. "You want me to ease the ache, the fire between your legs. You're hot and wet and ready for me, aren't you, angel?"

Lord, but his words alone could climax her. He drove her crazy and if she wasn't careful soon she would lose all sanity and let him have his way with her and then . . .

He'll discover his child resting in your belly.

Her silent reminder startled her and she struggled against him, against her own desire.

"Catherine," he said sternly, his hands reaching for her waist to settle her.

She slipped from his grasp and if Santos hadn't caught her she would have fallen to the ground. He helped her up and cast her a startled expression. He had felt her rounded belly, he knew.

She begged him with her eyes and a shake of her head not to reveal her secret.

He nodded and sent her a sad smile before releasing her.

She ran toward her aunt and Dulcie who had rushed out of the house to help her.

"Tomorrow, Catherine," Lucian called from the carriage.

Catherine didn't turn and acknowledge him, she ran straight into the house.

"Two days and you're telling me she still isn't well enough to receive visitors," Lucian said to the imposing manservant who blocked the entrance of the Abelard town house.

"The physician left explicit instructions that she rest and that she was to receive no visitors," Dunwith explained calmly.

"And when did the physician feel she would be well enough to receive visitors?"

"I couldn't say, sir. That information is privileged and for the Abelard family alone to divulge if they wish."

Lucian grew furious. Catherine belonged to him and he damn well intended to find out what the bloody hell was wrong with her. "I demand to see the marquis."

"He isn't home."

"I'll wait," Lucian said, and took a step to walk around the servant.

Dunwith took a step to his right, blocking Lucian's path. "He isn't expected back for a few days."

Santos came up behind Lucian, ready to help him charge the house if he wished, but Lucian held up his hand, sensing his friend behind him.

"Tell the marquis the Earl of Brynwood, Lucian Darcmoor, requests a meeting. I will be here the day after tomorrow at noon. And I will not be turned away."

Dunwith nodded. "I understand perfectly. I will inform the marquis."

Lucian turned and walked off with Santos, his heavy and purposeful strides evidence of his anger.

"He will not be put off again," Dunwith announced, turning around to face Catherine after locking the door.

Catherine stood in the doorway of the drawing room, her hand pressed to the cherrywood frame for support, her other hand unconsciously splayed over her rounded stomach. "Please order the servants to pack, we leave for Yorkshire tonight."

"What is the meaning of this, Catherine?" her father asked as he walked into her bedroom two hours later. "We planned to leave at the end of the week, why the sudden change?"

Catherine drew in a deep breath and released it slowly.

She was tired and weary of this whole matter. It was time for the truth. "Dulcie, please leave us."

Dulcie bobbed her head and closed the door behind her as she left the room.

"Sit, Papa," she said, patting the spot beside her on the bed. "There is much I must tell you." And she did. She spent the next hour detailing her capture, the reason behind it, and the pirate Lucifer's true identity.

"Good Lord, I had not thought the past would come back to haunt me so," her father said. "I had thought Lucian dead. I had hoped otherwise, but the evidence pointed to his death. That was why I helped Charles fight to retain the Darcmoor title and estates. I had assumed someone was posing as Lucian Darcmoor and laying claim to the properties."

"Have the Darcmoor properties been granted to Charles?" Catherine asked.

"The court has postponed their decision due to my request, but now . . . now I will inform them that Lucian Darcmoor is indeed who he claims he is and that his inheritance should be transferred to him immediately."

"Can you tell me now why you signed those papers?" she asked, needing desperately to hear a reasonable explanation.

"Forgive me, Catherine, but I cannot. I made a promise a long time ago and I cannot go back on my word."

Catherine understood better than anyone what her father's word meant to him and she didn't pursue the matter. Someday she would learn the truth. Until then she would assume her father's reason was a just one.

"You are right, it is best we return to Yorkshire. You need rest and you need distance between you and Lucian at least for the moment until the matter can be thought through and settled. I will send my solicitor to the court with papers in regard to his lands, then we will leave at once for home. The servants can see to the rest of the packing and follow later. Gather what you wish to take and I will have the carriage brought around."

Her father hurried out of the room, mumbling to himself.

Catherine sighed for relief. She was finally going home.

⚘ 27 ⚘

Lucian rode as if the devil was on his tail. Branches sped past him barely missing his face, some glanced off his shoulders, but he paid them no heed, he rode on.

The black beast beneath him could barely be contained when he rode into the stable at Brynwood. He settled the horse, riding him about the stable area to calm him, then he dismounted and threw the reins to the stable master to tend to the animal.

His hasty strides took him directly through the back of the house past startled servants who fled fearfully out of the new master's way. He rounded the center staircase and took the steps two at a time, causing a young housemaid to drop her bundle of linens in fright and execute a hasty sign of the cross as he passed her.

The whole manor claimed he was the devil himself with his long red hair and fiery disposition. Lucian paid them no attention. He had discovered in the month's time he had been in residence at Brynwood that he hated England, its weather, the people, and his own lands. He wanted to go home. Home to his island. Home with Catherine.

"Santos," he bellowed from the top of the steps, causing every female servant in the house to cross themselves protectively.

Santos appeared at the bottom of the staircase, casting an optimistic glance up at him.

"I've had enough," Lucian announced, and Santos fled like the wind up the steps.

He followed Lucian to his bedroom, closing the door behind them.

Lucian began to shed his clothes as he spoke. "Get the *Black Skull* ready and bring her to the eastern cove and anchor her there. We sail for home tomorrow evening."

"Catherine?"

Lucian threw his shirt off. "She's coming with us."

"You've spoken to her?"

"No," he snapped irritably. "That damn servant, Dunwith, insists she's much too ill to receive visitors and won't let me in."

Santos frowned. "Do you think she is ill?"

"No. She's being obstinate. I had thought time and sending her flowers and small gifts with notes expressing my concern would soften her enough to at least see me. But she has not acknowledged one gift or request to speak with her. My patience is at an end."

"Then you plan to abduct her?"

"Not myself. I'll send Bones and Jolly. I've had them watching the Abelard house. They've managed to locate the whereabouts of her bedroom, as no one has seen her outside her home since her return. I don't think she will give them as much trouble as she would give me if I came for her."

"What if she refuses to go with them?"

"They've been given explicit instructions to bring her to the cove or else!"

Santos nodded, knowing with that warning issued the men wouldn't fail Lucian.

"But first I plan on sending her one last gift," he said, walking to the chest of drawers beneath the window and opening the top one. He withdrew a black velvet box and handed it to Santos.

Santos looked puzzled. "Why give her another gift if you plan on abducting her tomorrow?"

"The gift speaks for itself, my friend."

Santos opened the box and there on a bed of red silk lay a strand of white pearls.

"Oh, my lady, the earl comes by every day and insists on seeing you," Dulcie said, pouring her mistress a cup of tea with a shaky hand. "He grows angry when Dunwith tells him you are too ill to receive visitors and then he asks if you have received the gifts he has sent. When he learns you have and have purposely not responded . . ." She bit on her lower lip nervously and shook her head.

Catherine sighed, resting back in the large chair that faced the open terrace doors in the sewing room. She had been shocked to discover that not only had Lucian, upon learning of her hasty departure from London, followed her to Yorkshire, but that within the week his estates and title had been returned to him and he had taken up residence at Brynwood, becoming her next-door neighbor. She had repeatedly refused to see him, ignoring his gifts and flowers though he had managed to touch her emotions with them. That he should take the time to court her as a gentleman impressed her and confused her. She had feigned illness these last few weeks and in that time her pregnancy had advanced considerably, making it impossible to see him.

"I had hoped his persistence would fade, but he appears intent on speaking with me."

"Maybe you should just talk to him—"

A shake of Catherine's head stopped any further suggestion from Dulcie. "I am in no condition to receive him."

Dulcie looked at Catherine's rounded belly. "He's bound to discover you carry his child, my lady. And then what?" Dulcie crossed herself.

"I don't know," Catherine said wearily, and waved the filled teacup away.

"I've upset you, my lady, I'm sorry," Dulcie apologized.

"Nonsense, I'm fine," Catherine assured her, and quickly changed the subject. "Were you able to speak with any of the servants at Brynwood?"

Dulcie nodded. "I found out that one of the servants who worked there around the time of the old earl and his wife's marriage now works at Moulton Manor."

Catherine grew excited. "I'd like to talk with her."

"I thought you would so I arranged for her to visit with you tomorrow afternoon.

"Good, there is much I wish to ask her," Catherine said, already planning a list of questions in her head.

"Lady Catherine," Dunwith said, entering the room. "Charles Darcmoor requests an urgent visit with you. He insists it is of the utmost importance."

"He wishes to see me and not my father?" she asked, aware that Charles had been upset when her father had informed him that due to the fact that Lucian Darcmoor's identity was legitimate he could no longer help him to retain the property that rightfully belonged to Lucian.

"He specifically requested to see you."

"Give me a moment, Dunwith, then bring him in."

Dunwith left and Dulcie helped Catherine adjust a shawl across her chest, draping it over her stomach to conceal her pregnancy.

Charles rushed into the room moments later. "Catherine, you must speak to your father for me."

His face appeared flushed, his hands trembled, and she wondered if he had been drinking at the local village public house.

"Please sit, Charles. Would you care for a cup of tea?"

"Tea?" he snapped. "How can you offer me tea when your father has turned against me and caused me to lose my entire holdings?"

Dunwith walked into the room and over to Charles where he stood glaring down at Catherine. "If you insist on raising your voice to Lady Catherine I will have to ask you to leave."

Charles calmed down immediately and turned apologetic. "I am terribly sorry for my unreasonable outburst."

Dunwith positioned himself by the door, his intention obvious. He would not leave until Charles was finished visiting.

"Do sit, Charles, and calm down. Then I will gladly listen to you," Catherine offered.

He took the seat opposite her, his hands still trembling and his cheeks more flushed than before his outburst. "Do you know why your father turned against me?"

"He did not turn against you. Indisputable evidence of Lucian Darcmoor's identity was presented to him and he had no choice but to advise the court."

"But all my documents proved Lucian dead. This man cannot be Lucian Darcmoor," he insisted with an angry shake of his head.

"Then evidently your research into Lucian Darcmoor's demise proved inaccurate." Catherine would have continued with her explanation, but Charles's expression startled her into silence. His eyes glazed over, his lips pinched shut, and his hands balled into tight fists. He looked on the verge of springing forward and attacking her.

"I had hired a trustworthy solicitor to see to all my legal matters and to make certain all facts were accurate." He spoke slowly and articulately like a man attempting to control his anger.

Catherine sought to placate him, his troubled mood filling her with concern. She had never seen him so agitated and near to losing control of his temper. "I'm certain the solicitor attended properly to the matter. News and information when sent over a great distance has a way of becoming distorted."

"Perhaps, but this man has no right to my properties and the Darcmoor fortune. All of it belongs to me. My uncle, Elliot Darcmoor, especially requested that I gain full title and rights to the Brynwood estate."

"In the event of his son's death," Catherine corrected.

"Of course," Charles agreed quickly. "But Uncle Elliot had searched for his son and had discovered, and believed without a doubt, that Lucian, his only heir, had been killed in a pirate attack."

"But he wasn't," Catherine said. "He is alive, and rightfully the Darcmoor properties, title, and fortune belong to him. I'm sure if you speak with your cousin he will settle a handsome account on your for your troubles."

Charles sprang out of his seat. "Settle an allowance on me with my own money!"

Catherine jumped, startled, and grasped the shawl protectively around her.

Dunwith was beside him in a second. "I must ask you to leave. You have upset Lady Catherine and she is still recovering from her illness."

Charles turned on the man to argue, but thought better of it, especially after meeting Dunwith's determined expression.

"Again, Catherine, I beg your forgiveness," Charles said with a bow. "I am upset and not myself, I meant no disrespect."

"Come and speak to my father when he returns from London. He was called away for a few days on an urgent political matter," Catherine said, hoping her offer would appease his anger.

"Thank you, Catherine. You have been most generous and I will make certain to contact your father upon his return." With a perfectly executed bow he left the room with Dunwith close on his heels.

The morning dawned gray and cloudy and by afternoon a fine rain fell over the countryside sprinkling the early summer flowers and leaving a light chill and fog in the air.

Cozy and warm, Catherine sat by the hearth in the drawing room, the flames chasing away the dampness.

Lorna Belford, gray-haired and dressed in her Sunday best, sat stiff and straight on the settee directly across from the hearth. Her short legs, Catherine noticed, were stretched out with her damp boots tilted toward the fire to dry.

"I don't know what you want from me," Lorna said apprehensively and with an edge of defense.

Catherine had sat up in bed most of the previous night preparing for this meeting. She had compiled an endless list of questions and written numerous reasons as to why she sought to discuss the Darcmoors with a former servant of theirs. Now faced with the prospect of discovering information of Lucian's and her father's past she faltered, fearful of what she might learn.

"I don't know anything, my lady," Lorna insisted when Catherine didn't respond.

Catherine regained her courage. "With the new earl in residence at Brynwood I thought it would be best to learn about his family before inviting him to a small dinner gathering I have planned."

Lorna nodded. Social status she understood.

Catherine had Dulcie pour them tea and Lorna began to relax, enjoying the luxury of being served instead of being the server.

"Marissa Darcmoor was a beautiful woman with the most uncommon hair color I had ever laid my eyes on. Blood red. The servants would whisper with envy about it."

Catherine smiled, wondering if her child would inherit Lucian's and his mother's unique hair color.

"The earl, Elliot Darcmoor, was a strange one if you'll excuse me for saying so, my lady," Lorna said with a nod, and reached for a scone on the plate on the table in front of her. "I never did think he loved his wife. He treated her with an indifference that was downright mean and abusive. But oh, how she loved that son of hers."

Catherine waited anxiously while Lorna chewed her scone.

The elderly woman wiped her mouth with her napkin and continued. "He had the devil in him, he did. But he listened to his mother. His father . . ." Lorna shook her head. "His father didn't have an ounce of love in him for the boy. He acted as though the child wasn't his."

Catherine felt a chill run over her.

"Of course there were rumors, but then there's always rumors in a manor household. Some even talked of the woman Elliot Darcmoor kept two villages over." Lorna lowered her voice to a whisper. "There was even talk that the earl had fathered a child by his mistress."

Lorna took another bite from her scone and followed it with a sip of tea. "Lucian grew into a fine young man, he did. A bit wild and fancy-free, but a fine, handsome man. He treated his mother royally and she loved him as only a mother could. Her heart broke when all the trouble started. Downright dirty business and unfair. Lucian may have got himself into some debt from time to time but he always paid off his debtors. There was no reason, no reason at all he should have been sold into servitude. His mother cried for weeks and then took ill. After that, Charles Darcmoor, a distant cousin, began to visit and soon the earl fired all the old servants. I moved on to Moulton Manor and heard of

Lady Brynwood's passing while working there. I don't think she ever recovered from losing her son."

Catherine listened to Lorna's story carefully. She asked the woman a few more questions, offered her another scone and more tea, and an hour later, bid her farewell and extended a special thank-you for all her help.

"Dulcie," she said when the young woman came to clear away the tea tray. "Please tell Dunwith I wish to speak with him."

Dulcie nodded and took herself and the tray off.

Dunwith had been with her father since his youth. Which meant he would have knowledge of the incident at Brynwood and possibly the reason her father had signed that horrible paper. She should have considered this possibility sooner, but then perhaps she wouldn't have been prepared to confront Dunwith before now.

"You wished to see me?" Dunwith asked, entering the room.

"Close the door, Dunwith. I wish to speak with you."

If her order disturbed him, he didn't show it. He did as directed, then came to stand in front of her.

"Please be seated."

He looked at Catherine as though she had lost her mind.

"Be seated, Dunwith, that's an order," she said sternly, reminding herself of Lucian and his authoritative tone.

Dunwith complied and sat on the settee, stiff and proper.

"I need answers, Dunwith. My father refuses to give them to me. Lucian is filled with anger and I fear a confrontation between him and my father is imminent. I need to know what happened in the past that caused the problem we all now face today."

Dunwith remained silent.

Catherine sighed. "I feared you would not cooperate with me. I know how loyal you are to my father and I admire that loyalty. I too sought to protect my father. Shall I detail the cost of that protection to you?"

For the first time in all the years Catherine had known Dunwith his stoic expression faltered and he stared at her with wide eyes. "It isn't necessary, my lady."

"But it is necessary if you persist in refusing to discuss this matter with me," she insisted.

"It is not my place."

"I understand how you feel, but please understand my predicament. I carry Lucian Darcmoor's child."

Dunwith blushed.

"Lucian is the pirate Lucifer and he seeks revenge against my father. I need to know the reason behind this hatred and only you can provide the missing information that will unlock the secret and allow me to understand how this whole mess began. Then possibly more hurt and suffering can be averted and everyone can begin to heal."

Dunwith stared at her with what Catherine could have sworn was admiration.

"Help me, Dunwith. Please."

Dunwith thought a moment, nodded, and slowly unraveled a tale that brought tears to Catherine's eyes and understanding to her heart.

"My lady, excuse me," Dulcie said peeking her head into the room thirty minutes later. "Here's a package for you from the Earl of Brynwood. It was left for you with an urgent message that you open it immediately."

Dunwith stood.

"Thank you," she whispered.

He nodded and took the package from Dulcie as she approached, then handed it to Catherine. "Would you prefer I open it?"

She shook her head and unwrapped the plain brown paper

to reveal a black velvet box. She lifted the lid with a shaky hand, stopping a moment to take a deep breath.

What had Lucian sent her and why? Her trembling hand proceeded to open the lid farther and when her eyes caught sight of the contents, she gasped.

She dropped the box to her lap as she lifted the long strand of pearls from inside, letting them wrap around her fingers and fall over her wrist and down her arm.

"He's coming for me," she whispered. "Lucifer is coming for me."

❧ 28 ❧

"Shhh, you're going to wake the whole bloody household," Bones whispered, giving a poke to Jolly's belly.

Jolly ignored the jab, sniffed the air, and walked to the source of the tempting aroma. "Fruit tarts."

"Shhh," Bones warned again. "We should have never come through the cooking quarters. I knew it was a mistake as soon as I heard you sniffing like a bloodhound."

Jolly spoke in the same low tone as Bones. "Haven't had fresh fruit tarts since—"

"Since last week when that Bertha woman over at the captain's manor made them for you. Now quit sniffing out food. We have work to do, and remember the captain's warning."

Jolly reluctantly withdrew his hand from the cherry tart.

"The captain will have our heads if we don't bring his lady to him safe and sound. And besides, don't you want to go home? I hate this bloody place."

"I'm with you on that and anyway the tarts back home are a lot sweeter and meatier than the tarts they make here."

"Good, then let's get Lady Catherine and get going," Bones said, moving around the large wood table and toward the door.

"You think she's in her bedroom?" Jolly whispered as they entered the hallway.

"Where else would she be this late at night?"

"We'll have to wake her," Jolly said as he walked on tiptoes behind Bones, rounding the staircase to climb to the second floor.

"We'll be gentle," Bones assured him, about to climb the stairs.

"That won't be necessary, gentlemen."

Both men collided with each other in their haste to turn. Jolly's bigger and wider girth sent Bones to bounce on his bottom.

Catherine stood and walked out of the corner shadows. The full moon cast enough light through the tall narrow windows in the dining room that it extended into the entrance foyer, bathing the three in a dim light.

Bones rushed to his feet, his eyes widening with Jolly's as they took notice of Catherine's rounded stomach.

Catherine placed a protective hand on her belly, smoothing the pink linen smock she had placed over the lavender silk shift Dulcie had stitched to accommodate her expanding waistline and give her more comfort when sleeping.

"The captain didn't tell us she was with child," Jolly said nervously to Bones.

"The captain doesn't know," Catherine informed both men.

Each man looked at one another and shook their heads.

"Where is the captain?" she asked wearily, tired from her late-night vigil.

Bones answered. "He's at the cove waiting for us to bring you there."

"And if I refuse to go with you?"

Bewildered, both men stared at her.

Jolly finally spoke, removing his stocking cap to twist it nervously in his hand. "The captain says we were to bring you back or else. We have no choice. We've got to bring you to the cove."

Bones agreed. "Jolly's right. The captain, he was adamant about us returning with you. We can't fail him."

Catherine sighed. She had realized she had no choice but

to confront Lucian tonight. She had planned to stay hidden in the night shadows and demand that he talk with her father and settle this problem once and for all. Whether she would have been successful in convincing him or not was another matter, but then that depended on why he had come to England in the first place.

"Why are you to meet him at the cove with me?"

Bones looked down at his scuffed boot when he spoke. "Guess he feels it's the safest place.

Catherine immediately worried for his safety. "He's all right, isn't he? No one knows of his identity?"

"Always best to be safe than sorry," Jolly said. "Why don't we just take you to him and then you two can talk."

Bones rushed to agree. "Right he be, mum. Let's get you to the captain."

Catherine hesitated. She felt safe in her house, but down by the cove, by the sea where he was so much at home, he'd have a distinct advantage. But she needed to talk with him, convince him that he must speak with her father. He had to learn the truth. He had to. Then he could heal and possibly one day forgive.

"Let me change my slippers to ankle boots and get my cloak. I'll only be a moment," she said.

The two men separated, clearing a path to the stairs for her. She disappeared into the darkness and they anxiously paced the entrance hall waiting for her to return.

"What do you think the captain will do when he sees her condition?" Jolly asked.

"Don't know," Bones softly. "But I do know one thing." Jolly quit pacing. "What?"

"The captain loves her."

Both men smiled and sat on the bottom step to wait for Catherine to return.

Catherine wrapped her long black cloak around her,

concealing her stomach and warding off the late-night chill from the sea. Bones and Jolly fussed after her as they walked with her to the cove.

"Be careful."

"Watch your step."

"Take your time."

"Do you need to rest?"

Their concern and attentiveness was touching, but worrisome. She didn't want Lucian to learn of the baby. Not yet, not until the matter between her father and him was settled.

The full moon played tricks against the light fog that blanketed the cove, making it difficult to see the shoreline and anyone standing along it.

Catherine grew fearful as she walked closer to the sea. The dampness seeped beneath her cape and chilled her skin to gooseflesh. She took several more steps, the sand soggy under her feet.

A gust of wind rushed in from the sea across the shore, whipping her cape around her and sending her silver hair flying about her face. As the wind settled a tall figure stepped out of the darkness and advanced on her.

"Catherine."

She halted where she stood, his strong voice sending her legs to trembling. And when he walked fully out of the shadows he stood before her as Captain Lucifer, the legendary pirate.

A single braid ran down the side of his blood red hair, he wore tight black breeches and black boots. A white shirt lay open to the black sash that encircled his waist. He looked dangerous, a force to consider, and certainly not an equal opponent for a pregnant woman who was madly in love with him.

"Lucian," she managed to say without the quiver that ran through her reaching her voice.

"I have attempted repeatedly to see you." He walked closer to her, standing only a few feet away. "I had been told you were ill."

"I'm feeling better."

"Good, then the voyage will be pleasant for you."

"What voyage?" she asked tensely.

"I'm taking you home."

"I am home."

He shook his head. "No, you're not."

She felt her heartbeat quicken and her pulse race. "Yes, I am, Lucian."

"No, Catherine. There is much to settle between us."

She took a step back. "Settle matters with my father first."

His features hardened in anger. "Your father and I have nothing to discuss. It is you and I that concerns me."

She inched back away from him with another step. "I have nothing to say to you. Speak with my father."

"To bloody hell with your father. It is you I wish to talk with."

Bones and Jolly hurried around the captain.

Bones attempted to speak. "Captain, there's something that—"

"Prepare the longboat and be quick about it," Lucian snapped.

"But, Captain, you should know—"

"Not now, Bones."

Jolly tried to grab the captain's attention. "Captain, it's important—"

He turned on the two of them, his look as cold as ice. "Do as you're ordered, now!"

Catherine sighed with relief, aware that the men were attempting to warn him of her condition.

"Say your piece and be on your way, Lucian," Catherine said bravely even though her legs still trembled.

"The hell I will," he said. "You'll come back with me to Heaven and we will settle this torturing matter once and for all."

"I will not return with you. I am staying here with my father," she insisted, wishing she could convince him to meet with her father and learn the truth.

"Not likely, Catherine." His hand sprang forward like a snake striking its victim.

Her wrist locked in his powerful grip. "Let me go, Lucian."

"No."

His simple refusal frightened her. It was issued with a deadly calmness that warned of his determination. "Let me go," she said again and yanked fiercely to free herself.

"You're coming with me," he said, her wrist firmly clenched in his hand, her efforts useless.

Panic seized her. If he succeeded he would learn of the baby. Then what? "You can't force me," she cried.

He laughed in a low rumble. "So soon you forget you were my captive once before. You think me incapable of capturing you again?"

"Don't do this, Lucian," she pleaded.

"You leave me no choice, Catherine." He pulled her to walk alongside him.

She ripped at his fingers holding her writs. "Let me go. Please, you don't understand."

"No, I don't," he said, dragging her along with him. "I haven't understand anything since the day I met you. You have bewildered and bewitched me."

She raced to keep up with his long strides, her back and legs aching. "Lucian," she cried, but he ignored her and pulled her to the shore where the longboat sat waiting.

Bones and Jolly exchanged worried glances when they saw the struggling couple approach.

Lucian swung her carelessly up and into the boat. Catherine settled her cape more closely around her and hugged the side of the seat he had deposited her on. What was she to do now?

Her mind raced frantically for a solution. She had been stupid for coming here with Bones and Jolly. She should have refused to accompany them. Then Lucian would have had no choice but to seek her out. At least then she would have had the safety of her house and the servants around her. Lord, had she been foolish.

The boat rocked and dipped as it headed away from shore.

Catherine huddled in her cape, her hand on her stomach. Truth be told, she wanted to see Lucian. She missed him. Seeing him in London had only made her realize just how much she missed him.

Lucian settled himself next to her on the seat. "Cold?" he asked.

"No," she said, and kept her head turned from him. The longboat rose and fell against the rough sea as the men struggled to row it out to the ship.

She wondered how her father would react when he learned of her abduction. Would he demand her return? Would he attempt to follow her?

A light rain began to fall and the boat continued its struggle. Catherine's stomach began to protest the uneasy motion. She rubbed her belly, hoping to ease her queasiness. It did little good. Her condition worsened. She felt horrible, as if at any moment she would be violently ill.

A soft moan ran from her lips.

"Catherine?" Lucian questioned, looking down at her.

Catherine kept her face averted from him, fearful of showing her distress.

"Catherine, look at me," he ordered sternly.

She couldn't turn her head if she wanted to. She had no doubt that within seconds she would retch terribly.

"Catherine." His hand to her chin forced her to turn her head.

"I'm going to be ill," she said softly, and rushed to drop her head over the side of the boat.

Lucian moved closer beside her, slipping one hand inside her cape to wrap around her stomach for support. His hand stilled as his fingers splayed over her rounded belly. "Good God, Catherine, why didn't you tell me?"

She lifted her head up, throwing it back against his chest. Before she could answer another wave of nausea attacked her and she once again dropped her head over the side of the boat.

Lucian held her firmly but carefully around her protruding waist. When she finished he dipped the end of his sash in the sea, rinsed it, and gently wiped her face.

"Easy, angel," he cajoled. "We'll be at the ship soon and you can rest."

She was sick twice more and by the time her stomach finished protesting she lay exhausted against Lucian's chest.

The boat pulled up alongside the ship and Catherine ran her glance slowly up the rope ladder, past the balustrade to the tall masts. She moaned.

Lucian pressed his hand to her stomach. "Feeling ill again?"

"No," she sighed, "But much too tired to climb that rope ladder."

He kissed her temple and caressed her round belly. "I'll get you up the ladder and to the cabin. Where you'll rest. Then, Catherine," he warned sternly, "we will talk."

She remained silent, being in no condition to argue. When she regained her strength then she would have her say.

"Bones, bring the boat about as easy as you can," he ordered, "and hold her steady so I can get Catherine up the ladder. She's in no condition to climb on her own."

"Aye, Captain," Bones said, and added with a shake of his head, "Jolly and I tried to warn you of her delicate condition back at the beach."

"You knew?" he shouted, turning an angry glare on them both.

Bones and Jolly shivered in their boots.

Catherine placed her hand over his hand that rested protectively on her stomach. "Lucian, please, they tried so hard to help me. Don't be angry."

He heard the weariness in her voice, felt how she lay limply against him, felt the dampness of her chilled hand through his silk shirt and he worried that in his haste and anger he had caused her and his unborn child harm.

He commanded when he spoke but not with irritation. "Secure the ladder as steady as possible while I carry Catherine up it."

"You can't," she said as he helped her to stand.

He laughed with a shake of his head. "Angel, you constantly underestimate me."

A rough dip of the boat caused her to sway, moan, and fall against his chest. "Lucian, I feel horrible."

"The baby?" he asked anxiously, wrapping his arm around her.

"Does not take kindly to the sea," she said. "Please get me to the cabin and your bed."

"What I longed to hear," he teased. "You begging me to take you to my bed."

She smiled, rubbing her face against his chest, inhaling

his familiar scent of sea, fresh air and male, feeling as if she had come home and was once again safe.

With a firm arm around her waist, he lifted her against him. "Put your arms around my neck and hold on tightly."

She did as he directed, settling her face in the crook of his neck and closing her eyes.

He grasped the ladder with his one hand while he held her easily against him with his other. He made the climb in minutes, taking the rope rungs with sure and experienced steps.

Santos waited on deck to offer assistance. Lucian required none. He was over the railing and on deck lifting Catherine up into his arms in minutes.

"Weigh anchor as soon as the men are on deck and get us the bloody hell out of here," Lucian ordered before walking off with Catherine to his cabin.

He gently lowered her to stand in the middle of the room, his arm remaining around her. "You need to get out of these damp clothes." His hand moved from around her waist to the ties of her pink linen smock.

She looked up at him as he worked the strings free. She thought to say something, to brush his hands away, but she remained silent.

He watched her eyes study him with uncertainty. His fingers worked steadily until finally each enclosure had been freed. He spread the smock open.

"Thank you for the pearls," she said as he stared down at the strand of pearls that rested just above her rounded stomach.

❦ 29 ❦

Lucian hooked the strand of pearls on his finger. "Do you seek protection against me?"

She grabbed the necklace away from him, hugging it to her chest. "I seek peace for myself and my family."

Lucian turned away from her, roughly discarding his damp shirt. "I regret my decision in returning you to your father."

Catherine made no move to shed her damp shift though she shivered from the chill of it. "Why? Your plan was extremely successful. My father suffered numerous remarks attacking my virtue and I suffered countless propositions."

Lucian turned, having pulled off his boots and stockings and tossed his sash to the floor. "Your father deserved what he suffered, but not at your expense."

"If my father suffers, I suffer. Can't you understand that?"

She looked on the verge of tears and she shivered. Immediately his concern turned to her condition and that of his unborn child. "Take that shift off now."

"No!"

He growled an oath beneath his breath as he walked over to her. "You're chilled. It's no good for you or the child. We'll talk tomorrow."

"Until this rift between you and my father is settled I have nothing more to say to you."

"I have nothing to say to your father, madam, but I have plenty to say to you. And we'll begin with my child nestled so comfortably in your belly."

She took a step back and toyed with the pearls, her

emotions too near the surface to control. "What of the child?" she demanded defensively.

"Why didn't you tell me of him?" He stepped closer.

She backed up again. "I saw no reason. You made your intentions clear. You wanted revenge. What difference would it have made if I carried your child?"

He moved up beside her, "I no longer want revenge." His hands rode low on her hips slowly inching up her damp shift. "I only want you and our child."

"Lucian." She whispered his name on a shaky breath.

"I've missed you, angel. Bloody hell, but I've missed you. That's why I came for you. I can't live without you." He eased her shift up and over her head, dropping it in a heap on the floor.

He stripped himself of his breeches and eased her down on the bed, following her. He slipped them both beneath the quilt, his muscular leg wrapping around her slender one and his hand caressing the swell of her belly. "Let me warm you, angel."

Tired and weary from her long night, and astonished that he had admitted that he missed her, she snuggled against him, surrendering to his superior strength and his familiar protection. "I'm so tired, Lucian."

He ached to make love to her, throbbing in a readiness he had not experienced since he had last been with her. Surprisingly her figure so ripe with his child had fueled his desire beyond reason. But her fatigue was all too evident and she obviously required rest.

"Sleep," he whispered against her temple, cradling her safely against him. Tomorrow would be time enough to tell her he loved her. Time enough to lay the past to rest. Time enough to speak of marriage and eternity together. Time enough to make love to her.

*   *   *

"Two damn bloody weeks since we returned and she's been an obstinate little bit—"

Santos shrugged. "What did you expect? You sent her away and then you decided you wanted her back. Now you think she should fall willingly into your arms."

Lucian watched Catherine from the veranda on the side of the house. She sat contentedly reading beneath an age-old shade tree. She wore a simple cotton dress, her hair braided to lie over her shoulder, and her skin had warmed to a golden honey from her constant days in the sun. She looked healthy, vibrant, and tempting.

"I wanted her back the moment the ship sailed away from the island. My foolish pride disrupted my senses, blinded me to the obvious."

"And what was the obvious?" Santos asked, leaning back in his chair, waiting to hear what most on the island knew.

"That I love her beyond reason." He stared with concern as she stirred restlessly, seeming to suddenly find herself uncomfortable.

"Well?" Santos waited for him to continue.

"Well what?" Lucian asked, watching her shut her book and lean her head back against the tree. Something was disturbing her.

"Well, what do you plan to do about it?"

His eyes still on Catherine, he answered Santos. "I plan on marrying the stubborn woman one way or another."

Santos grinned widely. "I take it you've proposed to her and she rejected you."

"She has rejected every attempt I've made to solidify our relationship. She insists that until I speak with her father, our relationship will remain in limbo."

And it had. She had managed to avoid him day and night, feigning fatigue more often than not. They hadn't been intimate since her return and the tension their celibacy had caused crackled like thick ice suddenly beginning to crack.

"Odd, don't you think?" Santos remarked. "She knows your dislike for her father and yet she insists that you speak with him. Why would she do that?"

"Probably some wild notion that if we talk I may find it within me to forgive the man. An impossibility that she obviously refuses to accept."

"What will you do?"

Lucian moved toward the veranda steps when he noticed her hand stroke her belly slowly and her eyes flutter shut as though warding off a discomfort. "I intend to propose to her again, and this time I refuse to take no for an answer. Heaven will celebrate a wedding soon."

He almost vaulted off the steps, but controlled his haste and concern, walking over to her casually. He leaned down in front of her, his hand reaching out to cover hers as she stroked her well-rounded stomach. "Does the baby cause you discomfort?"

She smiled, taking his hand to rest it along the lower right side of her tummy. "He's a little devil. He's curled himself up into a tight little ball right there and refuses to move. I've massaged him and explained politely that it is most uncomfortable for me, but still he persists in having his own way. He is much like his father."

Lucian smiled proudly. "I will teach him there is a time and place to demonstrate his willfulness. And inside his mother's womb is not one of those times."

Unhurriedly he eased her into his arms, adjusting her to fit snugly in his lap. With one supportive arm around her, his hand sought her discomfort. His finger dug gently into her belly, tenderly massaging the small ball that had tightened stubbornly. Skillfully and with quiet strength he eased his child to stretch and rest comfortably in his warm nest.

Catherine rested her head in the crook of his neck, her lips a mere breath away from the pulsing vein that raced with his life's blood. She hungered to place her lips against it, to taste the familiar flavor of him, to surrender to her outrageous need to feel him part of her once again.

But she successfully restrained herself. She had staunchly refused to continue their relationship as it had been before he had sent her away. She stubbornly maintained her position that he must speak with her father. This matter required an immediate settlement. Lucian not only needed, but was entitled, to learn the truth.

"Does that feel better, Catherine?" he asked, his hand resting lightly just beneath her breast.

"Much," she sighed.

"Good, I want you content and happy here." His hand drifted up, cupping her milk-filled breast in his hand, his finger deliberately skimming her nipple.

"Why?" she asked, the heat of his touch, too long absent, raced to fire a tingling warmth between her legs.

"This is your home. Here we will live out our lives as husband and wife, raise our children, grow old and die together, being buried on the small rise beyond the garden, joined together for eternity."

Catherine almost cried for she felt as he did, that death could not separate them. She loved him well beyond this earthly plane.

His hand wandered up to lift her face to his. He kissed her as though it were their first joining. Tenderness and warmth embraced her lips and tears blurred her eyes as his gentle kiss turned persuasive. "Marry me, Catherine. I love you."

His declaration so simple, yet so fiercely issued, rushed the tears from her eyes.

"No, angel, don't," he whispered, kissing away her tears.

"My heart breaks when you cry. And surely you don't wish me to suffer a broken heart."

She shook her head, not trusting her voice. She couldn't bear having him suffer the heartache she had suffered when he had sent her away and yet how could she prevent it when her answer . . .

"I cannot marry you, Lucian."

He had expected her denial, though he had hoped. "Once you declared your love for me and I foolishly ignored it. Do you still love me, Catherine?"

Her lips trembled with her answer. "My love for you grows in strength with each day. I will always love you, Lucian."

Her words reassured him. He had known, known deep inside himself, that she still loved him, but he had needed desperately to hear her admit her love. "Then why refuse my offer of marriage?"

"I wish I could make you understand the importance of your speaking with my father."

"Enough about your father," he said, raising his voice in annoyance.

"I cannot. You cannot. You must settle this matter or it will forever linger between us and one day rise up and tear us apart as it once did. You will never forget I am Abelard's daughter."

He grabbed her shoulders tightly and gave her a gentle shake. "Who you are matters not to me any longer. I will never, *never* send you away from me again. I was foolish, blind to my own emotions. I love you, Catherine. You are my life and we will never be separated again. Now, damn it, marry me!"

She forced herself to focus on the importance of what she was about to do. Her decision had been made solely with

Lucian in mind. As she had sought to help her father, she now sought to help Lucian.

Bravely she raised her chin. "You must speak with my father first."

He set her aside and stood, so irritated by her continued stubbornness that he feared if he kept her beside him he'd throttle her out of anger. "I have heard all I intend to hear about your father."

Catherine petulantly raised her chin higher and crossed her arms over her breasts.

Her silence and surly actions annoyed him all the more. "You had the proof of your father's guilt in your hands. His signature proved him a monster. What more did you need?"

"I needed my father to admit his guilt, for without his words I would believe no paper."

"Bloody hell, Catherine, did you bother to ask him when you returned to England?"

Her answer surprised him. "I did."

"And?" He waited, hands on his hips, anger in his eyes.

She struggled to stand. He offered no help, knowing she would refuse him. When she was finally upright, her hands braced on her hips, mimicking him, her head tilted high, she answered him. "You will need to ask him yourself as I did."

Fury raced through him. He glared at her and Catherine thought in that one moment that he might just raise his hand to her. She winced, expecting his attack.

His eyes narrowed and his tone turned icy. "Never, *ever* think that I would dare to raise a hand to you. I am not the monster your father is."

With that he stormed off toward the stables.

Catherine sighed and her eyes teared. Weariness seeped through her and she shivered. She'd had enough of this bickering over the past. If only her father would come after her.

She drew her head up abruptly, her thoughts racing. The idea, taking form, developed immediately into a full-blown plan. She smiled and giggled with the delight of a school-child and hurried off to the house.

"Zeena," she called with excitement, running inside and peering into each room she past.

She rushed up the steps and down the hall, as fast as her condition would allow, finding Zeena in the second floor sewing room.

"Zeena, I need your help," she cried, collapsing into the chair beside the startled woman.

"The baby?" she questioned anxiously, and stood.

Catherine waved her concern away. "No, the baby is fine and not due for a few months yet. I need your help in getting a letter to my father."

Zeena raised a brow. "I cannot betray Lucian's trust, especially where the marquis is concerned."

"Not even if Lucian will benefit from my intentions?"

"Do not play games with me, Catherine. If you wish my help then honesty is the only way you shall receive it."

Catherine debated entrusting to Zeena the information she had learned, worried that she would relate it to Lucian.

As if reading her thoughts Zeena spoke. "We do not know each other long, but trust is something we share. Trust me, Catherine, before more people suffer needlessly."

Catherine smiled and reached out her hand to Zeena. "I have a tale to share with you."

Lucian sat in the metal tub, the hot water easing his sore muscles after the exhausting ride he had taken earlier in the afternoon. He rested his head back on the rim, watching the sunset through the open louvered doors of his bedroom.

His hard ride had tired his body, but not his mind. In the last seven years he had established a reputation for striking fear and obedience in the hearts of man. His name was synonymous with evil. Though the tales it generated were exaggerated, they were not entirely unfounded. He had done what was necessary to survive and he would do what was necessary to make Catherine his wife.

He sat up, grasping the sides of the tub and easing his large body up and out, his feet resting on the braided cotton rug. He reached for the towel on the small nearby table and drew it around his waist, ignoring the rivulets of water that ran like glistening tears down his chest.

Catherine found him standing in the middle of the room nearly naked, the water running off him like a mighty god whose ominous presence had just emerged from beneath the dark depths of the sea.

Lucifer.

Gooseflesh raced over her, stinging her flesh, reminding her just how vulnerable she was around him. Unconsciously her fingers moved to her pearls, twisting the strand nervously around her finger.

Lucian kept a penetrating gaze on her. He unhooked the towel at his waist. It dropped to his feet and he casually stepped over it, walking toward Catherine.

His slow advance tickled her flesh with anticipation. It seemed forever since last they had been intimate. And she missed their lovemaking. Missed it desperately.

He stood in front of her, his hand reaching out, his fingers raking through her hair to the back of her head and drawing her near to him. "You have denied yourself and me far too long."

Her condition and limited strength was no match for his imposing size so she hastily relied on words to prevent his intentions. "Will you speak with my fa—"

"Don't, Catherine," he interrupted sharply. "Don't allow your father to come between us. Not now. Not at this moment. There's only you and me. And I'm going to love you, angel. I'm going to love you all night."

He gave her no chance to respond. He took her face in his hands and brought his lips to hers. He kissed her with the intensity of a man denied too long and she responded with the same.

No longer able to deny her own needs she selfishly took what he offered, drinking in his taste as though starved with thirst.

"Damn, but I've missed you," he whispered between heavy breaths.

Again she had no chance to respond, he ravished her mouth.

She let him, wrapping her arms around his neck.

He lifted her into his arms, his mouth never leaving hers. He walked to the bed and lowered them both to the sheets sweet with the scent of jasmine.

Reluctantly his mouth left hers. "I want you naked. I'm hungry for you."

She managed a response, suddenly self-conscious of her awkward shape. "Lucian, my body is—"

"Beautiful," he whispered, rushing the dress off her. His hand gently cupped her breast. "You're filling with milk. If only I could taste it now. I'm so hungry for you."

He took her sensitive nipple in his mouth and sucked with a tenderness that sent the shivers through Catherine.

She ran her hand through his hair, holding his head against her as he fed.

He sampled her other breast as well and then moved on, caressing, kissing, splaying his hand over her extended belly. Her skin felt smooth like warm silk and her womanly scent mixed with the thick scent of jasmine sent his senses spiraling.

His hand ran down along her inner thigh, gently nudging

her legs apart, gently cupping her heated crown of silver blond curls, gently inserting his one finger in her wetness.

She moaned his name unable to speak coherently.

Another finger joined his other and her moan took on a throaty tone as it came from deep inside her.

"I need to taste your richness, angel. Tell me you want me to. Tell me to taste you."

His decadent suggestion fueled the passion that surged through her. She was beyond control, beyond caring. "Taste me." She breathed heavily and arched her hips up to him.

His mouth instantly sought the small nub, the center of her desire, and he licked it with infinite slowness while his fingers played skillfully within her.

She cried out helplessly, unable to stand the pleasure.

"Relax, angel," he warned. "I intend to have my fill of you."

And he did, his tongue and fingers bringing her close to climax, then easing back to begin again.

"I can't stand it any longer," she begged him.

"But I haven't had enough of you," he whispered. And he hadn't. He throbbed unmercifully for his own fulfillment, but he ached much worse to taste her until saturated and he could stand it no more.

"Lucian." His name ran from her lips harshly.

"Promise me I can taste you all night and I'll ease your ache," he teased, his thumb having replaced his lips, stroking her swollen nub.

"Whatever you want, Lucian. I'm yours, tonight I'm completely yours," she promised, her need so great she would give him anything at that moment.

"It's dangerous to surrender so completely to the devil. You may lose your soul," he warned seriously.

Her emotions soaring, she answered in a gentle cry, "I surrendered my soul and my love with my virginity."

Her words pierced his heart like an arrow. She had loved him since their first time together and she had given freely to him because of that love.

He closed his eyes against all the pain he had caused her and sought now to only bring her pleasure.

"I love you," he said softly, and gently spread her legs to ease between them. He slipped his arms beneath her knees and drew her up toward him.

"Lucian," she cried out.

"Soon, angel, soon," he cajoled, adjusting her position to accept him easily and without pain or discomfort to her or the child.

When he was ready he entered her slowly, thoughtfully, wanting only to bring her immense pleasure. And he did.

His strokes were sure and steady. She arched against him, wanting him deep inside her, wanting him strong against her.

He read her response correctly and moved with more intensity, more promise of satisfaction. He stroked fiercely, dominantly, surging in and withdrawing with controlled thrusts.

His rhythm increased.

Catherine's cries grew, the overwhelming size of him compelling her to scream her satisfaction, her need to release around him.

He felt her tighten, draw him in. Hot, wet, and pulsating. He could barely contain himself. "Catherine," he commanded sternly.

She understood and obeyed, squeezing around him, feeling herself release, feeling herself climax in a shattering explosion that took her breath away.

Lucian followed along. Mindless to his surroundings, mindless to everything but the forceful spilling of his seed deep within Catherine's womb.

The night wore on, Catherine wondering where Lucian got his stamina and Lucian wondering when he would ever get enough of her.

They laughed, they teased, they loved, falling asleep just before the sun rose on the horizon. Just before the cargo ship left the shore with Catherine's note to her father.

> *Papa, come at once, I need you.*
> *Love, Catherine.*

❧ 30 ❧

LUCIAN STOOD ON shore shaking his head as he watched his stubborn woman swim. He had ordered her to cease all strenuous activities and what had she done? Exactly what she wanted to do.

He stripped off his clothes and ran diving into the water, his powerful strokes taking him to Catherine in no time. He grasped her gently about her thickened waist and trod water until his feet touched sand and he could easily stand.

She clutched around his neck smiling and gave him a quick kiss.

"You taste like the sea," he said, nibbling at her lips and feeling a contentment he had not thought possible.

She pressed her finger to his lips, preventing his playful bites. "I never imagined I would enjoy swimming so much."

Lucian spoke seriously. "Did I not order you to cease swimming now that you have grown so abundant with my child?"

Catherine turned a little-girl grin on him. "I seem to recall something."

Lucian narrowed his brow. "I made myself perfectly clear."

"You always make yourself perfectly clear, you handsome devil," she teased, and kissed him soundly.

He tore his mouth away. "That won't work, Catherine. I expect my orders to be obeyed."

She kissed the corner of his mouth, lingering to enjoy the salty taste of him. "Swimming is not at all strenuous or harmful to the body. The baby favors the activity completely."

Lucian splayed his hand over her belly and was answered with a hearty kick.

"He's a little devil," she laughed.

"Like his father?"

She deposited a feathery soft kiss on his lips before responding. "He is much like his father. He keeps me up at all hours and demands that I stroke and ease him."

Lucian felt himself harden, recalling several evenings past when Catherine had stroked and eased him so skillfully. He had burst in her hand like a young schoolboy, and she had smiled in delight before arousing him again and settling herself over him.

"I want you, Lucian," she murmured against his mouth.

"Marry me," he demanded.

"When you speak with my father," she answered as she had each time he had asked her in the last few weeks. Knowing very soon her father would arrive and she would have her way.

"I'll never let you leave me," he warned sternly, slipping his hand between her thighs.

"I don't want to leave you. I love you." She gasped against his lips when his fingers intimately captured her.

Words were quickly forgotten as the two lovers joined in the midst of the sea, the hot sun beating down upon them, the seabirds serenading overhead and the ship in the distance drawing closer to Heaven.

Santos sprinted across the lawn, vaulting the wide bed of pink flowers before reaching the front step and racing up it. He threw open the door and ran straight for Lucian's study.

He knocked and opened the door simultaneously.

Lucian moved out of his chair swiftly, reading the anxious look on Santos's face. "What is it?"

"Abelard's here." Santos stopped in front of his desk. "The boat is rowing him to shore now."

"He dares to invade my home," Lucian said in soft anger.

"He's here by invitation."

Santos swerved around while Lucian stared past him at Catherine standing in the doorway. She wore a pale yellow dress with a matching smock trimmed at the collar with embroidered apricot flowers. Her hair was drawn back with a yellow ribbon. She appeared ready for visitors.

"You invited your father here?" he asked cautiously, his temper near to erupting.

"Yes," she answered.

Santos shook his head.

"It is time this matter is settled," she insisted, walking into the room. "It is time you spoke with him."

Lucian maneuvered his desk and walked up to her. "Madam, your condition warrants my patience, but if you think I'll accept Abelard as a guest in my home you are sorely mistaken."

Lucian stared down at her from his towering height, but she refused to allow his size to intimidate her. "He is my father and I wish him to visit with us."

"He is the man who condemned me to hell," he argued.

Catherine braced herself for she knew her words would hurt him, but she also knew that in the end they would help heal him. "You have served your sentence. It is time to face your accuser."

He looked as though the fires of hell had raced up to engulf him, so red did his face flame. "So help me, Catherine—"

"That is precisely what I am attempting to do," she said

gently but with a sternness that warned she was adamant in her decision.

No one had time to respond. A loud commotion in the entrance hall caught their attention, as did Bones when he ran into the study rushing to speak.

"Abelard says he demands to see his daughter, and now. And there's an older woman who feels that this is the greatest adventure she's ever been on and is asking all sorts of questions about pirates, and then there's a young pretty lady's maid that keeps crossing herself, and a tall, older manservant who stands directly beside Abelard and doesn't say a word." Out of breath Bones stopped talking.

"He demands in my home?" Lucian said with an angry growl.

Catherine attempted to soothe his fury. "My father is accustomed to giving orders."

"As I am, madam," Lucian snapped. "And since this is *my* home he will obey *my* orders."

Catherine took a deep breath against the chore she faced.

"Are you all right?" Lucian asked, his hand swiftly seeking her rounded belly and stroking her gently.

Catherine leaned against him. "Please, Lucian, speak with my father."

He found it hard denying her anything. He loved her so much. And Abelard was here and he had many questions. He was about to answer when Jolly rushed into the room.

"The marquis says his daughter better be brought out to him immediately, or there'll be hell to pay."

That did it. Lucian completely lost his temper. He pushed Catherine aside and stormed out of the room.

She shook her head. "Please, Santos, help me. It is important for them both."

Santos nodded and they both hurried from the room.

Lucian halted abruptly when he came face to face with

Abelard. He had not expected a tall man, with well-defined features and a stance that spoke loudly of his aristocracy.

His clothes were tailored to his height and lean frame and his eyes . . . were chilling in their ice blue color. And when he spoke it was clear he was a man accustomed to issuing orders and being obeyed.

"My daughter, where is she?" Randolph Abelard demanded.

Aunt Lilith, to Catherine's relief, interrupted the confrontation. "Randolph, mind your manners. We're in this gentleman's home. And as you can see for yourself Catherine looks healthier than any pregnant woman I have ever seen."

Catherine attempted to move past Lucian to greet her father. But his hand captured her wrist, preventing her from moving. His possessive action wiped the smile off Abelard's face.

"This is *my* home, Abelard," Lucian announced, causing eyebrows to arch from his obvious disrespect in not addressing the marquis by his title. "Catherine obeys me, as do all who reside here. Is that clear?"

Again Aunt Lilith and her chatty nature interfered and Catherine blessed her. "Of course, my dear boy. We are delighted to be here and would not think of disrupting your household. Right, Randolph?"

The marquis stared blatantly at Lucian, his eyes having lost their icy chill. He almost looked sad as though looking at the imposing pirate brought him sorrow. "As my sister said, we are delighted to be here. Catherine?" He summoned her with an outstretched hand.

Catherine looked up at Lucian, seeking his permission, not wishing to embarrass him by demanding that he release her. Instead she whispered, "Please."

He hesitated a moment, his grip tightening as though he

fought with himself to let her go. But he did. He released her hand and she fled to her father.

Abelard captured her in his outstretched arms, hugging her fiercely to him. "I was worried."

"No need to be," she reassured him. "I am safe and happy."

Her remark pleased Lucian and he stood waiting impatiently to take her away from Abelard.

"You will stay and visit with us," she insisted. "I have much to show you here and you could use a rest."

"We plan to stay as long as you need us," Aunt Lilith said, reaching out to her niece for a hug.

Catherine went to her and Lucian relaxed, relieved Abelard no longer held her.

"I'm glad you've come, Aunt Lilith," Catherine said, squeezing the woman's ample waist.

"You don't think I would allow your father to go off on an adventure as grand as this one and not take me along," she said with a laugh.

Catherine smiled, loving her aunt's unconventional ways.

"And you, sir," Aunt Lilith said to Lucian. "You will tell me all your pirate tales and adventures, won't you?"

Lucian couldn't help but like the woman. She was outspoken and her manner direct. She hid nothing and she spoke with honesty. "Gladly, madam."

Catherine smiled proudly at his display of sincere charm.

"You are a handsome one, you know," her aunt said with a twinkle in her eyes. "I'm glad my niece captured you."

"That she did, madam," Lucian said with a laugh, and sought to win Lilith to his side. "But she refuses to marry me and save my reputation."

Catherine glared at him.

"Is this true, Catherine?" her aunt asked. "He has proposed to you and you've turned him down?"

"Perhaps she doesn't wish to marry him," Randloph said sharply.

Lucian waited for her response, wondering if she would state the conditions she had insisted upon. Her answer pleased him.

"I wish for you two to speak with each other," she said. "That is why I sent for you, Papa."

"Catherine, we've been through this," he sighed. "I have nothing to say to this man. He has caused you much pain and I wish he would leave you in peace."

"And what of the pain you caused?" Lucian accused.

"I did what I had to do," Randolph argued.

"Why?" Lucian demanded angrily.

"It is of no concern now."

"To me it is."

Randolph shook his head. "It is over and done. Let it go."

"Bloody hell I will," Lucian said in an icy calmness, and stormed past everyone out the front door.

"Father," Catherine scolded, only addressing him so formally when angry.

"I will not speak about it, Catherine, and that is my final word on the matter," he said, and stubbornly stumped up the steps, Dunwith close behind.

Catherine gave Dulcie a quick hug. "I'm glad you've come. Santos will see you to your rooms. Aunt Lilith, I will see you later. I must—"

"Be off with you, Catherine, he needs you," her aunt interrupted, and turned her chatty attention on Santos.

Catherine found Lucian in the stable, stroking his stallion's neck.

"Animals love unconditionally," he said, knowing she stood behind him.

"As I love you," she whispered softly.

He turned, walked up to her, and drew her into his arms. He had wanted her to follow him, to leave everyone else behind, demonstrating that she cared solely for him. And she had.

"I never meant to cause you pain," she said on a choked sob.

He brushed a restrained kiss across her lips. "Bloody hell, it is I who have caused you pain."

He kissed her fully then, sweeping into her mouth and capturing her senses.

"No more pain, angel," he whispered between ravishing her mouth. "I promise you, you will suffer no more pain."

Lucian found his promise difficult to keep in the weeks that followed. Her father openly sought to persuade her to return to England with him.

Though polite out of necessity, both the marquis and Lucian found it nearly impossible to deal with each other. Too much buried resentment and too many secrets lay between them and until addressed the tension would continue to mount.

"Why do you put up with this nonsense?" Santos asked one evening before supper.

Lucian sighed, relaxing back in the wicker chair on the veranda outside his study. "Catherine is only six weeks from delivery. I don't wish to upset her at this delicate time."

"Bah," Santos said with a wave of his hand. "Catherine is much stronger then you give her credit for. Send her father packing, marry Catherine, and return peace to Heaven."

"If he suggests one more time that she return to England I may just do that."

Santos smiled. "I'll tell the crew to ready his ship."

Lucian laughed.

"At least someone is laughing," Zeena said, walking out onto the veranda.

"What's wrong?" Lucian asked, his thoughts immediately of Catherine.

"That father of hers is insisting she'd get better care in England during her delivery and that she should return for her baby's sake."

"He's upsetting her?" Lucian asked standing.

"Very much," Zeena insisted angrily. "Her hands are shaking and she looks close to tears."

"That does it," Lucian said, and stormed to the parlor where he knew all of them would be waiting before supper.

"Think on it, Catherine," her father said. "If there is a problem with the delivery there would be a trained physician to tend you. Not some island native."

"She's not going anywhere," Lucian said, marching into the salon and straight up to Abelard. "Catherine is staying here with me."

"Don't be so selfish," Abelard said, not backing away from Lucian's imposing stature.

"You are the one who is selfish," Lucian accused. "Have you bothered to ask Catherine if she wishes to leave here? Have you bothered to notice how much you've upset her since you arrival?"

"She requested that I come. She wrote that she needed me."

"For what reason, Abelard? Think about it. For what reason?"

"Because I am her father and she trusts me."

"You're a fool," Lucian snapped. "She told you plainly the day of your arrival that she wished us to talk. That is the reason she sent for you. Not for herself, but for you and me."

"At the moment my concern is for her and her condition, and as the father of her child you should be—"

"I will take care of Catherine and my child. Your opinion doesn't matter."

"I'm her father," Abelard shouted, turning a furious red.

"Her stepfather," Lucian corrected. "And a poor excuse for one."

"Enough," Catherine cried out. "I've had enough."

Lucian turned. She stood in front of the settee, striking in all white with a white ribbon entwined intricately with her braid.

"The bickering has been endless, driving everyone within this house crazy. And it is all my fault."

Her father attempted to speak, she silenced him with a wave of her hand. "I will have my say, Papa. I thought you both cared enough for me to end this torment. But both of you are so stubborn that I find myself having to issue an ultimatum."

Lucian raised a brow in warning.

She shook her head at him. "It will be my way or else."

"Have your say, Catherine, but don't think you will be leaving this island," Lucian said forcefully.

Catherine forged ahead, realizing she had no other choice and hoping she wouldn't be forced to carry out her threat. "Settle this thing between you tonight or tomorrow I sail for England with Aunt Lilith and Dulcie. Once there I will reside with my aunt, never speaking to either of you again."

"Catherine," Lucian threatened furiously through clenched teeth.

She held up her hand to him, her green eyes pleading softly and turned her attention to her father. "Tell him, Papa. Tell him the truth."

Abelard gasped. "You know."

"Yes, I know, and now he must hear it from you or I

will"—she took a deep fortifying breath—"never call you Father again."

Her remark shocked Lucian as did her strong defense of him. At that moment Lucian realized the extent of her love for him and he felt his heart swell with the same unconditional love for her.

"I'm willing to talk with you, Abelard," Lucian offered.

Catherine sent him a grateful smile. "Papa?" she said, looking to him.

"I made a promise, Catherine," he said with an aching sadness.

"I know, Papa, but Lucian has a right to know. Please tell him."

Abelard nodded slowly.

Catherine walked up to her father and kissed his cheek, then she walked over to Lucian and kissed his lips. "This is difficult for him. You will understand why shortly. Please remember how loving someone can hurt," she whispered, and fled the room, her aunt following.

✿ 31 ✿

THE DOOR CLICKED shut behind Catherine. The two men stood alone.

"A drink?" Lucian offered.

Abelard declined. "I want a clear head when we speak."

"Then shall we begin?" Lucian suggested, and directed him to two high-back chairs arranged alongside each other near an open window.

Abelard sat silent, staring at Lucian.

Lucian waited, judging by Catherine's words that the tale the older man had to tell wasn't going to be easy for him. He took some comfort in knowing that whatever it was Abelard had done, he had been troubled by it these many years.

"I knew your mother," Abelard began.

"Well?"

"Yes. She was a beautiful woman. You have her strange hair coloring."

"I remember my mother's hair, though it was touched with gray the last time I saw her," he said sadly, recalling their last good-bye.

"Your mother and father's marriage was arranged. Marissa never loved Elliot, your father."

"I never thought my parents loved each other. They accepted their position in life as so many did."

Abelard nodded. "True enough. But your father grew bitter over the years. He had loved a woman. A woman not befitting his station. His father warned him that if he chose to marry her, he would disinherit him. Elliot went into the marriage with your mother blaming her for preventing him from marrying the woman he loved."

Lucian listened, wondering what all this nonsense had to do with him. Many men were forced to marry women they didn't like, much less love. His parents had been no different. He had understood that from a young age. And from a young age he had known his father had mistresses.

"Your father kept the woman he loved as his mistress after Marissa and he were wed. She died in childbirth, leaving him a son. As the years passed his hatred for your mother grew as did his hatred for you."

Lucian looked at him oddly. He had known no love for his father, but hatred for his own son? That was surprising and hard to understand.

"Your mother contacted me, fearful for your life."

"My life?" he asked oddly.

"Yes." Abelard choked back the pain. "Your mother begged me to help protect you."

"From who?"

"Elliot. He wanted his illegitimate son to inherit his title and land. Fearing that Elliot would have you murdered, Marissa asked me to find a way to protect you and help her petition the court to secure your inheritance."

"So you falsified documents of my debt to you," Lucian said.

Abelard nodded. "I could control how long you were away from England and return you when it was safe."

"What went wrong?" Lucian asked, realizing a quirk of fate had condemned him.

Abelard's voice nearly caught on a sob. "You were to be assigned to my best and most trustworthy captain. All was settled. You would be safe." He shook his head, casting his glance to the carpet at his feet. "The captain was killed by a robber the night before the ship was to sail. My agent handling the vessel had to find a replacement immediately. There was no time for a proper and thorough check on the man. He was assigned to the ship and hastily told you were to be treated exceptionally."

"I think he misunderstood the order," Lucian said with controlled anger.

"No, he did not. I discovered too late that he was a vile creature who hated the genteel. And by the time I did attempt to return you to England, the ship had already been captured by pirates."

"An interesting story," Lucian remarked. "But I'm confused. You're telling me my own father hated me enough to want me dead?"

Abelard stood and walked to the open window. "Yes, I am."

"Not a good enough explanation," Lucian stated calmly. "I want to know what you aren't telling me."

Abelard rubbed his temple. "I had promised your mother those many years ago I would never reveal the secret."

Lucian stood, impressive in his size and dressed like a gentleman in his blue brocade jacket with white breeches. "Tell me, Abelard. Tell me the true reason my father wanted me dead." Though he had no love for the man, the idea that his own father would have him killed tore at his heart.

Abelard stared at Lucian.

"Tell me, Abelard. You owe me that much."

"I owe you much more," he said softly.

"Then begin with the truth. Why did my father want me dead?"

His answer was swift. "Elliot Darcmoor wasn't your father and he knew it. He wanted no bastard to inherit his title and lands."

"Who is my father?" Lucian demanded.

"I am."

Lucian felt the shock down to his very soul.

"I loved your mother more than life, but duty and family obligations forced us apart. She never told me she was pregnant. I didn't learn that you were my son until she came to me all those years later for help."

Lucian attempted to comprehend, but it was difficult. The man who had been responsible for his suffering was his own father.

"I need that drink," Lucian said, heading for the cabinet that contained his best brandy.

"I could use one myself," Abelard agreed.

Lucian poured them each a glass of brandy.

Both men downed their drinks in no time and Lucian poured them each another one.

Abelard continued. "Your mother was beside herself with worry and regret when you were captured by the pirates. I spared her the news of your suffering on my ship. I didn't think she should know."

"I'm glad you didn't tell her. It would have been too much for her to bear."

"I have far worse news for you, Lucian," Abelard said reluctantly. "I have just learned of it myself and feel betrayed by a man I thought kind and generous."

"What is it?"

"Elliot had his son move to Brynwood just before you were taken by the pirates. He introduced him as a distant cousin. He appeared well-mannered and personable. He was well received by the gentry. I have sound reason to believe Charles masked his hatred for everyone at the manor while he slowly poisoned your mother and then arranged for the accident that took Elliot's life."

"And how have you come by this information?" Lucian contained his anger, unable to bear the thought that his mother had suffered alone.

"I had an altercation with Charles—"

"Charles Darcmoor is Elliot's son?" he asked startled.

"Yes, I had helped him during the years he lived at Brynwood following your mother's and Elliot's death. He made me believe that he cared for your mother and that her death hurt him terribly. He requested my help in financial matters, being a frequent visitor to my home. I had once considered him a possible candidate as a husband for Catherine."

"But?" Lucian said, anxious for him to continue.

"But when Catherine explained to me who you were, I knew I had to help you in your petition to have your lands and title returned to you."

"Why?"

"You are my son. There was no one else to help you. And I wanted you to have those lands. You deserved them."

"And Charles?"

"He grew furious, bursting into my home one day and confronting Catherine."

"She never mentioned this incident to me," he said, annoyed that she hadn't confided in him.

"Catherine tolerated Charles as a friend. He had been quiet and passive in nature until that day. His unusual behavior troubled me and I made a few inquiries. He had made several purchases of a highly toxic herb from the apothecary. And he had cancelled the carriage ride he was to take with Elliot, sending him on alone to his death."

"All this is speculation."

"Instinct," Abelard corrected.

Lucian's own instincts took hold. "Do you have reason to fear for Catherine's safety? Is that why you attempted to convince her to return to England with you?"

Abelard rubbed his pounding temple. "I heard Charles had hired a ship with a motley crew and had sailed for parts unknown. I was preparing to sail when Catherine's note arrived."

"Why should he want Catherine?"

"He blames me for losing his lands and title. He knows how much I love my daughter, as did you. And he blames you as well, and he knows Catherine is with you."

"There is much for us to discuss, Father," Lucian said, testing the sound and testing Abelard.

"Yes, there is, my son," he answered with a smile.

"Good," he said, easing back in the chair, "then begin by telling me all you can about Charles Darcmoor."

Catherine yawned and stretched herself awake. The early morning sun flooded the bedroom through the open windows, the morning heat sprawling through the room.

She turned to discover an empty spot beside her and she smiled with a yawn. Lucian and his father still talked. This was a promising sign. Perhaps before the week was out there would be a wedding on Heaven.

"Lying abed all day will do you no good."

Catherine bolted up in bed and stared at Charles Darcmoor lounging casually against the window. A nervous fear gripped her stomach and sent it to fluttering. "What are you doing here?"

"I've come for what is rightfully mine."

"Which is?" she asked, wondering how to notify the house of his unannounced presence without endangering herself.

"Revenge against the man who stole everything that was rightfully mine."

"You're Elliot's son," she stated clearly.

He walked into the room. "And I always thought you a beauty with no brains. Did you know I was born only minutes before Lucian, making me the rightful heir?"

"But you're a bastard, and bastards don't inherit when there is a legitimate son," she said bravely in defense of her Lucian.

Charles stared at her with hate, enraged by her remark. "Then I must dispose of Lucian, and you of course. Now get out of bed. We sail immediately."

"She's gone! Good Lord, she's gone!" Lilith shouted, stirring the house as she rushed in a frenzy down the stairs.

Lucian and the marquis burst out of the salon as Bones and Jolly rushed through the front door. Santos, with Zeena close behind, came running from the back of the house, slipping on his shirt as he joined everyone in the entrance hall.

Lilith waved a note at Lucian. "He took her. Good Lord, he took her."

Lucian snatched the note from her waving hand.

Come get her.

Lucian handed it to Abelard. "Charles has arrived."

"Oh, dear," Lilith gasped, and Dulcie rushed over, placing an arm around the woman in comfort.

"Captain, a ship dropped anchor last night off the west side of the island, but didn't signal to land. We've kept an eye on it but nothing happened and it sailed a short time ago," Bones nervously informed him.

"Get the *Black Skull* ready. We sail immediately," he announced, and sprinted up the stairs.

Lucian returned in minutes, his guests taking several steps back in fear as he descended the stairs.

Lilith gasped and clasped her hands to her chest.

Dulcie crossed herself and mumbled a hasty prayer.

Abelard glared wide-eyed not at Lucian his son, but at Lucifer the infamous pirate.

He wore all black—boots, breeches, and shirt that lay

open to expose a broad chest heavy with muscles. His long hair looked as though he had raked through it with his fingers, wild and untamed it framed his face. A face so handsome he could steal a woman's heart with one look and icy eyes that could freeze a man to the bone.

The marquis took a shaky step toward his son. "I'll not be left behind on the island like a helpless woman while you rescue my daughter."

"And I'll not waste precious time arguing with you," Lucian insisted. "If you go, you follow my orders without question."

"Agreed," Abelard answered hastily.

The men took off after Catherine while the women offered silent prayers for her safe return.

The *Black Skull* sliced through the water like a demon bent on revenge. Within the hour they were close to catching Charles's ship and the crew sounded a boisterous cheer.

"I don't like this, Santos," Lucian said, standing on deck, studying Charles's ship as the *Black Skull* came closer to overtaking it. "We caught up too easily."

"You think he planned it this way?" Santos asked, nervous himself that the chase had gone too smoothly.

"He's up to something. Make certain the crew stays alert."

"Aye, Lucian. Every man stands ready to obey your order."

Catherine stood on deck at the railing in her nightdress, feeling awkward and vulnerable in the thin material. She watched as the *Black Skull* gained solidly on Charles's ship. She could almost make out the men on deck and she craned her neck searching for Lucian.

"Soon, Catherine," Charles assured her. "Soon Lucifer will watch you perform a most amazing feat."

Fear crawled over her flesh. "What do you mean?"

He laughed. "I wish to bait the chase. Fill Lucifer with rage. Make him lose control."

Catherine took a step back, his crazed wide-eyed look frightening her.

He grabbed at her wrists, she struggled but her cumbersome shape hampered any chance of defense. With her wrists firmly locked in his grip, he shouted for rope.

Her heart plummeted and fear tightened her throat.

Two brawny men roughly took her from Charles and tied her wrists so tightly that the hemp cut into her skin.

"Are you a good swimmer, Catherine?" Charles asked, but gave her no chance to answer. "Not that it matters."

"Charles." She had to attempt to reason with him, but the only words she found herself uttering were, "My baby."

He looked indifferently at her. "Don't throw her overboard, lower her slowly so Lucian can watch her descend into the sea."

Catherine froze from the dreadful thought of being dropped into the sea, swallowed alive, unable to breathe. She'd never survive.

"He's close enough to see clearly, lower her," Charles ordered, and stood by the rail to stare across at the *Black Skull*.

The men grabbed her and sat her on the balustrade and then with strength and skill they lowered her slowly, easing her away from the side of the ship.

She grasped the rope above the knot that locked her hands together. She wouldn't look down. She looked up at the clear blue sky and swallowed the lump in her throat. She sent several silent prayers to the heavens above and attempted to recall all the lessons Lucian had given her on swimming and breathing properly.

She gave a glance at the *Black Skull* hoping to see Lucian

one last time, hoping to shout her love to him. Her eyes were too blinded with tears and fright to see him, but she called out her love to him hoping he'd hear her as the water grabbed at her feet and pulled her under.

Lucian watched in horror as Catherine was lowered into the sea. He heard her call to him. Heard her fear. Heard her love for him. Shock and disbelief at what she was about to suffer froze him for a second and then his scream of outrage pierced the air and sent a rush of terror through every man on the *Black Skull*.

Lucian lunged for the side without thought or reason. Santos grabbed for him. Bones and Jolly jumped for the captain as well and other crew members flung themselves at him, preventing him from jumping after Catherine. It took ten men to contain him.

"Lucian," Santos yelled, attempting to get through to him. "Lucian, think. You can't help Catherine by throwing yourself into the sea after her. You'll never reach her. You can't help her that way."

His words finally penetrated Lucian's mind and he ceased his struggles. One by one the men released him just in case he had a change of heart.

Santos was the last to let him go.

"I'm going to kill him," Lucian announced calmly, his hands gripping the wood rail so tight that Santos thought for sure the wood would splinter. "I'm going to gut him and feed him to the fish."

Santos felt the same way, watching as Catherine struggled to keep her head above the water. He pointed to her. "Catherine fights to survive. You can do no less for her."

Lucian looked and caught sight of her pitiful struggles, causing his heart to rip in two from the pain she had to be enduring. She would slip beneath the surface and just when he thought she could breathe no more, her head surfaced to drink deep breaths of air before the sea swallowed her once again.

"Breathe, Catherine," he whispered his encouragement. "Breathe as I taught you. Don't give up. Please don't give up."

"Captain, an island up ahead," Bones shouted from atop the mast.

Lucian realized then Charles's intention. Charles was drawing him into a confrontation, using Catherine in such a horrid manner that it would enrage Lucian beyond control and reason, leaving him vulnerable to Charles's attack.

But Charles had made a dreadful mistake. He had harmed what belonged to Lucifer and in so doing released the devil's wrath from the fires of hell.

Catherine surfaced once again, a prayer trembling from her lips as her numb fingers fought to grasp the rope and hold her above the water. Her body ached, her arm muscles burned, she was completely worn out, her strength gone.

The water would swallow her soon and this time she would not have the strength to fight against it. This time it would claim her forever.

The rough tug startled her and slowly she was drawn upward away from the sea that gripped at her body, fighting to claim her. Weak, grasping the rope feebly, her wrists, arms, and shoulders torn with pain, she was hefted up over the side of Charles's ship and deposited on the deck.

Catherine breathed deeply and slowly, not caring that her soaked nightdress molded against her skin, leaving her almost naked before the crew. She was alive and Lucian was close by. He would come for her. She had no cause to worry. None. Then the pain ripped through her lower belly and she fainted.

She woke to shouts and chaos as the anchor was dropped

and the longboat lowered. Before she could gather her thoughts she was scooped up over a large pirate's shoulder and carelessly taken down the rope ladder to the longboat below.

She huddled in pain, cradling her belly with her arms and moaning almost silently to herself. "Hurry, Lucian. Please hurry."

The distance to the beach was short and in no time she was once again handled carelessly, being roughly deposited on the white warm sand. She stayed crumpled as she was, the pain having subsided momentarily and having no wish to disturb the blissful peace.

Shouts and hammering went on around her and she glanced up briefly, catching sight of the *Black Skull's* longboat being lowered and the men dropping down into it. Lucian would be here soon. Very soon.

"Stake her!" Charles shouted. "I want her clearly visible as he rows toward shore."

Abject terror widened Catherine's eyes and she screamed when a pirate grabbed her and dragged her to the stake not far from the water's edge. Two other foul-smelling pirates helped the other one to tie her against the stake. Her hands were secured tightly behind her back and her ankles were wrapped with rope, drawing them firmly against the stake. Another rope ran under her breasts just above her pregnant belly, flattening her completely back against the splintered wood.

She couldn't move and when another pain consumed her stomach all she could do was bite down on her lip and pray for Lucian's speedy arrival.

"He's coming," a pirate shouted. "The devil's coming."

Catherine lifted her head slowly and with tearful relief caught sight of Lucian. He stood tall at the bow of the boat, his eyes focused on her. His red hair blew wild around him and his eyes glared with murderous revenge. The sea wind rippled his black shirt against his chest and whipped his sash around his thick legs. He held his cutlass in his hand ready to battle, ready to free her.

She smiled as another pain attacked her and before she bit down on her lip to stifle her cry she whispered softly, "Lucifer."

❧ 32 ❧

LUCIAN VAULTED FROM the boat into the gentle rolling surf near shore. His boots sank in the water nearly to his calves, but he marched on, the water splashing out of his way.

His men followed behind him, each certain that Catherine's captor would not live out the next hour. Every man in the longboat had reached out for the captain when they had watched in horror as Catherine had been tied to the stake.

But Lucian had remained still, deathly still, his only words, "Charles is mine."

His men marched confidently behind him, each prepared to battle to the death for their captain and his lady.

Lucian ignored Charles and his crew, walking right past their startled faces, straight to Catherine. Nothing would stop him from reaching her. *Nothing.*

He showed no emotion, but his concern for her tender condition tore at his heart and ripped at his soul. She hung on the stake like a worn-out rag doll. Her wet nightdress was plastered to her very pregnant body and her silver hair dripped water along her face. But worst of all he could see and feel her pain and worry. It scarred him much worse than any lash to his back.

One of Charles's hired pirates stepped toward Lucian in an attempt to stop him. Lucian never halted his stride, he threw his fist out, forcibly backhanding the man and breaking his nose.

No one else dared to prevent him from going to Catherine.

"Angel," he said softly, and with a skillful slice of his cutlass cut the rope that bound her.

She fell against him, his arms crushed protectively around her. She didn't want him to ever let her go.

"Are you all right?" he asked, her body trembling.

Catherine raised her face and favored him with a weak smile. "My swim tired me out."

He shook his head at her ability to joke about her harsh ordeal. "The baby?" he asked anxiously.

She couldn't alarm him about her labor. His attention to the problem at hand was required. "He's fine."

He kissed her gently, tasting the broken skin along her lower lip. "When I finish killing this bastard, you can tell me how you really feel," he said. "Until then you will sit right here and rest while I send him to hell."

Bones and Jolly flanked her sides after Lucian eased her down to sit on the sand. He took off his shirt and slipped it around Catherine's shoulders, pulling it around her.

"Stay put," he ordered before walking off.

Only when he was a safe distance away from her did she allow herself a small moan against the pain that ripped through her.

Both men looked down at her where she sat crossed-legged and cradling her belly.

"Shhh," she whispered, holding her finger to her lips, warning them that no one was to know of her discomfort.

Both men nodded, too startled to respond any other way.

"So, my dear half brother, we finally meet," Charles said as Lucian approached him.

Lucian stood a few feet away from him, his eyes quickly assessing his opponent. Charles was inches shorter than him, his frame lean, a gleam of revenge in his brown eyes. Lucian deemed Charles an opponent not to be underestimated, but one not capable of besting him. Not with the rage that raced through Lucian's blood. "A shame you went through all this trouble, Charles, for nothing."

"Nothing?" Charles asked curiously.

"It appears Elliot wasn't honest with you."

Charles looked at him oddly.

Lucian laughed wickedly. "I am not your half brother. And Elliot Darcmoor was not my father."

Charles exploded. "What nonsense do you speak?"

Lucian stalked him slowly, walking in a circle around Charles in steady steps. "A shame your father didn't tell you of my true parentage, but then he probably was too ashamed that he harbored a bastard in his home to relate such a tale."

"You mean the Darcmoor title and lands are mine?" he asked greedily.

"Afraid not. I have no intention of forfeiting them, and without proof, everyone assumes that I am Elliot's son. But that should be of no concern to you anyway."

"And why is that?"

"I intend to kill you."

Charles laughed. "Did your whore's swimming show upset you that much?"

Lucian struck out so fast that Charles never saw the blow coming. Blood spewed from the cut on his cheek and he stumbled back onto his bottom.

Charles wiped the blood from his face with his sleeve, then jumped back to his feet.

Lucian discarded his cutlass and summoned him with a flick of his hands. "Come on, Charles, I'm waiting."

Charles threw his sword to the ground and inched around Lucian. "One other thing you should know."

Lucian stared at him, his hands ready to choke the life from him.

He delivered his news with no remorse. "I helped my father kill your mother. She was in the way of our plans."

Lucian's stomach twisted in a pain so sharp he almost screamed his torment. Instead he said, "I'm going to enjoy killing you."

Charles grinned. "It's a heady sensation. I sat watching your mother die."

Lucian lunged at him, flesh meeting flesh in powerful blows that sent the surrounding pirates cheering.

They broke apart, Charles spitting blood from the blow Lucian had delivered to his mouth. His breath came in short gasps when he spoke. "Your mother died with your name on her lips. Heartbroken that she wasn't able to see you one last time."

Lucian struck out again, Charles no match for his superior strength and raging fury. Charles's men, realizing he was in trouble, threw him a dagger as he stumbled away from Lucian's powerful blows.

Santos cried out to Lucian, tossing him a dagger.

One of Charles's men dove for it, causing both crews to join in a melee. Daggers and fists flew.

Bones and Jolly remained by Catherine, each man throwing feigned blows, anxious to be part of the brawl as they watched their crewmates fight.

Lucian circled Charles eyeing the dagger he held.

"I killed Marissa and I enjoyed killing that idiot father of mine. He thought he could control me. Have me jump to his commands. He was a fool. And now it is your turn to die," Charles said, and swung the dagger straight for Lucian's face.

Lucian side-stepped the awkward attack, but Charles returned with speed and Lucian shielded the blows with skill.

Lucian managed to maneuver them toward the water's edge away from the heart of the fighting. Charles panted heavily, but fought like a madman bent on revenge.

A sudden side blow quickly deflected caught Lucian's arm, grazing his skin. His leg swung out, taking Charles down, and Lucian followed heavily on top of him. Viciously the two men fought for the one weapon, rolling in the water, struggling in a wild frenzy.

Lucian squeezed Charles's wrist, smashing it repeatedly against a half-buried rock protruding from the water. The knife fell from his hand, disappearing beneath the shallow water.

Lucian smashed his fist into Charles's face twice. Charles returned the blows, barely grazing Lucian's cheek. They rolled, they tumbled, until frantic for victory, Charles made a sudden dive for the dagger in the water.

"Lucian!" Santos yelled, and flung him a dagger.

Charles stood, dagger in hand and a victorious smile spread across his face as he lunged wild and wide-eyed toward Lucian.

Remaining on his knees Lucian raised his hand, capturing the flying dagger just as Charles reached him. Charles attacked from above as Lucian aimed from below straight for Charles's gut.

Lucian's blade sunk in and with one powerful slice Lucian tore the blade upward, splitting him open.

Santos hurried to his friend's side, ignoring Charles's dead body at Lucian's feet and the blood that pooled in the water around him.

"You better hurry. The baby," Santos said nervously.

Lucian handed the weapon to Santos and stepped over Charles's body, stopping briefly to wash the blood from his hands.

Lucian rushed up to Catherine, dropping to his knees in front of her.

She frantically grabbed at his arm. "The baby's coming."

"Don't worry. You'll be fine," he assured her, and

carefully scooped her up into his arms and hurried to the longboat. Bones and Jolly followed, grabbing a few more men to help row as they passed by the fighting.

Santos was left behind to clear up the mess, the boat returning for him after Catherine was safely on the *Black Skull*.

"Lucian," she cried, doubling in his arms as another pain consumed her.

He attempted to soothe her, her intense pain frightening the hell out of him. "Easy, angel. I'll have you on the ship soon. You'll be all right."

She shook her head. "No. I fear it is too soon and the child and I will die. I don't want to die, Lucian. I don't want to leave you. I want to share my life with you and our child. I love you."

"You are not going to die," he said sternly, as though hugging her fiercely to him would save her from death. "I will not allow you to leave me. Not now. *Not ever*."

Once on deck, her father rushed over. "Catherine?"

"She's in labor," Lucian informed him, and wasted no time in taking her to his cabin, Abelard close on his heels.

A scream tore from her when he laid her on the bed. She curled on her side, rubbing her belly.

"Madam," he shouted at Catherine. "You will face this delivery with the same bravado and tenacity you faced me the first time we met."

"Don't speak to her that way," Abelard objected, feeling helpless to help his daughter.

"Get out," he ordered Abelard. "This is between Catherine and me."

"Papa," she cried, reaching out her hand to him.

Lucian grabbed Abelard's arm and forcibly walked him to the door. "If you love her, you will leave her to my care."

Abelard nodded though he winced when she screamed "Papa" again.

"Get me hot water and see about clean blankets and sheets," Lucian ordered, shoving him out the door and locking it behind him.

He hurried back to Catherine. "You will listen to me, madam."

"It hurts so badly, Lucian," she said, twisting as another pain tore through her.

"Catherine," he said, sharply. "You will obey my every word. Is that clear?"

"No!" she shouted back at him.

He smiled pleased. She still retained her obstinacy. She hadn't given up yet. He sat beside her on the bed, grabbing her hands, offering his for her to squeeze until she broke them if necessary. "Let me help you, angel."

She grasped his hands, pulling at him. "I'm frightened. So frightened I'm going to lose our child."

He leaned down and kissed her gently, running his tongue over her bitten lower lip. "With both our stubbornness I don't think there's a chance in hell we'll let our child die."

She smiled briefly, then bit her lip as another pain hit her.

Lucian tore his one hand free from her and stroked her stomach. "Easy, angel, easy," he cajoled, helping her through the intense contraction.

It passed and Catherine breathed a heavy sigh of relief.

"Let's get you out of this wet nightdress," he said, and without waiting for her agreement stripped it off her. He took a clean sheet from the trunk at the foot of the bed and slipped it beneath her bottom. Then he took another one and draped it over her.

In between her pains he fussed over her, talked with her, teased her, asked her about names for their baby and when she would like to give this baby a brother or sister. He recieved a punch for that remark though it was delivered with a smile.

Time wore on and the *Black Skull* set sail for Heaven. While the crew paced the deck in anticipation of the baby's delivery, the captain navigated his wife through each contraction.

"I'm too tired, I can't do this anymore," Catherine complained.

"You can and you will," Lucian demanded sternly, fearing her surrender would mean death for her and the child.

"I won't," she cried, feeling another pain charging across her belly. "I won't. I won't. I won't!"

"Yes, you will," Lucian ordered, grabbing her hands and holding onto them tightly. "Fight, damn you, Catherine. Fight."

She shook her head. "I'm not strong enough."

"You were strong enough to fight me."

"I used my head and it wasn't nearly as painful."

"That first time you stood in front of me, a virgin, never seen naked by any man, wasn't that frighteningly painful for you?"

She thought back, remembering her fear and her determination. "Yes, Lucian. I was frightened."

"But you did it anyway. Why?"

Her answer was swift. "To save my father."

Lucian sank down on the bed beside. "Now it's time to save our child."

And she did. A short time later with Lucian's encouraging words and his gentle touch their son slipped easily from her womb into his father's waiting arms.

Epilogue

Heaven was ablaze with burning torches, lively music, and a babble of laughter and merriment. The island was in the midst of celebrating the marriage of Catherine and Lucian.

"Randolph, stop fussing over your grandson and come dance with me," Lilith demanded.

The marquis held his seven-week-old grandson lovingly in his arms and was not about to relinquish him. "The boy is too comfortable to disturb." He tucked the light blanket around the sleeping baby and settled back in the bamboo chair to relax and watch the couples swirl about on the makeshift dance floor.

"Bah," Lilith said with a dismissive wave of her bejeweled hand. "You haven't let that baby be since his birth, and why? Simply because Lucian and Catherine chose to name the child after you."

"They chose wisely. Randolph is a superior name," he argued.

"Where are they anyway?"

"Who?"

Lilith shook a finger at him. "The newlyweds, Catherine and Lucian. I saw them dancing only a few minutes ago and now they're gone."

Randolph shrugged. "They have probably gone off to enjoy themselves, as you should be doing. Now go find someone to dance with and leave me and my grandson alone. I have a story to tell him of a beautiful woman with dark red hair."

"Doting old fool," she said, and walked off, wiping a joyous tear from the corner of her eye with her lace handkerchief.

Lucian carried his wife of eight hours up the staircase, her numerous petticoats beneath her white silk wedding dress rustling in protest of being squashed.

"Do you think anyone will miss us?" she said with a smile, her one arm hugging his neck while her hand toyed with the braid that ran down behind his left ear.

"I don't give a bloody damn if they do." He marched down the hall and turned into their bedroom.

"What if Randolph requires more nourishment?" she asked, suddenly nervous of being alone with her husband. The last few weeks since their son's birth had been a constant buzz of people fussing around her. She and Lucian had barely had time alone together. And at night when he climbed into bed beside her she was already fast asleep, her ordeal and birthing having spent her strength.

"I doubt he will require any more milk tonight. He was a greedy little fellow an hour ago, drinking his fill, and he has slept peaceably through the night this last week. But just in case he proves hungry Zeena has arranged for an island woman to nurse him this evening."

He glanced down at her plump breasts protruding modestly from her gown. "I will be the only one to feed on your milk tonight."

She blushed like a virginal young lady.

He lowered her legs to the floor, his arm remaining around her waist to hug her closer and brush a brief, lazy kiss across her lips. "I'm going to make your whole body blush tonight, angel."

His promise excited her. Their enforced abstinence had not been felt until these past three weeks when she once again began to feel her old self and had become more aware of her husband, especially when he had paraded in front of her naked on more than one occasion.

He stepped back and casually slipped off his black brocade coat. He looked so elegant and handsome in black brocade. The dark material complemented a white silk shirt and a white lace cravat. But what added to his arresting features the most was his pirate braid woven with a black leather strip.

"I do favor undressing you, *but,*" he emphasized, his shirt rolling easily off his wide shoulders, "I feel I would never survive the ordeal of ridding you of all those garments."

"Are you suggesting I undress myself, sir?" she asked, smiling and dramatically pressing her hand to her chest.

"Most hastily," he suggested, his hand ready to strip off his breeches. "Unless you want that lovely gown ripped from your body?"

"You wouldn't." She feigned shock.

"Ah, but madam, I would thoroughly enjoy tearing through the wrappings to reveal your precious beauty beneath."

"Lucian," she whispered, touched by his generous compliment, and walked over to him.

His arms went around her, his mouth came down on hers and they shared a kiss that tore at the very core of their souls and lasted until time no longer existed for them.

Finding breathing difficult, they parted, Catherine's head dropping to rest on Lucian's bare chest.

"I've missed the intimacy we shared so frequently," he confessed, his embrace possessive.

"As I have, dear husband." She kissed his chest, the taste of him ambrosia to her emotions. Her tongue sensually skimmed his flesh, unable to get enough of him.

"Catherine," he breathed through clenched teeth, attempting to pull her away from him.

She resisted, his taste too intoxicating to willingly abandon.

"Catherine," he said almost in a harsh reprimand as he yanked her away from himself.

Her eyes misty, her breathing erratic, she whispered, "I need you."

He swore, released her abruptly, and tore the fastenings on her gown as he stripped it off her. Her undergarments followed in quick succession, tossed to the floor with few not torn. He swung her up into his arms, her combs falling free, her silver hair spilling down over his arm.

The large bed welcomed them both, Lucian parting from her for a brief second to shed his remaining clothes.

He joined her, her outstretched arms greeting him in a greedy embrace. "I love you," she whispered, her lips eager to sample his.

"Not as much as I love you." He took her mouth, claiming it in a fierce kiss. A kiss that possessed, conquered, and cherished.

Time for lingering and savoring would come later, now they needed each other fast and furious. And that's how he took her.

He entered her swiftly, her own movements urging his haste.

She cried out painfully.

He stopped. "Catherine?"

She shook her head. "Don't stop, I need you so much it hurts."

He eased his thrusts until she opened to accommodate him and then he lost himself within her.

They moved like lovers long separated and recently united, their climax quick, explosive, and simultaneous.

Lucian, after regaining his breath, slipped off her and onto his back beside her.

Catherine, unable to relinquish their intimacy so soon, slipped over him, spreading herself atop him. Her head rested on his chest, one leg gently nestled between his two and her hand roamed his chest and belly.

"I wish a long sensual night with you, angel. I want to linger and explore. Taste and pleasure. I want to pursue love to its fullest, but only if you feel up to it. I do not wish to cause you pain."

Catherine laughed softly, reaching down to cup him fully in her hand. He swelled in her palm. "Remember when I suggested you let me pleasure you with pain?"

"You lack the experience," he challenged.

She lifted her head to stare directly into his eyes that pooled with passion. "I could learn."

His reply tested. "I can teach you much."

Her answer said it all. "I have a lifetime to learn."

He captured her face in his powerful hands and followed her custom of stating things simply, yet so meaningfully. "I love you."

They loved the night away, until, depleted of strength and energy, they slept.

As morning broke over Heaven, Catherine gently slipped from Lucian's sleeping embrace and climbed out of bed. She walked to the open window, standing to the side where she couldn't be seen, though the island's occupants hadn't stirred yet and probably wouldn't for several hours after last night's wedding celebration.

Still she desired her privacy. She ached to watch the sunrise and offer a small prayer of gratitude to the heavens above.

She had managed to accomplish the impossible . . . she

had found Heaven on earth and a loving *soul* to share it with.

Warm arms circled her naked waist and eased her back.

"Lucian," she sighed, feeling the length of his hard flesh rest against her.

"I thought our lovemaking would leave you in an exhausted sleep for hours."

"I needed to watch the sun rise."

He caressed her neck with his lips, his voice soft and filled with emotion. "When the sunlight touches your skin it reminds me of that first time I saw you naked in my cabin. You were bathed in sunlight, an ethereal beauty . . . an angel."

Catherine turned, her arms reaching up to drape around his neck, her lips drifting toward his. "I am an angel. I'm Lucifer's angel."